SEEKER

SEEKER

ARWEN ELYS DAYTON

CORGI

SEEKER

A CORGI BOOK 978 0 552 57055 8

Published in Great Britain by Corgi,
an imprint of Random House Children's Publishers UK
A Penguin Random House Company

This edition published 2015

1 3 5 7 9 10 8 6 4 2

Penguin Random House is committed to a sustainable future for our business, our readers
and our planet. This book is made from Forest Stewardship Council® certified paper.

Set in Adobe Garamond

Random House Children's Publishers UK,
61–63 Uxbridge Road, London W5 5SA

www.**randomhousechildrens**.co.uk
www.**totallyrandombooks**.co.uk
www.**randomhouse**.co.uk

Addresses for companies within The Random House Group Limited can be found at:
www.randomhouse.co.uk/offices.htm

THE RANDOM HOUSE GROUP Limited Reg. No. 954009

A CIP catalogue record for this book is available from the British Library.

Printed and bound by CPI Group (UK) Ltd, Croydon, CR0 4YY

To Finn, Emer, and Imogen,
the three terrors I have unleashed upon the world

"By now you should be convinced that our universe *may* have additional curled-up spatial dimensions; certainly, so long as they are small enough, nothing rules them out."

—Brian Greene, *The Elegant Universe*

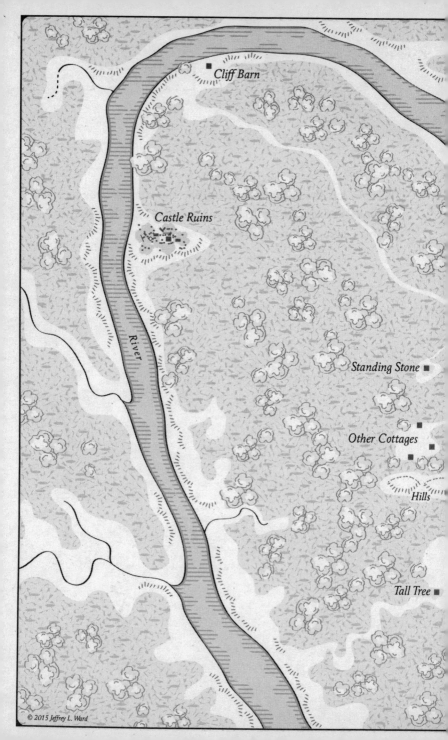

Cliff Barn

Castle Ruins

River

Standing Stone

Other Cottages

Hills

Tall Tree

© 2015 Jeffrey L. Ward

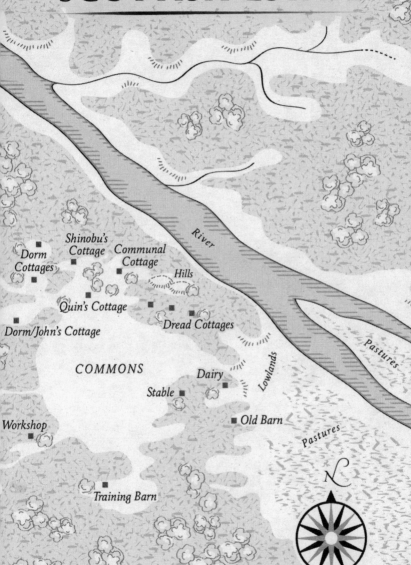

SCOTTISH ESTATE

River

Shinobu's
Cottage

Communal
Cottage

Dorm
Cottages

Hills

Quin's Cottage

Dread Cottages

Dorm/John's Cottage

Pastures

COMMONS

Dairy

Lowlands

Stable

Workshop

Old Barn

Pastures

Training Barn

N

0   ¼

Miles

PART ONE

SCOTLAND

CHAPTER 1

QUIN

It would be nice to make it through alive, Quin thought. She ducked to the right as her opponent's sword came whistling past the left side of her body, nearly slicing off her arm. Quin's own whipsword was coiled in her hand in its whip form. With a crack, she flicked it out, and it solidified into a long sword. *It'd be a shame if he split my head open now. I'm so close to success.* The enormous man she was fighting looked delighted at the thought of killing her.

The sunlight was in Quin's eyes, but on reflex she raised her weapon over her head and stopped her opponent's next strike before it cut her skull in two. The force of his blow against her sword was like a tree trunk falling upon her, and her legs buckled.

"Got you, haven't I?" her adversary roared. Alistair MacBain was the biggest man she knew. He stood over her, his red hair glowing like an evil Scottish halo in the dusty sunbeams coming through the skylight. He was also her uncle, but that didn't mean anything at the moment.

Quin scuttled backward. Alistair's huge arm swung his oversized weapon as if it were no more than a conductor's baton. *He really intends to kill me*, she realized.

Her eyes swept the room. John and Shinobu were staring at her from where they sat on the barn floor, both clutching their whipswords like life preservers but neither able to help. This was her fight.

"Useless, aren't they?" her uncle commented.

Quin got a knee beneath herself and saw Alistair's wrist flick, changing his enormous whipsword from the long, slender form he'd been using to a thick and deadly claymore—the preferred sword for a Scotsman about to strike a death blow. The dark material of his weapon slid back upon itself like oil, then solidified. He raised it above his head and drove it straight down at her skull. Quin wondered how many of her ancestors had been turned to mincemeat by swords shaped like this one.

I am thinking, and it's going to get me killed, she told herself.

Seekers did not *think* when they fought. And unless Quin stopped her mental chatter, Alistair was going to spill her brains all over the clean straw on the barn floor. *Which I just swept,* she thought. And then: *For God's sake, Quin, stop it!*

Just as she would tense the muscles of her hand to form a fist, Quin focused her mind. At once, things became quiet.

Alistair's claymore was hurtling through the air toward her head. His eyes looked down on her as his arms swung the sword, his feet slightly apart, one in front of the other. Quin saw a tiny shake in his left leg, as if he were off balance just a bit. It was enough. He was vulnerable.

In the moment before Alistair's sword should have crashed through her forehead, Quin ducked, pivoted toward him. Her wrist was already twisting, commanding her whipsword into a new shape. It melted into itself, becoming an oily black liquid for a split second, then solidified into a thick dagger. Her uncle's claymore missed her and made a heavy impact with the barn floor behind her. At the same moment, Quin launched forward, burying her weapon in Alistair's left calf.

"Ahh!" the big man screamed. "You've got me!"

"I have, Uncle, haven't I?" She felt a smile of satisfaction pulling at her lips.

Instead of cutting flesh from bone, Quin's whipsword puddled into itself as it touched Alistair's flesh—it, like Alistair's sword, was set for a training session and would not actually harm its opponent. But if this had been a real fight—and it had certainly felt real—Alistair would have been disabled.

"Match!" Quin's father, Briac Kincaid, called from across the room, signaling the end of the fight.

She heard cheers from John and Shinobu. Quin pulled her weapon away from Alistair's leg, and it re-formed into its dagger shape. Alistair's own blade was stuck six inches into the hard-packed barn floor. He flicked his wrist, collapsing the whipsword, which snaked out of the ground and back into a coil in his hand.

They'd been fighting in the center of the huge training barn, whose old stone walls rose around the dirt floor with its covering of straw. Sunlight streamed through four large skylights in the stone roof, and a breeze came in the open barn doors, through which a wide meadow was visible.

Quin's father, their primary instructor, stepped to the center of the floor, and Quin realized her fight with Alistair had been only a warm-up. The whipsword Briac was carrying in his right hand was a child's toy compared to the weapon he wore strapped across his chest. It was called a *disruptor*. Forged of an iridescent metal, it resembled the barrel of an enormous gun, almost like a small cannon. Quin kept her gaze locked upon it, watching the metal flash as Briac moved through a patch of sunlight.

She glanced at Shinobu and John. They seemed to understand what she was thinking: *Brace yourselves. I have no idea what's happening now.*

"It is time," her uncle Alistair said, addressing the three apprentices. "You're old enough. Some of you"—here he looked at John—"are older than you should be."

John was sixteen, a year older than Quin and Shinobu. He should have taken his oath already, by the normal schedule, but he had started his training late—he'd been twelve, while Quin and Shinobu had started at eight. This was a source of ongoing frustration to him, and his cheeks reddened at Alistair's comment, an effect quite noticeable on his fair skin. John was handsome, with a finely carved face, blue eyes, and brown hair with the faintest tint of gold. He was strong and quick, and Quin had been in love with him for some time. He flicked his gaze to her and mouthed silently: *Are you all right?* She nodded.

"Today you must prove yourselves," Alistair continued. "Are you Seekers? Or are you poxy lumps of horse dung we'll have to shovel up off the floor?"

Shinobu raised his hand, and Quin suspected he was going to say, *It happens I am a poxy lump of horse dung, sir . . .*

"This is no joke, Son," Alistair said, cutting Shinobu off before his quips could begin.

Shinobu was Quin's cousin, the son of the giant red-haired man who had just attempted to decapitate her. Shinobu's mother had been Japanese, and his face had taken the best features from the East and the West and combined them into something nearly perfect. He had straight, dark red hair and a wiry body that was already taller than that of the average Japanese male. He turned his eyes to the floor, as if to apologize for making light of the moment.

"For you and Quin, this may be your final practice fight," Alistair explained to Shinobu. "And for you, John, your chance to prove you still belong here. Do you understand?"

They all nodded. John's eyes, however, were fixed on the disruptor strapped across Briac's upper body. Quin knew what he was thinking: *Unfair.* And it was unfair. John was the best fighter of the three of them . . . except when there was a disruptor involved.

"Does this bother you, John?" Briac asked, slapping the strange weapon on his chest. "Does it hurt your focus? It's not even on yet. What will happen when it is?"

John wisely did not answer.

"Take your weapons out of practice mode," Alistair ordered.

Quin looked down at the grip of her whipsword. At the end of the hilt was a tiny slot. Reaching into a pocket in the old leather of her right boot, she drew out a small object like a flattened cylinder, made of the same oily black material as her sword. She slid this into the slot on the handgrip, her fingers automatically adjusting the tiny dials on the attachment. As the last dial moved into place, the whipsword in her hand gave off a delicate vibration, and immediately it felt different, as if it were ready to do what it was made to do.

She grabbed the tip with her left hand and watched it melt and puddle around her skin. Even "live" it would not harm her flesh. But everyone else's flesh was now fair game.

Quin's heartbeat was speeding up as she watched her father and Alistair taking their own whipswords out of practice mode. A "live" fight was no easy task. But if she did well, she was minutes away from her father's approval, from joining her ancestors in the noble duties of a Seeker. Since early childhood, she'd been listening to Alistair's stories of Seekers using their skill to alter the world for the better. And since the age of eight, she'd been training to develop those skills. If she succeeded now, she would finally be one of them.

John and Shinobu had finished adjusting their own whipswords, and the barn was now filled with a different sort of energy, a sense of deadly anticipation. Quin's eyes met John's, and she gave him a look that said, *We can do this.* He nodded subtly back to her. *Be ready, John,* she thought. *We'll do this together, and we'll be together . . .*

A high-pitched noise cut through the barn, so piercing that Quin wondered for a moment if it was only in her head. The look on John's face was enough to tell her different. The strange cannon-like gun her father wore, the disruptor, had come to life. The base of it covered her father's whole chest and had to be held in place with straps over his shoulders and around his back. The barrel was ten inches wide, and instead of a single hole, there were hundreds of tiny openings in the iridescent metal. These openings were randomly placed and of different sizes, and somehow this made it look worse. As the disruptor came fully alive, the high-pitched whine faded, replaced by a crackle of electricity in the air around the weapon.

Shinobu shook his head like he was trying to get the sound out of his ears. "Isn't that toy a bit dangerous with so many of us fighting?" he asked.

"If you fail in this fight, you are very likely to be injured," Alistair said, "or even . . . *disrupted.* Anything is fair today. Take a moment to understand this."

The three apprentices had seen the disruptor fired before, had even practiced avoiding it in one-on-one drill sessions, but they had never seen it used in a live fight. The disruptor was made to instill fear, and it was working. *Our purpose is worthy,* Quin repeated to herself. *I will not be afraid. Our purpose is worthy; I will not be afraid . . .*

With his whipsword, Alistair hooked something floating in a metal trough at one side of the barn. The object was a heavy iron circle, about six inches across, covered in thick canvas and soaked in pitch. He sent it flying up into the air.

As the iron circle arced high above him, Alistair lit a match. The disc fell toward him, and he caught it again with his whipsword. He touched the match to it, and the three apprentices watched as it burst into flames. Alistair twirled the disc around his sword, an evil glint in his eye.

"Five minutes," he said, looking up at the clock high on the wall. "Let no flames spread, keep yourselves alive and sane, have the disc in your possession at the end."

The apprentices glanced around the barn. There were bales of straw against the walls, loose straw across the floor, racks of old wood holding fighting equipment, climbing ropes hanging down from the ceiling, not to mention the barn itself, with its wooden beams and rafters supporting the stone walls. In short, they would be tossing around the burning disc in a room full of kindling.

"No flames!" Shinobu muttered. "We'll be lucky if we don't burn the place to the ground."

"We can do it," Quin and John both whispered at the same time. A quick smile passed between them, and she could feel John's arm pressing against her own, warm and strong.

Alistair tossed the disc high up into the rafters.

"Prove yourselves!" Briac roared, cracking out his own whipsword. Then he and Alistair ran toward the apprentices with their weapons raised.

"I've got it!" yelled Shinobu, leaping out of Alistair's way and running for the center of the barn, where the disc was now spinning down toward the straw covering the floor.

Quin saw Briac heading straight for John. Flicking his whipsword into the shape of a scimitar, Briac swung it in a wide arc aimed to slice John in half. She watched John's whipsword flash out to block, and then Alistair was upon her.

"I have it!" yelled Shinobu as he landed the burning disc on his whipsword. It slid down toward his hand, the flames burning his fingers, and he had to spin it back up to the tip of his sword.

Alistair slashed at Quin, and she moved to one side, changing her sword into a shorter blade and striking at his back. He was already pivoting to meet her attack, turning her weapon aside.

"Not fast enough, lass," he said. "You hesitate when you strike. Why? You'll have the most precious artifact in the history of mankind in your hands, won't you? You can't hesitate. And when you're *There*, when you step *between*, hesitation will be fatal." This was Alistair's mantra, which he'd been drumming into their heads for years.

John and Briac were exchanging blows. Briac looked like he had every intention of killing John as soon as he got the chance. Yet John was keeping up with him—he was a superb fighter when he focused. But a glance told Quin that John was fighting angry, and he was terrified of the disruptor. Sometimes you could direct anger and fear into useful energy. But usually, emotion was a disadvantage. It scattered your mind, made you spend energy unwisely.

Suddenly Quin realized that Alistair had backed her right into John, and now he was fighting them both. Briac was freed to turn toward Shinobu. The hum of the disruptor intensified to an unbearable volume.

"I'm tossing the ring!" Shinobu shouted. In the same moment, the disruptor on Briac's chest fired. Shinobu threw the disc high up toward the rafters above Quin and John as the barrel of the disruptor released a thousand angry sparks of electricity. These sparks rushed through the air toward Shinobu, buzzing like a swarm of bees.

Shinobu hurled himself down beneath the volley and rolled away. With no human target to strike, the sparks collided against the back wall of the gym in bursts of rainbow-colored light.

"Got it," John yelled, leaping away from the fight with Alistair and hooking the falling disc onto his own sword. A glob of pitch oozed off the metal ring and onto a bale of hay, immediately setting it on fire. John stamped out the flames as the disc fell down upon his hand, burning him.

"Shinobu!" he called, flinging the ring back toward the rafters. He jumped in front of Quin, taking her place under Alistair's punishing blows, as Shinobu caught the disc across the room.

Quin tried to rest her sword arm for a moment, but Briac was coming with the disruptor. Sparks launched toward her, crackling and buzzing.

If she let those sparks reach her, she would never be free of them. They would not kill, but they would be the end of her. *A disruptor field is worse than dying—* Quin stopped her thoughts. She was going to be a Seeker, a finder of hidden ways. There was only the fight; consequences did not exist.

She jumped to the side, grabbing a climbing rope and swinging out of reach. The sparks from the disruptor passed by and danced along the wall behind her, dispersing harmlessly.

She landed behind her father. He was already turning, flicking his sword out into a slender, evil blade. Before she'd regained her footing, he struck, his weapon slicing through her shirt at her forearm and cutting into the skin underneath.

Blood began trickling down her arm, and there might have been pain, but she had no time to think about it. The high whine of the disruptor was building again.

Shinobu was fighting Alistair now. John had the disc again, and he was spinning it around his whipsword to keep it from burning his hand as he stamped out another fire on a bale of hay.

Briac turned, fired the disruptor again, this time at John.

"John!" yelled Quin.

He tossed the ring blindly as he saw the sparks racing toward him.

Quin expected him to leap out of the way, but instead he was frozen, staring at those sparks, suddenly lost.

"John!" she yelled again.

At the last moment, Shinobu leapt away from his fight with Alistair and tackled John. The two apprentices sprawled safely out of the disruptor's path. The sparks struck the wall where John's head had been, disappearing in flashes of light.

Quin had forgotten the disc in her concern for John, and the fiery circle was bouncing across the floor, setting the straw in its path alight.

The disruptor was at its full whine once more. Quin saw the enjoyment on her father's face as he fired it at John again.

John turned, transfixed. He was staring at the sparks coming at him, hypnotized by their awful beauty. Permanent—that's what the disruptor was. If the sparks reached you, they took your mind and didn't leave. And John was waiting to be hit.

She saw Shinobu kick John to the side, sending him out of the disruptor's path a second time.

John fell to the floor, and this time he stayed down.

Quin retrieved the burning disc and stamped out the flames it had left along the floor. For the first time in the fight, she was angry. Her father was specifically targeting John. It was unfair.

She tossed the disc to Shinobu, ran across the barn, and slammed her body into Briac, knocking him and the disruptor to the ground. Sparks shot up toward the ceiling and bounced among the rafters in a chaotic pattern.

Quin brought her sword down at her father's face as hard as she could.

"Match!" Briac yelled, before she could strike him. Instantly Quin obeyed his order and collapsed her whipsword.

Shinobu caught the flaming disc for the last time. Quin looked at the clock, astonished to find that only five minutes had passed. It had felt like a year. John slowly stood up from the floor. Everyone was breathing hard.

Briac got to his feet. He and Alistair seemed to share a silent assessment of the fight. Alistair smiled. Then Briac turned and walked toward the equipment room, limping slightly.

"Quin and Shinobu, midnight," he called, without turning around. "We meet at the standing stone. You will have a busy night." He paused in the doorway of the equipment room. "John, you have bested the others and even me many times, but I saw no evidence of that skill here. You will meet me in the commons at dinnertime. We will speak frankly."

With that, he shut the door firmly behind him.

Quin and Shinobu looked at each other. Quin's anger had disappeared. Half of her wanted to scream in delight. She'd never fought like that before. Tonight she would take her oath. The life she had been anticipating since childhood would finally begin. But the other half of her was with John, who stood in the center of the barn, staring at the floor.

CHAPTER 2

JOHN

The sun was getting low in the sky over the Scottish estate as John walked away from the training barn. He and Quin had left the barn separately, as they always did, but he knew she would be waiting for him.

A thousand years ago, there had been a castle on the estate, which had belonged to some distant branch of Quin's family. The castle was in ruins now, its crumbling towers perched above the wide river that encircled the land. As he walked, he could see the very highest point of the ruins in the distance.

Now the estate was made up of ancient cottages, most built over the centuries from stones carried off from the castle. The cottages were dotted around the edge of a huge meadow, called the commons. It was spring now, and the commons was full of wildflowers. Beyond the meadow, the woods began, a tall forest of oak and elm that crept right up to overshadow the houses and marched away to the ruins and beyond.

Barns lay at one end of the meadow. Some had animals in them, but others, like the enormous training barn, were where the apprentices practiced the skills they would need as Seekers.

John walked through the shadows at the edge of the woods, then headed deeper into the trees. Even with his tremendous failure on the practice floor hanging over him, he felt his pulse quickening. He was entering another world, when he was in the woods with Quin, away from the parts of his life that usually overshadowed everything. He hadn't been alone with her in days, and finding her seemed more important than anything else at this moment.

She never chose the same spot to wait, but he must be getting close now. He was in their favorite part of the woods, where the canopies of the great trees touched overhead, blocking the sun and leaving the forest floor dark and quiet. A moment later, he felt hands encircling his waist and a chin sliding onto his shoulder.

"Hello," she whispered into his ear.

"Hello," he whispered back, smiling.

"Look what I found . . ."

She slipped her hand into his. Quin had dark hair cut chin length and a lovely face with ivory skin and large, dark eyes. Those eyes flashed at him mischievously as he followed. She led him to a stand of oaks that had grown in such a way as to create a tiny, secluded space in their center. She stepped through an opening between two of the trees and pulled John after her.

In a moment they were standing together inside the thicket. "It's not exactly the finest room at the village inn," she murmured.

"It's better," he said. "At an inn, you might be standing farther away."

There wasn't really enough room for both of them, and John was forced to pull her up against him, which was all right with him. He leaned down to kiss her, but Quin stopped him, putting her hands on either side of his face.

"I'm worried," she whispered.

He could tell. He could feel it coming off her in waves, like heat off asphalt in the summer. She was right to be worried, of course. The knowledge they were being taught was ancient, and highly protected. And in John's case, only perfection in his assigned tasks would win him the privilege of learning it. He was hardly a favorite of Briac's. His failure in today's fight was surely the excuse Briac had been looking for.

"I've never heard my father say anything quite so . . . final to you," she said quietly. "What if he means to kick you out?"

The anticipation of meeting her in the forest had pushed aside John's dread for a few minutes, but now it came back in full force. He was the strongest fighter of the three, yet he'd failed in the fight. He'd failed at the moment when he'd most needed to succeed.

He let his head fall back against a tree trunk. For a moment, he fought the sensation of a large stone pulling him to the bottom of the ocean. *No,* he thought, *I can't fail. I won't.*

His whole life was wrapped up in taking this oath. He was John Hart. He would get back what was taken and be at no one's mercy again. He had promised, and he would keep the promise.

"Briac has to take this seriously," he told Quin, working hard to sound reassuring, both to her and to himself. He must pull himself up from despair. "I was . . . horrible in that fight, wasn't I? He's got to be strict. He's the 'protector of hidden ways' and all that. But he's spent years training me. I'm almost there. It would be wrong to kick me out now."

"Of course it would be wrong. It would be completely wrong. But he's saying—"

"Your father's an honorable man, isn't he? He's going to do what's right. I'm not worried. And you shouldn't be either."

Quin nodded, but her dark eyes were full of doubt. He couldn't blame her. John didn't believe the things he was saying about Briac either. He knew very well the kind of man Quin's father was, but he clung to the hope that Briac would keep his promises. There had been witnesses to those promises, and Briac must honor his commitments. If he didn't . . .

He forced the thought away. Life had been good here on the estate with Quin—as good as his life had ever been, much better than he'd dared to hope for—and he didn't want that to change.

Quin had made friends with John on the day he arrived. They'd been kids then—John only twelve—but even so, his first thought had been of how pretty she was.

In that first year, she and Shinobu both came to visit John in his own cottage frequently, but it was Quin's visits alone he liked the most. She was fascinated with his descriptions of London, and eager to show him all of the estate.

When John's mother had been alive, she'd warned him to keep up his guard around everyone, and he did. But he liked to hear about Quin's family, about the lore of the estate. And Quin seemed to enjoy his company—not because he was wealthy or because his family was important but because she liked him. Just him. He'd never experienced that before. Even at twelve, John refused to let this move him—her interest might have been a trick, a way to get past his defenses and learn his secrets. Still, he spent time with her. With Shinobu he would practice fighting. With Quin he would take walks.

And she began to get . . . curves. He hadn't realized how distracting curves could be. He knew he was in trouble when he was fourteen, sitting in their languages class, and he found himself examining the way Quin's slender waist twisted into her hips. They were being asked to read aloud in Dutch, but he was imagining his hand tracing the line of her body. He tried to keep her from his mind, to stay as clear and calculating as his mother would have wanted him to be, but he couldn't believe that Quin's friendliness was false.

Then, when she was nearly fifteen, they were paired in an especially difficult practice match in the training barn. Alistair was sending them against each other again and again, demanding that they fight at the extreme limits of their strength.

"Come on, John. Strike her!" Alistair yelled, apparently thinking John was taking it easy on Quin.

Maybe he *was* taking it easy on her. It was winter, and her cheeks were flushed, her dark eyes bright with the exertion of the fight as she moved nimbly with her sword.

She struck him hard and he fell. Perhaps he'd let her hit him, because he didn't mind falling. He imagined tumbling onto the floor with her . . . Then the fight was over and they were both breathing hard, staring at each other across the practice area.

Alistair dismissed them, and John found himself walking outside the training barn in a daze, trying to carry himself as far away from her as he could. He could not see where he was going. He could only see Quin. The desire to be with her was overwhelming.

He stopped around the back of the barn, hiding himself behind the trunks of the barren winter trees. There he leaned against the stone wall, his breath filling the air with steam.

He didn't want to feel what he was feeling. His mother had warned him against love so many times. *When you love, you open yourself to a dagger,* she had told him all those years ago. *When you love deeply, you have thrust the dagger into your own heart.* Love did not fit into any of his plans. But how could you plan for this? It wasn't just her beauty he wanted. It was all of her: the girl who talked to him, the girl who would bite her bottom lip when she was concentrating intensely, the girl who smiled when they walked through the woods together.

He pressed his cheek against the cold stone of the barn, feeling his heart beating wildly, trying to rid himself of the image of her.

Then Quin was there, walking past the end of the barn, only a few feet from him. She was staring ahead, into the woods, also dazed. Their eyes met, and suddenly he knew—he knew she had come looking for him.

John reached out his hand and grabbed the sleeve of her coat, pulling her toward him. And then her arms were around him. Neither of them had ever kissed anyone before, but all at once, he was kissing her. She was warm and soft, and she was kissing him back.

"I was hoping you would do that," she whispered.

He'd meant to say something romantic and controlled, like *You're very beautiful,* but instead the deeper truth came tumbling out of him. "I need you," he whispered to her. "I don't want to be alone . . . I love you, Quin . . ."

Then they were kissing again.

There were heavy footsteps approaching, twigs breaking. It was Alistair; they could recognize his tread anywhere.

Suddenly they were apart, pushing away from each other. And by the time Alistair reached the end of the barn, Quin had disappeared around the other side, with a final glance at John.

That began their forest meetings. Quin was quite sure her parents wouldn't approve, so they kept their feelings for each other secret. But eventually it was obvious that everyone on the estate knew of their changed relationship—after a while, John sensed something colder in Briac's stare, and a subtle irritation in Shinobu's attitude.

John had tried to justify his feelings. Perhaps it *was* love he felt, but couldn't love also be an advantage? Wouldn't Briac have to care more about him when he understood how much he and Quin cared for each other? If he could eventually convince Briac to let her marry him, it would create an alliance, wouldn't it? An alliance with Briac wouldn't be pleasant, but it might be a way to fulfill his own promise, at least for a time.

Surely a feeling that made John so happy could not be bad.

Now, between the trees with his arms around Quin, he marveled at how right it felt. When they were alone, he could imagine that she would be by his side for everything to come. Eventually she would understand, even about her own father . . .

"I don't want you to worry," he told her, making her look into his eyes. "I'll be a Seeker, just like you. Even if it takes me a little while to get there. It's meant to be, the two of us together."

The trouble cleared from Quin's face a little. She almost smiled. "It's meant to be," she agreed. "Of course it is." Her certainty gave him heart. "Look," she went on. "You're stronger than Shinobu. You're a lot stronger than I am. You might be smarter than either of us. There are just some things you don't do quite as well."

"If you mean the disruptor—"

"I do mean the disruptor. We're all scared of it."

"I wasn't just scared," John answered, reliving the moment in his mind. "I couldn't move, Quin. I imagined those sparks covering me—"

"Stop." She said it firmly, and John realized his despair was rising again. He must focus, especially today. "You don't want to end up in agony with your mind turning on itself," she continued. "Of course you don't. But you have to think of the disruptor as a weapon like any other weapon. We use our mental control to avoid it in a fight."

"'My mind is a muscle that's always slightly tensed,'" John responded, quoting Alistair, who was their favorite instructor. "Only—I'm not sure that works for me when there's a disruptor involved."

"Try to concentrate on the higher purpose of our training," she told him gently, "on how lucky we are to have this as our calling. Being a Seeker is bigger than you or me, bigger than personal fears."

Her voice was growing passionate, as it often did on this topic. "We're part of something . . . *exceptional.* I get just as scared, but that's how I fight my fear. It's not just about disruptors, you know. You need the mental control when you go *There.* Or you'll never come out."

John realized he was looking at her with pity. She was a girl with stars in her eyes, born into the wrong family, and the wrong century. Yes, they were part of something exceptional, something bigger than themselves, but he would describe it in very different words—words such as "ruthless" and "vicious." Briac was both of those things. John knew she would be going *There* tonight, and then beyond, when she took her oath. Quin might not yet realize the purpose of doing so, but John did. His mother, at least, had been honest with him, where Quin's father had not been honest with her.

What would she feel when she discovered the truth? That there may have been noble Seekers once, but nobility was not Briac's style? That her skills were going to be used for a very different purpose?

Softly he asked her, "What do you think you'll be doing tonight when you take your oath?"

"Briac said it would be a task that requires all of our skills." He watched her eyes growing distant. "Whatever it is, I feel like every generation of my family for a thousand years is waiting for me to join them," she said. "My whole life has led up to today."

John too felt the generations stretching behind him, waiting for him to take his oath. He had promised—*Get it back and repay them for what they've done. Our house will rise.*

"And what about the athame?" he asked quietly, pronouncing the word "ATH-uh-may."

Quin was surprised, as he had expected her to be, for John was not yet privy to all of the secret knowledge that had been given to Quin and Shinobu. He watched her studying him, wondering where he'd learned the word.

"If you know about that," she said, "then you're already halfway to knowing everything."

"I know it's what Briac's talking about when he mentions 'the most valuable artifact in the history of mankind.' And I know it's a stone dagger."

"Even I have only seen it, John. A couple of times. I've never used it."

"Until tonight," he pointed out.

"Until tonight," she agreed. She was smiling now, her excitement at the upcoming events returning.

In the distance, they heard loud, happy shouts. Quin ducked down and leaned through the opening between the trees, and John crouched next to her. From this angle, just barely, they had a glimpse across the commons. The shouts were coming from the cottages on the far side of the meadow. It was Shinobu with his father, both yelling about how well Shinobu had done in the fight. Alistair might be gruff and brutal on the practice floor, but with his son, in his free time, he was a teddy bear of a man.

It had always seemed to John that Shinobu was in love with Quin, but since they were cousins of some sort, there was never a question of Quin feeling anything romantic toward Shinobu. And eventually, once he'd had Quin to himself, he'd been able to treat Shinobu with more friendliness.

"They're celebrating," John whispered. "We should celebrate."

"What did you have in mind?" she asked softly.

John slowly pulled her toward him and kissed her. This time she didn't turn away.

They had always stopped themselves from doing anything more. Quin was waiting. She had her oath to take and at least a year more under her parents' guidance before they would consider her an adult. But she and John had daydreamed about camping trips across the river, or rooms in an inn somewhere, someday, when they would finally be able to give themselves to each other.

Now, however, something was different. Maybe it was her anticipation of the evening to come, or the glow of her triumph in the fight, but John felt something more in the way she was kissing him. *She loves me,* he thought, *and I love her. I want her to be with me, even when she knows everything.* The forest floor was covered with years of fallen leaves, and John pulled her down onto that soft ground. He whispered, "Let's go to my cottage—"

"Shh," she said, putting a hand to his lips. "Look."

From where they lay, they could see a figure emerging from deeper in the woods, heading toward them. John pulled Quin up, hiding them from view behind the branches. They watched as the figure got close enough to identify. It was the Young Dread, with a string of dead rabbits slung over her shoulder.

From the look of her face, they had figured her age at about fourteen, though of course, with the Dreads, age was a tricky thing. The Young Dread had arrived on the estate a few months ago, along with the other Dread, the one they called the Big Dread—a burly, dangerous-looking man who appeared to be in his thirties.

Briac had been vague in describing the Dreads' purpose for being there, but they were, apparently, to oversee the taking of oaths. Briac, who showed deference to almost no one, seemed strangely respectful toward the Big Dread. The apprentices had decided a Dread was a kind of judge of Seeker training, with a history at which they were forced to guess, since their instructors gave no more than hints.

If the Young Dread was indeed fourteen, she was short for her age. Her body was slender to the point of looking underfed, but her muscles told a different story. They were like delicate ropes of steel holding together her small frame. She had hair of an unremarkable dishwater brown, but it was thick and hung almost to her waist. It looked as though it had never been cut and had rarely been brushed, as though she'd received all her grooming advice from the Big Dread, who obviously knew nothing about raising girls.

She walked toward them with the strange gait shared by both Dreads. Her movements seemed slow, almost stately, like a ballet dancer during a particularly sad or serious part of the performance. And then, without warning, she would move at an entirely different speed. As they watched, there was a bird call from the meadow, and the Young Dread's head whipped around, almost too fast for their eyes to follow the motion. When she had identified the source of the noise, she continued on her way, as steady and fluid as a marble sculpture brought to life.

"Watch this," Quin whispered, so softly that John could barely hear her, though his head was still only inches from hers. Silently, she pulled her knife from her waistband. She waited until the Dread had walked into a patch of sunlight that would make her momentarily blind to motion in the shadows. Then Quin drew back her arm and threw the knife at the Young Dread as hard as she could.

The blade arced through the shadows expertly, aimed just ahead of where the Dread was walking, so she would carry herself straight into its path and it would impale the side of her head.

Yet that was not what happened.

The Young Dread continued her steady approach until the weapon was almost upon her. Then her whole body exploded into action. Her right arm whipped forward and caught the knife out of the air. She spun around so quickly, she almost appeared to blur against the forest backdrop, and she released the blade back toward them much like a thundercloud releases a bolt of lightning. It was propelled at such high speed that they could hear it whistling through the air, and both John and Quin ducked.

It made a perfect arc from the Dread, around the edge of the cluster of trees, and buried itself to the hilt just inches from where Quin's hand still rested against the tree trunk. The vibration of its impact traveled all the way down the tree, and John could feel it in his feet.

"Nice shot," Quin called, waving at the girl. "Maybe you'll teach me how to do that sometime."

The Dread's eyes traveled slowly over their hiding spot, almost as if she were examining them minutely, even from that distance. Something about her gaze made them uncomfortable, and instinctively Quin and John moved a step away from each other, as though their intimacy could not survive her fierce stare. The Young Dread looked as if she might say something, but she never got the chance.

There was a new noise above the forest. The Dread and Quin and John looked up to see an aircar, throwing off a low vibration, circling to land in the commons. An aircar was such a rare sight on the estate that even the Dread stared at the vehicle for several seconds before turning away and resuming her steady walk.

John and Quin hurried to the edge of the meadow in time to see a man get out of the car and head toward Briac's cottage on the far side of the commons. When John caught sight of the man, he began to run, sticking to the trees but moving quickly, trying to get a better view.

Quin caught up with him. "What is it?"

The visitor turned for a moment, looking around the estate. John stopped running. Was he imagining things? The man's face looked familiar. But sometimes, when he was on the estate for months at a time, far from London and crowds, he found that every new face looked familiar.

"I don't know," he said. "Do you think you can find out who he is?"

"I'm sure Briac will tell us if it's important."

"I'm not," John said quietly. He glanced at Quin and said mischievously, "But if eavesdropping makes you nervous . . ."

"Nervous?" She pushed him indignantly, and he was pleased to notice her now studying the visitor with more interest. John wanted as few surprises as possible when it came to Briac. "Hmm," she said. "I'll come find you if I learn anything." She kissed John lightly on the lips. "I know Briac will do right by you tonight. He'll say something harsh, but he's not going to stop your training. Of course not."

With that, she ran ahead of him, toward the cottages. John could already feel himself bracing for the coming confrontation with Briac. He watched Quin go, her dark hair swinging, her body graceful—but not the slow grace of the Young Dread. Quin was full of life.

CHAPTER 3

QUIN

Quin glanced back at John as she ran from the woods and through the high grass of the commons. He was still standing where she'd left him at the edge of the meadow, in the shadow of a large elm tree. His eyes were following her, but his gaze had retreated within himself, as though he were thinking about something entirely other than her as he watched her go.

John's eyes were deep. That was how Quin had always thought of them. When he was with her, they would flash with humor and love, but at other times they were desolate and hungry, as though searching for something far away and out of reach.

It was his eyes that had first drawn her to him. Though John had only been twelve when he'd come to the estate, Briac had made him stay in a separate cottage out in the woods, all alone. Quin and Shinobu would visit him there often, intrigued by having another child on the estate, especially one so worldly, who lived in London and had been to many other places besides.

John had seemed wary of their company at first, and his look warned them away. He'd spoken very little of anything personal, but eventually, Quin had decided the storms in his blue eyes were not anger or fear of betrayal, as she'd at first thought, but simple loneliness. They'd begun to spend more time with each other, and she'd seen his look slowly change to something almost like happiness.

Now, moving across the commons, she could still feel the press of his lips on hers, his arms at the small of her back. She stole a final look as she neared her cottage, but he was gone.

A few minutes later she'd climbed through a window in the back wall of her parents' house. Crouching inside the pantry, which shared a wall with the cottage sitting room, she could hear the visitor from the aircar deep in conversation with Briac.

"There can be a disappearance," Briac was saying. "In which case, searches may go on indefinitely. That can be good and it can be bad."

Silently Quin pressed her ear against the narrow pantry door, which allowed her to hear better and see a small slice of the room through a crack between the door and the jamb.

Her father was sitting in the old leather armchair, beneath the rows of ancient crossbows strung along the ceiling, and next to the display chest decorated with carvings of rams—the symbol of Quin's family—and filled with knives. He was speaking to the visitor, a man in his twenties, who was warming his hands by a cheerful fire in the hearth.

The visitor wore clothes that appeared expensive, though Quin knew she was not a good judge of clothing styles. In her fifteen years of life, she'd spent almost no time off the estate.

"There can also be a clear-cut finish with no trail to follow," Briac continued, one hand running through the dark hair that Quin had inherited from him. Her father's head was still untouched by gray. He was not yet forty years old, as trim and strong as he'd been as a young man, though to Quin he'd always been an ageless, all-powerful presence, like the sky or the land. "It depends on what you need," he was telling the visitor. "We create a circumstance to serve your purpose. Do you know what you need?"

Briac was doing his best to appear friendly and polite to this visitor. Quin found the effect unsettling. She was used to her father's face and words being hard. He often frightened her. She accepted his demeanor as a necessity of her training: he was preparing her for a life that would be harsh, but it was harsh in service of something good. To be a Seeker was to be one of the chosen few who could step *between* and change things.

The visitor began to respond to Briac's question, speaking so softly that Quin could not make out the words. The man was very intent, but he seemed almost shy of speaking aloud. She pressed her ear more firmly to the pantry door.

Briac held up a hand. "Wait, if you would," he said. "I'd prefer if we continued this discussion outside."

The young man nodded, and the two of them rose to leave. When the visitor's back was turned, Briac took three steps across the room and gave the pantry door a hard shove, driving it into the side of Quin's head. She was sent sprawling to the floor.

She got slowly to her feet and staggered out of the pantry and into the kitchen, rubbing her head. In the other room, the cottage's front door opened and shut, and through a window, she saw Briac and the visitor walking together into the meadow. Apparently, Briac wanted privacy.

"Quin. What were you doing in there?"

Fiona Kincaid, Quin's mother, was sitting at the kitchen table with a mug of something in front of her. Quin caught a whiff of alcohol and knew her mother was drinking the strong cider of which she'd become so fond in recent years. On the stove, a stew was cooking for dinner, and there was bread in the oven, filling the cottage with delicious smells. These kitchen aromas were the background of her childhood, along with the scent of the tall grass that covered the commons and the rich earth beneath the trees of the forest. Only the faint trace of alcohol in the air took away from the sudden surge of happiness Quin felt. John would be successful. She and Shinobu would be successful. It was meant to be, and her life with John would be as she had always imagined.

"Were you eavesdropping?" her mother asked.

"I thought maybe it had something to do with tonight," Quin explained, dropping into a seat across from Fiona and drawing her knees up against her chest. Her mother's dark red hair was back in a tidy braid, and her face was blank.

Even without a smile, her mother had a beautiful face. Everyone said so. She was looking out the window now, at Briac and the visitor as they walked away. Then she turned back to her mug of cider, her expression growing serious.

"What did you hear?" her mother asked.

"Nothing," Quin answered. Then an unpleasant thought came. "You're not trying to marry me off, are you?"

This caught Fiona by surprise, and the hint of a smile formed on her lips. "Marry you off? Why, did you find the young man good-looking?"

"I—I don't know. I'm not really used to . . ." Her sentence died in embarrassment.

"Of course we're not marrying you off," her mother said with a gentle smile.

"Don't say 'of course,'" Quin responded. "That's what happened to you, isn't it?" In fact, her mother had never said that exactly, but this was the impression Quin had gathered from Fiona's description of her courtship and marriage to Briac Kincaid. She never spoke of falling in love so much as she spoke of her parents "making a match."

"Well, we're not marrying you to *him*," Fiona said, teasing her.

"I know how it used to be done," Quin went on. "Protect the bloodlines. Keep control."

In truth, she understood the value in being matched by her parents. Marrying someone her father trusted would help keep their knowledge and weapons under Briac's direct control. Briac and Alistair were, she had always been told, the last of the Seekers, and she and Shinobu must carry on this tradition in an unbroken line—and John, of course, but his line had already been broken, because his family had almost died out. In theory, she would be happy to marry someone who pleased her parents—but in reality she very much hoped that their choice agreed with her own.

Her mother took a long sip from her mug and shook her head. "We're not marrying you to someone, Quin. Even if your father might like the idea. Enough of your life has been planned out for you already, I think. You should choose your own mate."

Quin looked out across the meadow to where she and John had just been walking. The feeling of happiness was upon her again, and she decided to take a leap. She was only hours away from taking her oath. Soon she would be an adult in their eyes. "Mum, you know I've already chosen him, don't you?"

Her mother followed her gaze out the window, but there was nothing visible except grass and trees.

Slowly Fiona asked, "And is he?"

"Is he what?"

"Is John Hart your mate?"

Quin felt her cheeks flush hotly. "Ma."

"I believe you've been sneaking off together for a long while. Have the two of you . . ."

"No!" The conversation had taken a very fast and drastic turn. "Wait. What are you asking me?"

"Have you kissed each other?"

"Oh . . . Yes." Quin found herself smiling despite the embarrassment. "Yes, we have done that."

"And . . ." Fiona prompted.

"And what?" Quin was thinking of the way John had laid her on the ground, those lonely eyes of his focused completely on her . . . She looked down at her hands and said, "There's been kissing. A somewhat large amount. Don't you know already, Ma? You usually know these things without me saying."

"Sometimes I do, but not this time. Are you sure that's all?"

"I'm not an idiot. Briac's hard enough on him as it is. I don't want him chasing John around with a shotgun."

Fiona really did smile at that, her face lighting up as it rarely did. For a moment, Quin saw her mother's beauty at its full force, like a warm spring sun coming out from behind heavy clouds.

"Mum," Quin said, deciding that she was already so embarrassed, she might as well press on, "do you think Father will mind?"

"Mind what?"

"If I marry John?"

Quin held her breath as she said it, worried about her mother's reaction. But why shouldn't she speak about marriage? John was the perfect partner. He was from an old family like her own, wasn't he? Like her, he wanted to use his training to do good things in the world. Maybe they would live together here on the estate, or maybe she would live with him somewhere more exotic, but either way, they would work together, fight together, to help the world. *Tyrants and evildoers beware* . . . And of course, she loved him deeply. Surely her parents could see that.

Quin's eyes followed her mother, waiting for an answer as Fiona got up to tend the stewpot. It was a mystery to Quin what needed to be tended. It was stew, after all. You could cook it for days if you felt like it.

Her back to Quin, Fiona asked, "Has he asked you to marry him?"

"Well, no, not yet. But we understand it, I think."

"You're very young," Fiona said softly. "I've never known— I'm still a bit surprised it's John you're choosing."

Quin wasn't sure what her mother meant by that. Who should she choose, some stranger she'd never met? Some older man her father picked out? But she went on quickly anyway: "I don't mean now. Someday. Do you think Father will mind?"

Fiona turned to her, wiping her hands on her apron, her eyes looking anywhere but at Quin's face. "I think your father will have strong opinions on the topic, yes. And a lot has yet to happen between now and the time when you're ready to get married."

"That's not really an answer."

"But, Quin," Fiona went on, as though Quin hadn't spoken, as though she had to say the words immediately or they would disappear, "it doesn't matter what he thinks. Your life is yours."

Mildly astonished, Quin looked closely at her mother's expression, which had a nervous edge to it. Briac was, well, *Briac*. His absolute authority was part of the strange and privileged life into which she had been born.

"Ma . . ."

"Your life is yours," Fiona said again, almost urgently, taking a seat next to her. She glanced toward the window, then back. "If you . . . if you wanted to go to John right now . . . if you wanted to leave the estate with him . . . have a different sort of life together, right now. I would understand."

It was such a strange thing to say, she decided her mother must be more drunk than she looked.

"I'm not drunk, Quin."

"I didn't say that! But . . . now that you mention it, I do smell something in your mug."

"I'm not drunk," Fiona repeated.

"I never said you were."

"You did."

It was pointless to argue about whether or not she'd said those words, so she didn't bother. "I'm going to take my oath *tonight,* Ma. Didn't Briac tell you? I can't leave the estate."

"He did tell me." Fiona put a hand on top of her daughter's hand and held it there firmly. "But I am telling you this: you take your oath only if that's truly what you want to do."

Quin was momentarily speechless. Finally she managed, "What— what have I been doing here my whole life? Of course it's what I want to do. I—I know how lucky I am."

"Are you sure?"

Quin smiled as she would at a child with an irrational fear. Her mother had never taken the oath. Fiona taught them languages, math, and history, subjects with no direct ties to Seeker-hood. Though her mother did not like to speak of it, Quin had gathered, from comments made by Briac, that Fiona had completed all the training, but something had prevented her from becoming a sworn Seeker. Sometimes apprentices did not make it, and this had, to some extent, ruined her mother's life, perhaps even caused her fondness for alcohol. Quin loved her, though, and didn't want her mother to be sad on this particular day.

She clasped Fiona's hands gently. "I'm sure," she told her. "And I'll make you very proud of me. I mean to do great things."

Her words did not have the desired effect. Her mother's eyes searched hers for a moment, quite urgently. Then her gaze dropped back to the table, and she nodded to herself.

"Of course you will," she said, moving her lips into a smile. "And I wish you every happiness in your life, my darling girl."

Fiona got back to her feet and turned to the stove. Quickly, so quickly that Quin could not be sure it had happened, her mother wiped her eyes. Quin whisked Fiona's mug off the table, sniffed the remaining cider inside, and dumped it down the sink before her mother could drink any more.

Quin could hear the aircar taking off outside, and she gave her mother a kiss on the cheek, then ran to the front door. From there she watched the car ascend in slow circles above the meadow, until it disappeared across the sky. It headed south, to somewhere far from Quin's life, Edinburgh, perhaps, or London, or somewhere even farther away. Perhaps she would be going to those places soon too. Once she had gone *There,* she might go anywhere. And then the world would be open to her and she would be a player on its enormous stage, fulfilling her destiny.

She walked toward the woods, thinking she'd meet up with John again, tell him she'd learned nothing about the visitor to the estate. Halfway across the commons, she saw him. John and Briac were walking together. Briac's hand was on John's shoulder, and John's face was turned toward the ground. She could almost feel the heaviness of John's steps, as though her father were leading him to his execution.

I know he won't do the wrong thing, John, she thought. *You'll stay on the estate and finish your training. Everything will be all right.*

It was the last time she would ever think so.

CHAPTER 4

JOHN

Briac's hand was resting on John's shoulder as they walked along the commons. This made John uneasy. It was like having a battle-axe resting on your shoulder, just as hard and unforgiving. They'd been walking in silence, but eventually John couldn't tolerate the quiet anymore.

"I failed my mental control," he said. "I won't deny it. But it's only when you have the disruptor—"

Briac snorted, cutting him off, then walked a full twenty paces in silence. John was trying to decide whether he should simply repeat what he had said or come up with something new, when he felt Briac's hand squeeze harder on his shoulder. A pair of metal pincers would have been more comfortable.

"You've always thought this was owed to you, John Hart," Briac told him. His voice was soft, which was frightening. Nothing about Briac was naturally soft.

"My training *was*—"

"Not just your training," Briac interrupted, his voice dropping even lower, and his hand twisting into the flesh at John's shoulder.

"All this." He made a short gesture with his free hand, which seemed meant to encompass the whole of the two-thousand-acre estate around them.

"I have never wanted your land, sir." John kept his voice steady, but he could feel anger rising from the pit of his stomach. He worked hard every day to stay friendly around Briac, but it wasn't easy.

"Really?" Briac asked. "And you've made my daughter love you for pure and unselfish reasons?"

"Maybe she just loves me," John snapped. Quin's love was the one absolutely true thing in his life, and Briac had no right to take that from him.

Briac's fingers were digging into John's neck, but John refused to pull away. With Quin's father, fighting back only made the punishment worse and John's goals harder to reach. *When I get back what was taken, I will not be at your mercy anymore, Briac. And neither will Quin.*

"She doesn't belong to you, John."

"She doesn't belong to you either, sir."

Briac shoved John ahead of him, releasing his grip.

"It all belongs to me," he responded. "Haven't you realized that by now?"

They were walking near the edge of the woods on the river side of the commons. The sun had just dipped behind the hills, leaving the estate in twilight. To John's left, between the meadow and the distant river, lay a broad strip of forest. And at the edge, almost touching the meadow, were the three cottages of the Dreads. In all his years on the estate, they had lain empty, until the arrival of the Young and Big Dreads a few months ago. The third cottage was as dark as it had always been. John wondered if there was a third Dread somewhere, waiting.

The whole estate was much emptier now than it had been in years past. He'd heard from his own mother about there being several apprentices in training when she was a girl. And further back than her time, there had been dozens, filling the stone cottages hidden deep in the forest, which now stood empty. The current population of the estate consisted only of the three apprentices, Quin's parents, Shinobu's father, a few farmhands to help with the cows and sheep, and now the two Dreads.

Both Dreads were sitting outside their cottages, by the open fire pit. The Young Dread was dressed for battle, her whipsword and several knives arrayed along her waistband, her hair tied up inside a leather helmet. She was sharpening a long dagger with a whetstone by the light of the fire, her hands moving up the blade with steady, rhythmic precision. The orange firelight danced over her face, casting dark shadows around her eyes. Across from her, the Big Dread was putting oil to his own knife and chanting words to the young one, his voice as cold and hard as the blade in his hand. When he paused, the Young Dread would chant an answer.

Neither moved as they spoke, but as John and Briac went by, both Dreads' eyes followed them for a few moments. It sent a shiver up John's back.

They passed the third Dread cottage, empty and silent, and then they were away from the woods, walking across the meadow toward the dairy barn and stables. Even as he fought to keep his emotions in check, John felt a tingling of alarm. He knew now where they were headed. Briac's hand once again found John's neck, pushing him on.

"Briac, I will take my oath. I must take my oath."

"There is no 'must,' John. There is only failure or success. You have failed."

Those three words hit him like a blow to the gut. Until he'd heard the word "failed," he had held out hope that Briac would be fair, that he would keep his promises and finish John's training.

"I am the strongest apprentice," he said quietly. "You know I am."

"That you are," Briac agreed. "A strong fighter. Also a distracted fighter, an emotional fighter. Both deadly for a Seeker, to you and your companions."

They passed the stone stables, where John could hear the whickering of the horses, comfortable in their stalls. For a fleeting moment he imagined that Briac would take him in there and ask him for another show of his horsemanship. But they did not stop at the stables.

They passed the dairy barn with its special stink, unpleasant and yet friendly somehow. Briac continued to walk, his hand now a force at John's back. Their destination was a structure with a very different feel.

Ahead of them lay the old barn. Half its roof had fallen in, but the back half of the building was still intact. From a window high up in the wall in the remaining half, a weak light spilled out into the dusk, a light tinged with metallic blue.

John stopped. Briac's hand pressed more firmly on his back. But John would not move.

"I don't want to go," he said.

"We are going."

"I've seen it."

"And you will see it again."

"No." John hated the childish sound of his own voice, but Briac knew exactly how to make him feel helpless. *Whatever the circumstance, you must control it.* His mother had told him that. He must find a way to gain control again.

Briac took his hand from John's back and walked on ahead of him. "You may leave if you wish, but you will never learn what I have to say to you."

John stood there for a full minute, watching Briac grow fainter in the gathering darkness. He spent most of his days on the estate trying to forget what was in that barn. But it was there, whether he avoided it or not. Still, his feet did not want to move forward. His whole body longed to turn around and run. Finally, he hurried to catch up just as Briac was unlocking the barn door.

Inside, starlight came in through the collapsed half of the roof, providing just enough illumination for them to find their way. From the shadowy corners came the smells of old straw and wild weeds and rodents—smells he remembered from the last time he'd entered this place.

On the other side of the barn, a modern room had been built. It looked like a giant child's building block shoved inside a larger and older toy. This room's walls were smooth concrete, framing a large steel door. The two men crossed the barn, and John watched Briac enter numbers on a keypad. The steel door clicked open.

Briac gestured for John to enter first. As he stepped over the threshold, a hospital smell hit his nose, a mixture of disinfectants and decaying flesh. The weak blue light he'd seen from outside came from a bank of medical machinery stacked beneath the room's lone window, set high up in one wall.

A figure lay on the bed in the center of the room, too hard to make out in the dim light, except for a halo of sparks floating around its head and torso, flashing faintly in different colors. Years ago, when John had first been here, those sparks had been brighter, hadn't they?

When Briac switched on the overhead light, John's instinct was to close his eyes, but he forced himself to look. The figure on the bed appeared dead. The IV tubes and machinery, however, told a different story: the skeletal shape lying before him was alive, if only technically.

John's throat constricted. The figure's gender and age were impossible to tell, and the flesh seemed withered by sources other than time. The hair was gray and patchy; much of it had fallen out. The bones showed through the skin, and though the muscles had disappeared almost completely, they had pulled the body's joints into awkward positions. The face was especially skeletal, with sunken flesh and a prominent jawbone. Beneath the head, an old and unwashed hospital gown gave the figure a measure of privacy.

Briac said nothing for a while, forcing John to study the body. In the brighter light, the sparks were hard to see, so that John continuously felt his eyes were playing tricks on him, an effect that left him dizzy and sick to his stomach. He remembered being seven years old and seeing a web of bright flashes like tiny electrical explosions before he closed his eyes tight. *Repay them for this . . .*

"This is a Seeker who met a disruptor field," Briac said, interrupting John's thoughts. "Is this a pretty sight to you?"

"No."

"This body has been here for years."

"You've shown me before. You know you have. You've shown all of us." John fought to control his voice. Briac clearly took pleasure in displaying this tortured creature.

"Yes. I keep it for apprentices. A Seeker should know what he's dealing with before he takes his oath."

John felt disgust at Briac's self-righteous tone. "If you want your apprentices to know what they're dealing with," he said, "you should tell them what Seekers do *after* they take their oath."

Briac ignored this. "You ask for access to the most valuable possession of mankind without properly earning it. Even though this"—he gestured to the figure on the bed—"would be the consequence. For you, or for those who rely upon you. Like Quin."

"I have earned it," John spat. "I *can* earn it. You're simply pretending I can't."

"It takes some energy to keep this one alive," Briac mused, again focusing John's attention on the figure in the bed. "At first, there were unpleasant convulsions and twitches, when the muscles were still working, but that's over now. It's just the sparks, which are slowly fading. I have to feed a current of electricity through the body, besides the nutrients. Otherwise the sparks would drain the life out in a few days."

Briac lifted one of the figure's eyelids and stared down into the lifeless eye, which had lost whatever color it had once had, then let the eyelid fall closed.

"Stop feeding it," John said. He tried to keep his voice even, but he could hear the pleading in his own words. "The dead should be allowed to die."

"You find this inhumane?" Briac asked with false surprise. "This is an important training tool."

John stared at the body—at the patchy hair, at the hospital gown. Just as he had years ago, when he'd first seen this horrible creature, he longed to slide up the hospital gown and look for the evidence he felt sure was there.

As if sensing his thoughts, Briac stepped between John and the bed. John's eyes were drawn to Briac's old leather boots with their heavy soles and metal tips, so out of place in this tidy medical setting. They were the boots of a man who'd done terrible things. John felt another wave of nausea.

He forced his head up so his eyes met the older man's.

"It's a pity you didn't die in the practice fight," Briac said with a deadly soft voice. "That would have been convenient. No one could have blamed me."

"You're a beast," John replied quietly. "What's going to happen when Quin finds out what you are and what you expect her to be?"

"Am I a beast?" Briac asked, his voice even. "And you—so innocent?"

"You made a commitment. There were witnesses."

"I owed you your training. I have trained you to the best of my ability. You were sixteen last month. A Seeker should be sworn by his fifteenth year."

"I came to you late. I was older than Quin or Shinobu—"

"Not my concern."

"I was a *child*. It took time to convince my grandfather it would be safe for me to come—"

"You've missed your chance."

John stared at Briac. He'd struggled for years to hide his hatred. Now it came upon him so intensely, he was nearly paralyzed. That would not do. *There will be many things that try to pull you from the path. Hatred is one . . .*

Hatred. He was almost vibrating with it. Yet he spoke as calmly as he could: "That 'valuable possession' you're always talking about— whose is it, Briac? Who does it belong to?"

Briac's right hand shot out to slap John across the face, but John ducked aside, stepping closer to Briac.

"You should be helping me," John said. "Quin and I will be married one day. You could make a truce with me now, restore relations between our houses, earn what you have taken unfairly. Before I have to—"

"You have no house, John," Briac responded sharply, cutting him off. "I saw to that. You're alone, and Quin will not be yours. An athame ends up with whom it belongs. In this case, that person is me." They held each other's eyes. "I told your grandfather you've failed, once and for all. He was very upset." Briac delivered this final piece of bad news with obvious enjoyment. "He's expecting you back home."

A vast ocean of hopelessness began to rise around John. He had to get out before he was engulfed.

"Pack your things," Briac said. "I'll take you to the train tomorrow. Now go."

John did, stalking out of the makeshift hospital room and the decaying barn. He paused outside the doorway, sucking in deep breaths of the crisp night air, filling his lungs like an athlete preparing for a sprint.

And then he ran.

CHAPTER 5

SHINOBU

The village of Corrickmore was quiet that evening, except for a few wandering fishermen too drunk to go home and too loud to stay in the pub. Their voices echoed off the houses facing the waterfront, and they were answered by residents throwing open windows and yelling for them to shut up before the police were called.

Shinobu and Alistair walked down the opposite side of the street, directly along the water. Their bellies were full of mutton-and-onion pie from the Friar's Goat, the pub at the north end of town, and they were sharing a bottle of beer large enough for four or five ordinary men, and nearly large enough for Alistair.

"Mind you, not too much of the drink," Alistair said as Shinobu tipped the bottle up. "We've got a full night ahead of us." He clapped his son on the shoulder, causing Shinobu to spit a huge mouthful of beer all over his own shoes.

"Ah, take a wee bit more than that, Son," his father told him, tilting the bottle up to Shinobu's lips again. "And a bit more still."

Shinobu shook his head and handed the bottle back. He wasn't interested in beer, and he didn't fancy getting his shoes any stickier than they already were. He danced up to his father like a boxer in a ring and pounded the older man's stomach with his fists. This was very much like hitting Michelangelo's statue of David; Alistair towered above him, and Shinobu was in more danger of hurting his fists than he was of hurting his father. Alistair only chuckled as he took a long swig of the beer.

"Tell me what we're doing tonight, Da." Shinobu was moving all around the big man now, landing a punch wherever possible.

"Cannae do that."

They watched the fishermen, who had reached the corner and were getting louder as the final verse of their drinking song dissolved into chaos. Then one stumbled off home, leaving those remaining to argue their way through the first verse of something new.

"Don't look unhappy, do they?" his father asked, running a hand through his red hair.

"Who, the fishermen?" Shinobu asked. "They're drunk off their faces."

"And we're not?"

"*I'm* not. I've got work to do tonight."

"Ye think work cannae be done drunk? Sometimes being drunk improves it," Alistair said.

Shinobu smashed a fist playfully into his father's gut. "Come on. Hit me back!" Alistair took a lazy swing at him, which Shinobu ducked easily. "Your son's taking his oath tonight! You can do better than that."

"Yon drunkards don't look unhappy," Alistair said thoughtfully as he took another swing at Shinobu.

Shinobu bobbed away from his father's fist and looked at the three remaining fishermen, one of whom was now throwing up noisily into a public rubbish bin.

"They don't know the secrets of the universe, maybe," Alistair went on. "They're not part of our special . . . club. Still, they have a good time."

"Dad, one's wiping his vomit on the other one's shirt." He punched his father's shoulder with enough force to fell a lesser man.

"Oomph," Alistair said, absorbing the shock. They both studied the fishermen more closely as another one retched onto the sidewalk. "Aye, maybe they're a bit disgusting," Alistair admitted.

He crossed the street and led Shinobu away from the waterfront, up a smaller road with rows of tidy brick houses.

"Mind you," his father continued, making another attempt at whatever point he was trying to make, "those eejits are not the best example. But these houses here, they're full of people. All sorts of people."

"Dad, I've been here before, you know."

"Aye, that I do know," his father said with a smile. He tapped the side of his nose with one finger as though sharing a secret. "More than you let on."

Corrickmore was the closest town to the estate, thirty miles away. And it was true, Shinobu had visited it on more occasions than he'd mentioned to his father. There were girls in the village. And girls, Shinobu had discovered early on, were quite happy with the way Shinobu looked ("like an Asian film star"), with the way he moved ("like a tiger"), with the way he spoke ("such a gentleman!")—with everything about him, really.

"At any rate," Alistair continued, taking another long drink of the beer, "a lot are happy. Even without all the special things you've been taught."

Shinobu finally stopped dancing around his father and came to rest in front of him. He shoved hard on Alistair's chest. It was like halting a locomotive, and Shinobu was pushed back a few paces before Alistair came to a stop.

"You think I'd be happier without the things I've learned?"

His father looked down at him, then away. "I'm not saying that. Not exactly."

He stepped around Shinobu and continued walking. The town was quiet here, lit by a few streetlamps and the occasional glow of a television inside a house. The only noise was the water lapping against the pier a few blocks away. Alistair turned again, choosing another street.

"What I'm saying," he continued, "is I've raised you on the estate, filled yer head with my world." Alistair was not much of a talker. Shinobu could tell he was straining to pick the right words. "It's natural you want to do what you've been taught, but . . . you have a choice, Son. Did I never tell you that?"

"I don't need a choice, Da. I love it. The fighting, the way I use my mind. All the old stories." He punched his father several times in the small of his back to make his point. Alistair hardly seemed to notice.

"It's not quite like those old stories anymore," Alistair muttered. He was quiet for a moment, then: "Your mother liked to walk to town. Do you remember? She liked to see the outside world."

"Of course I remember."

Surprised at the change in topic, Shinobu stopped hitting his father and looked up to study his face. As a rule, Alistair did not mention Shinobu's mother, Mariko. She'd been killed in a car accident seven years before. Shinobu's memories of her were fading, but he clearly recalled certain things, like walking with her in the meadow on the estate while she explained to him what honor was. He remembered her very lovely Japanese face and her small stature—she'd looked like a doll next to his father. Even so, she'd always seemed just as strong as he was. Except near the end, when she was sick, just before the accident.

"Your mother didnae want you to spend yer whole life on the estate," Alistair said.

"But I *have* spent my whole life on the estate. I've spent my whole life training to go *There,* Da. My whole life, and now I'm ready. Tonight we're going together."

Alistair stopped walking. He bent his shoulders so his eyes were level with Shinobu's.

"It's not *There* you have to worry about," he said gently. "It's where we go *after.*"

"Tell me."

"I cannot. I wish I could, but I can't."

Alistair looked pained. He rubbed his face with his hands. They had stopped in front of a row house. The curtains were drawn, but they could see the shapes of a family moving inside, and there were kitchen noises: a kettle whistling, someone yelling that the biscuits were done.

"Do you recognize this place, Son?"

Shinobu surveyed the house, smiled. "A girl I know lives here." He turned to his father, surprised. "How did you know?"

"I know a few things," Alistair said. "Is she your girlfriend?"

Shinobu noticed a figure moving in an upstairs bedroom. It was the girl in question. Alice. He could see the top of her head near the window.

"Not sure," he said, and shrugged. "She seems to like me. She let me kiss her."

"Did she? Was it nice?"

"It was." Shinobu smiled again. As if there could be any question that kissing girls was nice.

"Look around the town a moment, Son. Please. Look at the houses, the people, the life they have. Once you become a Seeker, once you take your oath, you won't see the world in the same way."

— 49 —

Shinobu glanced around, amused with his father—he had seldom heard the man string this many sentences together at once—but also confused. "Dad, I don't know what you mean. My whole life, Quin and I have—"

"I know. And I know what you feel for Quin."

Shinobu felt his face flushing, and he looked away. He could speak freely about any girl . . . except that one.

"She's my cousin," he murmured.

"Cousins" was the word they had grown up using, though their blood relationship was not nearly as close as that. Alistair and Fiona were second cousins, which made Quin and Shinobu third cousins. And somewhere, many generations earlier, an ancestor had remarried, which meant they were only half as related as they seemed. Shinobu had made as careful a study of their connection as he could without calling attention to his interest. Nevertheless, Quin always called Alistair her uncle and Shinobu her cousin, which made him unlovable except as a family member. And though she thought he was "beautiful"—her word; he'd heard her use it—his beauty to her was like the beauty in a painting, something you admire but do not want to touch. It was the worst kind of beauty, he thought.

"Aye, she's your cousin," Alistair agreed softly, "and more. You've trained together since you were small. You won't want to leave her. But"—he glanced through an opening between the curtains at the people inside the house—"there's a girl in there who seems to like you. I want you to know, you could stay here if you wanted. You could stay, and I would go. I wouldn't take it amiss. Briac might take it amiss, but I would deal with that. It's your choice."

Alistair's eyes were pleading. Shinobu had never seen that look on his father's face before. It made him uneasy, as though the ground beneath his feet were subtly shifting.

"Da, please tell me why you're saying this."

"I can't," he answered. "I've sworn my own oath." His eyes were locked on Shinobu's, as if willing his son to read his mind. "But know: if you choose to come back to the estate with me, life will be different. You might love a woman as I love your mother"—Shinobu noticed he used the present tense, and wondered how drunk Alistair was—"but she will never know all of you."

This evening was supposed to be a celebration, but Shinobu felt his discomfort growing under his father's searching look. Why couldn't the big man break the tension with a giant belch or by peeing on someone's doorstep? But there was no sign of amusement in his father's face.

Shinobu decided the awkwardness would remain until he took his father seriously. He stepped back from the house, moving to the middle of the street so he could see Alice in her upstairs bedroom more clearly. She was bent over a desk, doing homework, maybe. She was a pretty girl, and nice, and she loved when Shinobu gave her attention. She said she had never met anyone like him, that no "gorgeous boy" had ever wanted to talk to her before.

Alistair was right. The world was full of people, and maybe a lot of them were happy. Certainly a lot of them were girls, and if he wanted, it would be easy to find the funniest, the prettiest, the happiest, and convince her to fall in love with him. But where would that leave him? *Empty*, he thought. There was one girl, the girl he had grown up with. Perhaps she would never love him like that, but already they shared a life, and a purpose. They would be like the Seekers of old, their skills and their good works becoming the stuff of legends. *Tyrants beware*, as the ancient Seekers had said. Shinobu and Quin would protect good people from harm. He could never leave that behind.

He turned and put his hands on Alistair's arms. "Thank you, Father. I've made my choice. I want to go home."

Shinobu was sure he was seeing a trick of the light, the dim and flickering streetlamp nearest them, because it looked for a moment as though Alistair was about to cry. Then his face cleared, and he nodded very gravely, as if the most important thing in the world had just been decided.

"Well then, my boy, let's get back home."

CHAPTER 6

QUIN

The day had been warm, but there was a deep chill in the night air as Quin followed her father along the path through the woods. They were finding their way by a trickle of moonlight that outlined the dark branches above them and gave shape to the small forest path.

There were owls in the woods, awake now and hunting. In the distance, as always, she could hear the faint sound of the river, curving along the point where the ruined castle lay, rolling around and down to the flatter land beyond their pastures and then moving on, to the distant loch and the sea.

She felt the forest floor through her shoes, soft, welcoming. She felt the night air on her hands and face. But there was more than that. She could feel the whole estate, the whole forest, the whole of Scotland. She was as big as all these things. She had worked half her life for this night. Everything she'd learned, all her training, had been leading her here. In a short time, she would take her oath, as so many generations of her family had done before her.

Though her father would never answer any questions about what she would do once she'd taken her oath, her head was filled with the old lore. Alistair had been a great one for telling stories, and as children, she and Shinobu had sat by the hearth on cold, dark nights as he'd regaled them with tales of Seekers who had toppled tyrant kings, Seekers who had freed ancient lands of terrible criminals, Seekers who had righted all manner of wrongs across Europe and elsewhere. She'd grown up knowing she was part of this ancient tradition.

Now she could see flames up ahead, a small fire in a clearing deep in the woods. Her father's shape as he walked ahead of her was more distinct now, his broad shoulders defined by the orange glow of that fire.

Soon they emerged from the path into the open space. There was a tall standing stone in the middle of the clearing, covered with lichen and moss. That stone had been here before the ruined castle was built. It was from a time when the land had belonged to the Druids. Her father said their most distant ancestors had been Druids. Her family had been here that long.

In front of the standing stone, the fire burned brightly. Shinobu and Alistair were already there, as were the two Dreads. Quin had known there was no chance of John being with them this evening. Even if Briac was continuing John's training—which of course he must be—John still had many things to learn before taking his oath. Even so, Quin's heart sank at his absence. Some part of her had hoped for years that he would take this step alongside her and Shinobu. *It doesn't matter,* she told herself. *John will finish his training soon and follow us.*

As Quin neared the group, she saw they were all dressed as she was, in simple black clothing, with leather armor over their chests and leather helmets. Despite their similar attire, the Dreads gave the appearance of belonging to another time entirely. Their shadowed eyes and motionless expressions made them look fierce and terrible in the firelight. If they were indeed a kind of Seeker judge, they seemed to be cut from an ancient and brutal cloth.

Quin moved to stand by Shinobu, and they glanced at each other. His hair was tucked inside his helmet, as hers was, and his dark eyes were in shadow, but she could tell he was working hard not to smile. His body was drawn up to its full height, as though his feet were about to leave the ground. She felt the same sense of anticipation and excitement. They nodded slightly to each other and knew without speaking that they were both thinking the same thing: *This is it.*

What would they be asked to do? Quin wondered. What was the modern equivalent of the great deeds they had heard about as children? Certainly they would start small, with minor heroics. Wasn't the world full of injustice? Surely there were countless small acts of bravery they could perform to help.

The Young Dread stirred the fire with those stately movements of hers, bringing the embers closer together and adding more wood above them. Then she took a long slender metal rod and placed the tip of it among the coals. Quin exhaled slowly. That piece of metal would be the final part of tonight's ceremony. She reached out and tugged on Shinobu's sleeve in a gesture of camaraderie. He responded by squeezing her hand. Then both watched the metal rod in the fire, waves of heat rising above it.

"Now we begin," Briac said, in a voice that was not loud but still commanding. The two Dreads stood up from the fire and faced the other four. Shinobu and Quin turned toward their fathers.

Alistair stood by a large wooden chest that he had carried to the clearing. After throwing this trunk open, he began to draw out their weapons. He tossed her and Shinobu their whipswords. Until now, these had been kept locked in the training barn; from this moment forward, the whipswords would be theirs to keep. He threw them knives and daggers as well, then took some for himself.

Alistair flipped up a shelf within the trunk and exposed another layer of weapons. He pulled out several, which he laid on the forest floor. In the firelight Quin saw that they were modern guns.

Guns? She glanced at Shinobu, who was equally surprised. Of course they had trained with guns. They'd trained with almost every sort of weapon. Yet these were not the proper arms of a Seeker.

She watched Briac select two pistols and secure them in holsters so cleverly concealed among the folds of his clothing and armor that Quin had not noticed them before. Alistair did the same. Then Briac gestured to the apprentices.

"Will you choose any other weapons?"

"Will we need them, sir?" Shinobu asked, finding his voice before Quin could find hers.

"Likely not," Briac said. "The choice is yours."

Slowly Quin moved forward and selected a small pistol and holster, which she positioned at her lower back. Shinobu did not take a gun.

Alistair closed the trunk and stood to face them with Briac.

"We are honored tonight by the presence of these two," Briac said formally, gesturing at the Dreads. He spoke as though he'd carefully memorized his words. "They have come here to witness the last stages of your training. Tonight they will observe the final formalities and administer your oath, if you are successful."

Quin studied the Dreads again. They were armed already, though not with guns. The Young Dread's right hand rested near her whipsword and her left near her long dagger. With her hair tucked away, she looked much younger than Quin, which made the blank look she wore disturbing, as though she were a child robbed of her natural emotions. The Big Dread had a very different expression, intense and *expectant.* Because he held his body so still, Quin had the impression that this was the only look he had ever worn, as if it had been carved into his features at the beginning of time.

"Our respected visitors are armed," Briac went on, still speaking of the Dreads, "but they will not participate in the next actions unless forced by circumstance. Let us prove our worth by ensuring that does not happen. Are we agreed?"

"Agreed, sir," Quin and Shinobu said together, though Quin had no idea to what they were agreeing.

"It is time to don our cloaks," Briac told them.

These were the ritual words. Despite her confusion about the guns, Quin felt her excitement returning.

Briac and Alistair pulled on their own dark cloaks, fastening them about their shoulders. Turning to the apprentices, they placed cloaks around Quin and Shinobu as well. Quin felt the weight of the thick cloth envelop her. She thought, *My life is finally about to begin.*

Then, with smooth, measured motions, Briac drew an object from within his own cloak. All eyes turned to stare at it.

It was a long dagger made of pale stone.

Quin realized she was holding her breath. The dagger was about a foot long and quite dull, clearly not made for cutting. Its handle was cylindrical, built of several stone discs that had been stacked on top of one another—dials that Quin knew could each be turned independently. The dagger was bathed in the orange light of the fire, which it seemed to drain of color and to magnify, creating a pale light around its blade.

It was called an athame. The tool of the Seeker. John had poked fun at Briac's description—"the most valuable artifact of mankind"—but there was nothing amusing about the ancient dagger now.

Quin had seen this athame twice before, both times with Shinobu, when they'd done especially well in a practice fight. Both times, they had gotten only a brief glimpse. Now her training with the stone dagger was about to begin. In all of human history, only sworn Seekers had ever used it. It lay at the heart of their power.

"The athame," Briac recited. "The finder of hidden ways."

Then, quite unexpectedly, he pulled another object from his cloak. This one was not a dagger, though it was something similar. It was made of the same pale stone, slightly longer than the athame, with a simple handgrip at one end, and a flat, dull, gently curving blade.

Quin and Shinobu glanced at each other in surprise. They had never seen or heard of this object before—Briac had kept it entirely secret, a final mystery before they took their oaths.

"The lightning rod," Briac intoned. "Companion of the athame, whose touch allows the athame to come to life." He held the implement up for another moment as they stared at it. Then he asked, "Are your weapons ready?"

A final check of their weapons, and Shinobu, Quin, and Alistair answered as one, "Ready!"

The Dreads did not move or respond. They were simply watching.

Briac slid the lightning rod back into his cloak. Then he adjusted the dials that formed the haft of the athame. Each dial had many faces, and on each face was a symbol. Briac was lining up a specific set of symbols along the handgrip.

"Do not think! Do not hesitate!" commanded Alistair. "Hesitation is the enemy of the Seeker!"

I will not hesitate! I will not hesitate! Quin told herself. She glanced at Shinobu and knew he was repeating the same words in his own mind.

"Prepare yer chants!" called Alistair.

Briac held the athame and lightning rod above his head and struck them together. At the moment of their impact there was a vibration from the athame, low and penetrating. It filled the space around them and grew, resonating throughout the clearing. The stone dagger was coming alive.

Briac moved the athame, directing the vibration. With it, he drew a huge circle in the air before them. And as he drew it, it became not a circle but a circular doorway, a humming hole in the fabric of the world, opening onto blackness beyond.

An anomaly, Quin thought, amazed to see it just as her father had described it. The doorway he had drawn would take them from here to *There.*

The border of the circle swirled in tendrils of black and white, the ragged edges of the world cut through by the vibrations of the athame. Then the edges tightened into a solid line, framing the gateway and seeming to pulse with energy that flowed inward, toward the blackness beyond.

Quin began her chant, and next to her Shinobu did the same.

> *"Knowledge of self*
> *Knowledge of home*
> *A clear picture of*
> *Where I came from*
> *Where I will go*
> *And the speed of things between*
> *Will see me safely back."*

One by one, the Seekers and the Dreads moved through the anomaly. Quin was last, stepping over the edge of the opening and into the darkness on the other side. When she had crossed through, she turned. Behind her, the anomaly hummed, and the humming began to lose its rhythm. She could still see the woods and the firelight through that circle. Then, slowly, the tendrils of black and white stretched out, shuddered as they grew into each other, and the opening was gone. They were in darkness.

I am a Seeker of the dark and hidden ways between, she thought. *Evildoers beware . . .*

She began to feel a strange tug on her mind, almost a relaxing of her mental control, a sensation of time changing, growing longer, slowing down. A sense of eternity washed over her, like the cool waters of a lake. She could imagine losing herself in those waters . . .

She forced herself to begin her chant again:

> "Knowledge of self
> Knowledge of home
> A clear picture of
> Where I came from
> Where I will go
> And the speed of things between
> Will see me safely back."

The chant brought her back to herself. She was Quin. She was *now*.

They were *There*, and the only sounds were of her companions breathing. Very little was visible except for the athame itself, glowing faintly. She could discern, just barely, the shape of her father's hands upon it, shifting the dials in the haft again, choosing a new set of symbols. And then she heard the athame and lightning rod strike each other. Once again the dagger's vibration enveloped them all.

In the darkness, she watched the athame making a circular slash, cutting its way from where they were, from no-space, from no-where, from no-when, from *between*, from *There*, back into the world.

A new anomaly opened in front of them, a circle framed once more in pulsing tendrils of black and white, but this time the energy of the cut seemed to flow outward, from the darkness into the world. Through the opening was visible a wide expanse of lawn rolling through gardens and down to an enormous manor house in the distance. The house was quiet. It was the middle of the night.

They stepped through the anomaly and onto the grass. Quin watched the doorway behind them lose its stability and collapse in upon itself, the edges growing together in a discordant hum, disappearing. She turned and found Shinobu standing next to her, also watching.

Quin looked toward the manor house. She wasn't sure what she had been envisioning, but it was not this. *What was I expecting?* she asked herself. If she were honest, she had been hoping to chase down a criminal on her first assignment, or save a woman from being beaten and raped, or protect a child in the midst of an ugly civil war in some third world country. Small deeds to begin with, but worthy. She'd expected, she supposed, to be thrown into chaos, not such tranquility. And maybe she'd expected to arrive somewhere impoverished, not at a beautiful estate.

She looked again toward the quiet house in the distance. Perhaps they would be stopping some terrible injustice when they reached that large and peaceful house standing in the moonlight. Perhaps that house was hiding something awful.

Shinobu's eyes met hers. He too seemed unsure.

They were both hesitating.

"We're *thinking*," she whispered. "And it's going to make us fail."

"We're not going to fail," he whispered back. "There are all sorts of bad people, aren't there? Evildoers beware."

"Evildoers beware," she agreed, nodding to convince herself. *Our purpose is worthy,* she told herself. *I will not be afraid.*

Briac and Alistair were already moving silently toward the manor house, the Dreads close behind them. She and Shinobu followed their fathers in the running crouch they had used so many times in training.

I will not hesitate! she told herself. She discovered that her whipsword was already in her hand.

CHAPTER 7

QUIN

Quin was on all fours next to the fire, retching onto the ground. Shinobu was on his knees next to her, gasping for breath.

They were back in the clearing now, but it was impossible to tell how much time had passed. Was it an hour since they'd left the estate? A day? A year? Any of those seemed possible.

Beside her, Shinobu collapsed onto the ground, his face in the dirt and dead leaves.

The embers of the fire still glowed red, so they couldn't have been gone longer than an hour. The Young Dread was adding more wood, bringing the blaze back to life.

Quin could not get her breath. She looked down at her arm. Blood covered it from elbow to fingers and was now drying to a sticky paste, but she couldn't see a wound. She'd been cut earlier, she remembered, in the practice fight. But that had been the other arm. This was not her blood.

Shinobu, his face still in the dirt, was sucking in deep breaths like a drowning man, though on quick inspection, he didn't seem to be injured either.

Quin suddenly noticed a patch of long blond hairs stuck in the drying blood on her arm. She retched again. Then she scrubbed at her skin with a handful of dead leaves, trying to clean those hairs off her. She'd had a gun, but it was gone now.

Briac pushed her over with his foot, sending her to the ground. "Stop it," he said, his voice tinged with irritation. "Both of you."

Next to her, Shinobu tried to slow his desperate breathing. He had taken off his helmet. His red hair was plastered across his forehead, and his face looked pale, even in the warm light of the fire.

Alistair was standing nearby, but he was not looking at Shinobu or Quin. Instead he was staring into the coals.

Briac turned to the two Dreads, who stood again on the other side of the flames in their formal position. They looked as steady, as calm, as they had before they'd left the estate. In fact, if Quin had not seen them walking in their deliberate, graceful way across the grounds of that manor house, if she had not seen them standing silently in the great room inside that house as it had echoed with screams, she could have believed the Dreads had never left this clearing. The Young Dread still wore her blank look, as though her mind were mostly somewhere else, far away from these dark woods.

"Have the standards been met?" Briac asked them.

The Big Dread stepped forward.

"The standards have been met. Their skills, in body and mind, are sufficient to use the athame." His voice was strange, with an odd emphasis on each syllable, as though English were not his native language. As if speech itself were unusual for him.

Briac bowed his head, accepting their judgment.

"Bring the brand," he ordered.

The Young Dread pulled on thick leather gloves and removed the long piece of metal from the fire. The end of it, the end that had been resting among the hot embers all this time, bore the shape of a small athame.

Briac lifted Shinobu upright so he was kneeling before the fire.

"Shinobu MacBain, I invite you to say your oath and become a sworn Seeker."

As he looked into Briac's eyes, Shinobu was wearing an expression Quin had never before seen on his perfect face: hatred.

Then Briac moved to Quin, pulling her up next to Shinobu so she too was kneeling.

"Quin Kincaid, I invite you to say your oath and become a sworn Seeker."

She stared at her father, his dark eyes and hair, his fair skin, so like her own. But he was nothing like her. She felt the same hatred she had seen on Shinobu's face. All her life, he had been lying to her. The existence she'd imagined for herself was an illusion.

"Say your oaths," Briac commanded.

Neither of them spoke. The smell of the blood on her arm was in her nose, and she retched again, this time bringing up the remains of her dinner.

Briac slapped her.

"Say your oaths."

They did not speak.

Briac nodded to the Dreads. The Big Dread came up behind Shinobu, put a knife to his throat. The Young Dread moved to Quin, and she felt a blade at her own neck. From the corner of her eye she could see Alistair. He had retreated to the edge of the clearing and was looking away.

"Say your oaths," Briac commanded again.

The Young Dread pressed the knife harder against Quin's skin. She could feel the edge of the blade, unyielding against her throat as she swallowed. *I was blind,* Quin told herself, feeling hot tears well up in her eyes, *but I have done these things with my own hands.* She could see in her father's expression that he was willing to kill her if necessary. Once she had gone *There,* she must take her oath or die.

She could refuse; she could let this fourteen-year-old monster of a girl kill her. Was Quin willing to end it now, to never see her mother again, to never see John again?

The knife was cutting her skin. Blood was trickling down her neck.

"Say your oaths!"

She had been trained to obey Briac. She began to speak the oath.

Once she started, Shinobu's voice joined in and they were saying it together, as they had always imagined they would.

> *"All that I am*
> *I dedicate to the holy secrets of my craft,*
> *Which I shall never speak*
> *To one who is not sworn.*
> *Not fear, nor love, nor even death*
> *Will shake my loyalty to the hidden ways between*
> *Rising darkly to meet me.*
> *I will seek the proper path until time does end."*

Briac held out the stone athame. Quin noticed the tiny carving of a fox on its handgrip, a delicate detail in this moment of barbarity. The emblem of her family was a ram, the emblem of Shinobu's family an eagle—why, then, did this athame bear a fox? And then Briac was pushing their heads toward the dull blade of the stone dagger, forcing them to plant a kiss on its cool surface.

Quin had always known her father was hard, but she'd clung to the certainty that his purpose was noble. Now she understood that there was nothing noble here; perhaps there never had been. And Briac was not merely hard; he was brutal.

The Dreads were holding them down. Quin felt the Young Dread's small, strong hands pulling her left arm forward and holding it in place. Then Briac pressed the brand into Quin's left wrist, burning into her flesh the shape of an athame. She cried out as he held the metal to her skin. She was a Seeker now, marked for life.

She had thought this brand would be an emblem of pride, but now it meant something entirely different. She was damned.

CHAPTER 8

JOHN

John emerged from the trees, coming out of the forest gloom into late-afternoon sunshine. The tiny stone barn was up ahead, right at the cliff's edge. The river was a low roar here, and as he got closer to the barn, he could see the water far below, carving into the base of the cliff as it headed east and south toward the lowlands of the estate.

The barn might once have been an outpost of the castle, a home for a lookout, maybe. But while the castle had fallen into ruin, the ancient barn was still standing, its slate roof as heavy and solid as the stones of the barn's walls.

After his conversation with Briac the night before, John had been too upset to see anyone, and had spent the evening alone. Today he'd stayed in his own cottage, packing up his few belongings. Briac would be taking him to the train station late in the evening, and then John would be gone from the estate—until he figured out a way to get back.

After what he suspected had taken place before Quin's oath last night, he'd hoped she would come to him in the morning. All day, he'd imagined her storming into his cottage, outraged at her father's dishonesty and furious as well that Briac was kicking John out. Yet she had not come. Did it mean she was happy following her father? Had John lost her? This thought left him with an ache so intense that he'd driven his fist into the wall to make the feeling go away.

At last, when he could no longer tolerate her absence, he'd gone looking for Quin. She hadn't been in any of the cottages or barns near the commons. Eventually he'd come to this little outpost on the cliff.

"Quin?" he called as he got near the barn's open doorframe.

There was no answer.

He entered the barn. On the ground floor were a few decaying stalls once used for animals. The space was brighter than he'd expected. There were large circular openings—windows with no glass—at each end of the structure, up beneath the peak of the roof. The sun was coming through the western window, casting a yellow light into the rafters and onto the high sleeping loft.

He found her in that loft, a small space with a wooden platform wedged up against the wall. There was a fresh bale of straw on the floor, which Quin must have dragged up there herself. The bale was broken open, and straw was strewn across the platform, making a simple bed. There was a lantern on the floor, unlit now but with a pack of matches beside it. She was obviously planning to spend the night here by herself.

Quin was seated on the platform, her knees drawn up to her chest, staring at an old and very battered portable television. She didn't turn her head as he climbed up into the loft.

Quin watching television alone in this remote barn was so odd that John was momentarily at a loss for words. And when he finally opened his mouth, he stopped himself. She was watching a news report on the shabby set, and something about it caught his attention. There had been a change of power in a large French company, one of those huge organizations that controlled a little bit of everything in almost every part of the world, much like the industrial empire ruled by John's own grandfather. The head of this French company, the news was reporting, had disappeared, along with his family. Some sources speculated about sudden health problems. Others feared there had been a violent crime, because traces of blood had been found in the man's country estate. Either way, the location of the man, his wife, and their children was unknown, and this unexplained absence left the business dangerously at risk of a takeover.

That French businessman—wasn't his name familiar to John? John had never been much interested in his grandfather's business talk. It had been the background noise of his childhood, which he had always tried to ignore. His mother had considered such work beneath him. And yet for years, his grandfather had been discussing business around him. Surely that name was familiar?

"Quin?"

Without looking at him, her hand reached out and switched off the television.

He sat next to her on the platform. Tucking her hair back, he gently kissed the spot where her jaw and ear met, and as he did, he noticed a small bandage on her neck. Quin gave him no response. Instead she stared out the window.

"Did you take your oath?" For a moment he wondered if her strange demeanor meant she'd failed. But without a word, Quin extended her bandaged left wrist. "May I look?" he asked her.

She glanced at him quickly, then away. Her fine white skin was particularly pale, without the flush her cheeks usually wore. Her pretty, dark eyes were like coal against snow. She shrugged.

He peeled back the bandage. There, terribly blistered, the shape of a dagger was burned into her skin.

"You did it," he said.

"I did it," she agreed, her voice lifeless. "Everything he asked me to do."

John had expected her to be upset. But she was more than upset—she was in shock. The task Briac had assigned must have been particularly bad. He wondered what he himself would have done in the same situation. Would he have been able to go through with it? *Do what has to be done,* his mother had insisted. *I will,* he told himself now. *Even when it's hard.*

"It wasn't what you thought it would be," he said softly. It was a statement, not a question.

Quin took her arm back, tucked it close to her body.

"No," she agreed.

She studied John's face then, almost as if she were trying to recall how she knew him. One of her hands came up to his cheek. "What happened to you?" she asked at last. "What did Briac say, when you met him yesterday?"

"He's kicking me out."

"That's ridiculous. He has to finish your training." She said the words automatically, but they seemed to have no real meaning to her. They were like lines from a play she'd performed years ago.

"Ridiculous, right. Because your father's an honorable man, isn't he?"

They held each other's eyes, and finally they were sharing the truth about Briac between them. Quin was trying not to cry, but she was losing. She moved into John's arms, and he held her tightly against him.

"All your life he's made you think one thing while preparing you for another," he told her softly. "Now you know."

She was shaking against him, and her tears were coming faster.

"Are you saying you know what we did?" she whispered as she cried. "How can you know?"

"I don't know exactly what happened last night," he said. "But I know what Seekers do—what Briac does. And I can see the shock on your face."

He held her away, just enough so he could look into her eyes. But she would not meet his gaze now.

"How do you know what Seekers really do?" she asked.

"My . . . mother," he answered reluctantly.

"Your mother," she whispered. "You never speak about her. Catherine."

"Yes." It felt strange, telling Quin anything about his mother, when he knew his mother wouldn't have approved of Quin. *When you love, you open yourself to a dagger.* Hearing his mother's name on Quin's lips made him feel uncomfortable, as though she were exposing something private.

As though sensing his thoughts, Quin said, "My mother has said her name a few times, but she didn't like to talk about her either. Your mother told you . . . specific things about what Seekers do?"

A lump was forming in John's throat. His mother had done a great deal more than tell him about Seekers. She had, unintentionally, *shown* him.

"She told me . . . some things," he answered, fighting to keep his voice even. "Do you want to tell me what you did last night?"

"No," she said immediately. Then, more quietly, she added, "I never want to speak of it." She wiped her cheek roughly with the heel of her hand. "Was it always like this? All these hundreds and thousands of years?"

"I don't know. But it's Briac's way. He should have warned you."

"Why?" The word sounded choked as it came out of her.

"Why should he have warned you?"

"No—why are you here, John, if you knew? Why would you stay?"

"I—I don't want to do . . . whatever he asked you to do," he told her haltingly. "But this is my birthright, Quin. Just as it's your

— 71 —

birthright. I have to take my oath. I have to become a Seeker and have an athame. Things must be put back—"

"*Have* an athame?" she interrupted, her expression changing into something like pity. "Do you think my father is likely to loan you his? Do you think he'll ever let it out of his sight?"

"There are two here, Quin. Two athames on the estate. And one doesn't belong. Is that another thing he's been hiding from you? One is from Alistair's family, but the other—"

"It doesn't matter, it doesn't matter," she said, cutting him off and not really listening, "because I'm leaving. In the morning I'll leave." She was speaking quietly but intensely, to herself more than to him, as though talk of the athame had suddenly blotted out everything except her desire to go.

"I want you to leave with *me,*" he told her. "I want you to come away with me. But—but not yet." He put a hand gently under her chin and lifted her head so she had to look at him. "Quin, you have to stay and let him teach you the rest. All about the athame. So we understand it."

A strange, strangled laugh came out of her. "I'm never going to use it again."

"You will," he said softly. "It's what we were born to do."

"No," she said, tearing her eyes away from him. "I won't do any of it again."

John hesitated. He was about to ask her for something he would find very difficult to do himself. But there were larger things at stake.

"Quin, please listen. Can you . . . avoid the worst? And still learn to use the athame?"

"Avoid the worst?" she repeated, her voice rising. "There's no avoiding the worst with Briac!"

"But if you stay, if you learn a little more, I—I have a plan."

She was having difficulty focusing on him. "What do you mean?" she asked.

"Did you know they have to tell you now? Once you've taken your oath."

"Tell me what?"

"Whatever they know, whatever knowledge they've been taught. Once you take your oath, you only have to ask."

"Is that true?" There was a flicker of interest in her voice.

"My mother explained it to me." In fact, it was one of the last things she ever said to him. She'd been bleeding all over the floor, and he'd been frantic to make it stop, but she'd acted like the injury didn't matter. *He must tell you anything you want to know,* she'd said. *But you must take your oath.*

"Yesterday that would have fascinated me," she murmured, her eyes dropping to the straw beneath her. "But today . . . there's nothing more I want to know. And, John—you don't want to know either. You should trust me in this."

He was starting to feel desperate again. "There's so much more we need to know!" he told her urgently, his voice getting loud despite his best efforts. He pulled the whipsword from her waist and held it up between them. "Your whipsword? Alistair says every whipsword in existence was created a thousand years ago. How? A modern weapons company couldn't make one today. I know—my grandfather owns one of those companies."

She took the whipsword back and clipped it into place. "We have knowledge others don't." She said it without interest.

"But *how* do we have that knowledge? And how many of us have it?"

"What do you mean?" she asked him. "There aren't other Seekers anymore."

That was what Briac and Alistair had told them, many times. They were the last of the Seekers, and most of their knowledge and history had been lost. John was quite certain this was Briac's convenient explanation to prevent apprentices from asking difficult questions. But Quin had always been in such awe of her father that she'd believed him completely.

"Then why are we worried about disruptors?" John asked her.

Her eyes were still blank. "Because disruptors are the most dangerous weapon a Seeker has, created to instill terror." She was simply parroting Briac now.

"You just said there aren't any other Seekers," John pointed out gently. "Why would we ever fight someone with a disruptor if we are the only Seekers left?"

"Outsiders could get their hands on disruptors," Quin answered slowly, as though this were the first time she'd thought of it.

"That's possible," he agreed. "But it's not the most logical explanation, is it?"

Quin's eyes gradually came back into focus on him. "You think there are more of us? More Seekers?"

"There must be more of us, Quin! And I'm not the first person to ask these questions. There was—" He stopped himself. He wanted to tell her, but he couldn't bring himself to mention the book. That was between him and his mother. He took both of her hands in his. "There's history. You ask if it has always been this way. Why hasn't Briac taught us our history?"

"It's lost. So much of our knowledge is lost."

"Is it? Now you can *ask*. You have to stay here, learn what you can. In a few months, you won't need him. Then you can leave the estate and come teach me. You're a sworn Seeker now. You have as much right to give me my oath as anyone else. We'd be together. In just a few months we'd be together."

Quin was listening to him, considering this. She laced her fingers through his.

"What would we do then?" she asked him. "After I've taught you. After you take your oath?"

"We would take one of the athames for ourselves. And we could do . . . We would decide what to do. Together."

"Like what?"

"We . . . would choose the right course of action," John said, trying to pick the perfect words, words that would convince her. Eventually he would tell her everything and she would understand and help him. "I have—"

"You *have* everything. What is your grandfather? One of the richest men in England? Why do you want the athame? You want me to stay here, to do whatever Briac asks me to do. *Why?*"

"I don't have everything, Quin," he countered, frustration creeping into his voice. "My family—my mother's family—we haven't had everything for a very long time. And my grandfather . . . The situation is—it's *complicated.*" That word was not really sufficient to describe John's relationship with his grandfather, but it was the best he could manage at the moment.

"Will you tell me what happened to your mother, John?"

She'd asked him before, when they were much younger, and he had refused to explain. But Quin seemed to sense that the answer was now important, that it was directly related to becoming a Seeker and to both of their lives.

With effort, John breathed slowly, evenly. "She was killed," he said. "Before I knew enough about her. She was killed in front of me. Or nearly."

"Oh." Quin's face fell. "I'm sorry, John. I'm so sorry."

She put her arms around him again, and he pulled her close, feeling her warmth. He was sidestepping the details of his mother's death. In this case, the details were everything, but he wasn't ready to say them aloud just yet.

"When someone you love is taken, you realize what's important," he whispered. "You don't want someone else deciding who lives and who dies. You'll never be safe."

"No," she agreed, her cheek against his. "You'll never be safe."

"What if *we* were to decide, Quin?" he breathed. "We'd do a better job. We'd make the right choices. Good choices. Eventually we could—we could make the kinds of choices Seekers were supposed to make all along. We'd put things back the way they should be."

Quin's lips brushed his cheek. Then she leaned back and held his gaze.

"Would we make the right choices, John? I'm not so sure."

"Of course we would. We're not like Briac."

"But what you're saying, it's . . . it's like something Briac might say, don't you see?"

"It's not like Briac—"

"If I stay, if I teach you," she said, cutting him off, "we'll become like him, even if we start out with good intentions." Her voice became distraught as she added, "John—I think I'm already like him. I can feel it, and it's too late for me."

"Quin . . ."

She looked away, out the window and across the river. A new thought seemed to overtake her, and she turned back to him, her voice growing urgent. "We could be together . . . if we left right now. I'd leave my whipsword, everything. We'll forget what we learned here. We could climb down to the river and go. Right now. Wouldn't that be the best way?"

They looked at each other for a long while as John imagined himself saying yes. He could be with Quin. Their lives would be simple, and probably very happy. But he'd committed himself a long time ago, with a promise.

"Quin . . . what's here on the estate—I need it. I can't leave it behind. Even though he's kicking me out, I have to find my way back."

His words hung between them until Quin whispered, "Even if I can't be part of it?"

Forcing himself to nod was one of the hardest things John would ever do. "Yes," he answered. "Even if you can't be part of it. I *am* part of it. I'm sorry."

She was silent. Then at last she said, "When I leave tomorrow, I won't be coming back."

There was no hope in her voice, and John realized that she wouldn't be convinced, not yet. He would find a different way to get what he needed, and hope that she would be far away and safe. Maybe that was better.

On reflex, his mind was already racing ahead with possibilities. There was a prickling sensation in the pit of his stomach, a premonition of dangers to come. He could see one course of action open to him, and it would be a dance for his life the whole way.

He stood and moved to the barn window, placed his hands along the edge to brace himself. A moment later, Quin rose from the bed and put her arms around him. The warmth of her felt good.

He turned, and his lips found hers. They held each other in a melancholy embrace as the sun set over the land.

Will this be the last time I get to kiss her? he wondered.

CHAPTER 9

JOHN

The ship hung fifty stories above London, floating on quiet engines between the tall buildings of the financial district. Its shape was a cross between a zeppelin and an oceangoing vessel. It was huge, and especially at midday its lustrous metal hide made it occasionally blinding to those outside. It was called *Traveler*.

On board *Traveler*, John walked through one of the upper corridors and knocked at his grandfather's office door. He had returned to the ship the night before and was now steeling himself for his meeting with Gavin Hart. John never knew what to expect from his grandfather after he'd been away for a while.

Gavin opened the door himself and pulled John inside the room, glancing both ways down the corridor, as if to make sure no one had seen them.

"John, it's so good to see you."

He shut the door, but he looked over his shoulder again quickly, as though someone might be lurking in the room just behind him. Then he put a hand on each of John's shoulders and squeezed, which was the old man's version of an embrace. The effort seemed to overwhelm him. He started to cough, a scratchy, throat-clearing sound.

"Good to see you too, Grandfather. Are you upset with me?"

"Sit, sit," the older man said softly, straining to stop the coughing.

He helped John into a chair in front of his antique desk, then slid into his own on the other side. Behind Gavin's head were enormous windows, through which John could see London's skyscrapers sliding by. The tallest of the buildings were like stalks of metallic wheat, swaying gently with the currents of air.

We will let him think Traveler *is his, John, but it was built for you.* His mother had told him that when he was a small boy. She had set him up on a high stool so their matching blue eyes were level. *Seekers cannot use their athames to board* Traveler. *I have given you a home that is exactly what you need to keep you safe. And I've given you a family with stature, which is another kind of protection.*

Gavin was eighty-four years old, with white hair cut short. As always, he wore a finely tailored suit and tie, but today the knot of his tie was uneven and his suit was rumpled, as though he'd been sleeping in it. He was acting anxious, fiddling with his lapels as he coughed again. John noticed that the old man's hands were dirty, something he'd never seen before.

"I'm not upset with you, John. Of course not. But things *are* disturbing now."

"You told Briac to send me back?"

Gavin looked surprised. He had an expensive pen in his hands now, and he was loosening and tightening the cap in a nervous gesture. "I— No. Of course, I always want you back. It's the two of us— we're the ones who look out for each other, aren't we? But no, Briac Kincaid made it clear that you must come back. Now, now, now. Forever, forever, forever." This was followed by a little laugh that turned into another bout of coughing.

Gavin's speech patterns were erratic, and he was coughing a lot. He'd always been prone to twitches and strange physical mannerisms, and John understood the source of these. But today he seemed much worse than he ordinarily was, and John experienced a stab of panic— was there something new wrong with the man's health?

"And *they* know," his grandfather said, leaning across to John and almost whispering the words, as though he were afraid someone else would hear.

"What do you mean, 'they'?" John asked.

"My nephew Edward, and his son," he explained. He coughed again, the sound deep in his throat and very unpleasant. "They know you were sent home, unsuccessful."

"How can they have any idea what I was doing on the estate?" John asked, his voice rising before he could stop it. "You don't even know, Grandfather."

"Well, I—I don't know, it's true. You and your mother never told me much. But I know you're following in her footsteps, and I—I've had to explain things to Edward." Gavin's face was turning red now, and John realized he was holding his breath in an effort not to cough. He was also looking over his shoulder again, as though someone might have snuck into the room in the last couple of minutes without his noticing.

"Explain things to Edward?" John asked, wondering if this conversation was about something real or was simply part of Gavin's paranoia, which had been strong in past years but which now seemed to be reaching new heights. "Why do you have to tell your nephew anything?"

"He's challenging the family charter, John. Haven't I explained this to you? Because, you know, your mother and father were never married."

Gavin had made John his heir at the time of his birth. Back then,

Gavin had had an old and prestigious family name with a long history in England, but not much money, and no one had cared if he chose an illegitimate grandson as an heir. But as John's mother, Catherine, had helped Gavin amass great wealth, as the two of them had built *Traveler*, which dominated the London skyline, things had changed. Other members of Gavin's family began to challenge his decisions, and especially his choice of heir.

Gavin had, in fact, mentioned these challenges to John a number of times, but John had been immersed in his training on the estate, confident that he would succeed in becoming a Seeker, and he'd chosen to ignore the details.

"But—you're fighting him in the courts, aren't you?" John asked, trying to be patient with a topic he found tiresome. "Didn't you say that a few years ago?"

"Yes, yes, yes. I'm fighting. Fighting and fighting. But I'm afraid I may—finally—be—losing—John." He was having trouble getting the words out, as a violent fit of hacking overtook him. John jumped up, moved around the desk to slap him on the back, and pushed the call button for a servant.

Now that he was standing closer, he noticed that the pupils of his grandfather's eyes were larger than they should be. John lost his train of thought in a rush of alarm. What if things were truly not going properly?

A servant was already entering with a tea tray. It was Maggie, who had looked seventy years old for all of John's life, but who must be closer to ninety now. She had cared for John since he was a toddler, maybe earlier, maybe since birth. Watching her pour Gavin's tea with her graceful, old-world motions, John calmed himself. His grandfather couldn't be dying, or John would have heard about it from her.

Gavin took the tea gratefully and sipped it for a while, standing and walking to the window. He was still coughing, but the spasms were dying out as he swallowed the warm drink and his eyes followed the buildings outside.

Maggie was fiddling with the teapot just behind John as he stood by his grandfather's chair. He shot her a look and mouthed: *What's happening to him?*

She leaned close to his ear, and her words reached him so softly that John could barely make them out. But they had been communicating this way for years, and he was highly attuned to her murmurs.

"The dosage has become much less effective again," she said in her practiced undertone. "I'm increasing it steadily. I believe he will be all right—eventually—but his thoughts are erratic for now. He can be a bit mad. Be careful what you say."

John nodded, his eyes fixed on his grandfather.

Maggie left the room as Gavin turned around. Slowly he made his way back to his desk and lowered himself into his seat, still drinking the tea, and John returned to the seat across from him.

"Are you all right now, Grandfather?"

Gavin nodded, then very gently cleared his throat. After a moment, he looked over his shoulder again, before bringing his gaze back to his grandson.

"If our holdings are in danger, my nephew has some rights in regard to the decisions that are made," he said in a low voice, as though the two of them were part of a conspiracy. "That's the way the law governs a family like ours. And I'm afraid our holdings *are* in danger. I've told Edward I have every, every, *every* faith in you as the best heir our family could produce. That you'll put things back on course. You will. Right back on course. And I've said you've been receiving private tutoring. In Scotland."

"That sounds reasonable. How can he complain about that?"

"It's just that—we've experienced some *setbacks* in the last year.

Fairly large financial setbacks. Setting us quite far back. A setback, setting us back." He smiled absently, as though this were a remarkable play on words.

"You're a terrible businessman, Grandfather." John didn't say it cruelly. It was simply a fact. He and his mother had known it years ago. Gavin wasn't a good businessman, but he loved John, and Catherine had considered that his most important attribute. She had believed that she, and the athame, which gave her access to anyone, almost anywhere, could make up for his other failings. Maybe she would have, if she'd lived.

"I'm a terrible businessman?" his grandfather asked, looking wounded. "Is 'terrible' really fair, John? Perhaps I'm not so good as everyone assumed. Your father was supposed to take care of the business side of things. With your mother's help."

That had been the grand plan, as John understood it. Marry his father's name and family prestige to his mother's skills and create an unstoppable alliance—power and wealth. John had never understood why the wealth and position mattered so much, but his mother had insisted that they were important, that they helped protect him, just as *Traveler* helped protect him.

Gavin was looking thoughtful and sad, as he always did when mentioning John's dead parents. John had never known his father, Archie, who'd died before he was born, but Gavin told him frequently how much he resembled his father. And Gavin seemed to miss Catherine too, as though he'd considered her a real daughter.

"I have to show some sort of success, John. I kept waiting for you to be finished . . . at the estate. So you could help me, like your mother used to do. I hoped we could make a plan. Restore our fortunes."

Gavin had never wanted John to train with Briac. He'd tried to keep him away from the estate and safe on *Traveler*. But when their fortunes had begun to wane, he'd reluctantly agreed that John should go, that he should follow in Catherine's footsteps.

Gavin had paused to pull at the knot in his tie, as if it were choking him, but now he continued. "John," he said, "when Briac called me two weeks ago, to tell me you'd have to leave—"

"Two weeks ago? Grandfather, Briac told me only two nights ago that I'd failed. Don't you see? He never had any intention of fulfilling his obligation to me—to us. He was never going to let me succeed. He had my failure planned ahead of time."

"Please let me finish, John." Gavin drummed the fingers of one hand on the desktop and pursed his lips, apparently trying to choose the best words from a list of equally dreadful choices. "If I can't increase our fortunes—quickly—you won't be my heir and I won't stay in control. They'll take *Traveler* from me, take everything from me. So I—I did something I know you won't like—something I said I'd never—" He paused, then rushed forward. "We have a French competitor, a large group of companies, and I—"

The door to the office opened with a soft knock. A young man walked in, crossed the room, and began to speak quietly into Gavin's ear. With a start, John realized he'd seen this man before. A few days earlier, in fact. He'd come to the estate in an aircar and spoken to Briac privately.

John thought immediately of Quin, sitting in the barn loft, watching that news story on the television, about the French businessman and his family who had disappeared, or more likely been killed. At once, he understood what his grandfather had done. He felt anger rolling up from his gut, gripping him fiercely. It was all he could do to stay silent until the man left the room.

When he did, John stood from his chair and leaned across the desk, staring down at Gavin. He could feel his face turning red, burning. Gavin looked ashamed and shrank into his chair, his eyes darting away from John's.

"Grandfather—you—you had Briac go after that French family? When Briac called about me, you *hired* him? You gave him money to do what he does? To get rid of them?"

"I was desperate, John. I didn't have you or your mother to do it for me. We're in a corner! Now those companies are an easy target for us to acquire. Our fortunes—"

"I don't care about the money!" John yelled, pounding both fists on the table. "I don't care about business! Catherine warned you *never* to use someone else. *Especially* not Briac. He's— Don't you see? This is more reason never to train me, never to let me succeed. Why should he, when you come to him? You're letting him take control of our lives again—"

"I *do* care about the money, John," Gavin retorted, standing up across from him. He was keeping his voice low so he wouldn't begin coughing again, but it carried the intensity of a yell. John realized that his grandfather looked strong for the first time in their conversation, but he also looked insane. When Gavin took another sip of tea, he was holding the handle so tightly, the cup shook. "I *do* care about the money. It was what I was promised when I chose your mother for my son. I thought I could keep things going when she died. I can't. I couldn't. I'm sorry!"

He took another sip of tea, but he coughed as he did so, and the liquid splattered all over his desk. He looked at John with wild eyes, wiping the desk frantically with his sleeve. "They will not push me out! The ship, this wealth, this is my legacy, John. Mine, and yours. But if you fight me, if you scold me, I can't be responsible for what I do!"

His expression was completely mad now, eyes wide, tea dribbling down his chin.

John couldn't look at him. He let his eyes drop away, and when they did, his gaze came to rest on the cabinet behind his grandfather's desk. The doors were ajar, and inside he could see several open boxes and messy piles of clothing and mechanical items. These were all completely out of character for Gavin's office, which was always businesslike and perfectly clean.

Curious now, John looked over all of the items visible through the open cabinet doors. There was a dirty tool kit on the bottom shelf, the kind a mechanic might have for fixing old cars, with oil-stained wrenches and a small blowtorch for welding. And there were actual car parts as well—a vintage gearshift, a grimy contraption from inside a gasoline engine. Next to these were jumbled piles of T-shirts and jackets, which looked like they belonged to a male teenager.

John understood at once. These were Archie's things. They had belonged to his father, to Gavin's son. Archie had liked cars. It was one of the few things Gavin had told John about him. He'd mentioned this hobby proudly, years ago, and John had been happy to know something about Archie, but in truth, fixing old cars was so far removed from the focus of his own life that it had made him feel sad, as though he and his father would have been strangers.

Gavin had boxed and stored his son's possessions years earlier, saying it was the only way he could continue to live his life after the devastation of Archie's death. But here he was, wallowing in the memory of his long-dead boy.

Now that he was looking, John spotted streaks of grease on Gavin's suit and traces of it under the old man's fingernails and on his palms. He'd been handling Archie's things, maybe sitting alone in here for hours with these items, lost in the past. This was so unlike Gavin Hart that John wondered, *How far gone is he?*

John didn't care about the family wealth. But, in truth, he needed his grandfather's resources and men. He needed them right now, in order to get the athame. Even though Gavin was clearly in no state to have a rational conversation, or to be responsible for any sort of business, he was still in control at the moment.

After I get the athame back, I can walk away from all of this, can't I? John asked himself. And yet . . . *Seekers cannot use their athames to board* Traveler, his mother had said. There was value in the ship. *Traveler* might still protect him. And it had been built on his mother's hard work. The idea of others taking control made him angry.

He reached across the table and carefully wiped the dripping tea off Gavin's chin. The old man was still on his feet, but his eyes were now turned down to the desk. One of his hands swiped across it as though he didn't understand how the surface could be wet. John felt a surge of pity. Maybe, as Maggie had said, Gavin would eventually be all right, but even if he weren't, even if he were going crazy permanently, John didn't see how he could abandon him, when his madness was Catherine's fault.

John sat down again, feeling drained.

"You want to restore our wealth?" he said at last. "Give me a few weeks. I'll get back what was stolen from my mother. And I'll try to help you."

Gavin seemed to return to himself. He lowered his body into his chair, and his eyes focused on his grandson. Finally he spoke. "A few weeks?"

"A few weeks, Grandfather. I have to make a plan and gather the right men. You'll have to give me men."

"John, they're watching everything I do, waiting to pounce on me. To show I'm—I'm—I'm incompetent. I don't know if I can give you—"

"Grandfather! You have to pull yourself together. You're still in charge. If I get what I'm looking for, you can forget about the rest of the family. They won't matter. We can do whatever we want."

"Yes, yes, all right. I'll figure it out," he said, looking around the room once more for lurking spies. The old man noticed then that the cabinet doors were open behind him, revealing all of Archie's things. With a guilty glance at John, he pushed the doors closed and turned away from the cabinet. He muttered, "Don't yell, John. Please. It sends my mind spinning."

Seeing Gavin sitting at the desk, his shoulders slumped forward, John softened. Gently, he said, "You'll be all right, Grandfather. I'll make things right."

From Gavin's office, John walked through corridors toward *Traveler*'s bow, then moved upstairs. On the top floor of the ship, his apartment met him with a breathtaking view of London. Though he had been quite young, he still remembered when *Traveler* was built, back when Catherine, and the athame that was rightly hers, had made it possible for Gavin to accumulate their family holdings.

John walked through the suite. Though he had come home from the estate for yearly holiday visits with his grandfather, his rooms had sat mostly empty while he was training in Scotland. Everything was as he'd left it.

From his kitchen, at *Traveler*'s current heading, he had a view across the Thames. In the distance, he could just make out the tip of the building where he'd last seen his mother. He stood there awhile, thinking about that secret apartment, the one he had discovered and to which he'd snuck out one night, unaware of the ultimate consequences of that simple act of disobedience. He watched the building as *Traveler* glided on its way, until the ship made its turn at the bottom of its figure-eight pattern and began heading back the way it had come.

John pulled himself away from the view and moved through the suite to the last room, his bedroom. Sliding aside a section of the wood-paneled wall, he revealed his closet, at the back of which was a large safe set into the steel hull of the ship. Surely servants, workers, possibly even Gavin himself, had stared at this safe at one time or another, wondering what John might have inside. His grandfather claimed to have no curiosity about Catherine's methods, no desire to know her secrets, yet John bet the old man had hired expensive locksmiths to try to get this safe open so he could see what was hidden within—hoping to find some magic talisman that could restore things to the way they were when Catherine was alive. But his mother had designed the safe along with *Traveler*'s architect, and you would have to take apart the ship itself to force it open.

John entered a combination and presented his eyes to be scanned. The thick metal door hissed open. There was only one object inside, the last thing he owned from his mother. Lying in the center of the safe's padded interior was a disruptor.

John felt a deep revulsion at the sight of the weapon, but he took hold of it anyway and hauled it out. It was as heavy as it looked, its iridescent metal solid almost all the way through, with its harness of thick leather adding to its weight. He carried it to the bed and sat with it on his lap. Touching the disruptor made him nervous and slightly sick to his stomach, but despite this, he forced himself to examine every side of it. Life or death, sanity or insanity—he was holding these things in his hands.

Do what has to be done, his mother had told him. Briac had always been against him, Quin wouldn't help him now, and Gavin was barely sane. It was up to John to fulfill his promise. He would likely have to do unpleasant things, but he would do what had to be done, in the best way he could.

What would Quin think if she could see him? Quin. He imagined her sitting beside him, pictured himself leaning down to kiss her.

There will be many things that try to pull you from the path. Hatred is one, and love is another.

He forced himself to focus. The disruptor had been created to instill terror. If it did its job, he would not need to fire it. And Quin— she had already told him she would be far away.

CHAPTER 10

MAUD

Around midnight, the moon had still not risen, and she was alone in the near blackness of the forest. She moved with the silent tread she had learned as a little girl. It was the only way she knew to walk anymore. Since she had been stretched out so many times, her body would only carry her along as it perceived time should flow: smoothly, steadily, rhythmically.

The children on the estate called her the Young Dread. It was not her name, of course. She did have a name, though no one used it anymore. She could remember it if she wanted to.

She thought of the three apprentices—two were sworn Seekers now—as children, though by some accountings they were older than she. That was a riddle with no clear answer.

Maud. It came to her, floating up into consciousness like a piece of treasure rising from the floor of the ocean. *My name is Maud.*

She'd heard them call her companion the Big Dread, though he was, in fact, the Middle Dread, and her dear master was the Old Dread. Those young Seekers had not yet been taught all they would come to know about the Dreads.

Across her shoulders she carried a young deer she had brought down with an arrow. It was growing heavy as she walked, but weight meant little. She did what she must, regardless of discomfort.

To a normal eye, there was not enough light in the forest for her to find her way. For the Young Dread, however, even the faint background glow of the stars was sufficient. Perhaps it was an effect of being stretched out so often, or perhaps it was her old master's teaching, but her eyes were as sensitive to light as they needed to be. It might be they had learned to take all the time necessary to collect the light around them until they had enough for the work at hand.

Far away there was a noise. She paused midstep to listen, her foot hovering inches above the ground. She could hear the distant song of the river, night birds hunting among the trees, and insects even, moving through the soil at her feet. But this sound was something different. It had come from south of her, in the wildest part of the estate. As she listened, she heard it again. It was the sound of trouble.

She shifted immediately, her motions accelerating. In an instant, the deer was off her shoulders and on the ground. Before it had even touched the forest floor, she was sprinting through the trees, heading for the giant elm at the edge of the clearing to the south. Her body moved so quickly, she could scarcely feel the ground as she sped over it. Then she was at the tree, leaping to its lower branches. Like a jaguar, she scaled the trunk to the very top and stood concealed among its leaves, looking south toward the source of the noise.

There were horses there, six of them, with men on their backs. She scanned the entirety of the estate from her vantage point. These men and horses would be visible to no one else yet. They'd chosen the ideal route to enter the estate undetected.

She threw her sight, as her old master had taught her, sending it out across the distance to touch these men. At once, she was able to examine them closely, as though they stood directly in front of her. They were carrying weapons and wearing masks—but one was familiar to her, even with his face covered.

They had a disruptor. The familiar one was securing it with straps around the body of another man.

She threw her hearing at them, bringing their words to her ears as though she stood among them.

"It's bloody heavy," the man said as the disruptor was tightened across his back.

"Remember, it's only value is terror," the other one said, the one she recognized. His voice was quiet, and it was all wrong. He sounded like a demon, not like a person, his voice hissing and scratching. "Do not fire unless I order it. Do you understand? There are innocent people here. All I want is the stone dagger."

The man grunted an acknowledgment, and his fingers explored the disruptor's controls. The other men were checking their weapons as the horses moved about restlessly.

The estate was under attack.

She would throw her thoughts. She would reach out with her mind to the Middle Dread, her companion. It was the fastest way to alert him, and he would decide if he wished to alert the others on the estate. Mentally she reached toward him, sending her mind across the distance to his small stone cottage. He was there; she could feel him. Yet with the slightest touch of her mind against his, she recoiled. To her old master she could communicate easily this way. To the Middle it was different. The dislike between them was so great, the thoughts died in her before she could send them.

She would have to tell him in person. He would strike her, she knew, as he did when she said anything to him that was not in response to a question he had asked. But he was unlikely to give her a full beating when he heard what she had to say.

The Young Dread swung down from the tree, dropping from branch to branch until she had landed on the soft forest ground. She was already running.

CHAPTER 11

SHINOBU

Shinobu had three practice dummies set up across the floor of the training barn. It was past midnight and he had the place to himself. He moved from one figure to the next, traveling over the floor with a dancer's grace, then exploding blows into the dummies' bodies as he moved past them. He had no weapons tonight—only his fists.

The largest dummy was roughly the size of his father, and he paid it special attention. One strike for every day of the last month. He pummeled the figure's midsection, driving the rough mannequin back along the floor. Then he was on to the next one. This one was close to Briac's size, and it was easy to imagine Briac's face on it as Shinobu rained punches into the canvas. And the third one, the smallest dummy, who was that? Maybe Quin? He felt an outpouring of pity as he attacked it. He worked its face, hitting harder and harder. The more deadly Shinobu was, the faster his fight would be finished. He was putting the figure out of its misery. With an uppercut, he knocked it to the ground.

"Nothing was what we thought," he muttered to the small dummy as it lay on the floor. "I stayed only for you."

In the silence that followed, he stood still and listened, a knuckle dripping blood onto the floor. There was a distant roar. Like a storm. Or like . . . fire? As he moved toward the barn's door, he heard voices yelling across the commons.

CHAPTER 12

QUIN

"You're filthy. Do you know that?" Quin asked the horse as she grabbed its muzzle. "It's a bit hard to tell now if you're a horse or a pig."

She was in the stable, grooming Yellen, the enormous bay horse her mother had given her when she'd turned ten. Yellen nipped at her in a friendly way as she curried his back. Beyond Yellen was a fresh pile of hay at the back of the stall. Quin wondered if she could sleep there tonight. She had done that a few times when she was much younger, curled up next to her huge horse. It was more appealing at the moment than sleeping at home.

A few tears slid down her cheeks and landed on the floor of the stall. Roughly she wiped her eyes with the back of her hand. This had happened a lot in the last month—nothing, and then suddenly tears. Another one rolled down her cheek, but she ignored it; she was tired of her own weakness.

"Turn!" she ordered. Yellen stared at her blankly, his ears twitching. She pulled his head around and moved to his other side. "You've forgotten English, haven't you, you great lump?"

With the horse, she still had a sense of humor. With people, her humor had dried up. She hadn't spent much time with Yellen that year. John had gotten her attention instead. But John was gone. Quin herself was supposed to be gone, and yet here she was. Now the horse was the only one she knew who didn't make her think of things she'd rather forget.

"Easy," she soothed as Yellen stamped a foot. "Or I'll leave you muddy."

She had vowed to herself that she would leave, but she'd stayed. The night John left, she'd slept alone in the loft of the barn on the cliff. In the morning, she'd been woken by sunlight coming in through the eastern window.

She lay there for several minutes, feeling the warmth on her closed eyelids. As the sun slowly came up, she stayed motionless, until its light bathed her arms and hands. Then the heat of its rays sparked pain from the athame brand on her left wrist. Even bandaged, it began to throb.

It's still there. It will always be there, reminding me of what my hands have done.

She could leave, she thought then, but it would not change things. She would know what she was, and every time a stranger looked at her, she would wonder if they knew it too. And if she left, what would happen to Fiona and Shinobu? They would be left on the estate without her, stranded with Briac.

So, she had stayed.

Briac had taken her and Shinobu on five more assignments since that first night. She understood it all now: the wealth behind the estate, how her family survived. And there was nothing virtuous about it.

With each new assignment, thoughts of leaving had grown more remote. She'd been raised to obey Briac's word as law. It was difficult to break that habit. And the more she helped him, the more assignments she carried out, the more she was becoming like him and the less she deserved to get away. John had said she was born to use the athame, and she wondered if she was also born to be like Briac.

Now, in the stables, she watched her arms moving the brushes across the horse's back and was overcome by the feeling that her limbs were disconnected from her, as though her body belonged to someone else. Her new scars were healing. There was the line on her forearm, where her father had cut her during that last practice fight, the small cut on her neck from the Young Dread's knife, and there was the brand on her left wrist. The blisters from the brand had gone, leaving only the shape of an athame, still bright pink and tender. The scars also felt foreign, like marks on another person's body.

Without noticing, she'd stopped brushing Yellen and was staring at her right hand, inside the strap of the bristle brush. She moved her little finger to assure herself that the hand still listened to her some of the time.

"John . . ." she said aloud, then stopped, embarrassed.

She often imagined he was with her, his warm arms around her as she laid her head on his chest. When those daydreams ended, she would feel cold, and wonder if his eyes were lonely now, without her. Even so, she was glad he was gone. John had still wanted to become a Seeker, even after she'd warned him. In leaving, he had saved himself from a profound mistake.

Yellen stamped his front foot again and twitched his ears.

"Easy," she murmured.

The horse stamped again and began pulling at his lead rope. She heard the other horses in their stalls, whickering and stamping also. Then she noticed a smell.

Smoke.

She stopped moving and listened. There were distant shouts, and something else—a low roar that she now realized had been present for some time. Quin slipped out of Yellen's stall and over to the stable door.

Sliding the door open, she felt a wave of heat and found herself staring out at a wall of fire. It took a moment to understand what she was seeing. The trees near the barn were burning. Not just burning— they were being completely consumed by flames.

People were yelling across the commons, and she could see shapes in the distance—many horses running, with men on their backs. The estate was under attack.

Quin slid the door shut and leaned against it for a moment, assessing the situation. The fire was only yards away from the wooden structure of the stable. The horses were stamping and whinnying, some of them kicking at their stalls.

Putting a hand on Yellen's nose to calm him, she slipped his bridle over his head, then quickly threw a blanket and saddle onto his back.

She peeked through the doors at the opposite end of the stable and saw darkness. The men and fire had not reached that side of the barn, so she pushed those doors open and herded the horses from their stalls. The smoke was getting thicker and they were beginning to panic, but Quin swung a rope at their flanks, driving them into a run toward the open doorway. Out in the night air, they milled about her, too frightened to move farther from the stable.

Something flashed across Quin's line of sight, about twenty yards away. As she reached for Yellen's reins, an oak tree near the dairy barn burst into flame. She glimpsed a torch high up in its branches, and now she could see the person who had thrown it, a figure in dark clothing and a mask, riding away across the commons on horseback.

The weather had been dry for many weeks, and with a roar, the tree began to burn fiercely, sending the horses into a terror. One bolted wildly, crashing through the others. Quin was caught in the crush of bodies as all of the animals, Yellen included, took off for the forest.

She fell, but someone was there, catching her.

"Quin!"

"Shinobu!"

There was ash in his hair and smears of it across his face.

"Come on," he said. "We have to get to the woods!"

Through a cloud of smoke, they ran until they reached the trees. Then they paused beneath the branches, coughing.

"A cottage is on fire," he told her. "Yours, I think. I saw it across the commons."

Like her, Shinobu had his whipsword at his waist. An old crossbow that looked about to fall apart and a quiver of bolts were slung across his back. He had raided the meager weapons supply in the training barn.

"Who's attacking?" She asked the question, thinking of hordes of shadowy victims coming to the estate to get revenge upon them. But of course there was no mysterious answer. As soon as the words had come out of her mouth, she knew who was attacking. She felt a sick twinge in her stomach. *Even though he's kicking me out,* John had said, *I have to find my way back.* Quin realized some part of her had been waiting for him. But not like this. Was he really burning down the estate?

"We'll get a better look from the other side," Shinobu told her, not meeting her eyes.

"My mother?"

"I haven't seen her."

She started to run again, but Shinobu caught her arm.

"Wait," he said. "Wait. What do we want to do?"

"We'll find my mother, and then our fathers—"

"Why?"

"What do you mean, why?"

"I agree we should find Fiona, but why do we want to find Briac and Alistair?" he asked.

"We're under attack! They're better fighters than we are."

"*We're* not under attack. *They're* under attack. Which means they're distracted." He stared at his feet, a lifetime of loyalty making it difficult for him to finish the thought out loud. At last, he looked directly into her eyes and said, "We don't talk about it, Quin, but why should we stay, after what they've made us do?"

Quin struggled for a moment with an automatic instinct to follow her father. But Shinobu was right. He was saying the words she should have said. He was suggesting they do what she should have done a month ago. The estate might burn, but this was not a home anymore.

She said slowly, "We could find Fiona and get away."

"If we're lucky, Briac and Alistair will think we were killed," he told her. "This is a chance for us. A perfect chance. It won't come again."

She nodded her agreement. "All right. Let's get my mother."

They ran until they had circled around the edge of the commons and were nearer the cottages. There they came to a stop, crouching behind a fallen tree. The men on horseback were setting fire to the buildings. Her own cottage was burning. Behind it, farther away, she could see Shinobu's, also ablaze. And the others, the cottages deeper in the woods, many of which had not been used for decades. All burning.

"Do you see her?" Quin asked.

"No—yes. She's there!"

Halfway across the commons, heading toward the pastures beyond the dairy, was Fiona. Her beautiful face was twisted in a look of terror, and the ends of her hair were on fire, orange flame upon red hair, streaming behind her as she ran. Why was she running across the meadow instead of into the woods? With a sinking heart, Quin noticed her mother's wobbly gait. She was drunk.

Quin started to go after her, but Shinobu put a hand on her shoulder, holding her still.

"They see her too!" he whispered.

He was right. Three of the men on horseback were galloping after Fiona.

"Look," Shinobu said.

The lead horseman was now clearly visible. He wore a mask, but they would have recognized him anywhere.

It was John. She had known it would be him, but actually seeing him in a mask, burning the estate, was a different matter. And he was riding straight for Fiona.

"It's Briac he hates," Quin said quickly. "He's always hated him. He won't hurt my mother. I know he won't. Should we help him, Shinobu? He only wants . . ."

She trailed off as the three horsemen caught up with Fiona. Two men grabbed her and pulled her roughly into a saddle. All the way across the meadow, she could hear her mother cursing at them.

Quin was on her feet. Shinobu seized her arm and pulled her back down again. "What are you doing?"

In the distance, Fiona screamed. One of the men had slapped her, and now her hands were being tied.

"I—I have to go talk to him."

"No!" hissed Shinobu, keeping a tight grip on Quin's arm. "He's *attacking* us. He's *burning* the estate. He might do anything, do you understand? Hurt your mother, hurt you. He's not your boyfriend now. He's different! If we want to get away with Fiona, we need better weapons."

Quin stilled, Shinobu's words sinking in. "You're . . . you're right."

With great effort, she turned away from John. He was . . . She didn't know what he was at this moment. Was he against her, or only against Briac? Would he truly hurt them?

She watched Fiona still struggling with the men across the commons. They were plainly willing to injure her, and Quin was determined to get her mother off the estate alive.

"Do you know where they keep the guns?" Shinobu asked. "Are they at your house?"

"They weren't in the training barn?"

Shinobu shook his head. "Come on. We'll check both houses."

He took her hand, and together they ran toward the burning cottages, still keeping to the trees. They passed the cabin that had been John's. It too had been set alight, and very recently. The furniture inside was burning, and smoke poured out the door. There was no reason to burn everything. It was an act of pure hatred.

At the edge of the forest, they sprinted across an open space to Quin's cottage. But it was hardly a cottage anymore. By the time they reached it, Quin's home was completely engulfed in flames.

CHAPTER 13

MAUD

The Young Dread stood with the Middle Dread far from the cottages and the barns. They were atop a small hill within the forest, their backs against tree trunks, their cloaks wrapped around them, all but invisible. From her vantage point she could see the homes burning— all of them, except the cabins of the Dreads.

There was a dull throbbing in her cheek where the Middle had struck her. She'd arrived at his cottage after her furious run, but before her mouth could open to form the words explaining that they were under attack, his fist had found her cheek. She'd begun her explanation anyway. Within moments, at the Middle Dread's orders, they had gathered up every one of their weapons and melted into the forest.

A woman was yelling down on the commons. It was the woman with red hair—Fiona was her name. The Young Dread watched as two men beat out the fire in her hair and lifted her onto one of the horses. Maud threw her sight and hearing, watched closely as one of the men struck Fiona, and the young man she recognized—despite his mask and the harsh metallic sound of his altered voice—tied up her hands.

"Don't hit her!" that one said in his strange voice. "I don't want to hurt her!" Then to Fiona, "Please, please stop struggling. I only need Briac."

"I wish to help them," the Young Dread said. The words came out of her rhythmically, sedately, just as her body walked and her mind thought. Her voice did not seem to carry emotion, even though she felt it. "Several of them are sworn Seekers."

The Middle's arm swung around and slapped her other cheek. She had known he would do this. In her altered time sense, she had watched his arm coming toward her like a storm in the distance. She could have moved out of the way, but there was no reason. He would find another time to hit her, and more severely, if she did not accept his slap now.

She desired to help the inhabitants of the estate—especially if she could do so without harming the apprentice in the mask. But this was not their duty, in fact. Sworn Seekers were meant to have autonomy. The duty of the Dreads was to observe, to oversee the oaths of new Seekers, and only in certain circumstances to become involved. What was happening now—a squabble over control of the athame by two families who could make equal claims—was not their domain. Even her old master would agree with the Middle on that. Their duty was only to protect the athame of the Dreads, which hung safely inside her companion's cloak, close to the hand he had just used to strike her.

It was not their duty to interfere. Yet they had interfered in the past. A thought came to the surface slowly: *A woman with light brown hair, a boy hiding under the floor* . . . They were not supposed to interfere, and yet they had. *And look what happens.* Out on the commons, the young apprentice in the mask was yelling orders to the others. *The boy becomes a man, and the man is angry* . . .

CHAPTER 14

QUIN

Through the window of her burning home, Quin could see flames consuming their kitchen table and licking up from the seams in the wooden floor. The sitting room walls, with their old display cases of weapons, were fully ablaze, as were the timber beams of the roof. The house was throwing off so much heat she couldn't get close to it. Any guns that might have been hidden inside were as good as gone.

Shinobu had gone separately to search his own home, so Quin was alone as she scanned the area around her cottage. A short distance away was a stone shed that had not yet been reached by the fire. Even so, waves of heat came at her as she grabbed the old lock on the shed door and twisted the combination into it. Quin threw the door open, exposing their weapons.

Her whipsword was already at her waist, but she grabbed knives and her cloak. She felt carefully around the shed's walls, trying to locate a hidden compartment where Briac might keep other weapons. It would be very like her father to hide things from her, yet she found nothing.

A loud crack, almost like a shotgun going off, cut through the roar of the fire. Quin backed away from the shed in time to see the cottage roof caving in. The huge crossbeam beneath it had split, and enormous sheets of slate were tumbling inward.

The chimney fell sideways as the roof gave way below it. Quin leapt backward as the entire column of masonry crashed into the shed, leveling it as though it were made of paper. She staggered out of the way as hot stones rained down around her.

But as the falling masonry settled, she discovered something flat, hard, and painted now visible below the rubble of the shed. She dropped to her knees and dug. There was metal. She covered her face as fresh air poured into the house fire and a new blast of heat hit her. Then she grabbed handfuls of earth and stones to uncover a vault, sunk into concrete beneath the soil.

There was no obvious way to open the vault. It must have been designed to be accessed only by Briac's touch. This chamber was more secure than necessary for guns. There was only one item on the estate precious enough for this sort of hiding place.

The temperature was getting unbearable. She drew her whipsword and flicked her wrist a few times, shaping the weapon into a thick dagger that tapered to a needle point. Then she smashed the sharp tip straight down onto the edge of the vault, where the hinges for the door must be. The sword bounced off, leaving a tiny dent.

She set the tip of the dagger back into that dent. The material of a whipsword could be manipulated down to the molecular level, if you could master the subtle motions required. Quin cleared her mind and focused, ignoring the waves of heat that threatened to light her hair on fire. She put her wrist through a series of minute movements, ordering the sword to narrow its tip and extend farther.

The wind changed, and smoke buffeted her. She closed her eyes and shifted her wrist again, envisioning the tip extending farther, drawing itself out into a point so narrow, it could cut its way through metal.

She felt the sword move down through the surface of the vault, almost imperceptibly. She manipulated it again, tapering the edges so they were just as sharp as the point. As she did, the sword began to travel downward in a steady, continuous cut. It had pierced the metal. She dragged the weapon along the seam slowly, slicing as she went. A hinge gave beneath her hands, and then a second hinge. All at once, the cover came loose. Prying it up with the whipsword, she threw it aside.

The athame and lightning rod were there, waiting for a Seeker, their master, to pick them up and use them.

If she and Shinobu really meant to abandon the estate and everything on it, Quin knew she should not take the athame. She could leave it for her father and he would continue to use it as he always had. Or . . . or she could give it to John, who so desperately wanted it.

She covered her face against the heat and tried to locate John through the smoke, but the air was black around her.

She turned back to the vault. She could give the athame to John and ask him to release her mother. Or she could give it to him, calm him down, and ride off with him on the back of his horse. They would be together. His anger, this attack, they were only the result of Briac's unjust treatment.

But words came back to her from that afternoon in the barn by the cliff. *What if we were to decide, Quin?* John had whispered. *We'd do a better job. We'd make the right choices. Good choices.* It was easy to think you'd make the right choices when given power, but John didn't understand what it was to hold life and death in your hands and to decide which one you would deliver.

And if he did get the athame, he would need Quin to train him to use it. She would be helping him take his first steps *There* and beyond. She would be leading the way.

"I'm sorry," she whispered as she took the stone dagger and rod from the vault and concealed them in her cloak. "I won't be the one who turns you into Briac."

There was something else inside the metal box. It was a thick book with a leather cover and a leather tie around it. The cover was worn and shiny, as though many hands had touched it lovingly over many years. She flipped through the pages, discovering it was a journal of some kind. Much of it contained a neat, girlish script, but numerous other hands had left their mark as well. Some of the early pages held the sort of cramped script that had been in style long ago. And there were other pages written in beautiful copperplate, marred only by ink stains from a leaky fountain pen. There were also loose sheets of a fine, soft parchment—vellum, she thought, recalling one of her mother's history lessons. These loose sheets were elaborately decorated, folded carefully, and tucked among the other pages.

In her quick examination, she noted dozens of hand-drawn illustrations, many of them crude animal forms. Her eye was caught by one in particular, a diagram in an upper corner of one page: three interlocking ovals. Like a simplified drawing of an atom.

There was a yell in the distance. Quin carefully tucked the book into a pocket of her cloak, and she was away, running from the cottage toward the trees.

Shinobu had gone to his own house, to see if he could find the stash of guns. When she arrived at his cottage, however, she found that it too was a bonfire, falling in upon itself. Shinobu was not there.

Across the commons to the south, there was a loud boom, as of something large and heavy falling to the ground. Quin turned, but there was too much smoke to find the source of the noise. She could, however, see as far as her own cottage, and there she spotted her father. He was emerging from the trees to the east of her location and making his way toward their burning house, ducking low to keep out of sight.

Briac wore ordinary street clothes, and Quin realized that her father had been off the estate on one of his frequent trips—trips that usually led, a short time later, to another assignment that she and Shinobu would be asked to carry out. She didn't know the secret means by which her father was contacted for these assignments, but clearly he had long ago established a method for the right sort of people to find him.

Briac stopped some distance from their family cottage and looked south across the commons. The changeable wind had blown the smoke clear for a moment. Briac, and Quin as well, from her vantage by Shinobu's burning home, could now see John's group of horsemen gathered by the workshop. It was difficult to make out details at this distance, but one horse was carrying two people, one of whom had long, red hair. Her father watched the horsemen briefly, then continued on toward his cottage, without another look in her mother's direction. *He doesn't even care,* she realized.

Briac would be searching for the athame and lightning rod when he reached their house, and Quin planned to be well away from him before he noticed they were gone.

She and Shinobu had agreed, should they get separated, to follow Fiona. Quin began to move in that direction as the smoke closed in thickly again, hiding her from sight.

CHAPTER 15

JOHN

The door exploded outward from the workshop, pulled off by ropes attached to running horses. Inside, John and his men found Alistair MacBain huddled over a workbench, headphones over his ears as he concentrated on a small mechanical device. A deep vibration emanated from this device, reaching well past the workshop itself. John could feel it in his own lungs.

As the doors crashed onto the ground, the big man jumped to his feet in surprise, then turned to face the six of them. Alistair's eyes quickly found the man with the disruptor and then took in Fiona being held on the farthest horse. He turned to John as he removed his headphones.

"You need a mask to fight me?" he asked. "Where's your honesty?"

"I should ask you the same question," John said, the small box strapped to his throat altering his voice into something demonic.

"Cannae use your own voice, even?" Alistair asked. "Did I train a coward all those years?"

John had known they would all recognize him, and still he couldn't bring himself to enter the estate undisguised. He was here to get what was rightfully his. He knew he would have to terrify the inhabitants of the estate to do that, and it was easier to face them, to scare them, to order them, in a mask.

And the mask was liberating. He'd kept his hatred of Briac under strict control for so long, but now, disguised, he could allow it to the surface. He'd set fire to his own cabin, deep in the woods. Briac had kept him there for years, isolated, like a stray animal allowed to sit at the edge of camp, close enough to see the campfire but not to feel its warmth. It was frightening how good it felt to let the hatred out, to watch that structure burn.

His men had set fire to the other cottages before he'd been able to stop them, and he'd found it was a relief to watch them all burn, to destroy Briac's home entirely. They were just houses, after all— his men had made sure they were empty before setting them alight. Though John didn't mind the idea of hurting Briac, the others on the estate were a different matter. He wanted to keep them safe.

He was relieved that he hadn't seen Quin anywhere. She must have gone, as she'd told him she would do when they'd last been together. She was somewhere far away and safe.

Now, sitting astride his horse outside the workshop, his eyes turned to the device on the table behind Alistair. It was like a vise grip, but instead of metal it was made of the same oily black substance as a whipsword. Held tightly inside it was an athame.

John had never been allowed in the workshop before, had never seen this device. He looked again at the headphones, which were now hanging around Alistair's neck. The vibration, he realized, was coming not from the vise but from the athame itself. Alistair was doing something to the dagger, tuning it, maybe, and the headphones provided protection for his ears.

"Whose athame is it?" John asked in his distorted voice.

"It happens it's mine," Alistair said. Then, more softly: "You were wondering if it was hers?"

John slid off his horse and moved into the workshop, nodding to the man with the disruptor as he did so. This man ran his hand down the side of the weapon, and it crackled to life with a high whine.

"Careful now," Alistair said to the man. "That wee toy is dangerous. I bet he has not told you how dangerous."

John studied the athame inside the device. On the pommel was a tiny carving in the shape of an eagle—it was the symbol of Alistair and Shinobu's family. It was not the carving he'd hoped to find, but any athame was better than none.

"I told you, it's mine," Alistair repeated.

John studied the vise itself. It was more complicated than it had seemed at first glance. The stone dagger was held tightly in several places. And there was a sort of razor hovering over the athame's surface that could be used, John guessed, to shave off minute amounts of stone in order to make the dagger's vibration perfect. Used incorrectly, though, the razor could likely cause harm. John reached a hand toward one of the levers, then stopped. He didn't want to risk damaging the athame.

"How do I get it out?" he asked, keeping his voice quiet, which made the words sound like a growl.

"Can't tell you that," the big man said, keeping his eyes on the disruptor.

It was hard not to like Alistair, who had, at one time, tried to help John's mother. But John reminded himself that the big man had also been a faithful ally of Briac Kincaid for years. John was not going to leave without an athame; if Alistair helped him, everything would be easy and no one would be hurt. Slowly, keeping his hand steady, he raised his gun to Alistair's head. "You can tell me. I know you can."

"All right, you caught me. I can. But I won't."

"This doesn't have to be hard," John said, his voice scratching and hissing.

"I'm afraid it does," replied Alistair.

John nodded subtly. The disruptor let out a higher whine, preparing to fire.

"Will I be likely to explain it to you when I'm in a disruptor field, lad?"

"Very well." John hesitated, hoping he could trust his men to follow orders and kill no one without a direct instruction to do so. Then he gestured at the man who sat behind Fiona on horseback.

John avoided looking in her direction as the man pressed a knife to her throat and Fiona let out a strangled cry. He kept his eyes on Alistair.

"Remove the dagger from the device," he said evenly.

"I can't do that," Alistair replied. "No matter what I feel, the athame is more valuable than a life." His eyes, however, told a different story—they darted again to Fiona.

John steeled himself and gestured again. The man began to make a shallow cut across Fiona's throat. She struggled frantically within his arms, blood dripping down her fine, white skin.

It's only a little blood. He won't cut her deeply, John told himself. *Please don't cut her deeply!* He swallowed, kept his gaze on Alistair. The big man looked at the ground as the cut along Fiona's neck grew longer. At last Alistair nodded, giving in. He reached for the vise grip and began to unwind the levers holding the dagger in place. The knife at Fiona's throat stopped moving.

"Easy," John said to Alistair.

Alistair's hands moved slowly over the many levers of the apparatus. The athame itself began to move as the device loosened around it. At the moment when John expected the dagger to fall out onto the table, Alistair very gently took hold of the longest lever with both hands. Then he twisted the lever fully around, his huge arms straining as he yanked it toward himself in one sudden, brutal motion and the razor within the device bit deeply into the dagger.

At once, the athame began to throw off a terrible vibration. They could all feel it in their teeth, in their bones. It was like metal tearing or glass cracking. John's muscles tightened of their own accord, his fists clenching, his legs beginning to cramp.

Across the room, the man with the disruptor experienced the same tightening of his own muscles, just as his horse staggered backward, similarly affected. Involuntarily, the man's right hand clamped onto the disruptor, and the weapon fired.

John's teeth were gnashing uncontrollably. He saw disruptor sparks shooting toward him, but he could hardly get his legs to move. With a huge effort, he threw himself to the floor, landing like a bag of bricks.

The sparks passed above him and collided with Alistair.

The vibration from the athame stopped dead, as if snuffed out by an unseen force.

There was silence as everyone slowly regained use of their muscles. Then Alistair began to scream and beat at his own head.

John struggled to his feet and grabbed the device holding the athame. He saw then why the vibration had stopped. The razor arm within the apparatus had cut deeply into the shaft of the dagger, shattering the blade. Some of the stone pieces were still locked in the vise. Others had scattered across the workbench, along with a handful of gritty dust. The color of the stone itself had changed, become more gray, its surface dull. Whatever energy had existed inside that ancient artifact was gone.

Alistair was staggering toward the barn door. His red hair stood on end as multicolored sparks danced around his head and shoulders. He could not walk in a straight line, but kept turning back, striking out at the air, then staggering again toward the door. Fiona was crying freely as she watched him, and John's men stared in stunned silence.

John himself felt a rolling wave of nausea as he saw Alistair stumble through the doorway amidst those rainbow flashes. This sensation mixed with a regret so strong, it was physically painful. *Not Alistair!*

He ran for his horse and leapt up into the saddle. Bringing the animal close to the man with the disruptor, John slapped him across the face. He knew Alistair's condition was not the man's fault, and yet he couldn't stop his anger—at Briac, for putting him in this position, and at himself for losing control of the situation.

"How could you?" John screamed with his distorted voice. "He was a good man, and you've destroyed him." He put his hands to his head for a moment, then ordered, "Go find Briac!"

The explosion from John's blasting coil took out half the wall, but the withered figure made no move, not even a small flinch. The figure's position on the hospital bed and the faint sparks dancing around its head were just as they had been a month ago.

John stepped through the dust and smoke into the room. His eyes swept the medical machinery along the back wall, and then he took a seat on the edge of the bed.

He had never been alone with this creature. He'd always been in Briac's presence, and very much on guard. Now, gently, his fingers found the bottom edge of the ancient hospital gown covering the figure, and slid it up the withered left leg. On the upper thigh was a puckered scar, as long as a man's hand. It looked like a sword or knife injury that had been sewn up very carelessly.

He had known he would find that scar, and yet it still took his breath away. Briac had stood here twice, taking perverse pleasure in making John look at this decaying, tortured figure as John tried to pretend he had no idea who it was.

John dropped the gown back into place. Though he could not stand the thought of touching the body, he forced himself to put a hand on one of the bony shoulders. He studied the sunken eyes, the withered nose, the prominent jawbone. Nothing was left of what the face had once been.

He took out a knife and positioned it above the creature's chest. It would take only one hard thrust, he told himself, to drive the blade into the heart and put an end to it. He held the knife there for a full minute, trying to make that thrust, but he could not. Finally, he let his hand drop to his side.

He sat on the bed for a long while, unsure of what to do next. Slowly, as though he could not support its weight, his head fell forward until it was resting on the mattress next to the figure. He closed his eyes, pushed his forehead into the old sheet. The tears started gently but soon became fierce. His body convulsed in sobs, the sort of cries a small child might make when he discovered his world was ending.

At last, still crying, he stood up from the bed and blindly cut through all of the IV tubes. One by one he switched off every piece of machinery in the room.

When the equipment had all gone silent, he turned to look at the body in the bed, expecting to see some change. There was none. The figure was completely still, and the sparks still danced around its torso.

It might take hours, or even days, he realized, before the figure finally died and the sparks went out. Surely, after all this time, the end would be painless.

As he stood by the hole in the wall, he loosened the distortion box around his neck so his voice would not sound demonic. "Soon I will have back what is rightfully ours," he said quietly, his natural voice sounding foreign to him. "I will pay them for what they've done to you and put things back as they should be." He paused, looking at the body for the last time. "Goodbye, Mother."

Tightening the box around his throat again, he stepped back out into the night.

CHAPTER 16

SHINOBU

Shinobu grabbed his father's huge shoulders, trying to steady him. Alistair swung a fist at his son. Shinobu ducked, then found the big man's hands tightening around his neck. But Alistair's mind twisted away before he could do any damage. He released Shinobu and fell to his knees, beating his own head on the ground.

"Da. Do you know me?"

He pulled Alistair's head around so they were looking each other in the eyes. The moon had risen, lighting the floor of the forest. His father was still for the briefest of moments, his eyes wide and blank, cuts along his eyebrows from smashing his head into the dirt. Then he lunged. His hands reached for Shinobu's neck again, his fingernails grazing the skin. Just as suddenly, he stopped himself, groaning, and began beating his own legs.

The field distorts your thoughts. You form an idea, but the disruptor field changes it, sends it back to you altered. Shinobu was recalling Alistair's own words. He had drummed the perils of disruptors into their heads for years. *Your mind will tie itself in a knot, fold up, collapse.*

You will want to kill yourself, but how can you? Even that thought spins out of your control . . .

Smoke lay heavily over much of the estate, making it difficult to breathe or see. Shinobu had checked his own cottage, looking for the trunk full of guns, but had found nothing except a pillar of fire where his home had once been. He'd gone farther, to the cottages of the Dreads, hoping they might have weapons he could take. But those structures, while not burning, had been completely empty. The Dreads had taken their belongings and gone.

He and Quin had agreed to follow Fiona if they got separated, so he'd headed back around the commons and through the forest toward the workshop. Halfway there, in a section of the woods the smoke had not yet reached, he had come upon his father, staggering through the trees, caught in a web of sparks that would be the end of him.

Shinobu was ashamed to find that he didn't feel sorry for Alistair. If his father had been disrupted only a few short weeks ago—before their first assignment—Shinobu would have been devastated. But now his heart was numb. Truly numb. Alistair had let him make the wrong decision. Yes, he'd warned him, but so gently there was no way Shinobu could have understood. How could he possibly have understood?

His father had let him go on that first assignment and swear his oath. Alistair had known what it meant, and he had let it happen. And then he'd accompanied them and Briac on more assignments, without saying a word.

"Why did you not stop me?" Shinobu yelled at Alistair. "I would have listened if you'd explained . . ."

Alistair was gritting his teeth as though fighting a battle inside his head. He cried out, and in the same moment managed to pull a knife from his belt. He lashed at the air with the blade, hit his own head with the hilt. Then he raised the knife and struck down wildly at Shinobu.

Shinobu blocked him and pushed. Alistair landed in the dirt, but his hand was still pressing against Shinobu's with the knife. It was not the blade against his skin, Shinobu realized, it was the handle, and Alistair was shoving it into his hand.

Shinobu grabbed the knife, and his father rolled away, his fingers scratching at tree roots. Then he kicked at his son's legs. Shinobu took a step backward, out of reach.

He should end this for his father. That was what you were supposed to do for a comrade caught in a disruptor field—end it. The field was permanent, and only a monster would let someone suffer like this.

If I am a monster, Shinobu thought, *it's because of you. You stood by and let me do it.*

He tucked the knife into his belt and walked away.

CHAPTER 17

QUIN

Quin was following the sound of John's voice through the smoke, which lay so thickly around her that she was forced to creep along the ground, her cloak over her nose and mouth. She had been following that voice all around the commons, but at last she was getting close.

It wasn't John's real voice she was following, of course, but that strange, harsh metallic one he was using, as though it could separate him from what he was doing. She hoped Shinobu could hear that distorted screech as well and that he was nearby with an armful of weapons. She didn't want to hurt John, but weapons seemed a necessity if she wanted to get her mother back.

"I don't have what you're looking for." This was a new voice through the smoke—her father's.

"You have it," John said. "When you give it to me, you will have your wife back."

"Have my wife back?" Briac repeated, a mocking tone in his reply. "That's what you're bargaining with?"

There was a breath of wind, and Quin came into a patch of clear air unexpectedly. The moon was up now, and she discovered she was again near the smoking wreck of her own cottage at the edge of the field. Her mother was visible directly in front of her, still on horseback, with a man seated behind her. A short distance away, John faced Briac in the tall grass of the commons, the mounted men encircling them both.

Quin crouched low in three-foot-tall scorched stalks that had been a green meadow only a few hours before.

"You can kill my wife only once," Briac said. "Then what?"

You're a beast, Quin thought, staring at her father.

"You're a beast," came John's altered voice, speaking Quin's own thoughts aloud.

"Aye, I'm a beast," Briac agreed. "But I don't have the athame."

"All right," John said.

Quin watched as John pulled out a pistol and shot Briac in the leg. Her father cried out and collapsed into a sitting position, blood blooming through his trousers along his upper thigh.

"There's a matching scar for you," John told him in his inhuman voice.

She knew the sight of her father bleeding should bother her, but Quin could not stop herself from feeling a fierce satisfaction at his pain. *Briac would kill any of us if he had to,* she thought, finally admitting the truth to herself.

Her eyes went back to John. She couldn't see his face because he still wore his mask, but his hatred for Briac and his desperation for the athame seemed to radiate from his body. *Is he desperate enough to hurt my mother?* she wondered. She had the strong urge to pull the athame from her cloak and toss it to him. That simple action would put an end to the attack and make John happy all in a moment.

And then what? she asked herself. *What if we were to decide, Quin?* John had whispered to her in the barn. *We'd do a better job . . .*

"Where is the athame?" John demanded of Briac again, bringing Quin back to the present.

"I don't have it!" Briac yelled, clutching his injured leg. "Kill me, kill her, kill anyone you like! I still don't have it!"

It was time to act, while everyone's attention was on her father. Quin moved in a crouch toward her mother, staying low in the grass. As she approached, she could see a wash of red over Fiona's neck—her throat had been badly cut and was covered in blood. Had John done that to her?

Quin pulled a knife from its sheath at her waist, thinking, *I hope you're sober now, Mother.* Fiona turned her head and looked directly at her, as though Quin had spoken the words aloud. Seeing Quin's knife, she moved her head slightly, acknowledging that she understood. Her horse was the farthest back in the circle of men, away from notice at this moment.

"I was betrayed," Briac said frantically as John got closer. "I don't have it, I tell you!"

John shot him again, hitting his shoulder. Briac was thrown backward, and the new wound bled quickly, soaking his shirt.

"Don't worry," John told him in his awful voice, still approaching. "I'll stitch those up for you. I've got a needle and thread around here somewhere."

Quin saw her moment. She threw her knife, knowing she wasn't as skilled at this as the Young Dread but hoping her talents were sufficient. The knife arced through the smoky air and buried itself in the throat of the man holding Fiona. He tried to grab the blade, but before he had a chance, Fiona twisted her head and slammed it back against him, crushing the knife farther into his neck.

Staying low, Quin ran to her mother. She eased both Fiona and her captor—the man desperately clutching his throat—off the horse.

By the sounds he was making, he would be dead in a minute or two. Quin retrieved her knife and slashed the ropes from her mother's hands, and then they were running back into the smoke.

When they were past the burning cottages and among the trees, Quin paused to examine the wound at Fiona's throat. Blood was still seeping from it, but the cut was shallow enough to pose no immediate threat. Had John and his men meant only to make a surface wound? Or had Fiona simply been lucky?

"Your father . . ." Fiona whispered.

"We're leaving." Quin said it firmly, and though unspoken, it was clear she meant: *We're leaving without Briac.* "As soon as we find Shinobu."

She took her mother's hand, and they ran deeper into the woods, heading along the west side of the commons. Unless Shinobu had abandoned the estate, it was the only place he could be.

"John may kill your father," her mother breathed.

From their new location, they could see Briac again. John was approaching him with a knife. At that moment, Quin realized that she wanted John to finish him. Whether John was dangerous or not, sane or not, she wanted him to finish Briac. It would set her free; it would set all of them free. She was about to answer her mother—*If John doesn't kill him, I promise you I will*—when her attention was drawn to a large shape moving deeper in the woods.

"Look!" she whispered. "There's Yellen!"

CHAPTER 18

MAUD

The Young Dread and the Middle Dread were perched in the branches of a huge oak tree near the edge of the forest, watching the apprentice with the mask. He was holding a knife in his hand, approaching Briac, who lay wounded in the grass of the commons. Briac began to yell.

"You cannot stand aside! You cannot stand aside!"

Though her companion stood as still as stone, his breath so slow and soft that even she had difficulty hearing it, there was a tension about the Middle Dread as he watched Briac.

"You must help me!" Briac called.

He is speaking to us, the Young Dread realized. *No,* she corrected herself, *he is speaking to the Middle. Those two have secrets.*

And the Middle was listening. She moved her head slightly to observe him. His body was tensing. He was preparing to speed up.

"Sir," she said, forming the word with great concentration, "as you have said, we are only observers here."

He could not strike her from where he was perched in the tree, and this time he didn't even seem to consider it. His mind was on Briac only.

Out on the commons, the masked apprentice had also become aware that Briac was speaking to the Dreads.

He stood up and yelled into the air, "You must—"

But the rest of his words were swept away by the inhuman screech of his false voice. He tried to yell again, but his words were nothing but noise. The device changing his voice was no longer working properly.

"If he cuts me," Briac called out, "I don't know what I may say. Or what he may find. The book . . ."

The Young's eyes were on the Middle. He was poised between slow and fast, his feet at the edge of the branch. The Middle was scared of something Briac knew—of something he might reveal. *And the book.* She remembered the book, and the boy beneath the floor.

The apprentice ripped something from around his throat and yelled out with his true voice, "You must stand aside. You have rules. He has broken them first!"

The Young threw her sight at Briac. He was bleeding heavily from his leg and shoulder, visibly losing strength. If they waited long enough, he would certainly bleed to death.

"Sir, he is right," she said. "Briac first took the athame—"

The Middle sprang into action. He reached across the tree trunk and yanked her from the branch, throwing her to the ground. It was only ten feet, and she rolled into the fall easily, but the Middle's reprimand was unmistakable. From the ground, she looked up at him. He had a crossbow in his hands, and a bolt was already pulled into place.

"I decide," he told her. "You must obey."

"Help me!" Briac yelled again.

The Middle loosed the crossbow bolt, and one of John's men toppled off his horse.

"Fire on them," the Middle commanded her.

The Young Dread sped herself up, had her own bow in her hands, an arrow nocked almost instantly. She let the shaft fly and watched as it hit another of John's men in the shoulder, as she had intended, sending him to the ground.

The apprentice and his remaining men—only two of them now—were in disarray. The Middle loosed another bolt as one of the men tried to gallop away. The horse was hit, and the man went tumbling.

The apprentice had only one man left now. They were scrambling to disappear, the apprentice on foot, the other man, the man with the disruptor, still mounted. The Young Dread followed the apprentice with her arrow. She could kill him easily. She had only to release her right hand. And yet this was not her duty, no matter what the Middle said. To avoid interfering, he had stopped her from helping the others on the estate. For the same reason, he could not rightly order her to kill John. They had done too much already. The boy who was a man now, who was running for his life, was not their jurisdiction.

The Middle had sprinted into the open and was dragging Briac back toward the trees. She met him inside the edge of the woods, her bow back across her shoulders. Still at high speed, the Middle set Briac down and lashed out at her. The Young ducked his arm, but he had a dagger in his other hand and he'd already buried it in the side of her abdomen.

She stepped back, feeling the blade of his knife slide out of her, her hand grabbing at the wound. Blood spilled through her fingers.

The Young's own hand shot out with a knife and cut the Middle across his chest.

"You did not kill him," the Middle said. His voice was still speeded up, but his motions were already settling back into their se-date rhythm. His chest was bleeding, but he ignored the injury. "You should have killed him."

The Young Dread didn't answer him. She was ripping off a piece of her cloak and using it to stop the flow of blood from her abdomen. She tied another piece around her waist to hold the first tightly in place. She sensed her body growing weak, but as her old master had taught her, weakness meant little. You kept going regardless.

"Tie his shoulder," the Middle ordered. He knelt at Briac's left leg to make a tourniquet above the bullet wound. The Young knelt on the other side, stopping the blood at Briac's shoulder.

When they were finished, Briac had almost gone unconscious. The Middle leaned over him and pulled up an eyelid.

"Where is the book?" he asked. The wound on the Middle's chest was dripping onto Briac's shirt, but still the Middle paid no attention to the gash.

"Safe," Briac mumbled. "As long as I am."

"Where?" the Middle demanded.

"Safe . . ."

With that, consciousness left Briac. The Middle shook him vio-lently, but he did not wake up.

As the Young Dread watched this, she fell over onto the ground. Throwing her mind into her wound, she saw that it was trickling slowly now, matching her own speed. When he'd first cut her, how-ever, the blood had poured out, moving at the pace of her own battle motions. She could see an enormous puddle of it soaking into the ground nearby. Injury meant little, but with enough blood spilled, her body would simply stop working.

The Middle stood over her, tearing a strip from his cloak. As he did, he prodded the Young's wound viciously with one of his feet. He was looking down at her as she'd seen him look at small animals—as though her pain was delightful to him. She could not move away, but neither would she cry out.

From a pocket of his cloak, the Middle drew out the athame of the Dreads. It was smaller than the other athames, more finely made. Lying on the ground, the Young could see the carving in the base of the handgrip: three interlocking ovals. The Middle slid the delicate lightning rod from where it lay concealed in a groove at the back of the athame. When he struck them together, the vibration washed over her.

Carving a circle in the air, the Middle cut through the fabric of the world and opened a doorway to *There*. He grabbed Briac around the chest and yanked him up into his arms.

"You may die now," he said to Maud.

Then, holding Briac, he stepped across the threshold of the anomaly and into the darkness beyond.

The Young Dread could see the Middle through the doorway. He had set Briac down and was tying up his own bleeding chest wound with the strip he'd torn from his cloak. The Young grabbed at the earth, dragging herself toward that doorway, its border pulsing with energy flowing inward to *that place*. But her body would not follow her orders. She had moved only a few inches when the tendrils of dark and light began to lose their shape, seething into each other and collapsing. A moment later, the anomaly was gone, taking the Middle Dread with it.

He had promised not to harm her, but the chaos on the estate had given him an irresistible excuse. One day, when he had to explain to her master what had happened to her, he could blame her death on John's attack.

She let her head rest on the ground. The forest floor was cool against her cheek. Slowly, her eyes closed.

CHAPTER 19

SHINOBU

Shinobu was almost to the north end of the commons, following the sound of John's distorted voice, when his fingers found the inscription on the hilt of the knife. In the orange light of the closest cottage fire, he held the weapon up to his eyes and discovered letters and numbers carved into the handle. It took a few moments of study before he could properly discern them: *HK MMcB AMcB*. Next to these, the numbers of a year had been chiseled delicately near the end of the grip.

He traced the letters with a finger, as if he could not quite believe what he was seeing.

HK MMcB AMcB

And the year inscribed on the knife—six years ago.

MMcB. McB was MacBain, of course, his own last name. And *MMcB*, that could only be Mariko MacBain. His mother. And *AMcB*— was that for Alistair? And *HK* . . .

His father had thrust this knife at him, handle first. He had not been trying to stab Shinobu. Even caught in the grip of the disruptor field, Alistair had kept enough control of his mind to give his son this knife. With this message carved upon it.

His mother had died seven years ago, in a car accident, and yet this knife bore her initials and his father's and a more recent date. Was it possible . . .

"Oh, God." The words came out of Shinobu's mouth without his control.

He had left his father to die in the most terrible way possible. He'd refused to give him the tiny amount of compassion you would owe anyone, even an enemy. He had acted, in the face of Alistair's agony, like a spoiled child. Now bits and pieces from his childhood, scraps of conversation about his mother's family, came together and he understood.

She's Japanese, Shinobu, but her family has lived in Hong Kong for a long time, Alistair had told him once, when the two of them were alone together, walking along the shore in Corrickmore. *Sometimes I imagine you there.*

Shinobu looked again at the carvings on the knife. He could envision her bringing the blade somewhere to have it engraved. He could imagine his father receiving the secret gift, keeping the knife near him all these years, proof that she was safe and hadn't forgotten them. Could it be true?

He ran back the way he had come, throwing an arm across his mouth to keep the smoke out of his lungs, but the air was clearer in the forest, and he was able to move faster among the trees.

He found Alistair halfway up a hill, sprawled on the ground. Throwing himself to his knees by his father's side, Shinobu strained to catch sight of the disruptor field sparks, but there were only a few, and those were rapidly fading, even in the dim moonlit forest. With a sinking heart, he placed his hands on his father's body and pushed him over onto his back.

The big man lay completely still, his eyes partway open. His face was badly cut, and there was a large, bleeding patch on one side of his head, where his skull had been crushed.

Shinobu felt at his father's neck, but there was no pulse. Alistair was dead. As Shinobu watched, the final disruptor sparks went out.

A man caught in a disruptor field cannot usually connect his thoughts long enough to put himself out of his misery. But nearby, a small boulder, covered in blood, told the story. After what looked like many attempts, Alistair had managed to hit his head hard enough against that rock to get the job done. His father had done for himself what Shinobu had refused to do.

He sat back on his heels, hit by a vast, all-consuming remorse.

"I'm sorry . . ." Shinobu breathed. "I'm so sorry . . . Is she really there? All this time? Oh, God, I'm worthless . . ." He rested his forehead against his father's chest, momentarily paralyzed with shame.

Hoofbeats from the other side of the hill reminded Shinobu that he was in the middle of a fight and his misery would have to wait. He pulled himself away from Alistair and ran.

At the top of the hill, in the brighter moonlight coming through a break in the trees, he was greeted with a much more welcome sight. Below him, at the base of the slope, were Quin and Fiona. Quin was mounted on Yellen, pulling her mother up behind her. As Shinobu appeared at the top of the hill, Quin raised her eyes to him and beckoned. Then she reached into her cloak and pulled out the athame. It caught the moonlight and seemed to glow subtly in her hand.

Shinobu felt a surge of hope. They could get away from the estate together, right now. He started down the hill toward them.

"Quin! Quin! You're here!"

Shinobu's head whipped around. It was John, calling to her with his real voice, and he sounded confused. He was on horseback, as was the man with the disruptor, and they had just entered the clearing below.

John was urging his mount toward Quin, and Shinobu saw the moment when his eyes found the athame in her hands.

"You have it," he said. "Thank God you have it!"

Quin tugged on Yellen's reins, and the horse began backing away. She looked torn.

"It's all right," John told her. "You're safe. The athame's safe. We found each other. I thought you were gone."

Quin shot a glance at Shinobu, who was still concealed from John among the trees halfway up the hill. *She wants to get away,* Shinobu thought, *but she wants to get away without hurting John.* After what had happened to Alistair, Shinobu had no such qualms.

"I can't give it to you, John," she said, her voice shaking. "You shouldn't have it. I'm sorry, but you shouldn't have it." Her eyes met Shinobu's again, and he understood what she intended. They would get free of John and use the athame.

Before John could come any closer, Quin yanked Yellen's head around and dug in her heels, and she and Fiona were galloping away.

"Quin, wait! Listen!" John kicked his own horse to follow.

She's not listening to you anymore! Shinobu realized, with a vicious sort of elation. In an instant, he had pulled the crossbow off his back, stretched a bolt into place, and let it fly.

The bolt missed John, but the shaft buried itself in his saddle, cutting into his horse's flesh. John's mount reared and shrieked, running wildly into the path of the other man's horse. That man, unwieldy with the heavy disruptor around his chest, teetered in his saddle and almost fell. Shinobu took that moment to leap out from behind the trees, and he careened down the hill toward them.

Before he was halfway there, John had pulled out the crossbow bolt and regained control of his injured horse. Then he was off after Quin, racing toward the commons.

Shinobu ran headlong toward the second man, reached up, and yanked him violently from his mount. The man hit the ground and was nearly crushed by the weight of the disruptor, and then Shinobu was smashing the crossbow into his head, shattering the old weapon.

"That's for Alistair!" he yelled.

Then he leapt up into the saddle and galloped after John. Quin and Fiona were ahead, running flat out across the commons on Yellen. John was whipping his horse with the reins as a trail of blood flowed down the animal's white flank.

Shinobu kicked and whipped his own mount, forcing it to a full sprint as they reached the meadow. With a burst of speed, he came up alongside John. They were neck and neck. The wind had picked up, blowing the smoke on the commons away from them, and the moon was startlingly bright in the sky.

"I only want what's mine!" John yelled at him, his face still masked.

"What about Alistair?"

"I didn't mean for that to happen! Of course I didn't mean it."

Shinobu reached over, tried to shove John off his horse. But instead of being unseated, John grabbed Shinobu's arm and unexpectedly jerked Shinobu toward him, tipping him off balance. Shinobu clamped a hand onto John's shoulder to stop himself from tumbling off his mount. With his other hand, he groped for the reins of John's horse.

John yanked his reins away, and his mount veered, pulling Shinobu fully out of his saddle. Legs flailing as he came free of his horse, Shinobu clenched John's shoulder with an iron grip as his full weight slammed against John. To keep himself from falling, he locked his legs around one of John's and reached wildly for the pommel of the saddle.

Despite the jolting of the horse beneath them, Shinobu could feel John's hand scrambling for his gun. Then the cold metal was at Shinobu's shoulder. John was going to shoot! Shinobu's hand was on the pommel, his fingers touching the reins. He hooked one finger around the leather straps and wrenched the reins toward himself, jerking the horse's head down and to the side.

The animal reared, pivoted, and nearly fell, throwing both of them and sending them rolling over each other across the meadow. The gun went off harmlessly. And then they were hitting each other, like this was a brawl in a pub, except John's arm—the one holding the gun—was not working properly. He'd injured it in the fall. He fired the weapon again, wildly, and Shinobu slammed a fist into the damaged wrist, feeling it break. A shriek erupted from John as he let go of the gun.

Only thirty yards away, the man with the disruptor was running toward them across the meadow. Shinobu could hear the whine of the weapon preparing to fire. In an instant, he was up on his feet and sprinting toward Quin.

CHAPTER 20

QUIN

Quin pulled Yellen to a stop as a tingling pain, and then numbness, spread across her chest. She was suddenly finding it hard to breathe.

Shinobu was racing toward her on foot. She brought the athame up over her head and pulled the lightning rod from her cloak.

"Hold on to me tightly, Mother!" she said. She could see Fiona's arms around her waist, but she couldn't feel them.

Shinobu had covered only half the distance to her, and now John was back on his horse, kicking it into motion. John himself was injured, but he was in a desperate fury. Quin knew she could end this now; she could give the athame to him. He was begging her to help. But she couldn't do it. He had hurt Fiona and tried to shoot Shinobu, two people who had never done him harm. And if he could injure them in his attempt to get his hands on the stone dagger, what would he do once he possessed it?

"Hold on, Mother!" she cried again, and she kicked Yellen toward Shinobu. "Hurry, Shinobu!"

She managed to strike the athame down against the lightning rod, despite the fatigue creeping through her muscles.

Beneath the sound of John's horse racing toward them and her own labored breath, she could feel the vibration of the stone dagger. She was getting dizzy and her arms seemed to weigh hundreds of pounds, but she pulled Yellen to a stop. Grabbing his mane, she leaned forward and used the athame to cut a huge circle in the air in front of the horse.

Shinobu was almost to her, his red hair streaked with ash, his eyes fierce as he ran all out. John was not far behind.

The tendrils of light and dark were growing together, forming a circular doorway in front of them, the edges thrumming with energy that pulled inward, toward blackness.

"Quin, no! Please wait!" John yelled.

She could not feel her chest, and the numbness was spreading to her arms. There was pressure at her waist as her mother's grip tightened. Quin dug her heels into Yellen, and the horse leapt forward, a high, perfect jump, like Quin was taking him over a fence. He brought them neatly through the opening, just as the tendrils began to grow soft, hissing as they undid themselves.

"Shinobu!" She was trying to yell, but her voice came out muted.

Shinobu was there. He threw himself through the closing anomaly behind her. The black-and-white tendrils were now like a ragged river, carrying Shinobu with them into the darkness. Quin turned her head in time to see John, who had ripped off his mask and was still galloping toward them. His face was anguished as he looked at her through the diminishing doorway, his eyes not on her face now but on her chest.

"Oh, God, no . . . Quin . . ." she heard him say.

She looked down and saw a huge patch of red growing darkly across her shirt. She had been shot.

Then the anomaly mended itself, closing out the world of the estate and leaving them in darkness.

CHAPTER 21

QUIN

Quin fell from her horse and landed on nothing.

Her mother was there with her, somewhere. Quin could feel Fiona's arms groping to find Quin's body.

"I can't see you . . . I can't see you . . ." Her mother's voice already sounded odd, an echo of her real voice, thin and stretched out.

Quin couldn't feel her chest, but she could tell the numbness would not last forever, and when it ended, she would be in agony. She was starting to shiver, and her breath came raggedly.

"I'm shot," she breathed. "Maybe it's just as well . . ."

"Shh, shh," Fiona said.

There was a confusion of arms and legs, as though ten people had come through the anomaly with them.

"John might have killed you . . . It's all ruined . . ."

"Hush, Quin." Fiona sounded far away, though Quin was pretty sure it was her mother's hand on her stomach. "What's ruined, girl? You're here with me. We got away."

"I did bad things, Ma. So many. I can't get rid of them."

"A clear picture of, where I came from, where I will go . . ." She heard Shinobu whispering the time chant. He was getting closer.

Her own sense of time was changing. "How long . . ."

"How long what?"

". . . have we been here?" Quin finished weakly.

"I don't know," Fiona said from far away.

A hand connected with Quin's right arm, then another with her left. She could tell it was Shinobu, even in the darkness. There was something intelligent and sure about the way his hands moved as they traveled down her arms, taking the athame and lightning rod from her. She was getting so cold, and he felt warm.

"I don't know where to go," she whispered.

"I do," Shinobu told her. He pulled her close to him. "Can you stay awake?"

"I don't know . . ."

"Try. You have to try."

"It's all wrecked," she whispered.

"It is," he agreed.

In the faint glow of the athame, she saw his hands moving over the dials, adjusting them to a new set of coordinates.

The vibration engulfed her as Shinobu struck the stone dagger. Her eyes drifted shut.

"Quin, please stay awake." She felt him moving. "Fiona, you have to take her feet. Fiona!"

Quin forced her eyelids open, saw the new anomaly, heard its hum. They were carrying her. There was fresh air on her face. The next time she opened her eyes, they were outside, in an open space somewhere, with bright sunlight on her skin.

She was on the edge of consciousness. There were sirens, other voices, speaking a different language. Asian faces around her. Her chest was filled with a hot red ache that was overwhelming in intensity.

Her eyes stayed closed for a long while. Then a quiet room with candles, and a small man with gray hair, slanted eyes, a bright face. The pain was starting to go away. How long had she been here? Minutes? Hours? Days? Maybe she wasn't here at all; maybe she was still *There*. She could hear herself talking. Her eyes would not stay open.

The small man was murmuring something to her. Quin was not sure she had heard him right. Her ears seemed to be stuffed with cotton. Even so, a feeling of happiness enveloped her, and then she was unconscious again.

CHAPTER 22

SHINOBU

Shinobu waited until late at night, when the Bridge seemed most dead. He found his way through twisting corridors and dark stairwells. Eventually he was among the outer rafters, walking to the very edge like a gymnast on a balance beam.

From there, he could see the harbor and the hundreds of thousands of city lights on either side of the Bridge, more lights than he had ever seen in one place. The ocean water was bright near shore, reflecting the glow from buildings so slender and high, they seemed like monstrous blades of grass, waving gently in the night. But here, under the Bridge, the water was dark.

The image of his father was burned into his mind: Alistair with teeth gritted, face contorted in pain, covered in blood and scratches from beating his head against the ground. Again and again he felt Alistair thrusting the hilt of the knife into his open hand, trying, with his last trace of sanity, to help Shinobu. And Shinobu had done nothing for him.

It was John's fault. The attack was John's fault. But could he blame John for hating Briac? Could he blame John for attacking them? He couldn't. He might have done the same in John's position. He too had dreamed of going after Briac.

And he, Shinobu, was Alistair's son. He could have given his father mercy when it mattered most, and he'd refused. That had been his own choice.

He put a hand on a steel beam above him, bracing himself as he leaned out over the deep water running with the tide beneath the Bridge. He pulled out the lightning rod, concealed under his clothing, and flung it as far as he could into the depths. Then he leapt to another rafter and another, moving along the outer Bridge structure. When it appeared he'd reached the very center of the Bridge's span, he took out the athame. He threw it in a high arc out into the night air, then watched as it curved down and hit the water, immediately disappearing from sight.

Let the ocean take them and swallow the memory of those sparks. Let it swallow everything . . .

He made his way back to the Bridge's central road, and to the home of Master Tan. After moving up an outer staircase, he looked through the second-story window. Quin lay on a table in a candlelit room, her chest wrapped in a complicated bandage, acupuncture needles with burning herbs at their ends placed all over her body. He could see Fiona in another room beyond, asleep on a couch, bandages around her neck.

Quin had been dead, he was sure of it. When they'd carried her onto the Bridge, she had not been breathing, and she had gone cold. Now her eyes were closed, but there was a flush to her cheeks. As he watched, she even appeared to be speaking.

Master Tan was leaning over Quin's head, saying something quietly. Shinobu pressed on the window with his hands, sliding the glass up a few inches so he could hear.

"Child, child," Master Tan was saying, his voice like the words in a fever dream, "there is no need for this." One hand smoothed away the lines of worry creasing Quin's forehead. "You may forget if you wish . . . all of it."

Quin tossed her head from side to side.

"Forgetting is . . . as simple as deciding, as gentle as sinking into a warm bed," Master Tan murmured. "Child, you have gone and come back. Reinvention is the gift I can offer."

Quin's brow creased again above her closed eyes.

"The choice can be as quick as a heartbeat, or as long as a life. You may leave all of it behind," Master Tan whispered. "How do you choose?"

A troubled expression crossed her face, and then, as Shinobu watched, Quin muttered something to Master Tan and her features relaxed. After a short time, it looked like she had fallen into a natural sleep.

Was it possible? Could you wipe the chalk from the board and begin to draw anew? Shinobu pressed the heels of his hands into his eyes, trying to force out the vision of his father, head bloody, lying on the forest floor.

That was Quin in there, his cousin. (*Distant cousin!* he had always wanted to point out.) He should stay by her side. Maybe, when she finally recovered, she would see him the way he'd always seen her. After the night when they took their oath, he'd wanted to take her away, but he had not. Now there were too many unpleasant things he would have to remember every time he looked at her. And the truth was, he could no longer see himself the way he wanted Quin to see him. He had gone along on all of Briac's assignments. He had abandoned his father. He wasn't the man he was supposed to be.

He would leave. Quin would heal here with Master Tan, and then she and Fiona would be free to disappear into the world somewhere far away, where no one, including Shinobu, would ever find them.

"Goodbye, Quin." He whispered the words, and then he ran back down the stairs.

He walked quickly off the Bridge and out into the night in this new and strange city where his mother might be waiting for him, and where he hoped it was possible to begin life again.

INTERLUDE

OTHER TIMES AND PLACES

CHAPTER 23

JOHN

John had fallen asleep on the small bed. He woke when he heard the crash. Someone was out in the living room, making a lot of noise. There was another crash a moment later, followed by several more, then a voice, cursing. It was the voice he had been waiting for. His mother was home!

John swung his small legs off the bed and ran out into the other room. There she was, standing in the middle of the living room floor. A chest was overturned in front of her, with its wooden drawers pulled out and their contents spilled across the floor.

He noticed these details only in passing, because there was something much more important—blood. Blood was everywhere. For a moment, he thought it was paint, but it didn't look the way paint looked. It was more . . . real. His mother's trousers were covered in it. There was a puddle of it below her on the floor, and large splashes on the papers that had fallen out of the drawers. Her light brown hair was tied back, and it too was streaked with red.

"Mama!" he called, too frightened to get closer to her.

Catherine stopped her frantic search of the drawers.

"John . . ."

She was so surprised to see him, she didn't move for several seconds. She stared at him, her face drawn tightly about her mouth and eyes.

John's attention focused on the cut high on her left leg. Her pants were torn, and she'd tied a strip of cloth around the wound, but it was still bleeding. All over.

"Sweetheart," she said, "what are you doing here?"

"I—I found this address. On something in your pocket at home." He took a step toward her, then stopped. It seemed like she might be angry with him.

She was moving again, searching through the papers strewn across the floor. Her fingers closed around a thick book, bound in leather. She stared at it, as if unsure, now that she had found it, what she planned to do with it.

"I didn't want you here," she said, more to herself than to him. The words made John feel bad. He'd come to the apartment all by himself to surprise her.

She was having a difficult time catching her breath. She staggered over to John, and went down on her knees so her blue eyes were level with his. Her hands took hold of his small shoulders, and the rich metallic smell of her blood was in his nose. It was terrifying. "You're supposed to be on *Traveler*. Safe."

"I—wanted to see you. You were gone for so long. And you're hurt."

He could tell that she wasn't really listening to him. Instead her head was cocked to listen for something else, or maybe someone else. Or perhaps she was counting something inside her head.

"They will be here soon. How much time? Can we make it?"

Even at seven years old, John could tell that she was speaking to herself and didn't expect him to answer. She tucked the leather book into the waistband of John's trousers, then pushed herself up onto her feet.

"Come," she said, taking one of his hands. "I can't get you home, but I can get you close. Find a policeman. Tell him who your grandfather is. You need to keep the book safe—Maggie will know where to hide it."

"What do you mean?" he asked her, pulling at her hand, trying to get her to look at him. "We should go to a doctor, shouldn't we?"

Catherine was taking something from inside her jacket that looked like a dagger but was made out of stone. She began to turn the stone dials of the handgrip. Then she paused, squinting as if it was hard to see, even though the dagger was right in front of her.

"Can I do something?" John asked.

She looked down at the gash in her left thigh. A new puddle had formed near John's shoes. He noticed then that there was no blood by the apartment's door. The mess started and ended in the middle of the room.

Catherine lost her balance and fell hard onto one knee.

"No, no, no," she muttered. She put her hands on John's shoulders, tried to push herself up that way, but her legs would no longer obey. Her strength had deserted her. John felt panic overtaking him, unsure how to help.

"I can't take you," she whispered eventually. "I could risk it for myself, but I can't risk leaving you *There*."

Hot tears were leaking out of his eyes. They fell onto the floor near the edge of the blood. "Please, Mother, could we go to a doctor? They have bandages and things. They could fix your leg."

She had collapsed into a sitting position. She seemed hardly able to keep her eyes open. She slid nearer, brushed his hair out of his face with her messy hands, and leaned close.

"I have only a few minutes. They'll figure out where to follow me. It won't take them very long."

She buried her head in her hands, trying to think.

"Take the book over there," she told him, pointing to a cabinet against one wall. "Look in the cupboard."

With shaking hands, John removed the leather book from his waistband and crossed the room. In the bottom of the cupboard was a safe whose metal door stood open.

"Put it inside and shut the door. The red button locks it. He'll be looking for it . . . Gives me something to bargain with . . ." She was fading.

John did as she'd said, locking the book inside the safe. He turned back to his mother. She was panting for breath. "I need you to do . . . exactly as I say. Quickly. Can you do that?"

He nodded mutely.

"Good boy. In that bench . . . there's a door. I can't touch it, or I'll leave blood . . . You go open it. Wait—your shoes." She examined his shoes, which were miraculously free of blood. "Good. Go open it."

John walked to the long bench at the side of the living room and lifted the heavy panel that formed the seat. The space underneath was coffin-shaped, containing some odds and ends—a few pillows, a few tools, a blanket.

"You want me to go in here?" John asked.

"Not there . . . Underneath. Another door. You can feel . . . a tiny lever. It slides if you push it."

John felt around the bottom of the space. His small fingers located the hidden lever. He pushed it, and the bottom of the coffin slid back several inches into the wall.

"Leave the things on top, if you can," she said.

He climbed into the seat, then squeezed his way through the bottom door. There was another space beneath, big enough to hold an adult.

"Slide it shut now," Catherine said.

John pushed the pillows and other items to one side so they wouldn't be caught by the closing door. Then he ducked down and pulled the panel shut above him. He'd been worried it would leave him in darkness, but he found he could still see. There were small slots cut in the base of the bench, and through these he was able to look out into the living room.

His mother was lying on the floor several feet away. Her eyes were open but looked blank. Her chest heaved up and down, and after a few moments she closed her eyes, gathering her strength, and scooted herself a little closer to him. He could see her face through the slots.

"There's a lever behind you," she said. "It will shut the seat."

John turned and felt along the wall. His fingers closed around a flat piece of metal, which he pushed down. There was a bang above him as the heavy seat swung shut.

Catherine took up the stone dagger from the floor and positioned it so John had a good view. She was breathing strangely now, like the air wouldn't go all the way into her.

"Mother, can you please go to the doctor?" he asked. He was crying again, though he was trying to stop. "I'll stay here, if that's what you want."

"I need you to listen to me very carefully." A pause to breathe. "Do you see this dagger?"

"Yes, Mother."

"It's called an athame. Say it . . . so you remember it. 'ATH-uh-may.'"

"'ATH-uh-may,'" he whispered.

"This is your birthright, John. It's been in our family for . . .

hundreds . . . maybe a thousand . . ." She stopped, trying to get her breath. It took a few moments.

"Maybe you can tell me after the doctor," he suggested. There was quite a lot more blood on the floor around Catherine than there had been before he'd climbed into the hiding place. He moved closer to the slots in the wood of the bench and his foot bumped against something. Reaching down, John felt smooth, cool metal. There was a helmet of some kind on the floor of the hiding place. He pushed it aside so he could crouch as close as possible to the openings in the bench.

"We are an ancient family. Been betrayed . . . killed . . . robbed . . ." She stopped again. "No time, dammit . . . Maggie will have to tell you." She tilted the stone dagger toward him. "This was stolen, was gone for a century . . . I got it back." She extended the athame closer to him. "Do you see this?" She pointed to the pommel. There was a tiny animal carved into the stone.

"A fox," John said, the word catching in his throat.

"A fox. Our symbol. With the athame . . . power over life and death." She laughed quietly, which interfered with trying to breathe. "Except now . . . Now it's death for me."

"Mother, please—"

"*You* will have the power of life and death, John. You will choose. They have . . . betrayed me . . . They think we're . . . small and weak and helpless . . . easy to kill . . . Are we easy to kill, John?"

"No," he whispered.

"No. The athame will let you . . . decide . . . They are going to take it away, but you will get it back."

"How will—"

"I will make them agree . . . bargain . . . Briac. Briac Kincaid. Say the name."

"Briac Kincaid," he said softly.

"He was with others just now, so I think there will be . . . witnesses. I'll make him promise . . . educate you . . . if you ask. Once you take your oath, he must tell you . . . anything you want to know. *Anything,* John. But you must take your oath. And be strong enough to get it back."

"What is my oath?"

"It will make sense. The book . . . I know more than they do . . . Both." She was smiling. "As precious as the dagger in the right hands. I will have to give him this book now, but you must find it again, and also . . . We've written . . . A thousand years . . . I am so close . . ."

She had to stop. He could see her breathing, but it didn't seem to be doing her any good. The puddle of blood was getting wider. He wondered how much blood one body could hold. Finally she continued, "Your oath and our athame, the one with the fox. Promise me . . ."

"I promise," he said.

"Say it again, John."

"I promise. My oath and our athame, the one with the fox." His tears were coming freely now. He could hear them hitting the wood beneath him.

She let the athame settle on the floor next to her. Her chest was rising and falling quickly. "You mustn't be scared to act. . . . Be willing to kill. . . ."

"What do you mean?"

"It's necessary . . . to live . . . for money sometimes . . . as I did to get us *Traveler* . . . Those are small deaths . . . There will be bigger deaths . . . to repay them for this . . ." She gestured at the wide pool of blood spreading around her. "Do what has to be done. At no man's mercy, do you understand?"

"Yes." His voice was small.

"Our house will rise again, and the others will fall . . . as they should have done long ago." Her voice was getting quieter. It was only a whisper as she said, "Close your eyes."

"Can't you go to hospital—"

A vibration started in the room, low and penetrating. John could feel it in his stomach.

"Coming now . . ." Catherine said, her own eyes closing. "No matter what you see . . . don't make a sound. Tell Maggie what happened . . ." She trailed off, and it looked to John like she had fallen asleep. Then she stirred. "John, promise me. Not a sound."

"I promise." He whispered the words.

Catherine smiled.

John wiped his eyes with his hand, and he saw in the dim light coming through the slots that his sleeve was now red. His mother's blood must be caked on his cheek.

The vibration grew steadily, filling the space around him. Then, from nowhere, there were voices. Several pairs of feet walked across the living room floor, though the front door had not opened. The vibration faded, allowing him to hear the voices of two men. One was strange and slow, the other rough and quick. He could not see their faces, but one stopped between the bench and Catherine, and John was treated to a view of the man's boots—thick, old leather with heavy soles and metal tips. They were, he thought, the boots of a killer.

The other man's legs and feet were across the room, hard for John to see. But there was a third pair of shoes nearby, much smaller, made of an old-fashioned soft leather. These shoes looked like they might belong to a girl, but the figure who owned them never said a word, only knelt on the floor, its back to John, and began to tie up his mother's wounds. This small figure turned its head once, and John got a glimpse of two eyes beneath a leather helmet. He was worried those eyes had seen him, so he shut his own eyes tight, hoping that would make him invisible. He could not stop himself from crying. He wrapped an arm around his face to muffle the sound.

A man's voice was demanding, "Where is it?"

His mother was answering. Her breathing was harsh, but otherwise her voice was gentle. "There. You can break into the safe, which will destroy it, or you can make me a promise . . . before these witnesses."

John heard a new voice, another man's voice, from across the room, low to the floor.

"I am your witness, Catherine," the voice said. The words were strained, as though the speaker were in great pain.

John dared to open his eyes for one moment, in hopes of seeing who had spoken. He glimpsed a large figure with red hair lying on the floor, holding his chest as though badly injured. Then the smaller figure stepped directly in front of John. The girl again. He closed his eyes tightly and pressed himself against the back of the hiding place.

His mother spoke for a while, so softly John could not make out the words, and then there was a high-pitched whine, growing louder, and a crackling. The sound was terrible and he pressed his hands over his ears. After some time, John opened his eyes for a moment and saw colored light dancing around the room. Then he closed his eyes and tried to make himself as small and quiet as he could.

It was not until many hours later that he finally crawled out of the bench and out of the empty apartment with the bloody floor. From there he made his way back through London to *Traveler,* a seven-year-old boy without a mother and with a heavy promise weighing him down.

CHAPTER 24

MAUD

They were playing prisoner's base. It was Maud's turn to run out from the line of children into the town square with one of the boys chasing her. With a squeal, Maud took off through the mud. Glancing back, she saw her pursuer was the tall boy with the limp, Michael. Michael was still very fast, even with the bad foot. He had invented a kind of swinging run, and because he had long legs, he was keeping up with Maud just fine as she plunged through puddles and across the deep ruts made by carts.

The other children, all fifteen of them, began to spread out through the town square and the alleys leading off it, each chaser trying to touch the one he chased and claim a prisoner for his team.

Maud's seven-year-old legs were moving as quickly as they could, which was not quick enough through the mud and animal dung on the lower side of the square. The skirt of her dress, which had once been a very light color, was now covered in muck and bits of the leaves that were blowing all over the town on this autumn morning.

Risking a look behind her, she discovered the boy with the limp had stopped. He'd lost a shoe in the mire and was trying to get his foot back inside it without stepping onto the ground. Maud ducked into an alley, ran ten paces, then moved sideways into the tiny passage that led back behind the alehouse. There, she crept along the wall, her back pressed into the stone.

She heard the boy's footsteps coming down the alley. She tried to keep her eyes closed, thinking that would help her go unnoticed, but she couldn't resist a peek when his steps got close. Michael ran right past the opening to her tiny passage.

"Maudy, where are you?" she heard him call out from farther along. "You're out of bounds! The prison yard ends here."

Maud smiled, moving deeper into the small back alley. It would lead her to another street, and from there she could make it back to her base without being captured—and all while staying in bounds.

"Maudy!" the boy called again. "Be fair!"

His voice was farther away. He had continued up the main alley. He would be too far away to catch her when she came out the other side.

As she edged her way down the dim and muddy corridor, her nose filled with the smell of animals. On her left, the tiny passage let into a stone courtyard at the back of the inn, where several horses were tied up. The place hadn't been shoveled out in weeks, and the smell was overpowering. Maud snuck past the opening to the enclosure, intending to slip into the darker passage beyond, but something caught her attention.

At the rear of the inn was a room with its wall right up against the back alley. A shutter over a window was partly open, and she could hear voices inside, arguing.

"Do not think you will change the Old's mind," one voice said. "There have been Youngs before you, yet I am still here." Maud was intrigued. The man's voice sounded cruel, which scared her, but it also sounded foreign, which was interesting. He was speaking her language, but he had a funny way of doing it.

"You cannot stop me from talking to my own master," another voice said. This one was much younger. "We have both taken the same oath."

"Oath!" the older man said, almost spitting out the word. "Stretched, I am. Since years too long to count."

What does he mean by "stretched"? she wondered. Was this man long and thin? Had he been put to the rack? Maud's curiosity got the better of her. She crept closer. By standing on tiptoe, she could look through the crack between the shutter and the stone wall. It was dark in the room, almost as dark as the tiny alley where she was hidden, yet she could just see the faces of the two men. One older, the other one young—hardly even a man yet. But neither looked like he had been stretched.

"You were with a woman," the young one said. "I saw you. In the upstairs room." The younger man also had a funny way of talking. He didn't have an accent, like a foreigner might, but there was a slowness to his voice, as though he had thought everything out ahead of time, and now the words were falling out of his mouth in a steady way.

"No one cares what you saw," the older man said.

"We stand apart from humanity, so our heads are clear. It is our oath. The Old will hear of this." The younger man moved as if to go out into the horse yard, but the older man stepped forward, blocking him. Even though their voices were slow, their movements were so fast, Maud could not figure out how they had gotten across the room so quickly. She had to shift her feet ever so slightly in order to keep the two of them in view. A small knot of wood had been knocked out of the shutter, and by moving to her left, she could see them through its jagged hole.

"The Old will hear nothing," the older man said, his arm across the door that must lead to the stable yard.

"Let me pass," said the younger one.

"You pass when I permit." There was something shiny in the older man's hand that had not been there a moment before. Maud thought it might be a knife, but how had it gotten into his hand so quickly? She realized the younger man also had a knife in his hand. Like magic, the weapons had appeared.

"What happened to the Young before me?" the younger man asked, his knife held up against the other man's knife, his eyes searching the older man's face. "That was your doing."

"Was it?" the older man asked. "You were not there. The Old was not there. Who can say?"

The knives struck out. From where Maud stood, it looked like a blur of many arms, with flashes of light from the blades winking at her again and again. One knife seemed to disappear into the younger man's chest.

Then the younger man was falling to the floor. The older man had a hand around the boy's back, to help him settle to the ground without making a lot of noise.

When the younger man was lying on the floor, he whispered, "I have written it down. All of it." His voice was so quiet, it took Maud a moment to understand what he said.

The older man shook the boy roughly by his shirt. "What did you write?" he asked.

"Many things about you," the boy said, even more softly than before. "Others will know what you are . . ."

The older man shook him harder.

"Where?"

A smile crossed the boy's lips, but no more words came out. He was staring up at the older man, and somehow Maud understood that the boy was not breathing anymore.

Maud gasped. In her short life, she had seen several dead men. In the winter, beggars would sometimes freeze in the town square or out on the road. But she had never seen a man die before. Realizing immediately that she had made too much noise, Maud slid down the wall as fast as she could, to remove her head from view.

Hardly a moment had passed before the man was there, right above her. He had crossed the room in the blink of an eye, and he was standing against the shutter. She could hear him breathing.

The shutter swung open. Maud closed her eyes, trying to become invisible, pressing her whole body against the wall, as if she could squeeze herself into the stone. There was a wide windowsill beneath the shutter. She could feel it above her head. Was it wide enough to hide her body from the man's view? She was not sure. She could feel the wet mud on her skirt and on her arms, making her into little more than a dark blur in the dim alleyway. Maybe she would be hard to see.

All at once the man was gone from the window. Maud didn't wait to find out what he would do next. She scrambled to her feet and pressed on through the tiny alley, so narrow here she was forced to walk sideways. In her haste, she knocked over several buckets by a pig trough behind the butcher's shop next door, setting off a terrible racket of clanging metal and squealing animals. Maud ran then, terrified the man was after her, the close walls scratching her arms as she went.

At last, she came out onto a wider lane, rather full of people. This street was so muddy, it swallowed her feet to the ankles, but she hardly cared. At the bottom of the lane, she turned and was relieved to find the town square as busy as she had left it. She lost herself among the men and women milling about in front of the butcher's shop and hauling carts toward market stalls.

As she passed in front of the inn, a hand grabbed her shoulder. She turned, and with a jolt of fear found herself looking up at the man she had seen in the back room. He wore a long cloak over his shoulders now, but his face was the same.

"You," he said to her.

Maud could not move. She expected a knife to appear suddenly in one of his hands.

"Fetch me water," the man said. "I will wash."

The man had taken her for one of the serving girls at the inn. He was not going to stab her. She wrenched her shoulder out of his grasp and ran off through the square.

A moment later, a hand grabbed her again. Making a fist, Maud turned and swung at her attacker. She hit Michael, the limping boy, square in the face. He fell backward, into a deep, muddy puddle.

"I got you fair, Maudy. You're my prisoner!" he said as he slipped around in the mud and tried to get back to his feet.

"All right," she agreed, relieved to see her friend. "I'm your prisoner." She took Michael's hands and helped him up.

Together they walked toward the top of the square, where most of the children were gathering for another round of prisoner's base. The limping boy walked her triumphantly back to the others—he had returned with a prisoner and did not much mind that she had struck him in the face.

Weeks later, when she had begun to put the inn and the men with knives from her mind, Maud was marched out of her house to greet an honored visitor. She had been scrubbed quite clean in a tub of warm water that morning, and she was now wearing a fancy and rather uncomfortable dress into which her mother and maid had forced her with great difficulty. Her hair had been braided and tied with ribbons.

Maud's father was a cousin to their lord, the baron, and her family lived in a large stone house at the top of the hill, overlooking the village. Though Maud often snuck away to play with the villagers' children, she knew quite well she was not one of them. Maud could read, for instance, something few of the village children were ever likely to do.

It was because of her education, she sensed, that she was now being sent away with this visitor. It was the year of our Lord 1472, and it was quite ordinary, being sent away. Her older brother was gone to the monks right now, receiving his education, and her other brother was a squire to their cousin the baron, who lived in the castle on the hill beyond the wide river, which she could see in the distance.

Girls were often sent to serve great ladies in distant places, but this visitor was obviously not a representative of a great house. He was dressed in a simple robe, like a monk, which was tied at his waist. Over this he wore a long cloak, which seemed to contain a large number of interior pockets, all stuffed with objects whose strange outlines could be glimpsed through the cloth. And he was old. Being seven, Maud did not know how old, and she didn't trouble herself too much to wonder—it was enough to note that he had long hair streaked with gray, and a beard that reached past his neck.

Maud's father was affectionate with no one and was feared by all members of the household, herself included. Yet he was treating this old man in the simple robe like visiting royalty. Servants were called to fetch wine and food, a bed was offered, then more wine.

The old man responded to these suggestions politely, yet he waved off everything but a plain meal. All of his attention was fixed on

Maud as she was introduced to him. His eyes were the best part about him, she decided immediately. His eyes took her in all at once—they saw not just her clothes and shoes and hair, which were, after all, her mother's doing, but something more, something inside her. His face was very serious, but those eyes of his were smiling.

At first, Maud refused to go with him and was both shocked and pleased to see deep embarrassment on her father's face. The old visitor did not argue with her. Instead, unexpectedly, there was a flower in his hand. She had not seen how it came to his hand, but there it was, like magic, and he was presenting it to her.

Maud was unsettled for a moment—but only for a moment. The flower smelled sweet, and the man placed it behind her ear. Before she knew it, she was walking down the road with him, a small pack of her belongings slung over the man's shoulder. When she looked back, she saw both of her parents at the top of the road, looking after her as she walked away. Her father usually spent a great deal of time being angry about Maud's behavior, and this was the first time she had observed him being proud of her.

"You will see your mother and father again," the man told her, catching her looking back. "I promise you that. You will see them many times in the next few years."

He had a strange way of speaking. His words came out like a chant, or like a poem. And some of his words were funny to her, as though he had learned to say them differently than she had. This had made her uncomfortable at first, but she was already growing used to it.

"When will I next see them?" she asked.

"Soon," he promised. "And after some time, if life with me does not suit you, you may return to them. So you see, there is nothing to fear."

"How did you make the flower appear?" she asked him.

"It was only in my pocket."

"I did not see you take it from your pocket. It was not in your hand, and then it was."

"Ah. You are good at noticing things. I admire that," he told her, with a twinkle in his friendly eyes. "I can move quickly if I must."

"But you did not move at all!"

"I did. Very quickly. And so shall you, when I have trained you."

Maud smiled when she heard that. She had understood when she met him that he intended to give her an education. She suspected it would be a far more interesting education than the one her parents had been planning, which laid a heavy emphasis on needlework and musical instruments.

They walked a while quietly, with Maud feeling that it was a very pleasant silence.

"I hope life with you does suit me," she said after some time.

When she met their traveling companion, however, her good feelings ended. She had managed to forget, mostly, about the man in the tavern. Now he was standing right next to her. He was being introduced to her as a companion and teacher. The man's cruel eyes looked her over. Then he nodded to the older man, but he did not say a word of greeting to Maud.

Maud felt a moment of panic—did he recognize her from the front of the inn, when she'd ignored his order to bring him water? Did he recognize her from the back alley? But no, even if he had seen her then, she'd been dirty, in old clothing, and she didn't think this man could recognize children individually. One child, to him, was probably very like the next.

"We shall be taking good care of this Young," the old man said to the other man, in his steady voice.

The other man made only a grunt for response as he lifted a bag over his shoulder, and the three of them continued walking along the road.

Maud's hand slipped into the old man's hand, and she was comforted a bit when he squeezed it tightly. There had been three of them before, she understood. The old man, the middle man, and the young man she had seen in the inn. Now they were calling her "the Young." She was replacing that young man, who in turn had replaced someone else.

As they continued on, she did not dare look at the middle man. If what he'd said in the inn were true, there had been several youngsters like herself, all of whom were now dead. She thought suddenly of running away, back to her home, but that might make the man suspicious and cause him to come after her. And besides, she didn't want to leave the old man.

Perhaps sensing her change in mood, the old man leaned close to her and began to speak again.

"Now, child, if you are to stay with us, you must know that we stand apart from humanity. Why?" He tapped the side of his head. "So our heads are clear to judge. Tyrants and evildoers beware."

These were the same words she had heard from the young man in the inn. Maud stole a quick look at the other man, but his face showed no sign of listening to their conversation.

"In the beginning," the old man said to her, a smile playing across his lips, "there was the hum of the universe . . ."

CHAPTER 25

JOHN

"I'm not crying!" John said, burying his face deeper into the pile of clothing.

"John, come out of there." Maggie's voice was soft from beyond the closet door.

"I'm not crying," he said again, feeling his mother's blue scarf absorbing his tears.

The closet door handle rattled as Maggie tried to get in. He clutched his mother's belongings around him in the darkness. He'd managed to keep the door shut by wedging one of Catherine's scarves firmly beneath it, but now there was a crack of light as Maggie forced it open.

He hid his face in the cloth. He could hear her pushing the door; then her hands were beneath his arms, pulling him up. When he opened his eyes, John was looking into her lined face as she knelt in front of him inside her own closet.

"I'm not crying," he whispered again, though he could still feel wetness on his cheeks.

"What's all this?" she asked, her eyes moving over the pile of items heaped on the floor. "Your mother's things?"

There were scarves and hats and photographs and small items that had sat on shelves. They were the things that most reminded John of Catherine.

"They were putting them in boxes. They were taking them away!"

"John."

"Grandfather says I'm not allowed to look at her things so much. I yelled and stamped on his foot. I told him to go to hell."

Maggie's grip on his shoulders became more firm. Her soft eyes took on a look that was not nearly so soft.

"He loves you, boy," she said.

"He doesn't!"

"You know he does, John." She shook him slightly to make sure he was paying attention. "He doesn't want to see you sad for so long. It's been a year. He's worried about you."

"He wants to make her disappear."

"No. He's worried you'll try to be like her. He doesn't want to lose you as well."

"But I *will* be like her, Nana!"

"John, you mustn't call me that. Not here, not if you want to stay together. I told you so you would know you had more family. But our blood connection is a secret."

"I'm sorry. I won't say it."

"I'm not your grandmother, not really."

"You're Mother's grandmother."

"I'm older than that, boy. Come."

She took him by the hand and led him out of the closet. John let her seat him on the ancient embroidered quilt upon her small cot in her servant's chamber on *Traveler*. The room was on the bottom deck, where the engine noise was deep and constant.

There were several framed pictures hung on her walls, each of a castle. Some of these images were photographs; others were fine line drawings. Maggie walked to the first of the pictures and took it down. It was a photograph, in black-and-white, of a fortress with low, round towers and a partially ruined wall.

"Where is that castle, Maggie?" he asked.

"It happens it's in France. But the castle is only a reminder to me of what's behind it." She sat on the bed next to him and turned the frame over. Carefully, she removed the back. Hidden between a piece of cloth and the picture itself was a small stack of photographs. Maggie's hands shook slightly as she removed them and placed them facedown on the bed.

"You are younger than I like for this, John. I wouldn't show you these now, except it's necessary for you to know." She began to lay the pictures faceup on the quilt, one after another. "From early years we have no pictures, but the ones we do have tell enough of the story."

John couldn't at first make sense of the black-and-white images. They appeared completely chaotic. Then all at once they came into sharp focus in his mind. They were pictures of death. Dead people in a room that had been torn apart. It was not death like you saw on the television. It was much worse, much messier.

The photographs showed a man, a woman, and four children, in clothing that placed them more than a century in the past. They had been cut. Someone had cut them deeply, carefully, and abundantly.

The man and woman were pinned to a wall as though glued there, with their heads lolling forward. When John looked more closely, he could see the long knives sticking out from their shoulders, knives someone had thrust all the way through them and into the wall behind.

There was no red in these photographs—no color at all—but something in the quality of the black-and-white let John imagine the deep crimson of their blood as it cascaded from those wounds and onto the floor. The four children had not been pinned to the wall, but they lay in positions of agony, their clothing ripped where they'd been cut, their own blood turning the cloth dark. The youngest could not have been more than five. He lay facedown near his sisters, blood around his head in a dark halo.

On a clean patch of the small boy's white shirt, something had been traced with a finger dipped in that blood. It was a drawing of an animal.

"Who are they?" John asked.

Maggie picked up a picture that showed the small boy in detail.

"The little one survived," she said. "We—the photographer discovered he was still breathing. It was a miracle, though he was crippled his whole life. He was your great, great, great-grandfather, John."

John couldn't take his eyes off the figure of the small boy, even smaller than John, slumped on the floor next to his sister's skirt. "Is that a bear?"

"Yes. It is the sign of the house of the man who killed them," she said.

"We're a fox," John whispered.

"Yes, we are."

There were more photographs hidden in the other frames. One by one Maggie took them down and made him look. The images were a parade of horror, moving forward through time until John was looking at color prints. They were distant uncles, grandfathers' fathers, cousins of all kinds. Most were young in the pictures, dying in terrible ways—stabbed, shot, strangled, drowned. In many, there was an animal drawn in blood on one of the victims.

The faces began to blur, but eventually there was a young woman John recognized. Her blue eyes were wide in death, and her hands clutched a gaping wound in her belly.

"My—my mother?" he asked.

"No, boy, though they are very alike, aren't they? She was your mother's older sister, Anna."

The girl was beautiful, despite a gash across her cheek, and she was so much like Catherine that John had a difficult time believing it was not her.

"She recorded it," Maggie said softly. "I have her film. I want you to watch it."

There was a thin video screen hidden in one of the frames, which Maggie withdrew and set on John's lap. Tapping the screen, she brought an image to life. It had been filmed perhaps by a dropped phone, half concealed beneath a bed, but the image was clear enough.

John didn't want to watch but found himself unable to turn away. He was looking at his mother's sister, crawling across the floor as a young man with dark hair stepped between her and the camera. This man's words were lost as the girl screamed, but his actions were clear. He was cutting her, slowly, awfully, his back toward the camera. Once he looked to his right, speaking excitedly to someone in another part of the room, and a few of his words were audible: ". . . didn't listen . . . he's angry . . ."

Eventually the girl was quiet. When the man moved away, John could see what he had done. She'd bled to death from the wound he had made across her belly. And there was a shape drawn on her blouse with her own blood—a ram.

John was turning away, overcome, but there were more. The last photographs were of a room he recognized. It was his mother's living room, as he'd last seen it. The large pool of blood was spread across the floor, smeared where her body had been. He'd seen this himself, when he escaped from that room. But he had not seen the animal shape that had been drawn at one corner of the drying lake of blood: a ram.

Darkness began to creep in around his vision, and nausea rolled over him. Sometime later, Maggie shook his shoulder as he lay curled on her bed, his arms around his stomach.

"Sit up, John," she said.

Her words were kind but firm, and he did as she told him. She was kneeling, her eyes level with his. He had often thought of her as a very old woman, but at this moment she looked both ancient and young, alive with emotion.

"They have tried to make us nothing, John. They will only be happy when we're nothing."

"Who?" he asked.

"The other houses. We are at the center and beginning of Seekers. They want us gone. They've been trying to stamp us out for hundreds of years."

"They'll kill me too, won't they?" he asked her, his eyes filling with tears.

"They will certainly try when they get the chance."

John began to cry.

"Cry if you like," she told him. "But tears are a step toward death. Your mother took a different path. Do you understand her path?"

John looked again at the photographs spread across the bed, then back to Maggie. He nodded.

"To take my oath," he said. "To get back the athame and repay them for what they've done. To find her book, because they took it when they . . ."

"Yes," Maggie said. "All those things. But why?"

John looked up at her, unsure of the answer.

"With the athame and the book, John, someday you will destroy the houses who have harmed us. And put things to rights. You will become what we were in the beginning, powerful but good."

He sat on the bed quietly for a while, thinking of the man with dark hair who had killed his mother's sister. He had seen that man before, had seen his boots as they stood in Catherine's living room, before those colored lights and that awful high-pitched whine had put an end to her as well.

"You are eight years old, John. Too young, but that can't be helped. Choosing your mother's path means you must grow up quickly. You must be willing—"

"To do what has to be done," he finished. "Even kill. I know."

"It's easy to say. But there will be many things that try to pull you from the path. Hatred is one, and love is another. Both are everywhere, and both are dangerous."

"It seems like everything is dangerous."

Maggie smiled. "For you, yes."

"I have already chosen, Maggie," John told her. "I promised her"—he nodded to the photographs—"and I promise them." His voice sounded different in his own ears, as though he had aged over the past few minutes.

"Very good, John. Now you must listen to me about your grandfather." She took one of his hands in her own, forcing him to look up at her. "He cared about your mother; he needed her. Now she's gone, just as your father is gone. You're all he has left. He's a weak man, and he wants to keep you safe."

"I promised I would start my training—"

"You will. We'll convince Gavin. In time. For now, let him be happy having you close. His position, this home, they protect you while you're young. I had reasons for bringing your mother to this family." She gestured to the photographs still spread across the bed, then put her hands on either side of John's face, bringing their heads close together. "John, your grandfather thinks he is strong, but he's not. So we won't burden him with our secret plans. Do you understand? We will make them in private."

John nodded solemnly. He understood. "Our plans are secret," he said.

"In the meantime, I will ask him to bring instructors to *Traveler,* to teach you to fight. Would you like that?"

John nodded again, his eyes straying to the images of death lying on the quilt next to him. It would be good to know how to protect himself.

Maggie leaned close again and whispered, "And there's one more secret. You love your grandfather, and he loves you. But if that ever changes, we have a way to control him . . ."

"The boy wishes to apologize to you, sir."

John stood outside the door to his grandfather's rooms, holding a large box full of his mother's belongings. Maggie stood behind him. When Gavin smiled and stepped aside to let him enter, John felt her squeeze his shoulder. Then he walked into the room on his own.

"I'm sorry I cursed at you, Grandfather," he whispered. "I understand I shouldn't be looking at my mother's things all the time."

"That's all right, John," Gavin said, taking a seat on the small sofa by the fireplace. John climbed up beside him, leaving the box of Catherine's things on the floor by their feet.

Gavin put a hand on his grandson's head and cleared his throat in the way he often did, making a strange scratching sound. "Your mother has given so much to me, John. I want you to remember her." He was looking down at John, his face kind. "But when you stare at her belongings all day, I worry. You don't—you don't have to do the things she did. Dangerous things. She restored our fortunes. It's done. We can survive without risking you."

John looked up at the old man and nodded, as though he agreed. "I understand," he whispered.

Gavin pulled him close, and they sat for a while, peacefully look-ing at the fire. But soon the boy's eyes strayed to the open box on the floor. A picture of his mother and himself was visible at the top. In the image, they were sitting together on the floor of her bedroom on *Traveler*, and her arms were around John. Her eyes were looking at him now from within the photograph, and he could feel tears start-ing again at the back of his throat.

He got down from the couch and pushed the box toward his grandfather.

"You take these, please, Grandfather."

Gavin peered into the box, picking up the picture on top and studying Catherine's other belongings.

"You should keep them, John. It's only a few things."

"No," the boy whispered. "You're right. I shouldn't look at them so much. I don't want to be sad and angry all the time."

"Wouldn't you like to keep the photograph with you, at least?" he asked.

"Maybe when I'm bigger. Now I can remember her inside." He touched a hand to his chest. "Like you do with my father."

"Yes, like I do with your father," Gavin murmured. He did not keep pictures of his dead son Archie around. Archie, who had died before he could marry Catherine, before John was born. Gavin said pictures of his son made it too hard to carry on with life. John under-stood that now. He too must carry on with his life—and it was going to be a dangerous one, a life that would require his full attention.

Gavin shut the box, hiding the photograph of Catherine from view. But John felt she was still with him, her older sister was still with him, all those who had been tortured and killed were still with him. He had them inside himself.

CHAPTER 26

QUIN

"In the beginning, there was the hum of the universe."

Shinobu and Quin sat cross-legged on the floor of the practice barn. Alistair had dragged in the old blackboard. He was standing in front of it, looking as much like a teacher as it was possible for a large Scottish warrior to look. He had made a good start by wearing glasses beneath his messy and very red hair. He was, however, also wearing a tight, sleeveless exercise shirt that left bare his enormous arms. Beneath the shirt he had on his teaching trousers, which made an appearance every now and then. They'd been carefully pressed with a crease down the front of each leg, but the effect was ruined somewhat by the fact that Alistair was barefoot.

The big man repeated himself: "In the beginning, there was the hum of the universe." He looked at his two students. "What does that mean?"

Shinobu's hand went up.

"Yes, lad?"

"The vibration of all things," said Shinobu.

Quin put her hand up.

"Yes, lass?"

"All matter in the universe vibrates," Quin said. "Atoms, electrons, even smaller things."

"Aye. Correct, both." Alistair uncrossed his massive arms, picked up a piece of chalk, and began to draw an atom. He pressed too hard and broke the chalk twice before he'd finished the diagram. Quin smiled.

"Don't laugh at me, child," he said good-naturedly. "You'll make me feel small, won't you? Now. What is a hum but a vibration? When something vibrates, it needs at least two dimensions, does it not? At least up and down and side to side. Do you agree?"

Quin and Shinobu nodded, impressed by the sheer quantity of words coming from Alistair, who usually said as little as possible. Perhaps this lesson was as exciting for him as it was for them—hence his efforts to look scholarly. He turned and drew a diagram of a two-dimensional wave vibration.

Quin caught Shinobu glancing at her. They'd both turned fourteen within the last month, and though they'd been learning to fight for years, Briac had only now given his approval for the two of them to begin this particular instruction with Alistair. It meant he believed they would make it to their oath. Briac believed they were good enough to be Seekers. She smiled at Shinobu, excited for them both.

Alistair cleared his throat. "If you can't even concentrate on the lesson, Son, maybe you should tell her, eh?"

"What, sir?" Shinobu asked, startled. He looked away from Quin quickly.

As Quin watched, Shinobu's cheeks flushed bright red, and he seemed to shrink in upon himself. She guessed that his father had mentally caught him daydreaming about one of the many girls he knew down in Corrickmore. That would explain the absent way he'd been staring at her for the last few minutes—his mind had been wandering. He was so good-looking, it was no surprise those girls were after him. To give Shinobu time to recover, Quin raised her hand.

"How do you read minds, sir? And why can't I?"

"How I read minds: not at all," Alistair replied. "My son's face had his thoughts written on it clear. No mind reading required." He removed his glasses and carefully cleaned their rims with the hem of his tank top, giving his face a professorial expression as he did so. "Why can't you read minds? The answer is, maybe you can."

"I really can't, sir."

"Could be you *can,* girl, but there's no telling if you *will.* It might happen of a sudden, at any point before you're grown, when you're training your mind as we are." He put his glasses back on, and Quin realized there were no lenses in them—they were purely for show. "Once you're an adult, you'll know whether you can or not. I can't. Your mother, Fiona, had it come upon her all at once when she was a girl. Overnight, she could read a mind like she was reading a book. But I think not so much anymore."

"She still does, sir," Quin offered. "Mostly when I'm thinking things I don't want her to know."

"Ah, of course. Now, if my son's cheeks have stopped burning, we can continue the lesson. Tell me—could something vibrate in three dimensions?" They both quickly agreed that this was so. "How about four?"

Shinobu raised his hand.

"Ah, lad, you know this one. What is the fourth dimension?"

"Time, sir," he answered. They had learned this before, of course, but its relevance was not yet clear.

"Correct. Master MacBain gets a lollipop after class. Which he is welcome to share if he likes." Here he glanced knowingly at Quin, and Shinobu looked uncomfortable again.

Alistair pushed on. He drew a three-dimensional cube on the blackboard, then a long arrow beneath it. "Time. Any vibration happens through time. But there is a very strange thing in the universe—"

"Stranger than a man wearing a tank top with dress trousers, sir?" Shinobu asked.

Quin stopped herself from smiling. Since Shinobu's mother had died, Alistair had been both father and mother to him, and he gave Shinobu plenty of room to fool around. But whether Alistair would put up with it during a lesson was never certain.

Fortunately, Alistair smiled and gave a very large sigh. "Have you no respect? This is my formal tank top, isn't it? Now, please. There is a strange thing in the universe. The vibrations of atoms and electrons and even smaller particles dinnae quite add up. There is something wrong with them, isn't there? Until we understand that they are vibrating in more dimensions than those we see around us."

Quin's heart beat faster with anticipation. Alistair was going to tell them something important. She could feel it.

"There are the three dimensions we see, and the one we feel— time. But there are more. Curled up within the smallest vibrations of the universe, there are other dimensions. These slide through our own dimensions like movable, interlocking threads."

He turned back to the chalkboard and drew something like threads woven together into a piece of fabric. "Aye, and time. Here, it moves like this." He pointed to the long, straight arrow in his earlier diagram. "But there?" He shrugged. "Time might not be so simple. What if you could unfurl those hidden dimensions? What if you could open them up and step into them? What would they feel like? Where would they take you?"

Both students were silent for a bit, staring at Alistair and his simple drawing.

Finally Quin asked, "Can we really do that, sir?"

Alistair set down the chalk and crossed his huge arms over his chest. He smiled.

"That's all for today."

PART TWO

HONG KONG

18 Months Later

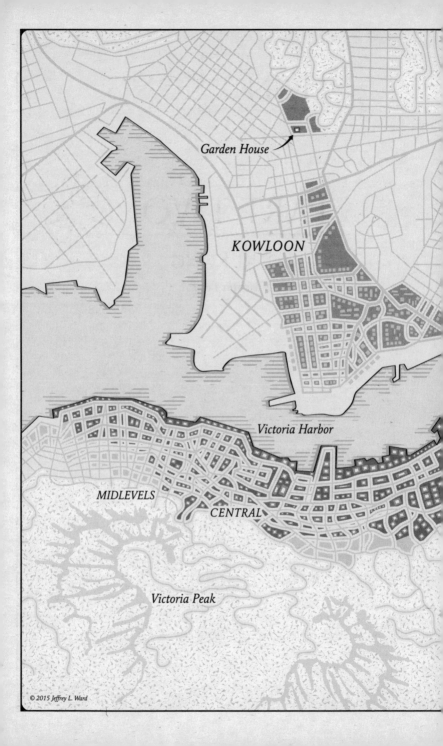

Garden House

KOWLOON

Victoria Harbor

MIDLEVELS

CENTRAL

Victoria Peak

© 2015 Jeffrey L. Ward

HONG KONG

KWUN TONG

Healer's House

Transit Bridge

HONG KONG ISLAND

0   1

Miles

CHAPTER 27

VICTORIA HARBOR

The tiny submersible moved through the depths of the harbor, photographing everything. It traveled in a zigzag pattern that allowed it, very slowly, to cover every inch of the harbor bottom. Each morning, it would surface to recharge its batteries in the sunlight and transmit its photographs back to shore. Then it would dive again, continuing along the ocean floor.

Somewhere on land, computers examined the pictures it sent, compared them to customers' requests, and decided if there was anything of interest down there. In a harbor as old as Victoria Harbor, in a city as large as Hong Kong, there was always something of interest under the water.

On this day, when the submersible came to the surface and bobbed in the wake of a large ship, it transmitted, among hundreds of thousands of images, a picture of a slender object made of stone and buried almost completely in sand. To the human eye, it was nothing, but enough of the object was visible for a computer to match it with an odd request from someone on the other side of the world.

CHAPTER 28

QUIN

Beneath her, the water was very deep and very cold. Near the bottom, where the sunlight never reached, it was black. Something was down there, and it was moving. She could feel it rising from the darkness and the freezing depths, slowly climbing upward. As it rose, it moved faster, into water that was deep blue, then lighter shades. In a moment, it would break the surface. From there, it would continue rising, up through the rafters of the Bridge, through each of the lower levels, until it was here in the room with her, all around her. She could feel it now, enveloping her and pulling her back toward the ocean, where she would drown.

"We're leaving!"

Quin woke.

She was lying in a bed near a small, round window. Her eyes moved over the room without recognizing anything. On one wall was a chart of the human body, showing acupuncture points and muscle reflexes. Near the chart was a calendar with a Chinese dragon along the top. There was an open closet with plain, dark clothing hanging in it. Next to the closet was a medical skeleton wearing a headband

and a blue smock, and above the skeleton were photographs of people who appeared to be complete strangers.

Quin turned her eyes upward, and the low ceiling came into focus. There was a map pinned there, covering most of the ceiling. In the style of an old etching, it showed a dense city that covered an island and spilled over onto the mainland nearby. It was a map of Hong Kong—she could see the name written in ornate letters across the center.

On the map, between the Kowloon section of the city on the mainland and Hong Kong Island, a large bridge was visible. *That's where I am,* she remembered. She was here, in her room, in the house she shared with her mother, on the Transit Bridge, which was a world of its own, running between Kowloon and Hong Kong Island, in the city of Hong Kong, continent of Asia. This was home, and maybe it always had been.

She turned her head to look out the window. Through it, she could see the high buildings across Victoria Harbor, and beneath her, the harbor's gray water, running away from her with the tide. She felt a little dizzy as she watched the current. It appeared to be morning.

"You were yelling something."

Her mother was standing in the doorway to Quin's bedroom. Fiona wore a bright silk dress, her deep red hair tied up in an elaborate coiffure that framed her porcelain skin and blue eyes. She hesitated at the door, looking quite beautiful. After a moment, she took a seat carefully next to Quin on the bed, almost as if worried that her daughter might bite her. Quin noticed that her mother's motions were sure and graceful—which meant she hadn't started drinking yet today.

"Are you all right?" Fiona asked. "You were saying something about leaving."

Quin closed her eyes, still feeling dizzy. The sensation from her dream had a hold on her, something rising and rising . . .

"Are you feeling all right?" Fiona asked again.

Her mother's cool hand touched her forehead. The dream disappeared and her dizziness faded. Her own life settled back around her. She opened her eyes.

"There you are," Fiona said, smiling down at her.

Quin wished her mother would take her hand off her forehead. When had Fiona last washed her hands? All the men Fiona spent time with, and the drugs down in the drug bars, everything her mother touched would be carried on that hand, small pieces of other people and places, now touching Quin. It made her feel ill.

She rolled away from Fiona, closer to the window, causing the hand to slip from her head.

"I'm not diseased, Quin," Fiona told her quietly.

"I didn't say that."

"You didn't have to." Her mother stood and moved back to the doorway. "I have an appointment. I'll be back for dinner. If you're feeling up to it, maybe we can eat together." When Quin made no response, Fiona turned and left the room.

She calls them appointments, Quin thought.

"They *are* appointments," her mother called as she walked down the stairs. "Just as any businesswoman might have." A moment later, the bells that hung from the front door rang as Fiona left the house.

Quin closed her eyes and pulled the covers over her head. She lay there for several minutes, but sleep would not return. Anyway, she wasn't sure she wanted to go back to sleep—that dream might still be waiting.

She could feel the place where her mother had touched her head. Those tiny particles were there, on her skin. They might be invisible, but Quin could feel them.

She threw the covers off and walked to the bathroom, where she spent several minutes washing her face and hands, avoiding, as she always did, the sight of her bare left arm. When she finally felt clean, she pulled on a long-sleeved shirt, tugged it down over her wrists, and then looked into the mirror.

"Quin," she said, like she was practicing her own name. Her dark hair was long, and her skin was as pale as it had ever been, from spending most of her time in the twilight of the Transit Bridge. Her dark eyes looked older, she thought, than her sixteen years.

From the skeleton in the corner of her bedroom, she retrieved the white headband, which she tied around her head. She took the blue smock from the skeleton as well and slipped into it. The smock and headband marked her as a healer. At sixteen, she was young for the profession, though of course she was still in training. Her eyes ran over the photographs taped to the wall. She recognized them now—her patients. She'd done something good for each of them. She was very lucky to have such a noble calling. In a small way, she was making the world better.

She leaned her forehead against the skeleton's bony skull and whispered, "I will help someone today. If I am lucky, I will help many people. If I am very lucky, I will—"

A knock on the downstairs door interrupted her morning ritual. Before she was halfway down the stairs, the knock came again, much harder.

"I'm coming!" she called in Chinese.

"Emergency!" said the voice from the other side, also in Chinese. It was one of the few Chinese words Quin knew well. She threw open the door to find an Asian woman around forty years old, carrying a small boy in her arms.

"Emergency," the woman said again, switching to English this time, after seeing Quin's Western face.

"What happened?" Quin asked as she took the boy from the woman's arms and immediately carried him to the back room. There, she laid the child on the treatment table that sat among the high shelves of Chinese herbs and racks of acupuncture needles she was still learning to use.

"It was some kind of drug," the woman told her. Her accent was nearly impossible to detect, almost as though she spoke English natively. She was panicked, but she spoke clearly—she was not someone who easily lost control. "His older brother—he must have left something in a drawer. Akio found it and swallowed it. I don't know what it was. Shiva maybe, or even opium . . ." Shiva was one of the drugs currently sweeping through the bars on the bottom levels of the Bridge.

"You know I'm only a trainee? We should get my teacher, Master Tan."

"I have already been there," the woman said. "Master Tan is away this morning. His mother pointed me here."

Quin could imagine Master Tan's ancient and tiny mother sending this woman to her. Quin was only three houses away from Master Tan's, but that did not mean this was the best place for the boy to come. The woman was now studying Quin's face, as though searching for something else there.

"Please . . ."

Quin had already begun to examine the boy's limp body, his eyes, his fingernails, the color of his skin, all the places Master Tan had taught her to look for telltale signs. It was odd—the boy had his mother's face, but his hair had a reddish tint. Something she'd seen before, maybe. She quickly inserted three acupuncture needles, at his head, wrist, and ankle.

"How long since he swallowed it?"

"Maybe a half hour," the woman said.

"I actually think we should go to hospital—" Quin began.

"Quin?"

"Yes?"

The woman nodded to herself. "Quin, Master Tan trusts you. His mother said so. So I trust you, Quin."

It was strange how the woman kept saying her name, just as Quin had been saying her own name a few minutes before, up in the bathroom. The woman put her hands on Quin's shoulders.

"Please. It's too late to go somewhere else. Help him."

Quin nodded. She concentrated, willing herself to enter a state of heightened observation. Master Tan called this her special gift. He said most healers worked a lifetime to achieve what she could do so naturally. When he had seen her potential, Master Tan, one of the great healers of the Transit Bridge, had taken her on as his student.

Standing over the boy, Quin calmed her breathing. Her mind emptied of everything except the child lying in front of her. Her perceptions began to shift. After a moment, she could see things that lay beneath the level of ordinary sight. She observed bright, copper-colored lines flowing around the boy, his body's electrical field. All people had such fields around their bodies—the fields could be measured with special instruments. But to see the field as Quin did was remarkable, a sign of intense mental focus. The boy's bright lines were broken by dark, irregular patches hovering over the organs that had been affected by the toxin.

"He must pass out the poison," she said. She'd helped Master Tan with dozens of similar cases—there were always problems with drugs on the Bridge—but she had never treated one so young. "Were you able to make him vomit?"

"No. I tried . . ."

There was not much time. The little boy was going into shock. Quin let her vision deepen. She could see her own energy field now, bright lines moving up and down her arms, and the small muddy whirlpool around the old injury in her chest. She concentrated and felt her energy sweeping down through her hands like an electrical river. Master Tan might be impressed at her ability to control her mind, but to her it seemed easy, like she'd been trained to do it all her life. Perhaps she had. Her existence before the Transit Bridge was all but missing from her memory, so she was free to imagine it any way she liked. She liked to tell herself she'd been training since birth to focus her thoughts in order to help people in this way.

She ran her fingers over the clouds above the boy's organs, letting her energy combine with his. The dark clouds moved, seemed for a moment to spread. The boy moaned.

"What's happening?" his mother asked.

Quin didn't answer. She directed her energy at the boy's stomach reflexes. His body convulsed.

She gently rolled him onto his side and grabbed a bucket. The boy convulsed again. And then he was vomiting, his whole body contracting as it forced out the contents of his stomach.

She saw the dark clouds changing, starting to break up. The boy's eyes were fluttering open. Quin felt his pulse in several places, then began to relax. He would be all right.

"Akio, Akio," his mother whispered, leaning over him. The boy mumbled an answer.

For a moment, as Quin's vision settled back to normal, the woman's face and the boy's reddish hair looked so familiar. She could almost imagine them in a meadow with the sunlight playing over the tall grass . . .

"Quin."

She looked up to see that the mother was kneeling on the floor in front of her. Akio was sitting up on the treatment table now, looking weak but much better. Time had passed without Quin noticing. She realized her eyes had been closed, her head propped in her hand. She was sitting in one of the chairs, and she was holding a full glass of water.

"I thought we'd lost you for a moment," the woman said to her.

"I'm sorry," she replied. "I . . . lost track."

"How old are you?" the woman asked. There was something odd in her tone, as though she were inquiring to confirm something she already knew.

"I'm sixteen," she answered. For a while, as she had recovered from her chest wound, she'd had trouble remembering her own age, but she reminded herself of it frequently now. She had been fifteen then, and she was nearly seventeen now.

"Sixteen." The woman appeared to be doing some kind of calculation in her head—perhaps wondering how long Quin had been studying. "You've done very well. Do you have friends here?"

"Friends? Not really." Quin was a little taken aback by the personal nature of the woman's question, but she was also disturbed by her own answer. Why was the idea of friends a foreign concept?

She stood and handed the woman the glass of water she'd been holding. "Have him drink all of this, and then three more this morning. I need to make him a tea. Can you come by in a few hours for that?"

As the boy finished the glass of water, Quin carefully washed her hands again. The woman had touched her shoulders a couple of times, but she was fairly sure the woman's hands had never actually come into contact with her skin. She wouldn't worry about germs on the fabric, even if she suspected they were there. If she let herself worry, she'd spend all day washing her clothes.

When she was finished at the sink, she pulled her long sleeves back down as far as they would go. The left sleeve covered a blemish that bothered her. She didn't like to look at it.

Soon the woman was carrying the boy Akio out the front door.

"Thank you. Quin." The woman said her name again in that strange, careful way, like she was enjoying the sound of it.

When the door shut behind them, Quin stood quite still for several minutes. *I've saved the life of a child,* she told herself. *I've saved the life of a child.* Maybe the woman would let her take a picture of the boy to put upstairs on her wall.

There was a tugging at the edges of her lips. It surprised her—her mouth had grown unused to smiling.

CHAPTER 29

SHINOBU

Shinobu was sweating. He could feel wetness trickling down his forehead inside his face mask, despite how cold the water was. He blinked the sweat out of his eyes and adjusted his headlamp as he swam deeper. His friend Brian was diving next to him, both of them wearing heavy reclamation tools around the belts of their dive suits. Brian's big gut made him look like a giant sea bass as he swam down into the darker water. *And I am a barracuda,* Shinobu thought. He had gotten so skinny in the past year that his ribs were visible even through his thick wet suit.

They had just entered the Trench, a deep cut in the bottom of Victoria Harbor where the ocean currents swept and buried all kinds of debris from the harbor floor. As they passed between the Trench's high walls, the water became much darker and much colder. In the light of their headlamps, the shadows were moving wildly, and Shinobu had to blink his eyes every few seconds to clear the perspiration.

"Brian!" he yelled. "It's haunted down here." He wasn't actually speaking, since his mouth was full of his breathing regulator, but a garbled stream of sound came out along with a lot of bubbles. As usual when he tried to have conversations underwater, Brian was ignoring him.

The sweat was driving Shinobu crazy. He lifted his goggles and let water wash over his face. Then he blew out the mask and swam to catch up with Brian.

A group of real bass was swimming by, their outlines eerie against the trench wall. Shinobu had done Shiva sticks that morning, burning and inhaling the drug's smoke in the horrible room he and Brian shared above a movie theater in the slums on the outskirts of Kowloon. Shiva changed the way you saw and heard things, so it was never a good idea to do Shiva before a day of physical labor, especially labor as complicated as diving, but Shinobu had a hard time enjoying himself unless he was scared out of his wits.

He grabbed Brian's shoulder.

"The shadows are following me!" he yelled, again sending up an avalanche of bubbles.

Brian pulled the clipboard at his waist around to the front and wrote on the back of it with his special marker:

SHUT UP.

"You shut up!" Shinobu said, spewing bubbles and accidentally inhaling a mouthful of seawater. He coughed it out. Then he laughed, terrified and exhilarated. Diving was as different from his old life as you could get. Even more different than throwing oneself off high buildings and bridges, which was how he'd spent his first six months in Hong Kong.

They were nearing the floor of the Trench. The bottom was covered with tall drifts of silt, which hid all sorts of treasure. In a city the size of Hong Kong, with a harbor that had been open to ships for hundreds of years, there was no end to what you might find. Using an underwater blowtorch, Brian and Shinobu had once salvaged an entire Rolls Royce, piece by piece, from the Trench's south end. Another time, they'd used explosives to blast their way through a steel hull of an ancient Japanese supply ship to recover a cache of World War II weapons.

Brian was following the navigation bar of a device strapped to his arm. As they swept the area with their lights, the shadows got crazy again. Shinobu could swear there were other divers hanging just out of sight, darting off whenever he turned his head.

He grabbed the clipboard from Brian and wrote:

THEY'RE WATCHING US.

Brian batted Shinobu's hands away. Below them, the drift contained shards of cookware and an old television with an eel hiding in the broken glass screen.

Shinobu grabbed up the clipboard again and flipped through the waterproof sheets to their work order. He had left the paperwork to Brian before they'd started the dive, and he hadn't even bothered to check out what they were looking for. On the upper half of the page was an image of the object they'd been sent to find, as photographed by a submersible traveling along the ocean floor. The item was partly buried, and hard to make out in the picture. Next to the photograph was a drawing of what the entire object was supposed to look like. It was some sort of dagger—the hilt of which was made of several separate stone rings stacked on top of one another, each ring carved with symbols.

Shinobu experienced a rush of panic. With his altered Shiva senses, it felt like an icy hand had gripped his intestines and was squeezing them. They had been sent to find the athame he himself had thrown off the Transit Bridge a year and half ago.

"We can't do this!" he said to Brian.

Just like before, nothing but bubbles came out, and Brian didn't even turn, so Shinobu reached for Brian's shoulder.

"Stop! We have to go back."

He was so agitated, he forgot himself again and breathed in a huge amount of water around his mouthpiece. While he coughed it out, Brian continued searching along the drift, ignoring him completely. By the time Shinobu could breathe normally again, Brian was waving to him with a look of triumph on his face, and he was holding the athame in his left hand.

Moving as fast as he could through the water, Shinobu swam over and hit the stone dagger out of Brian's hand. It spun away, sinking toward the bottom of the Trench.

Brian went after it immediately, but Shinobu caught his ankle and yanked him backward. Brian Kwon was big and friendly and very slow to anger, but he got angry now. He kicked out at Shinobu. Shinobu ducked aside and pulled Brian again, bringing him farther away from the athame, which was now stuck in the sand ten feet below them.

Brian shoved Shinobu. Shinobu grabbed Brian's arms and wouldn't let go. Brian twisted a big, meaty hand out of Shinobu's grasp and swiped at his chest, yanking the hose out of Shinobu's mouthpiece. A stream of bubbles flowed out, his oxygen spilling into the water. As Shinobu flailed his arms to try to stop the bubbles, Brian dove deeper.

The threat of death forced Shinobu to control his panic. He calmed himself, did not follow Brian, and instead reached a hand carefully around to his tank's master valve, which he cranked shut. The bubbles stopped.

It took a while to reattach the hose to his mouthpiece. When he had finally gotten his air back on and was gasping in deep lungfuls, Brian was swimming up toward him, the athame tucked safely into his belt. His big friend stopped in front of Shinobu and pulled his clipboard around. On the work order, beneath the picture of the athame, was the salvage fee they were being paid for recovering it. Brian's finger jabbed at the fee several times: they were getting triple wages for bringing the stone dagger back to shore in perfect condition. Then Brian turned and swam for the surface. *Sea Bass wins,* Shinobu thought. *He'll never swim away from that much money.*

Shinobu floated in place for a moment. The Shiva sticks were wearing off, and his head was starting to ache. He slowly made his way after Brian, turning his head from side to side periodically, in hopes of catching any stray divers who were lurking just out of sight.

It was in one of these moments that he saw it. The lightning rod was almost completely buried in a drift of sand. Only the end of the flat blade stuck up into the water, next to a broken toilet. Shinobu swam over and pulled the rod from the sediment.

The stone implement was exactly as it had been eighteen months ago—its trip to the bottom of Victoria Harbor and then along the seafloor to the Trench had done it no harm.

He looked up at Brian, swimming far ahead of him. Apparently, no one was searching for the lightning rod. And without it, the athame was useless. He gripped it in his hands and lifted a knee, thinking he would break it in half. But he stopped himself halfway through the motion. He had been able to throw it away all those months ago, but actually destroying it was another matter. He thought about burying it in the silt, but found he could not do that either. It was in his hands now, one of mankind's most precious artifacts, as his father had always told him.

My father . . . He did not want to think of him. And yet he could not escape the feeling that Alistair wouldn't want him to discard the lightning rod.

"Dammit!" he yelled, filling the water around him with bubbles.

This object had been used for . . . things he did not wish to think about. But those things were not, strictly speaking, the lightning rod's fault. Shinobu hovered in the water for a while, muttering bubble-laced curses to himself, the rod held between his hands. Eventually he slipped it into the pouch at his waist.

He caught up to Brian, and the two of them glared at each other as they hung in the water at their waypoint, waiting to decompress so they could swim the rest of the way to the surface. After a couple of minutes of angry staring, Brian wrote:

WHAT DID YOU DO THAT FOR?

Shinobu took the clipboard and wrote:

SORRY, SEA BASS. MY MISTAKE.

His big friend seemed to accept this, and by the time they were walking up the shore at the salvage site, Brian was smiling and thinking of ways to spend their money.

"More Shiva sticks?" he asked, shoving Shinobu in a friendly way.

"No, I'll never sleep."

"Since when do you sleep?" Brian asked.

"You have a point."

They were speaking in the combination of Chinese and English that was popular among young people in Hong Kong. That worked reasonably well for Shinobu. He was Japanese, not Chinese, of course, and all the Chinese he knew had been picked up in the last year and a half—but he was a quick study.

They'd exited the water in an area called Kwun Tong, which gave a view southwest along the harbor. From where they were walking, Shinobu could see the huge, high bulk of the Transit Bridge crossing the water, its upper canopy designed to look like a mass of sails from Eastern and Western ships. And beyond the Bridge, on the other side of the harbor, the slender skyscrapers of Central were just visible in the midafternoon haze.

Shinobu glanced at the athame, still tucked in Brian's belt, and wondered when it would be delivered to whoever had asked for it. *And who would be asking for it?*

His question was answered almost immediately. Walking down the salvage site toward them, across the piles of reclaimed electronics and car parts and pieces of old ships, were two men. The first was their foreman, a tiny Filipino who yelled at them constantly but was never actually angry as long as they brought up what he wanted from the harbor floor. The second man was white and young, and completely careless of his trousers and shoes as he walked through the mud.

It was John. Of course. For the past year and a half, he'd probably been checking with salvage companies all over the world, and now the athame had brought him directly to Hong Kong. And, inadvertently, right to Shinobu himself.

A distant part of Shinobu knew he should kill John. He should run up the shore right now and finish him, without a moment of hesitation. That would be the honorable thing to do. But already, he knew that he would not. It was because of John that Alistair had ended up the way he had. It was because of John—and yet, it was not *only* because of John. It was very much because of Briac, and even because of Alistair himself. His father and uncle had chosen to do certain things . . . things Shinobu did not allow himself to think about anymore.

Other things were John's fault—Quin's injury, for instance, and her obsession with him. And yet . . . Quin was no longer Shinobu's responsibility. He had said goodbye to her and left everything from

Scotland behind him, his father included. What he really needed right now was something to stop him from remembering.

"What should we do, then?" Brian asked, frustrated at Shinobu's silence. "Maybe one of the fancy opium bars?"

"Yeah, sure," Shinobu agreed absently.

He was still in his dive gear, and his red hair had been shaved short and dyed in a yellow-and-black leopard pattern. He had piercings in his nose and eyebrow, and he was taller and skinnier than he had been before. Still, he and John had spent years together, and in another thirty yards, John would be close enough to recognize him.

"Well, which one?" Brian was asking. "I hear there's a bar on the fourth level of the Transit Bridge. It's like an opium den from imperial China—"

Shinobu drew back an arm and punched Brian directly in the face midsentence. The blow dropped Brian's considerable bulk to the ground, and Shinobu jumped on top of him and began raining fists onto his head. As he had hoped, Brian grabbed Shinobu around the neck and rolled over, pinning him to the wet ground. Instead of swinging at Brian's face again, Shinobu grabbed handfuls of stinking mud and smeared it all over his own hair and face.

"What did you do that for?" Brian yelled. "We don't have to get opium. You can pick whatever you want!"

He was choking Shinobu now, and Shinobu stopped smearing mud on himself and began trying to pry Brian's large, sausage-like fingers from his neck. The foreman was running toward them, yelling for help from his workers. A moment later, a dozen arms were pulling Brian off of him.

Someone helped Shinobu up, and he sat on the ground, coughing and gasping, completely covered in mud. From this position, he watched John walk the rest of the distance toward them, his face showing concern that something might have been damaged in their fight. The foreman was examining the athame critically, making a big show of berating Brian for getting mud all over it.

"It was at the bottom of the ocean anyway, boss," Brian pointed out.

Then John was standing right above Shinobu as the foreman wiped off the athame and handed it to him. John took it almost reverently and held it up, examining the stone in the sunlight. It was undamaged, perfect. His thumb stroked the bottom of the pommel, where, Shinobu knew, there was a small, delicate carving of a fox. John's face held a mixture of hope and relief that was almost painful to see. Then he tucked the athame inside his coat and walked back up the muddy slope without a glance in Shinobu's direction.

Shinobu wiped a hand across his forehead as he watched the foreman counting out their fee and handing it over to Brian. Shinobu was sweating profusely again and felt an intense thirst coming over him.

"Here, let me help you." Brian put out a hand and pulled Shinobu to his feet. As soon as he was up, Brian punched him in the jaw, sending him back down into the mud.

Shinobu looked up at Brian and spit out a mouthful of sludge. "What'd you do that for?"

"What the hell's the matter with you, Barracuda?" Brian muttered.

"I just had a sea bass sitting on top of me!"

They both laughed. None of it mattered. Their work was over for the day, and the drug bars waited.

They hosed themselves off with the filthy water that came out of the salvage yard hose, and changed back into street clothes. Street clothes, for Shinobu and Brian, meant tight jeans and leather jackets, ripped T-shirts held together with safety pins, and bracelets with metal studs so sharp, it was a wonder they didn't poke their own eyes out. Shinobu liked to wear his thickest bracelet on his left wrist, where it covered up an old scar he preferred not to see.

He had gotten so thin that his jeans weren't as tight as they used to be, and he was able to slip the lightning rod down a trouser leg, with the end of the dull blade shoved into his left boot.

He noticed a message from his mother then, which had come through on his phone while he was underwater. It asked him to contact her urgently. It must have been important—she never tried to reach him. His mother, who was not dead, but very much alive, and with whom he had been reunited only a year and a half ago, had already grown disgusted with him. And he couldn't blame her.

He started to call her, but then Brian was banging on the changing room door, telling him to hurry up. He slipped his phone back into his pocket without another thought. Together, he and Brian walked off the salvage site and into the city, the stone rod tap-tapping against Shinobu's leg.

CHAPTER 30

QUIN

Quin was in the back room of her healing office, tidying up after mixing a bag of herbs for the little redheaded Asian boy. The bells on the front door rang, alerting her that someone had just entered the waiting room.

"Mother?" she called. For the first time in a long while, she was eager to see Fiona and tell her about saving the boy.

She moved into the front room and discovered it was not Fiona.

It was a young man. He was about her own age, quite nice-looking, with fair skin and light brown hair. He stood with his back to the entry door, and his blue eyes were looking at her like he was drowning and she might save his life.

Somehow she lost control of her hands and dropped a canister of herbs. It fell to the ground, spilling its contents across the floor.

"Quin," he said softly. "Is it really you?"

She'd been worried that his voice would be different, twisted, terrifying even, but it was not. He sounded quite ordinary, and very, very familiar.

He was watching her closely, as if worried she might do something dangerous or wild. His eyes followed her as she bent to pick up the herbs. She too felt like she might do something unpredictable. But what?

She took her time retrieving the canister from the floor and setting it carefully on a counter. Her motions felt awkward all of a sudden, like her muscles had stopped working properly in his presence.

"Quin," he said again. She knew his voice. She knew it so well. And him. Of course she knew him. He was important in her life somehow.

"Do you know me?" he asked. He took a step toward her.

"Of course." She said it automatically and found herself backing into the doorjamb of the room behind her. It was good to feel the solid wall there. She did know him. She could imagine herself walking over and laying her head on his chest. But there was good reason, her mind told her, that she did not remember him. "Of course I know you."

He took another step toward her, like he couldn't keep himself away.

"What's my name?" he asked.

Quin bit her bottom lip. His name was right there, on the tip of her tongue. It was something common, and yet she couldn't think of it. It was part of that gray area in her mind, where other people thought memories should be. The gray was like her own Victoria Harbor, drowning the first fifteen years of her life.

He was getting closer. The way he moved . . . She had seen him in a barn, in a field, far away from here. There was a river in the distance. These things were like marks left on an ink blotter after you've taken your paper away—she could feel them more than she could see them.

He was standing right in front of her, and Quin was pressed against the wall. He smelled of soap and salty ocean air.

"What's my name, Quin?"

She whispered, "John."

The sensation of dizziness rolled over her. Her knees gave out, and she was sliding down the wall. John caught her. She pushed herself up and away from him, moving into the back room.

She could not remember, and yet not remembering was exhausting. It was hard to walk. She was staggering. She knocked over another canister of herbs, heard it spill all over the floor. She should not be with him.

"I was so worried," he was saying. "I thought—ever since that night—"

"No." Instinctively her hand came up to stop whatever he was going to say. There was John's face. She'd seen it looking at her through a hole, while numbness spread across her chest . . .

"Thank God you're all right," he breathed, now following her as she tottered around the examination table.

She pulled another few canisters off a shelf as she tried to hold herself up. The old wound in her chest was aching. She was actually falling; her legs had collapsed.

Instead of hitting the ground, she was lifted into John's strong arms. It felt so natural. Even though he was dangerous. He was dangerous, somehow. And so was she. Together they would be very dangerous.

"I've got you," he whispered. "I've got you."

He was carrying her up the stairs to her bedroom, and it was like being on the deck of a rocking boat. She didn't mind that he was touching her, didn't care where his hands had been. She let her eyes close. Then they were in her bedroom, and he was laying her gently on the bed.

The dizziness was worse. This had happened to her before, during her first months in Hong Kong. *It's your past trying to overtake your present,* Master Tan had explained patiently. *You may leave it in the past, if you wish. You must simply wait for the moment to pass.*

"I'm here," he whispered. "I'm here with you. I've missed you. God, I'm so sorry . . ."

Why was it dangerous to be with him? It didn't make sense. She could sleep, because he was there to stand guard. Things were right again, because John was here.

"I missed you too," she murmured, holding one of his hands in her own as she drifted into unconsciousness.

CHAPTER 31

SHINOBU

Shinobu peered at the object in his hand through a haze of opium smoke. It was vibrating. He worked hard to focus his eyes and eventually discovered it was his phone. Who would be calling him? It was the middle of the day. The crew he and Brian usually hung out with didn't even wake up until after dark.

He exhaled another cloud of smoke from the opium pipe cradled in his arm. It was his seventh pipe, and he was reaching that perfect state when he was balanced between his body and the sky: no worries, no troubles, no people.

But the phone kept vibrating. It had been vibrating for hours, though that was in opium time. In real time it might only have been a few seconds.

"Please shut up," he whispered to it.

It didn't listen.

Clumsily Shinobu set the pipe on its tray and struggled up onto his elbows, irritated. He rubbed his eyes and stared at the phone.

"It's my mother."

He shoved at Brian Kwon, who was curled up next to him on the pallet, his own pipe lying by his face. Brian grunted in response and mumbled, "Barracuda mom."

The phone had stopped vibrating, and now it beeped, indicating there was a message. His mother never called. Something tickled the back of Shinobu's mind. Earlier that day, hadn't she called him another time? Two calls from his mother in one day was remarkable. Being hit by a meteor while salvage diving was more likely. The last time he'd seen his mother, she had found him unconscious in the kitchen, with burning Shiva sticks all around him and his little brother collapsed in the hallway from the smoke. Mariko had thrown a large cooking pot at him and screamed that he was never, ever to come inside her house again. That had been months ago, and he hadn't heard from her since.

Without realizing he'd done it, he was already lying down again. He brought the pipe back to his lips and took in another long breath.

His eyes drifted around the room. He had never been to this particular establishment before, with its fine draped silks and carved wooden pallets detailed in silver. There were many cheaper drug bars on the Transit Bridge. Usually he visited the cheapest, on the lowest levels, where you would lie on a pile of Styrofoam packing peanuts, crammed in with dozens of other opium fiends. But Brian had been eager to spend their extra pay from the day's salvage job. Here, attractive attendants in silk pajamas moved about, preparing new pipes and offering drinks. He noticed they were wearing filters over their noses so they wouldn't become addicted to the smoke.

Smoke, he thought, his peaceful balance ruined. *Smoke and fire. I should have killed you, John, but I hated Briac and Alistair more . . .* There was his father, with a web of sparks around his dark red hair. Shinobu could see that red hair now, like it was across the room from him.

He slowly realized that the red hair actually *was* across the room from him. Though his mind was still floating, his eyes very gradually came into focus, and he found himself looking at a woman reclining on a pallet on the other side of the opium den.

She was less than forty years old, her red hair the exact shade of his father's. She was beautiful—as beautiful as he had once thought his aunt Fiona. This woman wore a silk dress in the Chinese style. With her was an older European businessman, whose head was in her lap as she held an opium pipe to his lips. There was a yellow scarf about her neck, which marked her, he knew, as an escort. It was a legal profession on the Bridge. The man must be her client, buying her company while he enjoyed himself in the drug dens. She was speaking softly to him, a discreet filter perched above her lip.

"Sea Bass, she looks just like Fiona," he mumbled.

"Who?" came the sleepy response from Brian.

"That woman." He tried to point, but it was too difficult to get his hands to move when he was floating so far above them. He blew smoke in her direction, but of course Brian was lying behind him and could not see that.

"Who's Fiona?" Brian mumbled.

"Right there," Shinobu said, coughing.

The woman looked up just then, almost as if she'd heard what he said, which was surely impossible at this distance. Her eyes flitted around the room, paused at Shinobu's face, then continued on.

It *was* Fiona. Not someone who looked like her, but Fiona herself.

Shinobu's stomach did an unpleasant flip. The floating sensation ended. He came crashing back into his own head.

"It *is* her," he whispered, reaching out a hand to shake Brian's shoulder. "She's right there!"

"Please shut up, Barracuda," Brian muttered, batting his hand away. "Close your mouth. Close it up like . . . like something that keeps its mouth closed!"

Panic was creeping from Shinobu's stomach toward his head. He had not seen anyone from his previous life for a year and a half. Now, in one day, he'd seen both John and Fiona.

"Why today?" he asked Brian.

"A tortoise," mumbled Brian. "They're quiet. Be like a tortoise, Barracuda."

Shinobu concentrated, hoping to see his way through any opium tricks. If Fiona was an escort, it meant she must live on the Bridge. It was true he'd left Fiona and Quin here on the Bridge that night, all those months ago, with Master Tan caring for them. But Shinobu had never imagined they would stay. It was hard to become a Bridge resident. You had to have very particular skills. As he watched Fiona across the room, with her exotic, Western face, and her rare hair color and rarer beauty, he realized that perhaps Fiona had those skills.

He had assumed she and Quin would leave Hong Kong as soon as Quin was healed, find some out-of-the-way corner of the world in which to live. But here Fiona was.

"Go away," he whispered.

Again, Fiona looked up from across the room, and her eyes scanned the other pallets. Shinobu buried his head behind his arm.

"*You* go away," Brian grunted. "And when you get there, please shut up."

Shinobu waited behind his arm until Fiona's attention went back to the man lying with his head in her lap. Then he grabbed the side of the pallet and hauled himself to his feet, nearly flattening an attendant who was walking past at that moment. The small man signaled to other waitstaff, and together they steadied Shinobu into an upright position. He was, at age sixteen, more than six feet tall, and it took three men to keep him from falling onto the floor.

"Sir, perhaps you would like to lie down again?"

"No," he said, swinging an arm to brush them aside, and nearly toppling onto Brian as he did so. He caught himself against a wall. He kneed Brian in the leg. "Bri, come on. We're leaving."

"Shh, Barracuda," he said. "Tortoise. Mouth shut."

"I'm getting out of here!" He shook Brian's shoulder.

". . . make you into tortoise soup," growled Brian. One meaty arm came up to slap at him, but Shinobu dodged it, grabbing the wall again to steady himself.

"Then I'm leaving without you."

He staggered out of the bar, tossing a pile of bills at the attendant who followed him to the door.

"Sir, the Transit Bridge has strict rules about public intoxication. You risk having your visitor's pass revoked."

That was true. Shinobu paused and grabbed one of the oxygen masks hanging from the ceiling by the exit. He breathed through it for a few minutes while he leaned against the wall. Whatever was coming through the mask cleared his head immediately. He could still feel a tiny bit of the opium float, but his ability to control his arms and legs came back.

"Thank you," he said, and he made a respectable show of walking normally out into the wealthy crowds in the corridor beyond.

This level of the Bridge was lined with nightclubs and drug bars of the most expensive sort. His dirty clothes and leopard-spotted hair were already attracting unwanted attention. He pushed his way toward the airlifts, then remembered his phone.

Digging it from a pocket, he found his vision was now clear enough to read his mother's message. The last vestiges of his opium high disappeared when he saw what she'd written. Akio had been very sick. He'd gotten into something in Shinobu's room, and he had almost died. Shinobu tried to remember what he might have left there, but it could have been anything. Drugs had been his constant companions for the past year and a half, and he could have left any number of them in his mother's house. A combination of guilt and terror bloomed in his stomach.

He felt a rough shove and looked up to see Brian, who had staggered out of the bar after him.

"What next?" his friend asked. "Another bar? Or some food?"

"Wait." He read his mother's following message, and relief flooded into him. Akio was all right. It took Shinobu a few moments to catch his breath. "I have to pick something up."

"Food?"

"No, Sea Bass."

"Beer? We can drink like fish, Barracuda."

"I have to go home first."

The words seemed to confuse Brian.

"What home?"

They had been sleeping in that room above the theater for a month, curling up with the rats and cockroaches, which assured Shinobu that he was not, after all, in the Scottish countryside anymore.

"My mother's house," Shinobu answered.

Before Brian had a chance to question him further, Shinobu stepped into an airlift. He was whisked to the surface level of the Bridge. It was gloomy there as always, kept dim by the canopy above, which let in only a small amount of sunlight. Late-afternoon crowds of visitors were wandering down the thoroughfare, past restaurants serving every sort of Asian food.

Brian lurched out of the airlift a moment later, and together they joined the foot traffic walking the Bridge. Above the restaurants were apartments, most with lights on inside, where he could see figures moving about. Between the restaurants were healing offices of acupuncturists, herbalists, and practitioners with more exotic skills that Shinobu couldn't begin to describe.

"It's over there," Shinobu said at last, looking at the address his mother had sent and crossing to the other side of the road.

"That's not your mother's house."

"Shut up, Sea Bass. If you're very helpful, I'll buy you a beer when I'm done."

It didn't happen quite that way. Shinobu was about to have his third strange encounter that day.

He found the office he was looking for, a small clean storefront with an apartment above. He felt inside the metal drop box by the front door and pulled out a large plastic bag of herbs with Akio's name written across it.

As he walked away, tucking the bag beneath his jacket, the door to the healing office was thrown open. Before he could turn around to look, he was knocked to the street by a figure flying out that door, running like someone desperate to stay alive.

CHAPTER 32

QUIN

There were screams in the other room. She could hear the sounds of fighting very clearly from where she stood in the nursery. The child's eyes were staring up at her, terrified.

"What's happening?" he asked quietly in French. He had a lisp, as small children often do.

"Nothing," she answered, also in French. "It's all right. Come with me."

The boy was too frightened to move.

"Come with me," she said again, more roughly now. There was no time to lose.

She pulled the covers off him and reached for his hands.

There was a louder scream from the other room. It might have been a woman's voice, but it was hard to tell.

The boy started to cry.

"It's all right," she said. "I'll take you out of here."

He didn't want to go with her but didn't know how to refuse. She took his hands and moved with him to the doorway. She could see the others, off in the larger room at the end of the hall. No one was looking in her direction at that moment.

She threw the edge of her cloak around the little boy. Holding him tight, she ran down the corridor, down the stairs. In a moment, they were out the side door and moving away.

She picked him up as she ran across the grass. "Where are we going?" he asked.

"Away from here," she whispered into his ear. "I'll keep you safe."

As she ran with the boy in her arms, Quin knew she was dreaming. This was not real; this was not how it had happened. But for this one moment, she was making the right choice, the choice she should have made, and she was filled with happiness. It was not the truth, but it felt good to be brave and noble, even in a dream.

CHAPTER 33

JOHN

John stood against Quin's closed bedroom door, watching her sleep. She was, at this moment, smiling into her pillow as though caught in the grip of a delightful dream. *Is she dreaming about me,* he wondered, *as I have dreamed of her?*

But many of his dreams about her hadn't been pleasant. The last time he'd seen her, she had been on the other side of that strange portal, blood spreading across her chest. A stray bullet from his own gun had nearly killed her, and the memory of it was like an icicle to his gut. *How could I have let that happen?*

When he'd arrived in her office downstairs, he had expected her to scream and call for help, or to attack him—either would have been justified. Instead, though she seemed to know his face, she hadn't even remembered his name at first. Somehow Quin had started her life over. Was it possible she didn't remember the events of her last night on the estate? And if so, could that mean he was forgiven? That he had another chance with her?

"How did you manage to forget?" he asked her softly, returning to the bed.

Quin shifted in her sleep but didn't wake up. Gently John unbuttoned the neck of her shirt and pulled it back. He didn't want to look but felt compelled by guilt. By her left shoulder, he found the scar where his bullet had exited her body. The mark was round and puckered and still red. He guessed that it must bother her from time to time. A few inches closer to her heart, and she surely would have died.

"I thought I killed you," he whispered, feeling again the horror of that moment. "I thought you were dead."

He lay down next to Quin and closed his eyes. The smell of her brought back vivid memories of their last afternoon among the trees.

"I don't want to be alone in this," he whispered. "I need you back."

"Need you," she murmured. She was still asleep, the smile from her dream lingering on her face.

When he felt her hand against his cheek, he leaned forward and brushed her lips with his own. Quin pulled him closer and sleepily wrapped her arms around him.

"Why did we never . . ." she began, starting to wake up.

"I wanted to," he whispered.

She moved her head into the crook of his neck. "John." She said his name against his skin, like it was a foreign word she had just learned, "John."

He put his arms around her, feeling the length of her against him. *There will be many things that try to pull you from the path. Hatred is one, and love is another . . .* He wanted to tell his mother and Maggie to be silent. Couldn't he live a day or a week or a month in peace? Couldn't he have Quin to himself for a while? But the promise he had made lay like a glowing ember at the center of his heart, and their words were always in his mind.

He needed Quin's help. And there wasn't even time to prepare her for what he was about to ask. There were signs of Fiona all over the house. Quin didn't live here alone, and at some point, Fiona would be back. John had burned the estate and shot her daughter. He was quite certain Fiona would not give him a warm welcome.

In fact, it was even possible, if Fiona were clearheaded, that she had already sensed something amiss and was heading back to check on things. He must convince Quin now.

"Quin . . . will you help me?" he whispered. "I need your help."

Quin's lips were on his cheek. "Of course I'll help you," she whispered. "Anything."

She might still have been half asleep, but he allowed himself to hope.

He sat up and shifted to the side, giving her a clear view of what was lying on the chair by the door to her bedroom: the athame.

Immediately the spell was broken.

Quin moved away from him and slid up into a sitting position, her back against the wall, her arms around her body.

"What is that?" she asked. "Why is it here?"

"Quin," he said gently, "you know what it is. It might take you a moment to remember—like when you saw me downstairs. But you know what it is."

"I don't."

"Please don't be scared. It's just us here—"

Without warning, Quin was on her feet, bolting for the door. John scrambled to get there first, blocking her path.

"Let me out," she said. "Let me out of here!"

She pushed him, but John didn't move aside. His back was pressed against the door, holding it shut.

"It's just lying there," he said. "We're not even touching it. It's all right, Quin. Please."

But she was in a panic. "Get out of my way, John!" Louder, she called, "Ma! Fiona!"

"You don't have to handle the dagger. You don't even have to look at it. I only need you to teach me."

She wasn't listening. She swung at him, and her hand connected with his cheek. "Let me out of the room! Mother! Mother!"

Then her knees gave, as they had done downstairs. She fell to the floor. "That's not me," she whispered. "Not anymore. I do good things . . ."

John knelt down. "I'm not trying to hurt you. I want to be with you. I only—"

"I'm going to be sick . . . I'm going to be sick . . ." she was muttering. "Let me out, please."

She really did look like she might throw up.

He pulled her gently to her feet and walked her out of the bedroom. When he took her into the bathroom, Quin dropped to the floor by the toilet, clutching her stomach. Away from the athame, however, she calmed a bit. He crouched next to her, trying to get her to look at him.

"Why are you here?" she asked. "I don't want to feel what I feel around you."

"You stayed on the estate. You know how to use the athame—"

"Don't talk about it!" she whispered.

"I have to. Briac is gone. Alistair . . ." At the memory of Alistair, John fell silent for a moment, overcome by regret. *It was an accident,* he reminded himself. *And he could have helped me. He could have done what was right.* He pushed those thoughts from his mind and concentrated on Quin. "You're the only one," he told her. "Or Shinobu—is he here? Is he with you?" He hadn't thought much about Shinobu, but the sudden idea that he might still be with her brought on a deep pang of jealousy.

"I don't know what you're talking about," she breathed.

Maybe she'd forgotten Shinobu too. That was good. "Show me

how to get *There*," he told her. "Teach me. Then I'll go, if—if you want me to go."

"That's not me anymore," she told him. "I don't do those things."

"Teach me, and you—you never have to see me again."

"John . . ."

"My grandfather can't help me much longer. He can hardly help himself," he said desperately. "I *promised*, Quin. I have it back now. Please show me—"

"Stop!" Her hands were over her ears, and she was rocking back and forth on the floor. "I don't remember those things! I don't remember them. They're behind me."

He gently took hold of her shoulders.

"Don't you see that everything can be okay?" he whispered to her. "We're here—just us. Together, we can get past all the bad things that have happened. Start deciding what's right for ourselves."

"Stop, please—"

"I love you." He pulled her hands off her ears. "Will you please help me?"

He was holding her hands, kneeling in front of her. The look on her face was like that of a wild animal cornered in the woods.

"Come on," he said softly. "Won't it be nice to be together? Like we always imagined. Teach me about the athame."

Quin's eyes were frantic. Without warning, her head shot forward, slamming into John's forehead, stunning him in a blossom of pain.

She scrambled to her feet, reeled against the bathroom doorframe, and then she was away from him and running down the stairs.

"Quin!"

He was on his feet. He grabbed the athame and moved down the stairs after her.

But she was already at the front door. She threw it open and flew out. He reached the doorway in time to see her push through a crowd of pedestrians, then crash into one of them, sending herself sprawling onto the Bridge thoroughfare.

John could still feel her lips against his, but he hadn't been able to hold on to her. Again, he'd failed to convince her, and she was abandoning him.

He watched as she disentangled herself from the pedestrian and was back on her feet, running. She was getting away, but John was no longer seeing Quin or the Bridge. He was seeing the slumped figure of a five-year-old boy, lying by his dead sisters. He was seeing a dozen bodies, drowned, pinned to walls. He was seeing a young woman, so like his own mother, screaming as Briac Kincaid made her bleed to death. He had promised all of them.

Were there other Seekers who could teach him the secrets of the athame? Somewhere, John believed, there must be. But Quin was here, now. He needed her to help him, even if he had to force her. And he believed, deep down, she wanted to help. Wouldn't she understand in the end and forgive him?

John brought his eyes back into focus on the Bridge. He gestured to the men outside Quin's house—men he had brought, but whom he'd dearly hoped would not be necessary. They materialized around him from their hiding places and moved into the crowds, following Quin's trail.

CHAPTER 34

MAUD

The Young Dread's mind did not wander. It would travel in one direction as long as it needed to, and then it would travel in another. A single thought might linger indefinitely, if she were not yet done with it. The thought that had been holding her attention for a very long while was this: *I am going to kill the Middle Dread.*

Sometimes she imagined killing him in a sword fight, sometimes with poison, sometimes with a knife in his sleep. These were not daydreams—she was planning. For now, however, it was a plan without action. The Middle was far away, perhaps already training her replacement.

She had fed the cows and was now milking them. There were only two left, but these helped keep her alive. When the pail was full of milk, she carried it from the dairy barn across the commons toward the workshop. Like the dairy, it was one of the few buildings on the estate that had not been burned in the attack.

All along the commons, charred timber and piles of scorched stone stood in place of the warm cottages that had once dotted the landscape. At the edge of the forest, large swaths of trees had burned as well. The cottages of the Dreads had been left intact, but staying there seemed like sharing an intimate space with the Middle Dread, and so she had chosen the workshop instead.

Her stately stride was perfect for carrying milk, and the liquid hardly moved in the bucket. There was a dull ache in her left side, where the Middle Dread had cut her, but pain meant little. It was only the lack of training that bothered her. For a year and a half she had been here alone, aging.

Life without training is water poured on sand. The words ran through her head like a chant as she walked. *No time is mine. No place is mine. No one is mine.*

That night in the woods, when the Middle had left her and told her to die, she'd almost obeyed him. Her life had drained out of her injury, soaking into the forest floor. Her eyes had closed, and she'd wondered what happened to someone like her when death came. Would it come upon her in a single, clear moment, or would it be as it was when you were stretched out, suspended in an endless moment that lengthens into all of time?

On that night, hovering at the edge of death, she felt herself slowing down and realized her old master had trained her even for this. She brought her body almost to a stop, but not quite. Her heart still beat, once or twice a minute; air still came gradually into her lungs. She stopped dying and lay there in a state of near death.

In this way, she passed the whole night, and she was alive when the sun rose the following morning. Sometime that day, the farmworkers came to the estate, and eventually, in their search for survivors, they found her among the trees. They thought she was dead until she moved a hand to grab one of their ankles. She heard the men's yells of surprise, and then they were lifting her and carrying her away.

She spent a month or more in a strange, tall building filled with doctors, where they did odd things to her blood and her skin and her bones. Her first language was the old speech they had used when she was a child. She had then learned English in its many forms as it changed over generations, but it was difficult to understand the new words of those men and women who hovered around her bed and poked at her with metal devices.

And then she was back on the estate, with a long red scar on her side, fending for herself. She could hunt, and there were the cows. Survival did not trouble her, but being alone did. She was not lonely—solitude was pleasant after so many years in the company of the Middle. It was the fact that there was no one to teach her and no one with whom she could practice. Even the Middle, as unpleasant as he was, had fulfilled his duty toward her some of the time and passed on the skills of the Dreads.

"Your own teacher did that to you?" the apprentice asked her when he returned to the estate.

He had been looking at her scar, visible beneath the edge of her shirt, and his attention disturbed her. This apprentice, the one who had worn the mask and who had attacked the estate—his standing among Seekers was unclear.

He had shown up a few months after the Young Dread returned from the hospital. She'd found him sitting in the workshop among her own weapons one evening when she arrived home with a pheasant for dinner. John. That was his name. And he was there, among her things.

"Are you all alone?" he asked her.

Without response, she went about her normal routine, building the cooking fire, plucking the bird. He helped her, without speaking much. The Young Dread found herself on guard around him, but he fascinated her as well. She'd caught glimpses of him at earlier ages, but now here he was, perhaps the same age as she was. What had those intervening years been like for him, after—after that night, when she'd seen the glint of his small eyes beneath the floor?

Her fascination was intensified by the fact that she'd spent almost no time with people her own age. True, it was hard to say exactly how old she was, but if she counted up her time spent in the ordinary world, she would be fifteen now, by the usual reckoning.

When they were sitting near each other, eating the pheasant, they finally began to converse.

"The athame Briac Kincaid used was stolen from my family," he told her. "You know that, don't you?"

In her slow way, she responded, "It is our law that an athame must stay with its family, but Seeker families have become tangled things, apprentice. Within a family, we Dreads believe the athame ends up with whom it belongs."

"And it will," he said. "It will end up with me."

She said nothing to this.

"When I have gotten it back," he went on, "I will need training to use it properly. Don't you think it would be fair for you to help me with that?"

She sat in silence for a while as a thought formed in her head. Finally she told him, "That is not my duty."

It was then that he noticed her scar. She tried to hide it with her arm when she saw the direction of his eyes, but it was too late. He asked her how she'd received the injury, and she told him. She was not sure why she told him, other than her strange sense of obligation to him, which had begun on that night years ago.

"If your own companion left you to die, your duty to him is done, don't you think?" he asked. "But if you believe you owe him your loyalty, couldn't you teach me to use the athame, then return to him after I've learned the skill—if you wish to return to him?"

"If I wish," she repeated, trying to understand the meaning of those words.

"Or you could stay with me," he suggested. "Teach me. Be your own master."

Her hand flashed out, grabbed his left arm, and turned it over, her fingers like a vise. She studied his wrist, which was perfectly smooth, with no athame burned into it.

"You have no mark. You are no Seeker," she told him.

"Briac has done me an injustice." He must have seen something in her face, because he added softly, "You've seen part of that injustice, haven't you?" He looked down at the soft, old leather of her shoes. "I always wondered who the smaller person was. Until one day I realized I did know. It was you."

She didn't answer, but she recalled John as a young boy, huddled in that hiding place beneath the floor, closing his eyes tight as though that could stop the terrible things he was seeing. They had done too much then; they had done things that were not their duty at all. Could one do other things to make up for those?

"He wouldn't finish my training," John went on, "but you can." He was looking at her in that way ordinary people did, as though she would suddenly feel what he was feeling and understand what was important to him, just by looking into his eyes.

But she could not feel what John was feeling. She was the Young Dread. She had existed for hundreds of years in her fifteen-year life, and her duties were far different than his. She and the other Dreads took turns stretching out through time, waking to oversee the oaths of new Seekers, holding themselves apart from humanity, making just decisions. This apprentice was as new as a fresh shoot of grass. He could not possibly understand.

Except . . . her mind had responded. *Except many decisions were not just. Justice has become a shadowy thing, and so many things were done while I was asleep.*

She had moved away from John then and stood staring into the fire. Eventually he'd left.

After the apprentice had gone, she'd had one thought for a very long time: *What am I?*

Now, all alone on the estate, the Young Dread entered the workshop with her pail of milk. She had stopped thinking of ways to kill the Middle Dread and was thinking instead of what John had said. And when she had her small meal that afternoon, the thought in her mind was this: *I wonder if John will come back. What will I do if he does?*

CHAPTER 35

QUIN

Quin hit the bystander on the Bridge so hard they were both thrown to the pavement. She continued moving, rolling over his body and into the legs of several other pedestrians. John was in the doorway of her house, just yards away, and somewhere in the house behind him was that stone dagger. She'd left that dagger and most of her memory in the past, and she'd sworn they would stay there.

She pulled herself up to her knees but found she couldn't stand. Her head was pounding from slamming it into John's forehead a few moments ago, and it took her a second to realize that the Asian boy she'd knocked over was, in fact, holding on to her.

"Hey!" he said, clutching her more tightly. "What are you doing?"

Quin realized he was a boy only if by "boy" one meant "very tall teenager with scary clothing." She tried to pull herself free but only succeeded in pulling him closer. One of her shirtsleeves had gotten pushed up in her fall, and the sharp metal studs of the boy's bracelet were cutting into her left wrist. She was starting to bleed, and the pain made her look down at her arm. Next to her own wrist, she could see the boy's wrist, with its thick bracelet, and beneath the bracelet, on the underside of his arm, was a dagger-shaped scar imprinted on his flesh. With a sick jolt, Quin noticed the identical scar on her own wrist, in the spot she tried very hard never to see.

She stopped struggling finally and looked at the boy's face. He had jewelry in his nose and through his eyebrow, and his hair was dyed to look like a leopard. But none of these surface details mattered. He was . . .

He was looking at her as well.

"Quin," he breathed. His hands released her.

From the corner of her eye, Quin saw John in the doorway of her house. And there were other men in the shadows nearby. She untangled herself from the Asian boy whose name she did not actually know, and got back to her feet, pulling her sleeve back into place as she did so. She was already moving, her hands automatically feeling at her waist, as though expecting to find weapons there. *No weapons allowed on the Bridge,* her mind chattered. *You know this.* So why did it feel like part of her arm was missing?

Quin glanced back to see John and those other men moving through the crowds. The next few minutes were a blur. A herd of Western tourists was choking traffic on the thoroughfare. She pushed her way through them, sensing every moment that John's men were getting closer. Then she was falling down an airlift, moving so quickly the lift hardly had time to catch her before she moved out onto a lower level, where there was loud music and denser crowds. She caught glimpses of her pursuers, farther behind her now.

Another airlift down, then out into more frightening swarms of visitors outside the cheap drug bars. She kept turning to the right, realizing too late that her pursuers were herding her in that direction.

She moved frantically down another airlift, this one smaller and open only to Bridge residents. When she stepped off this time, she was in an empty passage and a man was running toward her from a stairway. She ran left—the only direction available to her—and found herself moving down a wide, dark corridor.

This was a part of the Bridge she had never seen before. It was empty of humans, inhabited only by huge pieces of mechanical equipment that filled the space with a rhythmic vibration and the hiss of steam. The man's footsteps were behind her, getting closer, the sound of his shoes combining with the pulse of the machinery. He would catch her, the past would catch her, and it was happening so easily. She hadn't even cried out for help.

Quin's eyes shut without her realizing. Even running for her life, she lost herself for a moment, or perhaps it was many moments. When she forced her eyes open, she was at the very end of the hall, among huge air-conditioning units giving off a heat that smelled of engine oil. She wasn't running anymore. She turned slowly, discovering there were men all around her. She was cornered.

There were five of them. A few were young, but all were much older and larger than she was. She recognized the one closest to her—she had glimpsed his face, with its growth of dark stubble, during the chase.

Her back was against one of the giant air-conditioning units. The men were in a loose semicircle around her. A few had knives at their waists, even though the screeners at the Bridge entrances were supposed to catch anything dangerous before it entered the Transit Bridge. Quin sensed herself preparing for a fight, as though instinct were taking over.

The one with the stubbly chin threw something to her. On reflex, she caught it. The moment her hand touched it in that dim light, she realized she was now holding the stone dagger. She threw it away as though it had burned her. The man intercepted it before it hit the floor, and he shoved the dagger back into her hand.

"Please don't throw it again," Stubble Chin told her.

Quin felt the cool stone as her fingers wrapped around the dagger's handgrip.

"Tell me you understand," he said.

Quin nodded.

"Very good. You will demonstrate," he ordered.

"Demonstrate?" she asked.

He gestured to the dagger.

"Demonstrate what? I don't know how. Does—does John know what you're doing?"

Despite the obvious fact that these men worked for John, some part of her mind told her that everything would be all right if she could only put down the dagger and find him. John was desperate—she'd seen that in his eyes—but he didn't want to hurt her. He loved her.

The men parted slightly to allow her a view behind them. John was there, crouched against a wall. He was staring at her, his eyes tortured.

"John . . ." She took a step toward him, but the men held her back.

"Please, Quin," he said. "I need you to do this. I need you to help me. Don't say no."

She was shaking her head. "I can't . . . I don't know how . . ."

"You can remember, like you remembered me." His voice was pleading. "You can show me. Just show me."

She could feel herself growing hysterical. "John, please! That's not me anymore."

"Quin, I need this."

"I can't!" she said, hearing how wild her voice sounded but helpless to change it. "I just can't."

John forced his eyes away from her. Staring at the floor, he nodded slightly. Then his head was falling into his hands as his men closed in, hiding him from view as before. Quin was dizzy again.

"Demonstrate," Stubble Chin ordered.

"I can't!" she screamed.

He swung his fist at her. Automatically Quin ducked to the side. His arm crashed into the metal of the air-conditioning unit behind her, making a tremendous noise. He roared with pain, and one of the other men grabbed her from behind, pinning her arms at her back.

Stubble Chin swung at her with his other arm. She was unable to pull free, and this time his fist connected with her stomach, doubling her over in a burst of pain. She couldn't breathe. He had knocked the air out of her. *The past can stay in the past.* Master Tan had promised her. She did not have to remember.

The man standing behind her released her arms, sending her crashing to the floor. There was another jolt of pain from the old wound in her shoulder, and her forehead was throbbing where she had smashed it into John's head. And the floor—it was touching her skin. Dirt, germs, all of it. Panic was taking hold.

"I'm just a healer," she managed to say. "Why—"

"Show us," the man said again.

She stared up at him, the dagger still in her hand. The thought came to her suddenly: *There's something missing!*

"I can't," she gasped.

Above the rumble of the machines around them, she heard a high-pitched noise. The fifth man, who'd been standing behind the others, stepped forward. Across his chest was strapped a large, ugly object that looked something like a small cannon. It was made of an iridescent metal that sparkled faintly, even in the dim ambient light. As the high squeal coming out of it grew louder, there was a crackle of electricity around its barrel.

"You don't want to use that," Quin said, the words coming on reflex. She had promised herself she would never hold this stone dagger again. She had also promised, she was quite sure, never again to lay eyes on that weapon across the man's chest. She felt her terror rising. *Colored sparks . . .*

On the concrete floor, Quin gripped the dagger. *I could use this to get out of here. If only . . . If only . . .*

The man ran his hand along the side of the weapon, and its hum intensified. There were dozens of tiny openings across the face of the thing. She saw a fork of electricity crawl over the man's fingers as they hovered near the trigger.

"I'll show you," she whispered. "I'll show you."

Two men helped her to her feet. There was a movement among the other men. John was edging closer to listen. His face was ashen, wounded, as though the men had beaten him instead of her.

"These dials," she said, touching the stone rings in the hand-grip with the symbols carved into them. There were six rings, with a different set of symbols around each. "You turn them. They are your . . . coordinates." She said the words without planning them. It was like tapping into a script that existed only subconsciously. Fear of death—*not death, something worse!* her mind told her—was bringing the explanation to the surface. "First, like this"—she lined up a set of symbols along the dials, somehow knowing they were correct—"which will take you *There*."

"What do you mean, *'There'*?" the man closest to her asked.

"Shh," said John. His eyes met hers, and she saw shame in them, but something else as well: he looked immensely grateful. He seemed again like a drowning man, one who had just been thrown a life vest. "Let her finish. That symbol on all dials, to go *There*. Please continue, Quin."

She looked at the dagger and the dials, but her explanation had dried up. All eyes were on her, waiting for her to go on, but there was something else she needed if she were going to show them anything more. *Something for my other hand,* she thought. *He doesn't want to hurt me; I can see he doesn't want to hurt me. I could help him . . .* For a moment, she was frozen as she stood there holding the stone dagger. *If I help him, I will become whatever I was before. And John, he will become . . .*

I'm thinking! she scolded herself. *It's going to make me fail.* She forced her mind to clear, and all at once saw a course of action. She was still free to choose what she wanted.

"I turn the dials," she said, gripping the dagger harder, "and then I take it in both hands and lift it above my head." John was watching her raptly. "I swing it, like this—"

She brought the stone dagger down as hard as she could, straight toward Stubble Chin's neck. His arms came up to protect himself too late. The butt of the weapon crashed into his throat.

Quin found her hands moving to the man's waistband on reflex, and then his knife was in her right hand. She kicked his body toward the other men. A second man dodged around Stubble Chin's flailing form and grabbed for Quin's arm. She whipped her right hand up, slashing him across the throat with the first man's knife.

There was a high whine, hurting her ears, and then sparks fired from the weapon attached to the fifth man's chest.

Disruptor! her mind screamed.

She dropped down onto the floor crawling on hands and knees. Someone was grabbing her, trying to pull her to her feet. A weight collapsed onto her, then rolled away. A man's arms and legs were thrashing on the floor as rainbow-colored electric sparks danced around his head and shoulders.

John was yelling at them not to hurt her. Another man was grabbing her and she was lifted off the ground. She slashed with her knife, but someone else caught her arm. She kicked, and the man dropped her. Then someone was kneeling on her back, pressing her face against the floor. She was getting dizzy again. She stabbed out with the knife, felt it sink into a shoe. A man screamed, but still she couldn't move.

The fight was going on without her somehow. Blows were being exchanged. The man pinning her down put a wet cloth to her face. A smell hit her, like medicine and gasoline mixed together. She held her breath and struggled, fighting a wave of dizziness. The knife had been ripped out of her hand. She was trying to push the man off her. She was desperate to take in a breath. She began to inhale. Whatever was on the cloth was entering her lungs—

Then the weight was lifted. She was on her feet, and someone's arm was around her waist. She shook her head, breathed deeply.

"Come on," the person holding her whispered.

It was the boy with leopard hair. He broke into a run, pulling her along. It took a moment for her to get her legs to work, but then she was running beside him. The sounds continued behind them as they sprinted down the dark corridor, toward a lighted area ahead.

"Who are they fighting?" she asked.

"My friend Brian. Probably chasing him now. But he's faster than he looks and knows the Bridge much better than they do."

He pulled her past the airlifts and into the corridor stretching along the opposite side of the Bridge.

"They were going to, you know, *sparks* . . ." Quin said as he pushed her to the right, into a small alley.

They were walking now, through a space too narrow to move any faster. They dodged right again, then squeezed through a tiny opening between a huge gas tank and a concrete wall. He pulled her to a stop and edged past her. At the base of the wall there was a large patch of darker black, which looked like an opening of some sort.

"Here," he said, still quietly. "This shaft goes down. There's a ladder inside. Grab hold after me."

He ducked, and a moment later disappeared through the tunnel. Quin followed, feeling her way into the darkness and onto a metal ladder. As she began to climb down the rungs, she could just make out his shape below her, moving quickly. She tried to keep up with him. At one point there was a chink of light across the rungs, a crack in the wall. Looking through it, she could see water. They were moving along the inside of the Bridge's skin.

The ladder shifted right and left a few times, and after they had gone a very long way, Quin saw open air below. They were coming out the bottom of the Bridge.

"Careful," he told her. "The last part is tricky."

Beneath her, he reached out of the ladder shaft, caught hold of something, and hoisted himself out of sight. Quin crawled down more rungs and found a break in the casing of the shaft, opening onto daylight. Leaning her head through, she saw him perched inside a framework of metal rafters. He grabbed her hand and pulled her up next to him. They were standing together among the rafters, Victoria Harbor a hundred and fifty feet below, the bulk of the Transit Bridge above.

He led her along a narrow metal beam. As he walked in front of her, Quin distracted herself from the drop beneath them by studying his clothing. He was dressed like a member of one of the gangs that bought drugs legally from Bridge suppliers and sold them illegally on the streets of the city outside.

"How did you know this was here?" she asked.

"I jump off things," he said without turning around, "and I climb around inside them, and sometimes I swim under them. I have lots of hiding places in Hong Kong."

He led her through the rafters to a place where sheets of plastic had been lashed to metal crossbeams to make a kind of bird's nest perch where someone could sit almost comfortably.

"Will someone else find us here?" Quin asked him. "I mean, people you . . . work with?" After escaping one gang, she was not eager to encounter another.

"No one else likes it here," he answered. "They're worried about falling to their death or something." He glanced down at the water of the harbor. One wrong step, and either of them would be tumbling into oblivion. He smiled. "Personally, I find it relaxing."

Quin climbed onto the plastic nest, noticing as she did that both of her hands were covered in blood. And there was filth all over her body. Now that she was safe for a few moments, she could sense the microbes on her skin.

"I need to wash," she whispered to herself, "I need to wash." She took a deep breath. She would not let herself panic again.

The boy was studying her, running one of his hands through that short and strange hair. She noticed his knuckles were torn in several places.

"You're different, aren't you?" he asked her.

"I'm so sorry to ask you this," she said, "but can you tell me your name?"

CHAPTER 36

SHINOBU

"Are you serious?" Shinobu said.

Quin had just asked him for his name. He started to laugh, but she didn't look like she was joking.

"I'm sure I know it," she said quickly, looking down at her hands, the backs of which were covered in thick, sticky blood. "I *did* know it. I'll remember it, if you give me a few minutes. It's just—it's hard to think with this filth on me. I'd really, *really* like to wash my hands."

Shinobu glanced around the bare rafters like he might have misplaced a sink and a big bar of soap somewhere nearby, then shrugged. Her jittery words seemed like an act. Quin had never been jumpy.

"Is there any on my face?" she asked, sounding more desperate. "It feels like there's blood on my face. Is it near my mouth? Can you see?"

"Stop it! Quin." Irritated, he shook her by the shoulders and watched as her eyes came into focus. There was, in fact, a good deal of blood on her face, but he thought it wiser not to mention it. "Don't you know me?" he asked. "I'm Shinobu."

"Shinobu." She said his name like it was the answer to a riddle that had been driving her crazy, and also like it was a very odd name for someone to have. "I heard that name. He said your name when he was in my house."

"He?"

"John," she whispered.

"Right, of course," he responded, feeling the deep annoyance he'd always felt when she spoke about John. Apparently she had no trouble remembering *him*.

She had become transfixed by her dirty hands again. "Do you have any water, Shinobu? Even if it's just a little."

"Forget about your hands!" He let out an angry sigh. He'd just saved her from a violent abduction, and she was worried about cleanliness? They had bigger problems, like John's presence in Hong Kong with armed men, and the appearance of the athame.

"Whose blood do you think it is?" Quin asked. "Could it be mine? Maybe I'm bleeding."

Shinobu felt a sudden pang of worry that she might have been injured without him noticing. He examined her more carefully than he had before. "You don't look hurt," he said after a few moments, relieved, but also a little disappointed—an injury might have explained her behavior. "At least not seriously."

"I don't think I am—except where he hit me," she responded, more to herself than to him, like she was picking her way through a mental fog. She looked a lot like the girl he used to know, but she sounded like a crazy person. "It seemed like I had a knife," she whispered, "and the knife cut one of them across the neck."

"The knife cut one of them, did it? Tricky knife. That *would* explain the blood everywhere."

"It's just . . . I saved the life of a child this morning. He would have died. But I fixed him." She couldn't keep her eyes off the mess on her hands as she spoke. "I'm not sure it counts, though, if I . . . killed someone else." The last words came out very quietly.

"If you're counting, I think you killed two of the men up there," he told her. "The one you hit first wasn't breathing very well when we left."

"I didn't mean to kill them! You believe me, right? The knife was just . . . there." She was looking at Shinobu now, her eyes wild.

He was annoyed by her unwillingness to admit that she had fought all five of those men by herself before he'd arrived. And it was unsettling to see her looking at him, with no deeper recognition of who he was. He felt a strong urge to slap her hard, to wake her up, but judging from the bruises coming in on her face, John and his men had already hit her several times.

"You're not this squeamish, Quin."

"You don't know what I am," she said petulantly.

He laughed dismissively. "You're right. Maybe I don't."

She was quiet for a moment, then looked up from her hands. "I'm sorry. Thank you for saving me. Shinobu." She pronounced his name very carefully.

He shrugged, no longer trying to have a normal discussion with her. "Sure. I had some free time."

"Is your name Japanese? Are you Japanese?" It didn't sound like she was trying to remember, more like an attempt at polite conversation.

"If you don't recall who I am, there's no point explaining." The words came out more roughly than he meant them, but he was trying to hide the fact that she was making him sad.

"I *do* know you . . ." she said, as if she had finally spotted the outline of something familiar through a haze. "Like I know John."

"Of course you'd remember John before you remembered me," he muttered.

"It's only that I saw him first. How did he find me? Wasn't I . . . hidden, sort of? I think I was hiding."

"He found you because he found the athame. Once he knew where it was, he probably had people start searching. You were nearby."

"Athame." She repeated the word, like it was something she had heard in a dream. "John called it that too."

"Probably because that's its name," Shinobu said.

He reached into his leather jacket and drew out the athame. It was here, in their possession again. There were streaks of blood on the stone dagger, but other than that it looked undamaged. He set it on the plastic sheeting next to her, and she immediately moved away from it.

"Why did you take it?" she asked, her voice pitching into panic. "I don't want it."

"I don't want it either. But I couldn't exactly leave it with John."

She didn't answer that, but her silence indicated that she might agree with him. That was something, at least.

"Maybe we should throw it into the ocean," she suggested quietly, like she was testing how the idea would sound out loud.

"You're not the first person to think of that. Here."

He put the dagger into her hands and gestured that she should toss it into the harbor. Quin got up from the nest and moved along a rafter until the water was clearly visible below. Shinobu watched her bring her arm up, preparing to throw the athame. But she didn't. Instead she stood there like a statue with her arm over her head, staring down at Victoria Harbor.

After a few moments she let her arm fall to her side. She looked at the dagger carefully, as though inspecting an object that was entirely new to her. He watched her fingers tracing the fox carved into the base of the handle. Eventually she returned to the plastic shelf and set the athame down.

"I can't throw it away."

"Why not?" he asked, knowing the answer.

"Once it's in my hand . . . I just can't," she said. She seemed to experience a moment of dizziness, but this passed.

"Shall I give it back to John?" Shinobu offered, a smile hidden in his voice. He was trying to irritate her now.

"No." She looked away. "He shouldn't have it. It wouldn't turn out well."

Shinobu laughed at the understatement and hoped Quin would laugh with him. But she didn't. It was as though the pleasant parts of her had fled, leaving only seriousness and detachment. When she'd been quiet for a while, he asked, "So what do you want to do?"

"*Why* is he here?"

"Quin, you know why he's here," he answered, frustrated. "*Think.*"

"He wants to learn how to use the athame." She said it quietly, as she looked at the dagger. "But I don't remember how to use it." Shinobu said nothing. "I could remember, maybe."

She was silent for a little while, perhaps thinking of all she had done in the past year and a half. Shinobu wondered if buried memories were nosing their way to the surface.

"If I don't want to remember, I'll have to go away, won't I?" she said finally. "He knows I'm here now. He'll keep looking for me and the . . . athame. Maybe I can be a healer in Tibet or somewhere, where he'll never find me." Then, almost in a whisper, she added, "I wonder if my mother will come with me. I haven't been very good to her."

Shinobu sighed and moved to sit near her on the plastic. The drugs had fully worn off. There was a new, very unpleasant feeling looming on the horizon. He picked up the athame and held it in front of her.

"There's a problem with that plan," he said. "I threw this to the bottom of the harbor—this huge harbor, where hundreds of thousands of ships come in and out and mountains of garbage end up under the water. And here it is, back in my hand, a year and a half later. True, I'm the one who rescued it—but not on purpose." He let the athame drop to his lap and ran a thumb along the blade. "And I promised myself I would never see you again, but here you are, sitting with me under the Bridge."

"You didn't want to see me again?" she asked, her mind still running in the wrong direction and her voice sounding hurt by the idea.

"You didn't want to see me either," he pointed out.

"How do you know that?" Her dark eyes were searching his face now as though she actually wanted an answer.

"You forgot my name, Quin."

"I've forgotten everything. Not you in particular."

"You had a patient this morning," he told her, trying another tack. "The one you saved. Who was it?"

"A little boy. Overdose. He got into his older brother's drugs."

Shinobu felt a surge of shame as he pointed at himself. "Japanese, reddish hair?"

He angled the top of his head toward her and watched as Quin slowly nodded, noticing that his roots were growing out red under the leopard dye.

"Your hair is red," she said. For a moment she actually sounded less detached, more present, as if his hair color were one small detail she could grasp.

"Yes, my hair is red, Cousin Quin. The boy's name is Akio."

"You're the brother?"

Shinobu pulled something large out of a coat pocket and held it up. It was the bag of herbs Quin had filled herself a few hours before, with Akio's name written across it in her own handwriting.

He said, "Somehow, no matter how far we're thrown, we all keep coming back to you."

She thought this over for a little while as she rubbed the backs of her dirty hands against her trousers. "Maybe everything is coming back to *you*," she suggested.

He shook his head. "You forgot me. John doesn't know I'm here. My mother pretends I don't exist. I'm a ghost, Quin. If John ever came after me, I'd—I'd become a ghost for real. I'm looking for an excuse." The way she was rubbing her hands was driving him crazy again, so he grabbed them to keep them still. "But you—you seem to be stuck with John unless . . . unless you get rid of him."

"What do you mean, 'get rid of him'?" she asked, clearly understanding exactly what he meant.

"Don't act so shocked," he responded. "He's forcing you to do something you don't want to do." Then he looked down at his dirty jeans. He was skirting an area of his own memories where he had forbidden himself to go. "You can get rid of him, Quin. Or you can give him what he wants. Usually you give him what he wants."

He could hear the bitterness in his own voice. But it was true—she'd always chosen John. Even now Quin was quiet, as though maybe she wanted to spend a little more time with John before deciding whether he was really dangerous or not.

She was shaking her head, and now, her voice rising, she said, "I can't 'get rid of' anyone. I'm a healer. I don't hurt people—"

"Right, of course. And that blood just happened to get on your hands. The knife just happened to cut someone. You had nothing to do with it."

"I didn't mean it! You don't even know for sure they're dead."

"Maybe that man's neck grew back. It could happen."

He turned away again. Whatever connection he had momentarily felt, it was gone. She was maddening.

"You don't know me," she said.

She was right. He didn't know her. She'd become someone else in Hong Kong. She did not want his help, not really, and she was not his responsibility anymore. There were too many unpleasant things to remember when he was with her.

To herself, Quin said, "I like my life here. Why did this have to happen?"

Shinobu heard an ugly laugh come out of him. "Neither of us can have our lives as they were, Quin. I can get you off the Bridge. And I have something to give you, if you want it. After that, we can go our own ways."

She nodded, looking through the rafters at the water beyond, which was turning dark gray as the afternoon waned.

Now that she was quiet, and looking away, Shinobu stole a glance at her. He could see a few traces of the old Quin, the one from a year and a half ago. There was even a little bit of the Quin he'd known before that. A light breeze was moving the dark hair around her face, as her dark eyes stared at the harbor. He could almost imagine that she and he were much younger, sneaking together through the tall grass at the edge of the commons—

He stopped himself. "The sun will go down soon. When it's night, we can go."

CHAPTER 37

JOHN

"We can't get the sparks off!" John said. "It doesn't work that way."

Their man Fletcher had at last stopped flailing his arms. He was now lying on the concrete floor with nothing but a few moans and muscle twitches to let them know he was alive. The sparks whirled around Fletcher's head in dizzy patterns that made John's own head ache. He felt sick: it had happened again, a man disrupted.

And he'd had to hurt Quin. Watching Gauge hit her had been worse than being punched himself. But she had almost helped him; she'd started to help him.

"Then what do we do? Carry him off the Bridge like this?" It was Paddon asking him.

"Not if we want to get out the ordinary way," John said. He wiped a hand across his brow and realized he was bleeding and his forehead was swollen. He'd taken a heavy blow to the head during the fight.

Paddon moved over to check the other man, Brethome, the one she had knifed. "Brethome's dead," he said flatly.

"And Gauge?" John asked. Gauge was the man with the stubbly chin, the one who had led the attack.

"He'll live," Paddon answered. "She crushed his throat, but he's breathing all right now."

They had lost a third man as well. The one who had fired the disruptor lay nearby, his neck broken by the tall Asian who'd come out of nowhere. Two men dead, one disrupted, one injured.

"Who were the others?" Paddon asked.

"I don't know."

The tall Asian and the other one, the big one, had looked like petty criminals, the kind that hung around the lower levels of the Bridge. When John had taken the crack to his head, Paddon had chased after the big one but he'd lost him in the bowels of the Bridge. As far as John could tell, Quin had simply walked away from the melee with the athame. Why? She hadn't even wanted to touch it. After a year and a half of searching, he'd had the dagger in his hands for a few hours, and already it was gone.

"Men are dead. This isn't going to be easy to explain to my grandfather."

"Probably not," Paddon agreed, bundling the disruptor into a backpack.

"How long is our guard on duty?"

They had bribed a customs agent at the Bridge entrance. They had to leave while he was still at his post, or there would be questions about their entry. And if their weapons were spotted . . .

"Twenty more minutes, give or take." Paddon was studying his watch. Then he examined the blood on John's forehead. "We have to clean up. Then go back the way we came, separately." He nodded to himself, calculating the needed time. "We can't stay any longer, John."

"Can Gauge walk?" John asked.

Paddon leaned over Gauge, who still had his hands at his throat, trying to ease the pressure from the blow Quin had struck with the stone dagger. The man tried to nod.

"Yes, he can walk," Paddon said. "But we have to . . . take care of the others."

"Yes," John agreed, hating the word as it came out of his mouth.

He leaned over Fletcher, who was moaning among the disruptor sparks. Grimaces swam across the man's face, hinting at the agony within. *Be willing to kill.* It was never easy, though his mother would have called this a small death. John consoled himself with the thought that, in this case, killing would be a mercy.

He reached for his knife.

CHAPTER 38

QUIN

Quin was in the nursery, listening to the sounds of the others some-where down the hall. There were two children in the room with her, a boy and a girl. They might have been twins, but it was hard to tell. They were huddled together in a corner against flowered wallpaper, the flowers looking like dark red stains in the moonlight.

I'm dreaming. It was a distant thought, somewhere in the furthest reaches of her mind. *I always dream of this night. Sometimes there's only one child, but two is the real number. There were two.*

"I'm frightened," the little girl was saying in French. Her long blond hair hung disheveled about her shoulders.

"So am I," said her brother. They looked terrified, saying the words to each other, but also to Quin, as though they expected her to do something. *They expect me to help them.*

There was a scream from another room. A woman's voice or a man's—it was impossible to be sure.

"Is that Mummy?" the little girl asked, her eyes opening wider.

"Of course it's not," Quin said in French, trying to soothe them, even as she herself felt sharp icicles of fear in her chest. "Come, I'm going to take you out of here. Hold my hands."

They were reluctant. *If only I'd been better at keeping them calm,* she thought in that distant part of her awareness.

"Come, take my hands," she urged again.

They wouldn't, but she took their hands in hers and led them to the door. Hiding them both under her cloak, she slipped out of the nursery and down the hall.

As she came around the landing in the grand staircase, she saw someone by the front doors below. She pulled the children behind the balusters and out of sight. The little boy was sobbing in soft, panicked gulps against her legs.

"Shh, shh," she breathed. "You have to stay silent. *Please.*"

The little girl was crying freely, but making almost no noise at all. "That's right," Quin whispered to her.

Quin peered around the stair railing and watched the figure by the doors stop and look up toward the second floor. Had he heard them? She turned around, her back against a wide baluster, willing him not to see her. A boot took a heavy step on the bottom stair, then another step. He had heard them! He was walking up the stairs. She grabbed the children's hands, ready to run down the upper hall.

Then there was noise from a room farther away, below them. The man's footsteps were retreating. She glanced down to see him moving away from the stairs, his long cloak swinging about his legs as he walked off into another area of the house. He wasn't just a man, of course. He was Briac. *Briac,* she thought, with the part of her mind that knew this was a dream. *That's his name, but there's something else I call him.*

As soon as Briac disappeared, she ran quickly down the stairs, the children clinging to her hands now. The little girl tripped on the final step, knocking over a vase perched on a small table against the wall.

Before the object had even hit the ground, Quin was grabbing both children around their chests and running toward the front doors.

She heard the vase shatter behind them, then those heavy footsteps approaching. He was coming for them.

"Quin!" Briac yelled. "Quin!"

What if I hadn't stopped? she wondered with the part of her mind that wasn't dreaming. *What if I'd kept going? I can keep going . . .*

She was through the doorway and out into the night air. The children were too heavy for her to continue carrying them, but now she could see Yellen. Like a miracle, her horse was waiting outside, pawing the ground impatiently. *Yellen was never there,* her mind told her. *But what if he had been?*

The angry tread of boots was getting louder. The children were still crying, but they felt her urgency now and were helping. Frantically, Quin threw both of them up onto Yellen's back, then swung herself into the saddle between them.

Briac's steps were like thunder. He was just beyond the doors.

"Hold tight!" she ordered the boy, who was sitting behind her. He wrapped his arms around her waist.

A shadow in the entryway, an angry voice, calling her name. She didn't pause to look back. She dug her heels into Yellen's sides, and the horse took off across the gravel path cutting through the moonlit garden expanse.

"Quin! You have to do this! There's no choice. Now."

It's my dream, she thought. *I can ignore him. I can do this right.* The children were holding on, the wind was in their hair, and Yellen was carrying the three of them far away. She could hardly feel the tears running down her cheeks.

CHAPTER 39

QUIN

"Quin, you f-fell asleep."

Someone was shaking her. Quin came awake slowly. She discovered that her face was wet and pressed up against a sheet of hard plastic. Wearily she pushed herself to a sitting position. She'd been crying in her sleep.

"Oh, God." Her hands were caked in dried blood, and some of it had moistened from her tears. There were reddish smears on the plastic beneath her. She desperately needed to wash, and every muscle ached.

They were in the rafters on the underside of the Bridge, and the sun had gone down. Her thoughts felt much sharper than they'd been earlier, as if her tears had cleared some of the clouds from her mind.

"We h-h-have to g-go, okay? You've been s-sleeping for a while."

Shinobu. The redheaded Shinobu, whose hair wasn't red now. He was sitting on the edge of the plastic sheet, shivering violently. The air was a bit cold, but he was wearing a heavy leather jacket, which should have kept him warm enough.

"Oh, G-God, you look awf-ful," he said as she sat up.

"So do you."

The healer in Quin looked him over in the faint light. There were dark circles under his eyes, and he was much, much too thin. He was shaking so hard, his hands were knocking against the plastic sheet.

"How are we getting out of here?" she asked him.

"Swim," he replied, smiling. His teeth were starting to chatter.

Quin laughed, then realized he was serious.

"We climb d-down the pillar, swim a l-little. Not far."

"You're in withdrawal," she told him, realizing it as she said it. Looking at him with an educated eye, she asked, "Opium?"

"H-hard to say," he answered, smiling weakly. "Sh-Shiva, opium, could be anything, really. Wasn't p-planning on rescuing you this afternoon. Supposed to spend the day in drug bars."

"Lie down." She liked the firmness she heard in her own voice. Even the blood on her hands bothered her a bit less as soon as she decided to take care of someone else. "Climbing down hundreds of feet isn't a good idea when you're shaking like that."

"P-probably right," he agreed.

He lay down in front of her, and Quin knelt at his side. She centered her thoughts and gradually shifted her vision. It was like letting her eyes go out of focus until hidden aspects became visible. She could see copper-colored lines of energy flowing around Shinobu's body. On a healthy person, these lines would form a regular pattern, almost beautiful in its symmetry. The field around Shinobu, however, was broken by dark patches almost everywhere.

She closed off her mind to everything else and concentrated on the energy running down her own arms. Spreading her fingers wide, she floated her hands above his body. Then she imagined her energy as a river flowing down and spilling over her fingertips, into the dark blotches that hovered over Shinobu's organs. Her river of energy would wash the dark areas away.

It took a strange sort of concentration, like a muscle that was always slightly tensed, to see the energy this way. She worked a long time in silence, until the patches began to break up and Shinobu had stopped shaking. He lay looking up at her as she finished, and in the half-light she could see past his clothes and hair and piercings. At last she saw a face she recognized. *Of course,* she thought. *Shinobu. My beautiful cousin.*

She was overcome by a feeling of sadness then, at his ribs visible through his shirt, at his filthy clothes, at his addiction. *You weren't always like this,* she thought. *This is new.*

"It suits you," he whispered. He lifted a hand to touch her cheek. He was at least as dirty as she was—probably much dirtier—but she didn't draw away.

"What does?"

"Using your mind for something good."

His eyes stayed fixed on her face, as if he wanted her to lean closer to him. He had seemed angry at her before she fell asleep, like he could hardly stand to be in her presence, but somehow that anger was gone.

"I don't want to bring you any more trouble," she whispered, leaning her head nearer to his. "If you get me off the Bridge, you'll be rid of me. I promise."

"I've been trying to get rid of you for a long while," he told her, looking away. "You won't stay gone."

That stung her, but Shinobu was right. She'd brought John and the past back into his life. He was a drug addict who had enough difficulty looking after himself. Whatever they'd once meant to each other, it was not his job to take care of her now. She must sort out her troubles on her own.

A short while later, they worked their way across the rafters to an enormous vertical piling. Metal rungs were buried in its concrete face, and Shinobu climbed down these, with Quin following a few steps behind. Though the sun had set, the moon was now out, and they moved down the rungs toward its reflection floating on the water below. In every direction, she could see the bright lights of ships moving about the harbor, but the water directly beneath them was empty and still.

As they neared the waterline, Shinobu pointed out a rectangle hovering just above the surface of the water, midway between the piling they were on and its twin, sixty yards distant. The rectangle was the top to some kind of shaft leading down beneath the harbor.

"Are you sure?" she asked. It seemed a long way to go through the uninviting dark ocean.

"It's a maintenance shaft for the subway and tunnels across to the Island side. The harbor's full of them. Brian and I once counted more than fifty, and we only stopped counting because we were running out of air. We can use it to cross under the water to Kowloon."

"Do I know how to swim?" she asked, knowing how strange the question sounded. But she truly didn't remember.

"Ha!" He smiled. "Let's find out!"

With that, Shinobu leapt off the rung and into the water. A moment later he surfaced, waiting for her.

Before she could change her mind, Quin jumped. There was a freezing jolt as the harbor enveloped her; then she broke the surface and discovered that she did, indeed, know how to swim. Together, she and Shinobu struck out toward the shaft, the moonlight on the water always a few strokes ahead.

Finally she washed. No shower had ever felt as good as this one. Quin scrubbed her skin and hair a dozen times, until every remaining trace of dirt and blood was gone. She was in the pool house, tucked in the back corner of a large garden. When she was sure she was clean, she stepped onto the heated floor of the changing room and pulled on a robe. She looked at her old clothing, lying in a heap outside the shower. Under no circumstances would she be putting those items on again. She stuffed them into a rubbish bin and washed her hands another time.

Shinobu had disappeared toward the main house. Quin moved quietly from the pool house and through the garden until she was below one of the home's lower windows. The house wasn't large, but it was beautiful, tucked into the nicest neighborhood she had ever seen in Hong Kong. They had arrived here after an hour-long trek through dark tunnels beneath the harbor, down ridiculously crowded nighttime Kowloon streets, and finally in the back of a taxi, with the reluctant driver eyeing his two damp and dirty passengers in the rearview mirror.

Shinobu was visible through the window, coming out of a large closet with a bag clutched to his chest. As she watched, he paused by a small bed that stood against one wall. Sleeping there was Akio, the boy Quin had seen that morning in her healing office. Shinobu leaned over his brother's slumbering form and whispered something for a long while. Then he kissed the boy's forehead over and over again. Quin ducked beneath the window when Shinobu stood up, so he wouldn't see her watching that private moment.

"Here," he said when he came outside. "Some clothes. They're mine, so they'll be too big, but they've been in Mum's house, so they'll be clean."

Returning to the changing room, she slipped into Shinobu's old jeans and a sweater, rolling up the sleeves that hung over her hands and tucking the long trouser legs into her damp boots.

Shinobu was sitting on the grass by the pool when she came out, the athame on the ground next to him. Lying by it was another weapon, one that looked like a whip with a sword's handle.

He was rolling up the left leg of his jeans as she approached. A flat stone blade lay against his calf, its tip shoved down into his boot. After drawing it out carefully, he set it next to the other items.

Quin took a seat on the ground nearby and pointed to the curled weapon.

"A whip?"

"Whipsword."

"Whipsword." She repeated the word. It seemed obvious now that he'd said it.

"I kept it for you," he told her. "When you were hurt. You should have it back."

"It's mine?"

"It's yours. You really don't remember?"

"It seems like I should know it. But I don't, exactly, not yet."

She studied the whipsword without touching it.

Shinobu was thoughtful for a while, staring at his scuffed boots. Then he said, "You were almost dead when we brought you to Master Tan. I think you actually *were* dead, for a couple of minutes, before he revived you."

Quin did not remember that. Yet something subtle was changing in her mind. Things that had once lain deep on the ocean floor were floating a little closer to the surface.

"Master Tan didn't know if he could bring you back," Shinobu went on, a slight tremor in his voice. "He said you didn't want to live."

That she somehow remembered. "How did he know?"

"He's Master Tan." Shinobu tapped his head. "He knows things—and you kept pushing us away every time we tried to help you. Later, you were lying on his table. I thought for sure you were gone. But when Master Tan told you that you could have a new life if you wanted it, that you could leave the old one behind, you started to breathe again." He looked away from her. "We're the Seekers, Quin, we're the ones who do strange things. But Master Tan put a spell on you."

"Why do you use that word?" she asked quietly.

"What word? 'Spell'?"

"No. 'Seekers.'"

He turned to her, as if gauging the honesty of her questions. When he saw she was serious, he said, "It's what we are, Quin."

Carefully he removed the thick, spiked leather bracelet from his left wrist. Then he reached over and pushed up the sleeve of Quin's sweater. Holding both of their wrists side by side, he traced the identical, dagger-shaped scars. Quin forced herself to examine the figure burned into her arm. It was not a blemish as she kept telling herself. It was something very different: she'd been marked.

"A Seeker," she whispered, trying out the feeling of it. She did not like it at all.

"Not what we are, I guess," Shinobu said more quietly. "What we *were*. What we hoped to be."

He was looking down at the grass, his head turned away from her. There was a sparkle of reflected light on his face, and Quin realized it was a tear running down his cheek. Its presence felt unnatural. It was like seeing a wild animal cry.

Shinobu brushed the tear away with the sleeve of his jacket, smearing more dirt across his face. She looked away, embarrassed.

"My mother was here the whole time. All these years," he said, so quietly it could have been to himself.

Quin made the connection. The woman in her healing office this morning—she'd known her before, a long time ago . . . in Scotland.

She felt an onrush of an emotion that was a mixture of sadness and dread. She was starting to remember . . .

"My mother was *dead*," Shinobu went on. "That's what I thought. That was what he told me. Only she wasn't. She was here with my brother. When she found out she was pregnant with Akio, she and my father made a plan to get her away. My ancestors owned property here. My father lived without her for seven years, so she and Akio would be free. He couldn't tell me, couldn't warn me, because Briac . . . But he was always trying to get us free as well, so we could be a family again."

"Free of Briac," Quin whispered. Briac, her father. She had seen him in a dream. *I promised myself I would kill him,* she thought. *So I could be free, and Fiona too.*

"I left my father there, dying." Shinobu's voice had gone hollow. Quin reached for him, but he moved away from her immediately. "One day I'll forget to eat, forget to check my air tank, take too many pipes at the bar. I'm not a Seeker. I don't think I'm even a person anymore. I'm a ghost waiting to die."

They sat together in heavy silence. At last, Quin said, "I feel the same. Except maybe I'm a ghost waiting to live."

Carefully she picked up the whipsword. The grip fit perfectly in her right hand. Without allowing herself to think, she let her wrist move automatically. The whip unfurled with a crack, and Shinobu ducked away from her as she sent it through five different sword shapes in quick succession. Then she gripped its blade, watching it melt around her fingers. She looked up at Shinobu.

"It knows me," she said.

"Of course it knows you."

She flicked the whipsword into more shapes—a scimitar, a rapier, a long sword. Then she grabbed its blade again, letting oily, dark puddles run over her hand.

"I was never a Seeker," she murmured. "I was a pawn."

He didn't respond. He was starting to shiver again, hopefully from the cold.

"I was my father's pawn," she continued. She wasn't sure if this was a memory returning, but somehow she *knew* it to be true. "I was always his pawn. And now John's . . ."

Quin flicked the whipsword into the shape of a dagger, then stuck it into the grass.

She overcame her reluctance and picked up the athame to study the symbols along its haft. Then she slid it through a belt loop.

She lifted up the flat stone rod that had been concealed in Shinobu's trouser leg.

"Lightning rod," he told her.

"Lightning rod," she repeated.

She slid the lightning rod through another loop, lodging the two stone weapons in her borrowed jeans like six-shooters. The whipsword got dirt on her clean hand as she pulled it from the ground, but she didn't allow herself to wipe it off. She'd been huddled in her house on the Bridge for over a year, scared of her own shadow. Today she had saved a child and killed a man, maybe two. Perhaps the dirt could wait.

She got to her feet.

"I don't want to be a pawn anymore."

She clipped the whipsword to her waistband, then drew the athame and lightning rod out of her belt loops. She watched as her fingers lined up the symbols along the athame's dials. Her heart was beating quickly all of a sudden. She was terrified, and it felt good. It felt like she was alive after more than a year asleep.

"Show me," she said.

Shinobu stood up and moved over to her. He studied the symbols she had aligned and nodded.

"Yes—that will get you *There*. Then you need the coordinates of wherever you're going *after* there."

"What do I say? Teach me again."

Shinobu stood behind her and held her arms against his own, positioning the athame and lightning rod so she could strike them together. With his body against hers, his shivering began to stop. He was so much taller than he used to be, she realized, and despite how thin he'd become, he was very strong, like a wall at her back, supporting her.

"In the beginning, there was the hum of the universe," he whispered into her ear.

With that sentence, it was as though he'd turned on a faucet in her mind. The words began tumbling out of Quin so they were saying them in unison: "The athame finds the way, cutting through the trembling fabric to take us *There*."

"Now the chant," he whispered. "Say it with me. *Knowledge of self, knowledge of home, a clear picture of . . .*"

"*. . . of where I came from,*" she continued, "*where I will go . . .*"

"Where will you go?" he asked.

His body was warm and steady behind her now, but Quin herself had begun to shiver.

"Where do you think?"

CHAPTER 40

JOHN

John stood in the office doorway, momentarily taken aback by the sight of his grandfather. Gavin was slumped over his antique desk, his form shadowy against the room's immense windows, his back shaking. He was coughing, but he also seemed to be crying. The room was filled with a burning smell.

"Grandfather?"

Gavin lifted his face off his arms in a sudden jerking motion. John took a step back involuntarily when he saw his grandfather's face. The old man's eyes were uneven, the pupil of the right eye twice as big as that of the left, and the whites of both were completely bloodshot.

"Shut the door!" Gavin choked out between coughs. "I don't want them to see me like this!"

John glanced both ways down the hallway first—he agreed that no one should be nearby to see his grandfather in such a state.

The old man was coughing again, but between fits, now that the door was shut, John became aware of a hissing sound somewhere in the room.

"Where's Maggie?" John asked, moving quickly to the bar against one wall and pouring a glass of water, which he brought to Gavin. "What's that noise?" His grandfather took hold of the glass frantically, with only his left hand, and swallowed several large gulps, coughing water all over his coat as he did so.

"Where's Maggie?" John asked again. The hissing noise was louder now, like air rushing through a pipe. Something close by must be making the sound, but the room was shadowy in the dawn light outside, and John could see nothing as he glanced around the desk.

"You left three of my men dead in Asia, John, and it's going to be the end of me," Gavin croaked, and then he was coughing again. The water was already gone, some down his throat, the rest spilled.

John took the glass and walked to refill it. "Grandfather, where is Maggie? I couldn't find her on the ship."

"Where's Maggie?" Gavin asked behind him, his voice rising into something like hysteria. "Where's Maggie, you ask me? I've sent her away. They want to push me out, want what's mine. Maggie included!" And then he cried out in pain.

John turned to see a bright blue flame in Gavin's right hand.

"What are you doing?" he yelled, rushing back to the desk.

In the moment it took John to cross the room, he saw Gavin directing the flame in his right hand toward the sleeve on his left arm.

It was a blowtorch. A tiny thing—just a hand-sized canister with a pipe snaking out the top—but the small flame was an intense blue, hissing loudly now. Gavin had been concealing it under the desk. In a flash, John realized it was the torch he'd glimpsed in the office cupboard a year and a half ago, one of the items that had belonged to his father, Archie. Gavin had progressed from caressing these objects to using them against himself. There was a burning smell again, strong and acrid.

"Stop it!"

He grabbed for Gavin's right wrist, but in a moment of wild strength, Gavin wrenched his arm away and stood up from the desk. He aimed the flame at himself again and screamed in pain as it burned through his coat.

John reached out to stop him, but Gavin flailed the torch, and John was forced to duck, feeling his face buffeted by a wave of hot air. He could now see a series of burns along Gavin's coat sleeve. Pink, raw flesh was visible underneath. How long had he been doing this?

"Grandfather, what are you doing? You're hurting yourself!"

"I'm not—I'm—not—" He was coughing again. "I'm focusing my mind. Archie used this, when he worked on his cars. He paid such close attention . . . If I can stay focused . . . I can see my way out."

Gavin's right eye drifted to the side, out of sync with his left. He was still waving the torch at John.

"My father didn't burn himself with a torch," John told him. "This isn't—it isn't you, Grandfather! How long has Maggie been gone?"

"Sent her away as soon as you left for Asia, John. Catherine said it—they're out to kill us. *All* of them."

In his increasing paranoia, Gavin had sent Maggie away, but in doing so he'd condemned himself. His mind was going entirely. John lunged, but the old man stepped backward, lengthening the torch's flame and swinging it in a wide arc.

"Grandfather, if Maggie's been gone, we need to get her back." He reached for him again, but Gavin kept out of reach. "You can't live without—"

"You killed my men, John—"

"I didn't kill them. I promise you." He grasped for Gavin and was met with another blast of hot air as the old man brandished the torch at John's face. "There was a fight—"

"They'll push me out now for sure . . ." Gavin began, and then he doubled over in a coughing fit.

John took advantage of the moment and seized him. Gavin thrust his arms up, straining to push his grandson away. He was much weaker than John, but desperation was driving him, and John didn't want to hurt him. His grandfather held on tightly, his left hand digging into John's flesh, his right hand rotating the torch wildly. Suddenly John felt searing pain across his forearm. The torch was on him. The flame was burning his skin.

He screamed and knocked his grandfather backward roughly. The old man fell, the blowtorch rolling down the front of his chest, burning him as it went, then clattering away across the floor. John jumped after it, switching it off, and kicking it toward the other side of the room. When he turned back, he found Gavin sprawled on the ground, small and weak and injured.

His grandfather looked up in terror. His right eye came slowly back into alignment with his left. The pupils were still mismatched, but both eyes were staring directly at John. "You too? Are you after me too, John?"

John knelt in front of him and took hold of his shoulders. "I'm not after you. This isn't you!" He made Gavin look at him. And then he spoke the words he'd been trying to avoid for years. "We—we poisoned you, Grandfather. Do you hear me? It's the poison making you think this way."

Gavin scooted away from John, still staring wildly, but the meaning of what John had said appeared to sink in. Gradually his face became calmer. "What?" he asked. "What do you mean?"

The room was still dim in the early-morning light, but John could see the bright red swath along his own arm, already blistering dramatically. His whole arm, from wrist to shoulder, had started to ache. He grabbed his grandfather's left arm and studied the row of burns there. They were bad, as were the burns down his chest. John would have to call a doctor for both of them.

He settled heavily onto the floor next to Gavin. "Your cough. That's one of the symptoms—spasms in the trachea. Your muscle spasms and tics. Dilated pupils. The mental disorder. They're from the poison."

"You poisoned me?" Gavin whispered, looking devastated. "Actual, actual poison?"

"My mother," John replied. He took a deep, slow breath, gritting his teeth against the agony now rolling up his arm in dark waves, in time with his heartbeat. He clutched the limb closer to his body. "Catherine did it, years ago."

He felt a vibration at his hip. With his good arm, John withdrew his phone from his pocket and studied the image that had appeared on the screen. For a moment, he forgot his pain and felt a rush of hope. She had contacted him. He hadn't thought she would, but she had. He could succeed, if he could keep Gavin sane for a little while and get his help one more time.

"Catherine poisoned me," Gavin said quietly, staring at the floor. His voice was heartbroken. His right eye was drifting out of alignment again. "Why would she?"

"It was before she knew you well, before you became close. She—she wanted a way to control you, if you became a threat."

"She gave me so much. I would never, ever—"

"It was a mistake, Grandfather. A bad mistake. The poison's been stealing your mind for years. She shouldn't have done it. She—she never thought she could trust anyone. It wasn't her best quality."

"I would never have gone against her," he said again, looking at the burns along his arm as though he were just now beginning to feel them. "Am I dying, then?"

"I don't know. The poison lives in your body permanently." John tried to say the words gently. He adjusted his own arm, attempting to find a position that hurt less. "You've been getting the antidote since long before she died. *Maggie* has been giving you the antidote. But it's not working like it used to. I don't know why. Now you've sent Maggie away, and you haven't been getting any at all."

Gavin looked up from his burns. John was expecting anger, but instead he saw relief flooding into the old man's features. "I'm not crazy?" his grandfather asked. "I'm not losing my mind?"

"You've been burning yourself with a blowtorch, Grandfather," John said. "I think you may be crazy. But it's not your fault. I'm sorry." It was strange to be the one apologizing when Gavin had just maimed him, but John could feel nothing but remorse at seeing the old man in this state of breakdown.

As John watched, paranoia began to sneak back into Gavin's expression. The old man's eyes went out of focus, darted about the room, and he whispered, "They're coming after me. They'll get rid of me."

"No," John told him firmly, gripping him with his good arm. "There's no one here right now, Grandfather. *Traveler* is still yours." He put his hand under Gavin's chin and turned the old man's face up to look into his own. "And I was so close. I had it in my hands."

He glanced at his phone, sitting on the floor next to him. Then he looked again into his grandfather's mad eyes. A harsh laugh came out involuntarily. His mother had wanted him to have Gavin for protection and stability, but his grandfather was providing just the opposite. He was another burden for John to shoulder.

"Maggie will come back here and help you," John said. "Then I know where to go. This time, I *will* get it back."

CHAPTER 41

QUIN

Time was growing longer. Quin could hear her own breath in the darkness, each inhale and exhale stretching out until they took minutes, it seemed, to complete. Eternity was all around her, like the water of the river that flowed around the estate.

Words from her oath floated into her mind, disconnected . . . *the hidden ways between, rising darkly to meet me . . .*

She had lost the thread of the time chant. She knew the words. They were on the tip of her tongue. Just there, just there, had been there forever . . .

Her breath slowly, slowly filled her lungs. *Why bother to breathe?* she wondered. It was easier to pause between breaths and hover there, letting the blackness float you away.

I will die here! she thought suddenly. The realization was strong enough to speed her up again. Her breath went out more quickly, then in again.

Knowledge of self. The words of the chant came back to her. *Knowledge of home.*

She forced the words to come through her mouth, out loud.

"A clear picture of where I came from, where I will go, and the speed of things between will see me safely back."

This was *now*. If there was no time in this no-place, still she had brought her own time with her. *My mind will clear,* she told herself. And it did. With a rush of gratitude, she understood that her work as a healer had kept her mental muscles sharp.

She could feel the athame and lightning rod in her hands. There was a faint glow from the athame, just enough light for her to see its shape.

She was saying the chant again: *"Knowledge of self, knowledge of home, a clear picture of where I came from, where I will go . . ."*

She knew where she must go. In the dim glow of the stone dagger, she turned the dials along its haft, feeling the shapes of the symbols with her fingers. These coordinates were the first her father had made her memorize, and they were burned into her mind below the level of consciousness.

". . . and the speed of things between will see me safely back . . ."

She lifted the athame and swung it toward the lightning rod. Halfway there, it struck something else. Quin reached out in front of her, and her fingers came in contact with cloth. Wool, like they used to wear when she was a child, thick and itchy. She dug her fingers in, finding something softer underneath, maybe flesh.

She held the athame close, trying to see what she was touching in its vague light. By its size and position, she was fairly certain it was the figure of a human, as still as stone. She could not make out details, but with her hands she discovered a head and shoulders, belonging to someone much taller than she was. She felt further and grew uncertain. There were too many limbs, and they were in the wrong places . . .

How long had she been standing here with the figure? How many breaths had it been? Ten? A hundred? It was impossible to count, especially with her lungs moving so gradually.

"Knowledge of self." The words came sluggishly, like bubbles through molasses. *"Knowledge of home . . ."*

She could not stay, or she would stay forever. She turned away from the silent figure, bringing the athame and lightning rod together. When the vibration enveloped her, she carved a new anomaly, drawing it as large as she could.

The tendrils of light and dark separated from each other, then became a solid border in front of her, creating a humming doorway. Its energy surged outward from the darkness, toward the world. There was a night sky beyond, and trees, a forest of trees.

"A clear picture of where I came from, where I will go . . ." she chanted.

She turned around and moved a few paces back, feeling her way behind the strange figure. Placing her hands against it, she thrust it forward with all her strength. It was heavy and awkward, but frozen so solid she could push it as you would a statue. She shoved repeatedly, sliding it along in fits and starts toward the hole between nothingness and the world. At last, with a final push, the frozen figure reached the lip of the doorway, whose pulsing edges helped carry it through. It tumbled downward onto the forest floor, and Quin jumped out after it.

Her feet touched ground, and she stood still a moment. She was in a clearing with thick woods on all sides. The east was growing lighter. It was almost dawn here. Her breath and heartbeat were speeding up, returning her to normal.

In the moonlight, she could see more clearly the figure she had brought with her from *There*. It was not one man but three, cloaked and hooded, their arms intertwined, one clutching the second's arm, while the second grabbed the third's shoulders. They lay there in the same positions in which they had stood, their legs pointing awkwardly away from the ground.

The first figure was an old man who was not familiar to her. The second she knew. Though she could not locate specific memories of him, his name came to her mind immediately: *the Big Dread.* This unlocked something else: a memory of the two Dreads, one of whom was much smaller. *A girl,* her mind told her. *I do remember her.*

The third man was Briac Kincaid.

Quin had brought her father back to the estate.

CHAPTER 42

SHINOBU

Shinobu was still sitting by the pool, staring at the spot where Quin had stepped through the anomaly and disappeared. It was painful to be in her presence, because of the memories she stirred up. Yet he could now feel the places where she'd been pushed up against him, like those parts of him were highlighted in his senses. Had she felt the same way when he'd put his arms around her to help her with the athame? Or was he still just a distant cousin, as pretty as a painting and equally untouchable? No. At least he was too dirty to be considered pretty now.

He was startled by a hand on his shoulder. His mother, Mariko MacBain, was crouched on the grass behind him, a dressing gown pulled tight around her in the slight nighttime chill.

If he had expected her to be mad at him, she was not. There was a cautious look on her face, though, like she worried that Shinobu might try to strike her. This made him ashamed.

"You came," she said softly. "Was that Quin?"

"Did you see?" he asked her quickly. The idea that she might have seen Quin step through the anomaly bothered him. His mother had successfully put their life on the estate behind her—he didn't want to bring it back.

"See what?" she asked.

"Did you see her leave?"

"No. I heard her near the house a few minutes ago." She moved closer on the grass, but not close enough to touch him. "She's the one who saved your brother this morning. She didn't know who I was, but I would know her anywhere. She's gotten quite pretty, hasn't she?"

Shinobu drew out the bag of herbs. The thick plastic had kept everything dry.

"The medicine you asked for," he told her. "I'm very sorry about what happened to Akio, Mother."

He could feel her eyes heavy upon him.

"'Sorry' does not repair the damage that was done, Shinobu. It was a very near thing with your brother this morning." She still didn't sound angry, merely exhausted. That was worse.

"I'll go through my room, make sure there's nothing else—"

"I've already done that, of course."

"I meant to drop off the herbs without you seeing me. Please forgive my continued presence here. I should leave."

He always became more Japanese around Mariko. There had been lectures, when he was a child, about things like manners and honor. Those lectures had meant a great deal to him, back when he'd believed his life would be full of honor.

"Perhaps you should leave. Before I become angry again. This morning I might have killed you if you'd been around."

"I'm sorry, Mother."

He got to his feet.

"Tell me—how did Quin get to Hong Kong?" she asked him before he could walk away.

"The same way I got here," he replied, sinking his fists deep into his jacket pockets to stop them from shaking. He turned toward the garden gate.

"At the same time?" She was on her feet, catching up to him. She was tiny compared to Shinobu, little more than five feet tall. Her very Japanese face was turned up to look at his, her eyes piercing.

"Yes," he answered. "We came here at the same time."

"You never told me. I thought you escaped alone."

"It doesn't matter. We were never together, not really."

"Are you helping her?"

"No—yes," he corrected himself. He stared down at his boots, still damp and dirty. "One thing, that's all."

"Even when you were small, I could see something between the two of you. Your father always liked her, poor girl."

"I'll go now," he said, turning away.

"You're thinking of your father," she called after him. "It's all right. I think of him too, all the time. It's what he wanted—you here with me and Akio."

"I know, Mother. It's what he wanted."

"Please, Shinobu. You can . . . change yourself. And come back to us." She was trying to sound firm, but he could hear the pleading in her voice.

When he had first been reunited with his mother, he'd tried to tell her about Alistair, about that last night on the estate, but he hadn't been able to make the words come. Mariko had sensed he was trying to make a confession, and she'd told him it wasn't necessary. She'd said his past was forgiven and they need never speak of it again.

It had felt wonderful, at first, to have that forgiveness. He hadn't understood that it would be another matter entirely to forgive himself. Only the drug bars offered that mercy. Drugs had made him unfit to be near his family and had almost killed his little brother, but the bars on the Bridge were the only places where he found a small measure of relief. How could he give that up?

"I'm not thinking of my father," he lied, walking for the gate without looking back. "I'm thinking of a ghost."

Brian Kwon was not a ghost, but he was getting close. After two hours of searching, Shinobu found him huddled on the filthy pavement behind a large waste receptacle two blocks from Queen Elizabeth Hospital, from which he had apparently run, trailing an IV tube and many half-wrapped bandages.

"I had to leave," Brian explained. "They started asking questions."

One of his eyes was bandaged, and a cut on his shoulder had been cleaned but stitched only halfway shut. It was trickling blood across his shirt. He had bruises all over his face and neck.

"You look terrible," Shinobu said.

"You should see the other guy," Brian managed.

Brian had led the last of John's men on a wild-goose chase back on the Bridge, while Shinobu had spirited Quin away. Shinobu examined his friend's torso and found more ugly bruises.

"It's not too bad," Brian told him. "The worst part was this." He pointed to a long, dark bruise that began on his forehead, then continued down his face and onto his chest. "I ran into a steam pipe while leading them into that east corridor. They didn't follow for long after they realized your girlfriend wasn't with me. They gave me a couple shots for the pain—the hospital did, I mean—not the guys on the Bridge."

"You make a good punching bag, Sea Bass," Shinobu told him as he pulled the big fellow to his feet. "But she's not my girlfriend."

"Whatever you say, Barracuda. I'm always getting into knife fights for girls who are just good friends."

"She's my cousin—third cousin. Well, *half* third cousin."

Brian groaned deeply as he managed to get fully upright. "What's a third cousin?"

"It's a . . . barely related kind of person, Sea Bass, who still thinks of herself as your relative."

"Oh. I'm sorry to hear that."

Shinobu was trying to steady Brian, who was grimacing, apparently more in response to Shinobu's poor prospects with Quin than from the pain. He took one unsteady step, then fell toward Shinobu like a wall of cinder blocks. Shinobu grunted under the weight but managed to shift his friend around until Brian was half riding on Shinobu's back.

How he was able to get Brian onto a bus and all the way down to the Bridge, he was never quite sure.

It was midnight when they got to the Kowloon end of the Transit Bridge, its canopy of sails disappearing into the fog that was rolling across the harbor.

"To whom shall I address your entry request?" the border guard asked him. The man delivered the question as though nothing could be more normal at this time of night than a dirty gang member carrying on his back an equally dirty but even larger gang member who was clearly injured.

"Master Tan," Shinobu replied.

The man leaned forward to take Shinobu's picture, which would be sent to Master Tan's residence for approval. Shinobu smiled winningly into the camera, Brian still moaning on his back.

"He'll probably remember me."

MAUD

In an earlier century, the Scottish estate was wilder and yet more populated. Life was centered on the castle, perched high on a promontory above the river. And yet on this day, the stone fortress was both motionless and noiseless when viewed from the outside. The residents kept themselves invisible when the Dreads were present, remaining indoors, and leaving only by the back gate when errands called.

It was afternoon on a cool summer day, and the Young Dread pirouetted in the castle's sand courtyard. Her left foot was on the ground, turning her swiftly in circles as her arms and her right foot blocked the objects thrown at her by the Middle Dread.

"Catch! Block! Block! Catch!" he called out to her, slinging large rocks and sharp knives her way.

The Young caught a knife and threw it back, blocked two rocks with her leg, then caught a third rock in her left hand.

"Faster!" he called.

Her left leg ached from her foot to her hip, but this meant little. In the training of the Dreads, some part of one's body was always in pain. She sent her awareness into the muscles, ordering them to move more quickly. To an outsider, her arms would look like a blur—if an outsider had dared to watch them.

The Middle threw a series of knives, each aimed with deadly precision at vulnerable parts of her body.

"Catch, catch, catch!" he yelled.

With each catch, she had to throw the knife back, aiming it just as precisely at him as he had at her. The Middle Dread kept up with her so easily, he had ample time to find unpleasant objects to hurl at her between knives. A small length of chain and a horseshoe came next.

"Block!" he called. "Faster!"

Her master was approaching. While most of her mind was occupied by the bombardment of missiles, a small piece of her watched the Old Dread draw near. She noted that his motions were slower even than they had been the previous day. For more than a week she had watched him wind down into dreamlike movements. He drifted to a stop nearby and very slowly lifted a hand, bringing her training session to a close.

The knives and stones stopped being launched from the Middle Dread's hands and were replaced around his body or on the ground. The Young Dread untwisted herself from the pirouette to walk toward her master. As she did, one final stone flew from the Middle's hands toward her head, fast and vicious, hoping to catch her unaware. She raised an arm at the last moment to bat it down onto the sand.

"We will walk," the Old Dread said. His voice was so quiet and slow it was difficult for her to hear him. His eyelids hung half closed.

Left alone, the Middle Dread pulled out his whipsword and moved off around the perimeter of the deserted courtyard. The Young and Old passed slowly through the castle's main gate and headed toward the woods.

"You will not like to hear this," he began. "It is time for me to rest."

"We have been stretched out so many times, Master," she said. "Is there no rest for you then?"

"There is. Yet not enough. The rest I speak of will be longer. You have made small jumps with me, a dozen years, a score, two score. I must stay in the darkness much longer."

"Will you sit, Master?" Nearby was a large stone that was handy for sitting, and they were walking at a pace so slow, it seemed pointless to continue on.

He shook his head. In an ordinary man, this motion would have taken a few seconds. For her master, it lasted half a minute.

"All my effort is required to stay upright and moving. If I sit, I am done. I will not rest until I am *There*."

The Young Dread looked over her shoulder and through the gate to where the Middle was practicing with his whipsword, sending it around his body so quickly, it gave the impression of a deadly black cloud. If her master truly meant to go, she would be left with the Middle, the two of them alone for years.

"How long?" she asked.

"Difficult to say. A hundred. Perhaps two hundred."

"Two hundred years!"

"Perhaps more, child."

It was a shocking number.

After the Young Dread had shown herself to be a good student, and she'd said goodbye to her family, they had spent a year in the darkness of *that place*, emerging to a world one year older, while she had not aged at all. She'd spent another year training. Then they had gone to that dark place for two years. And so on, alternating her training with what the Dreads called "stretching out" or "rest," and which really meant leaving time and place behind. The longest jump had been fifty years, so that, in all, a hundred years had passed since her master had first led her away from her family home, and yet she was just twelve years old. It was now the year 1570 or thereabouts.

"It is not so long as you may think. When your training has gone a little further, you may make a jump of as many years."

"How will my training go further, with you gone?"

The Old Dread stopped, placing a hand on each of her arms. "The Middle has many valuable skills. There is much you can learn from him."

The Young Dread said nothing to this. She hoped her silence would speak of the Middle's temper, his cruelty, and even things her master had never seen—like the young man at the inn, the previous Young Dread, the boy who had been stabbed for objecting to the Middle's behavior.

Her master's eyelids were open only a slit, yet she could feel him surveying her closely.

"You are strong," he told her, as though he had heard all of her thoughts. "You can defend yourself."

"Can I?" she wondered.

The other Young Dread, that boy at the inn, had been older than she was, and he had not been able to protect himself. Or had there been something else in the boy's eyes, a desire to be free? Had he been willing to die if it meant he would escape from the Middle?

There was a very long silence. She watched her master's chest moving in and out, like waves rolling up a wide beach. At last, he spoke again.

"It is why you have trained, child. You are the Young, for you are the youngest. Yet you are a Dread, just as I am, just as the Middle is. You decide what is just, as any Dread must. The Middle understands you will be alive when I wake. Or I shall be angry."

She had never seen her master angry, and so could not judge whether this would be a frightening prospect for the Middle Dread. Her master was old. Though she'd caught glimpses of his skill here and there, he'd been tired for all the years she'd known him. The Middle still deferred to the Old, but the Young Dread wondered how long that respect would last.

"I can guess the thoughts that pass through your mind, child," he told her. "I am a very different man when I have rested. I should have gone years ago. I was delayed by . . . your arrival."

Caused by the untimely death of the previous Young Dread, she thought.

"Now I am long overdue."

"How will you wake up, two hundred years hence, Master?"

The hint of a smile played across the old man's lips.

"That is a secret you will learn in time. When I am rested, there is much I will teach you. All of it. You will understand."

The Old Dread reached out a hand to steady himself against her shoulder, then sat heavily onto the ground.

"Call the Middle to me now, child. He has the athame. Lose no time. I must rest *now.*"

His eyes were almost entirely closed. His shoulders were moving downward, as though curling in upon themselves. The Young Dread turned toward the castle and ran.

CHAPTER 44

QUIN

Quin studied her father in the last of the moonlight.

"You're alive." The words fell out of her like stones dropped into a lake, creating ripples to the furthest reaches of her mind.

The memory of the last time she had seen him came back to her suddenly. He had been lying in the commons, which could not be far from where they were at this very moment, and his face had been distorted by a look of hatred.

Now, in the dawn, his skin was cool, his hands gripping hard at the fabric of the Big Dread's cloak. No breath escaped any of the three men. They exhibited no sign of life at all, and yet their skin was pink and healthy and soft to the touch. Their bodies were not frozen by temperature; they were frozen in time. She wondered how she'd come across them while *There*. What were the dimensions of that no-space?

Quin felt a strange war taking place inside her mind. A short time ago, she'd insisted to Shinobu that she was a healer and did not wish to hurt anyone. But she was now experiencing a very different urge.

She pried Briac away from the others, roughly pulling his fingers loose from the Dread's cloak and yanking him onto his back. His arms and legs held their strange positions as she moved him.

When she'd turned his body so he was looking up toward the sky, she pulled out her whipsword. She let her hand move of its own accord—her muscles knowing the motions more than her mind did—cracking the whipsword out into the shape of a long dagger. This she lifted above Briac's chest.

"I said I would kill you if John didn't," she whispered to him. That memory had fully surfaced, and it was tugging other memories up toward the light.

Briac's eyes were turned to the side, his mouth partly open, as though he'd frozen midsentence. She lifted her arm higher, planning to strike down with one well-aimed blow. But her arm hovered in place for a long while.

"Oh, God," she breathed, unable to finish the motion. It was impossible, with him lying there helpless. She rubbed her face with her hands. Leaving him alive would mean . . .

What would it mean? she asked herself. *More,* was the answer. *More of what we did before.* She wasn't sure what she'd done with Briac before, but the outline of it lay at the back of her mind, huge and dark, a slumbering giant she did not wish to disturb. *If he is alive, I'm afraid I will obey him, just as I have always done.* Still, she found she could not strike him like this.

Dawn was coming in earnest now. Quin tried to calculate how long she had spent *There.* Subjectively it was impossible to tell. Her memory told her both that it had been only a few minutes and that she'd spent days in that black nothingness. She had left Hong Kong near midnight. Hong Kong was seven hours ahead of Scotland, so eleven in the evening in Hong Kong would be four in the afternoon on the estate. Yet it was dawn now, which could only mean that her brief trip *There* had taken at least fifteen hours, or she could have lost a day and a half, or even more.

In the growing light, she noticed a dark patch on Briac's left trouser leg. She brushed her hand against his thigh, and it came away wet and dark. Blood. His shirt was similarly stained, at his right shoulder. He'd been shot a year and a half ago—she remembered that. So many memories were still hidden, but this one she suddenly saw in full clarity. John had shot him twice. *There's a matching scar for you!* John had said. *What did he mean by that?* she wondered.

In all these months, while Briac had been lost *There,* his blood had not even dried. It had simply stopped flowing, just as Briac and the others had stopped breathing, just as their hearts had stopped beating.

She examined the other men more closely. The oldest, whose face was hidden behind a thick woolen hood and a full, gray beard, looked unharmed. The other one, the one they'd called the Big Dread, had a cut across his chest, which had been poorly bandaged by a torn strip of his cloak. This wound too was still wet.

Quin wondered if these injuries were the reason her father and the Big Dread had become stuck *There.* It seemed likely the wounds had distracted them from their time chants and left them stranded.

She got to her feet, noticing for the first time exactly where she was. She had come through the anomaly into a clearing in the woods. A standing stone was off to her left, and down the path, in the distance, she glimpsed the commons. *This is where it all began. Right here,* she thought. With a last glance at her father, she started down the path.

As she reached the wide meadow, Quin saw the burned heaps of rubble that had once been cottages, but so far there was no sign of human life upon the estate.

Memories were surfacing faster now, and more images from that evening came to her mind—Quin hiding by her burning cottage, throwing a knife at a man holding her mother. Her right hand twitched at that memory, and she looked down at both hands, sensing their many hidden skills.

She passed by a structure with a gaping space where its large door had once been. The interior was dark, but otherwise it looked undamaged. The name came to her: *the workshop*. And up ahead was the practice barn, which had not fared as well. Its roof was gone except for a ragged remainder in a corner. Its stone walls were covered with black streaks, and the interior was strewn with fallen masonry.

Ducking through the barn's burned doorway, she found it chilly and darker inside. She could make out the shapes of weapons racks against the walls, all of them charred or falling apart. There was an equipment room at one end, full of rubble. Within that room, Quin found only one item of interest—a small metal chest in a corner, buried almost completely beneath stones and mortar.

Another memory appeared: Shinobu's father in the clearing in the woods, opening a trunk full of guns. Quin pried the chest open and found no guns inside this one, only a jumbled mess of holsters and scabbards. Almost without thinking, she buckled a belt of rubbery black material around her waist and hung her whipsword from one of its clips. Idly she practiced drawing the sword and putting it back.

Near the bottom of the chest, she discovered thin sheaths, designed to be worn inside one's clothing, up against the skin. She attached these to the inside of her waistband. The jeans she wore were so big she could easily fit the athame and lightning rod into these sheaths beneath her trousers. She didn't know what she hoped to find on the estate, but it was better, she decided, not to wear those stone implements out in the open.

The main area of the practice barn was strewn with debris, but there was a fairly clear path down the middle, as though someone had been there since the fire. She grabbed her whipsword from its new holster, closed her eyes, and let her body take over.

As long as she didn't try to think, her muscles knew what to do. Her hands flicked the whipsword out into the shape of a longsword, and she ran down the center of the barn, slashing the weapon in a routine that came as naturally to her as walking.

When she was finished, she stood by the open doorway, swinging her arms in circles to get rid of the soreness that was already settling in—she was terribly out of shape, and the old wound in her shoulder was aching.

The sky had grown brighter, and she became aware of motion in the distance. Someone was walking across the commons. As the figure drew closer, before Quin could see any facial features, she noticed the way it was moving—like a dancer, slow and smooth and stately. Then she saw the very long light brown hair. The name came to her mind immediately: *the Young Dread.*

The girl was heading toward the workshop, and Quin walked in that direction to intercept her. When the Dread crossed out of the meadow and through the trees along its rim, Quin had the strangest impulse to draw a knife and throw it at her. Her mind brought a very clear image of the Young Dread: the girl's lean, ropy muscles kicking into motion to catch a knife from the air and hurl it back toward Quin.

She had undoubtedly seen Quin from a long way off, and yet nothing in the girl's demeanor indicated this until she was standing almost directly in front of Quin. Her course had not changed, nor the direction of her eyes.

"Hello," Quin ventured when the Dread had come to a stop near her. The girl had a small deer over her shoulder. There was blood on its neck where her arrow had killed it.

The Dread did not answer but instead gave a slow and solemn

nod, stepped gracefully around Quin, then continued on into the workshop. She set the deer down, then moved to a back shelf, where Quin lost sight of her among the shadows.

"May I come in?" Quin asked after waiting a few moments for the girl to offer.

The Young Dread turned toward Quin, knocking something from the shelf as she did so, and her hand flashed out to retrieve whatever it was before it hit the floor. Quin was startled to see the girl mishandle anything—her motions were so precise that any error seemed out of character. The Young placed the object somewhere back on the shelf, then pivoted to face Quin.

"You may come in," she said.

The pitch of the Young Dread's voice was appropriate to a teenage girl, but its tone would never be described that way. Her words formed slowly and clearly, and they sounded unstoppable, once they had begun, like a trickle of water that would eventually cut its way through granite.

Quin entered the workshop almost timidly. The Dread was a petite girl, and yet crossing into her private space felt like stepping into the den of a jungle cat. Quin glanced around the room cautiously, noticing that a cooking hearth had been created near the gaping front door, with large stones arranged in a circle and thick ashes from previous fires.

Near the hearth was an area where the Dread had been butchering the animals she ate. There were several pelts drying above a chopping block, and Quin noticed the Dread herself was wearing a vest made by hand from deerskin.

There was straw in one corner with blankets folded on top of it, odds and ends scavenged from the estate along shelves, and a rack of knives and swords that looked to have been salvaged from the training barn.

The Young Dread tied her long, untidy hair in a twist behind her neck, then began working on the deer.

"Have you been here this whole time?" Quin asked.

The Dread did not bother to respond or even pause in her task. She continued skinning the deer with delicate, expert motions, in the way, Quin imagined, a Viking princess might. At any rate, the answer to Quin's question was obvious. The Dread was not the sort to take bus trips around the countryside or to do a theater tour of Glasgow.

Quin moved closer to the Dread, holding out her left wrist, where the athame-shaped scar showed clearly on her pale skin.

"You can see that I am a sworn Seeker."

The Dread's eyes swept over her wrist without stopping, then returned to the deer. When she spoke, there was a hint of surprise in her voice.

"You do not need to show me your mark. I am the one who gave it to you."

"Right," Quin said, remembering this only now and feeling like an idiot. "You gave me this mark. In the forest. You watched me take my oath."

"I did," the Young Dread agreed.

"Whatever I ask, you must answer me, isn't that right?" She remembered someone telling her that. John. John had told her, in the barn above the cliff.

"No," the girl replied. "That is a courtesy among Seekers. Another Seeker must answer your questions. Your father, for instance. We Dreads have our own knowledge."

"Oh." She wasn't sure whether she had once known this or not. It didn't feel as though she had. The Seekers and the Dreads, with two separate pools of knowledge. What did that mean exactly?

The Dread was quiet for a while as she began gutting the deer.

Eventually she said, "You may ask me a question. It might be I will answer."

Quin thought about what she should ask. What did she want to know? The answer was: *everything*. If she didn't wish to be a pawn, she must learn all she could. But one thing above all: "Is the athame with the fox carved into it the only one left?"

The Dread's head swiveled around to stare into Quin's eyes. This was uncomfortable—like being stared at by a tiger—but Quin resisted the urge to move back to safety.

"Do you have this athame in your possession?" the girl asked.

Quin did not answer.

"Who is your master, young Seeker?"

"I—I have no master." The words came out more confidently than Quin felt, but she meant what she said. "I am my own master now."

Perhaps she imagined it, but this seemed to please the Young Dread.

"No," the Dread said, "the athame with the fox is not the only one."

The deer was gutted, and the Dread was slicing the meat into cuts for cooking.

"How many are there?" Quin pressed.

"I cannot answer that, because I do not know." She was quiet again as she took logs from a stack of chopped wood and began to build a fire. "I have seen three in recent years," the Dread continued when the fire had sparked to life. "One was destroyed here—it was marked with an eagle."

Another memory: The eagle was the symbol of Shinobu's family. They'd had an athame, and it had been destroyed.

The fire was soon crackling, its heat causing Quin to notice how cold she'd been since arriving on the estate. The Dread brought out a metal grill, which she set over the flames, then laid slices of venison across it.

"Who has the other one?" Quin asked.

"The other athame is the athame of the Dreads."

"The athame of the Dreads," Quin repeated softly. Of course the Dreads would have an athame. "My family symbol is the ram. Why doesn't our athame bear that symbol?"

There was a long moment of quiet before the Young Dread replied, "That is not a question for me."

The girl's voice didn't invite argument. Quin tried another tack: "You said three athames 'in recent years.' Were there others?"

"I have answered a question," the girl said, as though that ended the matter. She settled into stillness, staring into the fire.

Quin fell silent as well, and soon the aroma of the cooking venison took up most of her attention. A few minutes later, when the deer meat was pulled from the grill, they both ate. And ate. Quin couldn't recall the last time she'd had a meal, and she burned her mouth in her haste to consume her portion. Grease from the animal dripped down her fingers, making her wish desperately for water and soap, but this didn't stop her from gorging. She wiped her greasy hands on her jeans and found it didn't bother her as much as she expected.

Finally, dirty and full, she studied the Young Dread's face and ventured another question.

"Was there ever a noble purpose for us?" she asked the girl. "I thought as a child—the stories of Seekers helping the world, 'evildoers beware,' 'tyrants beware' . . . Was it always lies?"

The Dread was silent for a long while—so long that Quin thought she'd decided not to answer. At last, however, the girl began to speak.

"We Dreads exist to ensure the three laws are followed. Do you know the three laws?"

Quin hesitated, waiting to see if a memory would appear, but none did.

"I don't think I do."

"Young Seeker, these are our sacred laws. Your father should have taught them to you before all else."

"There are many things Briac should have done that he did not," Quin answered quietly.

"That is so," the Dread agreed. "The three laws should rightfully be recited before you take your oath, but Briac Kincaid omitted them, and the Middle Dread made no complaint. Very well. In truth he is not the first to omit them." She paused, as though her own words disturbed her. "The laws are simple," she continued, "but when broken are to be punished with death. First law: a Seeker is forbidden to take another family's athame. Second law: a Seeker is forbidden to kill another Seeker save in self-defense. Third law: a Seeker is forbidden to harm humankind."

"But we—" Quin began.

"You have broken at least one of these laws, have you not? Perhaps many times," the Dread said. Then she continued, her words now measured as carefully as a medieval merchant might count out gold coins across a countertop: "It was not always so. Our laws were sacred once. Over time, shadows creep in. What was clear becomes muddy." Quin could see the firelight reflected in the girl's eyes. She was lost in the past. "Families intermarry. How can we Dreads know who rightfully owns an athame? There might be many with a valid claim. A Seeker kills another Seeker but has proof the other was a danger, or would become a danger. How shall we Dreads judge this? Was it self-defense, or was it murder? And humankind—it is very easy to claim that by harming some, you have saved many others. This is what every Seeker asserts when he damages humankind—'I did it for the greater good. It was necessary, I swear it.'"

"Who decides, then?" Quin asked quietly. "Who decides if the laws have been broken?"

"When my master is resting, as he has been for so long, the

Middle Dread decides," the Young continued. "The Middle Dread decides with judgment that is unreliable. He chooses not who is right or wrong but whom he favors, whom he wishes to have power. Lately he has favored your father. And before that, others like him."

"Then . . . your laws are worthless," Quin said.

"In my master's hands, the laws had great worth. He can look at a Seeker and see within the man. I have watched him do this. But the laws are worthless in the hands of the Middle Dread. That is true. And by his judgment, we destroy Seekers, and the families of Seekers, or keep them alive. It is why we are known as Dreads."

There was another silence, but eventually the girl continued. "You ask me, was it always lies? I have seen it both ways. There have been true Seekers. Honorable men and women. For centuries they fought unjust and cruel men and they helped those who were good. The stories you heard as a child are true."

Quin felt a flicker of happiness, but she knew the Young Dread was not finished.

"But there have been others," the Dread went on, "who used their athames to seek nothing but wealth or power. They have done shameful things. Simply because they saw some personal benefit in it."

"Like Briac," Quin whispered.

"And like many before him. But Briac may be the worst."

They were both quiet for a long while then, until the Young Dread wiped her hands on a rag and looked up, fixing Quin with a thousand-year stare. When she spoke again, she seemed uneasy about the topic.

"You have loved the other apprentice."

Quin was embarrassed. Only a short time ago, she'd let John carry her up to her room on the Bridge. She'd put her arms around him and pulled him close.

"Yes," she whispered.

"Do you still love him?" the Dread asked her.

She wanted very much to say no. After all, John had lain in bed next to her, had kissed her, and then he'd stood there as those men had beat her. And yet, some part of her understood his desperation. Eventually she shook her head and said, "I don't know what I feel."

The Dread turned her eyes away, and Quin thought she could see confusion in the girl's face. It was an emotion that did not fit well on one so self-possessed.

"Why do you ask about him?" Quin asked her. "Do you know him—more than just seeing him when we trained on the estate?"

"I do not know him," the Young Dread said firmly. "But we have spoken. And I wonder—I wonder what kind of person he is."

Quin tossed a twig into the fire, trying to figure out how to answer that question. "When I'm with him," she said after a while, "I can feel that he loves me. I see it in his eyes." She paused, watching the twig burn up in the flames. "But now I know he wants an athame more than he wants me, more than he wants anything else." She paused again, then added, her voice low and serious, "He came after us that night, here on the estate, for revenge. What would he do if he got an athame? It wouldn't be good. How could it be good?"

The Dread was looking into the fire once more. It was impossible to read the girl, but Quin sensed she was troubled.

Then slowly the Dread said, "I have seen him."

Something in the way she said it did not fit.

"Do you mean *recently*?"

The girl nodded.

Quin's stomach experienced a falling sensation, like she'd unwittingly stepped into an airlift that had dropped her down two stories.

"Where?" Quin asked. "Here?"

The Dread did not answer.

Quin was on her feet. She found herself backing away from the girl. Was she helping John? When had they spoken? Did this mean he would be after Quin again?

The Young Dread remained seated by the fire, her eyes on her hands. Looking around the room, Quin felt her attention caught by something that didn't belong. She allowed her eyes to travel slowly across all the walls, searching. There was something on the shelf along the back wall. There. An electric cord.

It was surprising that there was electricity on the estate at all—though the workshop was almost untouched, so perhaps that made sense. It was more surprising for the Young Dread to be in possession of anything requiring electricity. Why would the girl have such a thing?

Quin walked toward that cord, noting that the Dread turned her head to watch but didn't rise from her seat by the fire. Quin followed the cord along the shelf to a pile of rags. She slid her hands under the rags and pulled out . . .

A mobile phone.

Its screen was awake, and there were words printed across it: *Message Sent.* The time stamp was from an hour ago, when Quin had first walked into the workshop. And further, Quin was now looking at the date. She'd lost nearly two days when she went *There.*

The Dread was observing her from across the room. The girl's face was motionless, but Quin thought she now detected shame in the Dread's features.

"John gave you this phone? You've told him I'm here?" It was not so much a question as a statement. "You were stalling me."

The girl nodded slowly, like a judge confirming a death sentence.

"Why—why would you do that? He hasn't even taken his oath." She was trying to calculate where in the world John had been an hour ago and how long it would take him, from that hypothetical location, to reach the estate.

"There was an injustice," the Young Dread said, as though this would explain her actions.

"Isn't *this* unjust?" Quin asked. "I am a sworn Seeker. I only wanted time to remember, to decide what to do."

"I . . . I wanted . . ." the Dread began again. "I wanted to make up for things that were done. My master would know how to set things to rights. My master would have stopped Briac. But I . . . I am torn."

"Briac," Quin said, remembering that her father was lying in a clearing in the forest. "Right. I'll take care of that now. Before I have yet another person after me."

She turned to leave the workshop but had gone only a few steps when she made a new mental connection. She was angry, but she was finding it difficult to direct her anger at the Young Dread. Quin too had been torn about helping John. "Your master," she said, turning back. "Describe him."

The Young Dread began to do so, but before she had put two sentences together, Quin was running out of the workshop, calling back over her shoulder, "Come with me!"

The sun was fully up in the sky as the three men came into view. They still lay in the clearing near the standing stone, their arms and legs at odd angles. But Quin could tell immediately that something had changed. Her father's limbs appeared to have settled, as though his muscles were gradually growing softer.

And the men were breathing. Their chests were expanding and contracting so gradually, it was almost impossible to spot the movement, yet it was there, changing their appearance from statues to living creatures. Something besides their chests was moving as well: blood was trickling from their wounds.

The Young Dread let out a gasp when she caught sight of the old man with the beard. This man was moving the least—perhaps he had been *There* the longest. In a moment, the Young was kneeling at his side, holding his head very carefully in her hands. The girl put an ear to his mouth, listening for breath. She spoke softly to him in a language that sounded something like English. Then she shook his chest and spoke to him again, more firmly.

Quin drew her whipsword, knelt over Briac, lifted her arm. It was time to make good on her promise. If Briac woke up, he would remind her of things she did not wish to remember, would force her to do things she did not wish to do, and Quin didn't think she could stand up to him. She'd never been able to stand up to him. She must make an end of it now.

Briac blinked.

It was a slow motion. His eyelids traveled downward a tiny bit at a time, until his eyes were closed, and then they performed the same motion in reverse. His gaze turned very, very slowly, until he was looking up at her.

Now! Quin told herself. *Now, or you'll never do it!*

She struck down with her blade. Briac's half-frozen arms came to life on reflex. His right hand hit her whipsword away; his left grabbed her neck. Then he was perfectly still again, his hands frozen in their new positions. Danger had jolted him back into Quin's time stream, but only for a moment. She pushed his arms away from her and lifted the whipsword again.

"Quin!"

Her head snapped up at her name. John stood at the edge of the clearing, two other men spread out nearby. She recognized one of them from the Bridge. All three had guns pointed directly at her.

"Please, Quin," John said. "Please put your sword down."

CHAPTER 45

JOHN

"You brought guns this time," Quin noted as John approached. "You must be really scared of me."

"Well, you ignored the knives on the Bridge," he pointed out, trying to make light of the situation. He did not like pointing guns at her.

She had gotten to her feet and was standing perfectly still, her arms raised, whipsword on the ground by her feet. He watched her eyes move from him to each of the two men he'd brought with him. She looked much more alert than she had a few days ago on the Bridge. And more dangerous.

John's entire left arm was aching from the blowtorch burn, which was heavily bandaged beneath his shirt. It was a reminder that he had better succeed this time. His grandfather had lost his grip on sanity and would likely lose control of his empire as well. He wouldn't be able to help John much longer.

"You can't seem to stay away from me," Quin whispered when he'd come up beside her. Her words were meant to be cutting, but they still sounded intimate, and John could not stop himself from hoping that she would help him. Just once.

"I don't want to stay away," he whispered back. "I want to be together."

On the ground nearby, the Young Dread was crouched over an old man who lay awkwardly on the forest floor. There were two other men on the ground as well, who looked as though they'd frozen in the middle of a strenuous activity. Both men wore hoods obscuring their faces, but they were breathing, very, very slowly. The old man, however, was as still as stone. The Young Dread was speaking to him in a language that might have been English, but if so, it was an English so old John could not follow the meaning.

Quin was wearing ill-fitting jeans held up with a large belt, and after shoving his gun back into his pocket, John was easily able to slip his hand in along her waistband, searching for the athame. It was difficult not to think about his hand on her skin, but he pushed such thoughts away—he must focus. When his fingers came in contact with something hard, something made of stone and nestled up against her right hip, his heart sped up. Quin turned toward him, and John's men lifted their guns in warning.

"Don't take it, John," she said, her eyes pleading. "Don't take it." She put her hand on top of his, tried to push him away from the object beneath her jeans.

"You could make this so easy. Change your mind. Decide to help me."

"I promise I am helping you," she told him. "Things will get worse after you have the athame. Believe me."

"No, Quin. They'll get better. Finally."

Why couldn't she understand? Her hand was on his, and he imagined raising it to his lips. If she would only help him, he would be free to kiss her . . . Instead he slid the object up, out of her trousers.

It was the gray stone of the athame, slightly warm from lying against her skin. In his excitement at holding the dagger in his hands, he shifted his balance away from her to study it. With two quick steps, she was behind him, placing John between her and the men with guns. In the moment it took him to turn to her, Quin had grabbed up her whipsword and was running for the trees.

"Dammit, Quin! Don't do this again!"

He scrubbed at his face with his hands, torn. Then he gestured for his men to go after her. In an instant they were away. He wanted to go himself, but he doubted he could keep a clear head. Before arriving at the estate, he'd ordered his men to prevent Quin from escaping, even if it meant shooting her in a leg—and John would never be able to do that personally.

His eyes dropped to the object in his hand then, and he realized his mistake. He wasn't holding the athame. This was something else. It had the shape of a short sword, with a handgrip and a flat, curving blade that was duller than a butter knife. It was like the athame, certainly, but not the same. A decoy? But if so, why not make something more exactly like the real thing? And this object was of the same stone as the athame, he was sure of that. So what was this item he was holding in his hands?

"Master, Master," the Young Dread was murmuring nearby, still speaking to the old man in a low and steady voice, like a chant.

John stepped closer to the two other frozen men to get a better look. One, he now saw, was a Dread, the man they had called the Big Dread in his training days. The third man's face was still hidden behind a hood, but when John stood directly over him, he found himself staring down at Briac Kincaid.

The surge of hatred was immediate and overpowering. At once, John felt himself back in the old barn, staring at the withered figure of his mother in the hospital bed, being taunted by Briac because he was not good enough, would never be good enough, to take his oath. Briac had treated John and Catherine like they were small and weak and easy to kill. But no more. John's house was rising again, and it was time to put an end to Briac Kincaid.

He laid down Quin's strange stone sword, and his fingers brushed over the gun in his pocket. But instead, his hand went to his whip-sword. It had seemed only appropriate to bring it today for his return to the estate. With a graceful motion, he flicked it out.

Briac's arms were frozen above his face, as though warding off a blow. John knelt and pushed them aside, but very slowly the arms moved back into place, and Briac's eyes came into focus on John. He was waking up.

There were shouts from the woods and then a single gunshot. John looked up, panic rushing over him. His men were excellent marksmen, but still, they might make a mistake. *Please don't hurt her . . .* He strained his eyes in the direction of the gunshot, but he could see nothing except trees from where he knelt. He would have to trust his men to follow orders.

With effort, he forced his attention back to the clearing, and he noticed that the Big Dread was moving his arms and legs now. The actions were both jerky and sluggish, with jumps and starts followed by tiny, slow movements. He too was waking up.

John felt his attention drawn to something in the Dread's cloak, an object sticking out of an interior pocket. Its color and shape . . . John forgot both Briac and the gunshot as he crawled over to the Big Dread, reached into the man's cloak, and wrapped his fingers around a cool stone handle.

It was another athame. He could feel the dials beneath his grasp as he pulled it from the Big Dread's cloak. Briefly he took in its full shape in the daylight of the clearing . . . And then suddenly there was motion everywhere.

The Young Dread's head whipped upward so she was staring at him and the athame in his hands. She'd been entirely willing to ignore him until the moment he touched the stone dagger.

Behind John, Briac was moving, rolling himself slowly out of reach. At the same instant, the Big Dread swung up to a kneeling position in one smooth movement, bringing himself face to face with John. The Big Dread froze again, just as quickly, but his whipsword was now in his frozen hand, its point nearly touching John's chest and vibrating— a residual motion after being cracked out into a solid weapon.

The Dread himself looked completely inanimate again, as did Briac, and John thought it might take a few moments for them to move a second time. The Young Dread was still clutching the old man's robes, cradling his upper body on her lap, but John sensed she was preparing to lunge at him. His only chance was to run now, without giving any warning.

Immediately John was on his feet, clutching the newfound athame in his left hand, his whipsword in his right, sprinting out of the clearing.

For a long while, he simply ran, not daring to look back. Then, in a section of the woods where the trees were more sparse, he caught up with his own men.

"Quin?" he said urgently. "Did you—"

Gauge shook his head. "It was just a shot to pin her down." He nodded toward a wide tree trunk thirty yards ahead. John understood— Quin was cornered there. His panic eased.

He allowed his eyes to sweep over the forest behind him. There was no sign of anyone pursuing him. He looked back to the tree where Quin was hiding. No matter which athame he had, he would need a partner to teach him to use it. And he wanted Quin. Even if she'd never heard of an athame or Seekers, he would want Quin. *Don't turn your back on me, please,* he implored her.

John's other man, Paddon, was circling around through the woods to close in on her from the opposite side. Paddon gestured to Quin's location and opened his mouth to speak.

Like magic, a knife handle appeared at the back of his neck. Paddon spit out a spray of blood and pitched forward.

John turned to see the Young Dread moving with long, steady strides through the trees, another knife already in her hand, ready to throw.

There was a rustle of leaves from beyond the wide tree trunk. Quin was not waiting to see who would be the Young Dread's next target. She was flying deeper into the woods, heading away from them, in the direction of the barn on the cliff.

John took off after her. He could hear the Young Dread continuing behind him, but she hadn't killed him yet. He chose to take that as a hopeful sign.

CHAPTER 46

QUIN

Quin's legs were going to give out. She'd done more running in the past two days than she had in all of the previous year, and her muscles were not going to put up with too much more. Also, she was running out of woods. The trees were thinning ahead, with blue sky now visible through their branches.

The Young Dread had killed one of John's men, but the last time Quin had dared to look over her shoulder, the other man was still chasing her. And John, of course—he wasn't far behind.

The sight of that man flying forward, a knife buried in his neck, had not affected her as much as it should have. *So I am used to death?* she asked herself, immediately knowing the answer: *Yes, I am much too used to death.* There were still gray areas in her mind, but more and more was becoming clear.

A few moments later, she came out into the open. A hundred yards ahead of her was the edge of a cliff, and below that was a river. She could hear the water from where she stood. Near the cliff's edge was an old stone barn. And to the left of that barn was another path, leading back into the woods. The memory came to her—that way would take her to the castle ruins.

She hesitated. If she took that path, they would follow, and she needed a rest before running again. And what was her plan? John had the lightning rod. Without it, her athame was useless. She must get it from him. The only other choice was to give him the athame, teach him to use it, and be done with running.

She found herself walking toward the barn.

"Quin, stop."

It was John's voice. Without stopping, she turned her head and saw him at the edge of the woods, alone. He glanced back into the trees, searching for his remaining man.

"Maybe the Young Dread got both of them," she told him as she reached the barn doorway. She was close to the cliff now—the far side of the barn was nestled against the verge—and she could hear the river more loudly.

"Quin, just stop. Come on." He had pulled the gun from his pocket and was going through the motions of cocking it. The lightning rod wasn't in his hands. He must have it hidden in his clothes.

"Are you really going to shoot me?" she asked. "I don't believe it."

Without waiting for his answer, she crossed into the shadows of the barn. It smelled just as she had known it would, of damp soil and old straw. She moved through its cool interior to the ladder on the far side and climbed quickly up to the sleeping loft. From there she could see out the huge circular windows beneath the roof, giving a view down the cliff and along the river, to the distant hills beyond.

"I wanted you to help me back then," John said, calling up to her from the doorway below. "That day in this barn."

Quin was silent.

"What's the symbol of your family?" he asked.

"A ram," she answered.

"There's a fox carved into the pommel of that athame—the symbol of my family." When she didn't respond, he said, "You don't even want it, Quin. Why would you stop me from having it?"

It was true, she hadn't wanted it. She'd wanted to forget the athame and everything else. And she'd been a pawn. But now?

She peered over the edge of the loft to see him standing beneath her. He was holding the gun, but it was hanging at his side, like he was embarrassed about its presence.

"I'm coming up there," he said, taking hold of the ladder.

Quin braced herself, forming a simple plan. She took a deep breath, in and out.

All at once, he was up the ladder and stepping onto the loft. Instead of moving away, as he would be expecting, Quin moved forward and grabbed hold of him. Stepping back, she twisted around and threw them both off balance, sending John stumbling over the edge of the platform. He saved himself by clutching a rafter, but his gun fell, clattering to the barn floor.

For a moment, his legs dangled over the brink and he fought to get back onto the loft. Quin reached over and felt along his back as he struggled, around his waist, her hand searching for the lightning rod. It wasn't there. She brushed something hard inside his jacket, a solid object, but much too small. Had he given the rod to his men? Had he left it in the woods?

She ducked away from him. There was a long, narrow board connecting the sleeping loft at one end to a group of rafters at the other, beneath the second window. She was halfway across it when John spoke.

"I don't want to force you, Quin," he said. As she glanced back, she saw that he'd regained his solid footing on the loft and was stepping onto the plank behind her. "Wouldn't it be better to be together? I want you to choose to be with me."

"What about what I want?" she asked him as she crawled through the rafters toward the second window. "I want you to be the John I knew before. The one who wanted to do honorable things, to help people."

"I *am* him, Quin." He was moving across the board toward her.

She climbed onto the sill of the window. It was just an opening, without glass. From the sill, she reached out, grabbed the ridge beam beneath the eaves of the roof, and swung herself out of the barn.

She looked to her right, expecting to see the branches of a large elm tree. She and Shinobu had climbed that tree dozens of times as children. She had hoped to be down its trunk and into the woods before John recovered his gun and followed her.

But the elm wasn't there. There must have been a storm sometime in the last year and a half, for the tree had fallen over, tearing out a large chunk of soil with it. Now, with a jolt to her stomach, she saw that it was a straight drop out the barn window, past the remnants of the tree trunk, and down the face of the precipice to the water. A cold breeze was whistling up the cliff, and her feet were flailing in the open air.

She swung her legs frantically to the beam overhead, and as she did, she was given a view of the barn from a new angle. There was a carving next to the window, which until now had been hidden by the elm tree: three interlocking ovals were chiseled deeply into the stone of the barn, making a simple diagram of . . . It looked like an atom.

She didn't have time to study it. John was climbing among the rafters, only yards away from the window, and she was hanging over a cliff. She wrestled her way up onto the roof.

Picking a path across cracked slate tiles to the other side, Quin peered over the roof's edge and found that it was too far to jump to the ground. She might be able to lower herself down and drop—but there was no time. John was already climbing up onto the slate be-

— 310 —

hind her. On one side, it was too far to jump, and on the other was the sheer cliff drop to the river below.

She turned to face him. The idea of fighting John, when she hadn't trained in a year and a half, was almost laughable. Even so, she drew her whipsword and cracked it out. Maybe because she was thinking of Shinobu, she chose the shape of a katana, a Japanese samurai sword. As she swung it up above her head, it felt like Shinobu was behind her, encouraging her. She would be no one's pawn.

"You're out of practice, and I'm not," John said from the other end of the roof, his whipsword still curled at his side. Almost gently, he added, "I don't think you can beat me, Quin."

"You're a good person, John. Despite what you've done so far. If I give you the athame, you won't be, and neither will I."

"The athame doesn't make us bad. It only gives us the freedom to choose. That's all."

She shook her head, gripping her whipsword more tightly. "Really? Think about what you've done already, trying to get it. You shot me, you shot at Shinobu, you cut my mother's throat! You cut her, John!"

"I tried very hard not to hurt any of you! Why don't you see that, Quin? And why do you only care what *I've* done?" His face was changing. She could see him trying to fight his anger, but he was losing. "What about your father?" he asked, the words full of malice as he moved carefully across the roof toward her. "What's *he* done to get the athame? What have those others done?" John's whipsword was in his hand now, like it had a mind of its own.

She knew she was not yet in full possession of her mind. And yet, there was something more here—she sensed he was saying something more than she had ever known. He was about to tell her things she didn't want to learn.

"That's the point," she answered, checking her footing, bracing herself. "Whatever he's done, I don't want you to be like Briac."

"I am *not* a torturer," he told her, the words bursting from him as though he had no control. "I am *not* a beast!" John's whipsword cracked out, and he struck at her, his temper taking over. "I'm not like Briac!"

Quin's muscles reacted automatically, blocking. She might be a year out of practice, but her body had not forgotten. She threw his whipsword off with her own, sending both of them stumbling on the steep roof.

"You're not like Briac," she agreed, righting herself. "And I hope you'll stay as you are."

"You hope I'll stay as I am?" The words seemed to make him angrier. "You like me helpless, is that it? Beaten by Briac! My mother *murdered,* everyone murdered. My house in ruins!" He slashed at her, and she blocked him again. She didn't know what he was talking about. What had happened to John's mother? What had Briac done? "They've been deciding my family's fate for centuries. *Centuries.* But my house will rise again. Do you understand? It's time."

"Do you want a house of killers, John?"

"Are *you* a killer, Quin?"

At that moment, she saw a flash in the corner of her vision. It was the Young Dread at the edge of the woods, approaching the barn, but Quin didn't dare turn her head.

John struck at her harder. Just barely, she managed to throw off the blow, and as she did, she could see that he was favoring his left arm.

"You were going to kill Briac," he said. "I saw you." His sword landed another heavy strike against hers. Her left shoulder, the one with the old wound, was aching.

"Will you help me?" Quin called to the Dread, who was silently getting closer.

"You're passing judgment on me, Quin. But what about the things *you've* done?" John asked. He continued to swing at her, moving her backward.

How did he know what she'd done? How did he know when she didn't know herself, didn't want to know? He was pushing her toward the end of the roof. And in her mind, he was pushing her to another sort of cliff, one that separated the Quin of now from the Quin of a year and a half ago.

With two more steps, he drove her to the edge. There was nowhere for her to go.

"Please!" Quin called to the Dread. The girl was standing below them, motionless.

John raised his sword, but did not strike. "Tell me, Quin. What did you and Briac do?"

All at once, she knew the answer. The last curtain of gray was gone from her mind, and she could clearly see the events she had most wanted to forget.

She had done the things she was accusing John of wanting to do. She'd done those things with her own hands. The weight of them hit her like a physical force, and she almost fell to her knees. Of course she had forgotten. Of course she'd started her life over. Ignorance had been wonderful.

"We killed them," she whispered, letting the words hang in the air. She struck at John weakly, trying to step away from the edge. "If Briac's a beast, so am I."

"Who did you kill?" he asked, retreating a pace, giving her room.

"Lots of people, John, lots of times." Now that she was admitting it, she could not stop the words from tumbling out. There was a relief in saying them aloud. Finally. "Those children—I tried to run away. He stopped me. He said I had to. We'd already done so much. Their parents, the nurse . . . There was no escape . . ." She could see Briac as he was that night, at the base of the big staircase in the manor house. The children were hiding behind her. "I told them it would be all right, and I brought them back to Briac."

"He forced you," he said, his voice softer now, as though she could be forgiven for what she'd done. As though he understood and didn't blame her. "It wasn't your choice. Those deaths don't make you a killer."

"They thought I was helping them, John! I dream about those children. I tried to get away with them, but Briac caught me. He kicked the gun from my hands when he saw me faltering. And then he . . ." She couldn't say the words. Briac had taken those children and done what they did to everyone on those late-night assignments. Even if she hadn't . . . *finished* things with the children herself, there were all those others her own whipsword had cut and killed. On later assignments with Briac, there'd been no children involved, and this had been such a relief that she . . . she hadn't needed quite as much pressure to do what her father demanded. *I'm already damned,* she'd thought. *What does it matter now?*

"Briac's a monster," he told her. "He could have picked easier assignments, something more fair. He was trying to break you, hurt you."

"I wanted to be a *Seeker*—"

"Quin—you aren't the first Seeker to kill to survive. Where do you think my grandfather's wealth comes from? Where does your estate come from?"

"That's what Briac said!"

"But it's not what Briac did!" John yelled. "Killing for money, restoring your fortunes—that's surviving. Every house must do it from time to time. My mother did, when she had to. She picked assignments she could live with, killed . . . as fairly as she could, people who deserved what she did. But your father, those others—they kill anyone. And they killed *us*. Do you understand? Whole families of Seekers. Children, mothers, fathers. For no reason but jealousy, they've tried to stamp my house to nothing. And for that . . . can't you see I have to make that right?"

They were not striking each other anymore. They had both allowed their swords to fall to their sides, and they were both breathing hard. She didn't know the history John seemed to know. Briac had shared none of it with her.

"So . . . it's all right to kill?" she asked him, hearing the disbelief in her own voice. "As long as you select an acceptable victim? Or as long as you're killing for revenge? It's all right if the swords aren't turned against you?"

"I—I didn't choose this life, Quin. It was chosen for me. I will make the best decisions I can. I will try to be fair. But I've promised—"

"John, do you hear yourself? Do you think you can kill people and it won't change you? You think you can pick someone who deserves to die and that will make it all right? It doesn't work like that."

"I know our lives are harsh—"

"I wanted to do something good," she said, cutting him off. She was exhausted. "It was so simple when I was a little girl."

"You *can* do something good. The athame lets us decide—where we go, what we do. It *is* good."

The sun was behind John, casting him into shadow, but for the first time, Quin was seeing him clearly. She had been training with her father in the hope of doing something honorable with her life. It was all she'd wanted, even if the hope had been false. John thought he wanted the same thing—a noble purpose, justice—but he'd already seen Briac's path, and he was willing to set his feet upon it. He was like a sword that had been bent at the moment it was forged. Such a blade will always be bent, as John's heart was bent by the life and the death of the mother he'd never wanted to speak about. At this moment, he was still the John she had known, but he wouldn't stay that way if she helped him now.

"No," she told him, shaking her head. "It's not good."

Using the last of her strength, Quin struck at him suddenly with her whipsword, aiming for his injured side. He was caught by surprise and blocked the blow poorly, his left arm weak. She pressed her advantage, grabbing both ends of her sword and pushing at his blade. John lost his balance for a moment, and on reflex, Quin hooked one of his feet with her own and sent him sprawling. He slid down the roof toward its edge, dislodging a huge sheet of slate as he went. By the time he got a solid hold on the roof and stopped his descent, half his body hung out over the cliff.

Quin moved to grab him, worried he would fall, but she saw his grip on the roof was firm, and he was already pulling himself up.

Quin!

She turned in time to see an object arcing through the air. It was the lightning rod, the one John had taken from her. The Young Dread was throwing her the lightning rod. Only after Quin caught it did she realize the Young had not actually called her name aloud. It had been shouted directly into her head, and she had heard it.

She drew her athame from her waistband. She now recognized all of the symbols on the haft, and she made a quick adjustment to the dials.

Below her, John was clawing his way to a safer part of the roof, away from the cliff. In a moment, he'd be back on his feet.

She struck the athame and lightning rod together, and a vibration washed over her. She ran to the edge, just above the cliff, and looked all the way to the river below. Then she reached down with the athame and drew a circle in the air. The dagger cut an opening, hovering below her, the black-and-white fabric of its edges pulsing and growing solid as she watched.

John was pulling himself to the peak of the roof as Quin leapt off the far end of the building. Her stomach lurched as she began to fall, her hair whipped by the cold breeze coming up the cliff. Far below her, she could see the swiftly flowing river pressed up against the steep rock face. Her body told her she had just jumped to her death. But she was falling into the anomaly, and a moment later, she had crossed its threshold and was not falling at all.

She turned. Above her was the opening she'd cut in space, and through it she could see the barn roof against the sky. At the edge of that roof stood John, looking devastated. He moved a few steps back, preparing to leap, but the circle was already starting to unravel, the threads hissing back together. John stopped himself at the edge, as the doorway closed above Quin, plunging her into darkness.

CHAPTER 47

JOHN

It was too late to jump. The yawning hole hovering in midair below the barn roof was collapsing. John watched as its edges lost shape. Like threads sticking out of torn cloth, thin arms of black and white were growing across the center, vibrating with energy as they stitched themselves back together. After a few moments the hole was gone.

Quin had left him again, just as she had that night on the estate, when she'd taken Yellen through another dark doorway. She'd looked back at John then, but she'd been calling for Shinobu, not him. It might be she would never choose him. This realization sat heavily in his chest as he stared down the cliff to the river.

His mind went through her last moments on the roof, before she'd jumped. She had hit the athame against that other blade. It was clearly the athame's mate, equally important for traveling *There*. Why had his mother never mentioned that second object to him? The answer was simple: *She'd been bleeding to death in the middle of the living room. There had been no time for details.*

John walked away from the roof's edge, bringing the Young Dread into sight on the ground below.

"You helped her. I thought you would help me."

The girl had been watching Quin's escape, but now she turned her eyes to meet his own. She said nothing.

"Where is the justice of the Dreads?" he asked her, his anger rising again. "You could have killed me in the woods, but you didn't. You know I'm in the right, and yet you let her take the athame that should be mine. Why?"

There was a look of uncertainty on the Young Dread's face, but still she didn't speak. She was staring up at him as if deciding her next move.

From its hiding place inside his jacket, he pulled out the other athame, the one he'd removed from the cloak of the Big Dread. This dagger was different than the one Quin had taken. It was smaller, for one thing, perhaps ten inches long, and looked delicate in comparison. There was something dissimilar about the dials as well, wasn't there? There seemed to be more of them, each slender and interlocking perfectly with the others. And at the very base of the dagger, instead of a carving of an animal, there was a pattern of three ovals.

John moved the dials in turn, tracing the outline of the symbols carved upon each face. Each symbol was a place, perhaps, or a possibility, and together the possibilities were nearly infinite.

The sound of twigs snapping jolted him from his reverie. Two figures were walking among the trees, just now emerging into the clearing. The first was the Big Dread. He moved with long, awkward strides, a hitch at the beginning and end of each, as though the joints of his body might grind to a halt at any moment.

The second figure was the old man, who must, John thought, be a third Dread, the Old Dread. As John watched, this man took a very slow step, the entire motion occurring at glacial speed, then this was followed by several steps so rapid that he momentarily outpaced the other Dread. Then the process repeated, and he fell behind again as he took another slow step.

Together the two men gave the impression of a cinema reel running at inconsistent speeds. Once they had cleared the trees and seen John on the roof, however, they shifted simultaneously to a new and almost blinding pace and were, all at once, right beneath the barn.

"No nearer," John called down to them, holding their athame in clear view. "Or I will break it."

The Old Dread was closest to him, examining John with eyes that seemed to look straight through him at the distant clouds beyond.

There was a long pause as the man gathered his voice. Then the words came out of him in a steady stream, like a chant: "That would be bad for everyone."

"Mostly it would be bad for you," John said. "Please back away."

The Dreads did not move.

The Young Dread spoke up now. "An athame is difficult to destroy," she told him.

"It's stone, isn't it?" He looked around, moving nearer to the roof edge overhanging the drop to the river below. "Even stone will break if thrown far enough."

John now noticed the Big Dread had a wound across his chest that was dripping blood, but the man was ignoring it. The Big Dread's face, as he stared up at John, looked like a statue carved to illustrate the emotion of hatred.

"Perhaps," the Old Dread agreed. "Or perhaps not. You would be foolish to try. The object you hold is the only one of its kind."

John waved the athame above the drop. "Not the only. Quin has another one."

"No," the Old Dread said. "Similar, but not the same. The one you hold is special."

As John looked again at the stone dagger in his hand, he noticed a separate piece, a long, slender blade of stone. Cleverly designed, it was fitted along the athame's blade so perfectly they seemed at first glance to be one. Yet when he pressed downward on it with his thumb, the slender piece slid free.

The Middle Dread made a jerking motion, and all at once, there was a knife in his hand. Even in his half-woken and injured state, the man, John understood, could kill him quite easily. Yet the Old Dread signaled the Middle to stop.

"Do you value your life?" the Young Dread asked him.

"Do *you* value my life?" he asked her. "First you help me, and then you work against me. Aren't you allowed to make up your own mind?"

"If you value your life," she said, ignoring his words, "you will not use the tools in your hands. Without training, they will end you quickly, and when they do, you will lose the athame and lightning rod somewhere under the ocean or in the fiery heart of a mountain. We will never recover them."

John tapped the athame and the other object—the lightning rod, she'd called it—together gently, still holding them both above the drop to the river. Immediately, a low vibration began. He could feel it running through his lungs and heart, altering his breathing and heartbeat. It was in his ears as well, distorting other sounds. He pulled the athame and rod apart and waited for the vibration to die out. It took nearly a minute to do so, unsettling him the whole while. And this was from a gentle tap. What was it like when you struck them together for real?

The Young Dread was right—even with an athame in his hands, he could do nothing without training.

Quin had refused him. She didn't want to help, and he didn't want to force her. And yet there were only a few people in the world who could show him how to use the tools of a Seeker. Briac Kincaid was one, but he would die before helping John. The Young Dread should help him, but she had just shown that she would not. So, Quin. It always came back to Quin.

Carefully he slid the lightning rod back into its slot on the athame's blade until he heard it click into place. Then he drew his whipsword and cracked it out into solid form.

"You would fight the Dreads?" the Middle asked him, finally breaking his silence.

"Do I have a choice?" John responded.

The Old Dread made a tiny motion with his hands again, which seemed to say, *Leave this to me.* He brought his eyes back to John. "Return our athame and we will not harm you," the old man said.

John could almost believe that the Old Dread meant it. He glanced toward the Young Dread. She was impossible to read, but he sensed she would follow the old one. Then he looked again at the Middle. In that man's face, he saw nothing but his own death. He was quite sure that this Dread, and others like him, were the ones who had all but eradicated his house. John made up his mind.

"Thank you for your kind words," he said.

With that, he threw the athame as hard as he could over the cliff. The dagger flew end over end through the air, then began a downward arc out of sight.

The Old Dread's arms whipped up, pointing toward the falling athame in a gesture that ordered the other two to follow it. He needn't have bothered—the Young and the Middle were already racing toward the edge of the cliff, searching for a path to the river below.

The Old Dread turned his eyes back to John, but he moved no

closer. John didn't wait to see what else the old man might do. He ran to the edge of the roof farthest from the cliff. From there, he lowered himself and dropped to the ground. It was a long way down, but he landed well. Scrambling to his feet, he sprinted toward the woods without looking back.

PART THREE

WHERE ALL ROADS LEAD

CHAPTER 48

SHINOBU

"I'm not running errands for you," Shinobu said, elbowing his way through the crowd on the main Bridge thoroughfare. A few people turned to stare at him. "Does it look like I'm speaking to you?" he barked at them. When they turned away, a few frightened, more of them annoyed, he began muttering again. "Still on the Bridge, still running your errands. You promised me I'd be rid of you. Yet here I am."

He was, in point of fact, speaking to Quin, though some part of him realized she was not actually present. He hadn't bothered using the air mask that hung at the exit of the opium bar, and he was weaving dangerously between other pedestrians as he made his way toward Quin's front door.

When he saw her house swimming crookedly across his field of view, looming among many such buildings in the middle section of the Bridge, he made an effort to steady himself. The Bridge authorities didn't look kindly on intoxicated visitors walking around outside their designated areas.

"You've always taken me for granted," he told Quin. His words were rather blurry, but since Quin was absent from the conversation, he was fairly sure she wouldn't mind. "Asking for what you need. 'Find my mother.' 'Save me from being killed.' 'Give me a shower.' What about what I need?"

He lurched to a stop at Quin's door and rested his head against the wood for a moment, just to help him stay upright. Then he knocked softly. *What do I need?* he wondered. After all, Quin had only asked him to let her mother know that she was all right. He'd done that days ago. But he'd continued staying at Quin's house.

The door he was leaning against was abruptly pulled open, startling Shinobu, who had forgotten that he'd knocked. He fell through the doorway into Fiona's arms, ending up down on one knee, with Fiona pulling him up by his shirt. She didn't look very steady on her feet either.

"What about what I need?" he said to her.

"What do you need, Shinobu?" Fiona asked him. Her red hair was disheveled, hanging loose about her face. "Tell me."

She got the door closed behind him, pulled Shinobu through the front room, and eased him down into a chair in Quin's examination room, nearly losing her balance as she did so. The treatment table had been turned into a bed, with sheets and blankets, and Brian Kwon was lying there, much like a baby whale, still recovering from his injuries.

"What do I need?" Shinobu repeated, trying to remember how he had gotten from the front door to the chair. "I need . . ." He wasn't sure. It was something to do with Quin. He remembered her body pushed up against his, his arms around her. He could still feel the imprint she had left upon him.

"You don't need opium, that's sure," Fiona commented, her words slurring a bit. "You've had more than enough of that."

He focused his eyes with great effort, looking around the dimly lit room with its shelves of herbs, and the giant form of Brian studying him from the bed.

"Only two pipes," Shinobu told her.

"Your body tells a different tale."

"It might have been twelve. A number with a two in it. Maybe twenty or twenty-two point two. Two hundred twenty-two . . ."

"Hmm," Fiona said. She moved into the kitchen, attempting to tie her hair back as she did so. Then she busied herself making tea.

Brian was propping himself up on an elbow. "Be nice to her," he said. "She's . . . not feeling well."

"She's drunk."

It had been three days since the fight on the lower levels, and the nasty cut on Brian's shoulder was healing. His many broken ribs were wrapped tightly in a fashion that made him look like an enormous Chinese sausage.

"Sorry I didn't bring you any, Sea Bass," Shinobu said, assuming his failure to bring home drugs was why Brian was looking at him disapprovingly. "You know they don't let you take pipes out of the bar. You must be dying for something."

"I'm invited to Master Tan's house for dinner," Brian told him. "He says I can start walking more today."

"Well, don't expect any opium from him."

Brian wasn't laughing. "I'm not looking for opium. I have my tea."

"Whatever you say, Sea Bass."

Brian grimaced and swung his legs off the bed, so he was sitting on the edge. Very carefully he lowered one foot to the floor and then the other. His grimace deepened as he put his full weight onto his feet. But after a few moments in a vertical position he seemed all right.

"Not too bad today," he muttered.

Shinobu watched him hobble across the room to his clothes,

which were clean and folded on a nearby chair. With what looked like tremendous difficulty, Brian began pulling his shirt over his head. This involved many Chinese swearwords.

"Would you like some help?" Shinobu asked.

"I would not," Brian responded. "You'd end up breaking more of my ribs."

"That's probably true."

Fiona returned with tea, which she forced into Shinobu's hands, sloshing some of it over the rim. With her help, Brian finally got all of his clothes on, shoes included, though Fiona seemed to make the process take longer. When he was dressed, Brian placed his feet gingerly one in front of the other and walked out of the room.

"Since you're up now, I'll bring you down to the lower levels tonight," Shinobu called after him. "What do you say? Fiona can't keep us locked up here forever."

"What do you mean 'locked up'?" Brian called back. "She doesn't even want you here. You just keep showing up."

"So you'll come with me?"

"I'm done with opium."

"Fine—I was thinking Ivan3 tonight anyway."

Brian ignored him. With a jingle of bells, the front door opened, and before it swung shut, Shinobu heard him breathing heavily and cursing again as he walked off.

"Tea. Now," Fiona ordered, pushing it toward his face.

Shinobu took a sip and then spit it back into the cup. It was one of those healthy concoctions Master Tan had been making for Brian.

"Where's your tea?" he asked her.

Fiona looked daggers at him. She had put her hair up, but a large portion was still hanging down along one side of her face. "You will drink that tea or you will leave this house. And hopefully be arrested on your way off the Bridge."

"Is it only tea for opium addicts? Not alcoholics?" It seemed ridiculous for her to lecture him when she was too drunk to stand up straight.

"You've no need to call me that," she said, making an attempt to speak clearly. "If I have a little something from time to time, whose business is that? You fill your body with all sorts of nasty things."

"It's the same," he protested.

"It is not."

"Your poison comes in a bottle. Mine comes in a pipe, or sticks, or needles. That's the only difference."

"It is *not* the same." She was busying herself by making Brian's bed, but the sheets were not cooperating. "You don't see what I see. You don't listen to things you'd rather not hear, do you?"

"I listen to things I'd rather not hear all the time," he retorted. "Come visit my mother with me, and I'll show you."

"Your mother?" she asked, confused for a moment. Then she grabbed back on to her train of thought: "Do you have a daughter, Shinobu? A daughter who's hidden her past but sees things in her dreams? What if when she sees those things, there's the chance you'll see them also? That you'll know exactly the sorts of things she's done? What sorts of things I've let her do?"

Shinobu watched Fiona as she finished making the bed. Strands of red hair continued to fall down around her face, but she was getting less drunk by the moment.

"You get to see what's on the surface," she went on. "You've never been married to Briac Kincaid, have you? If you had been, you wouldn't want to see inside his mind, I promise you. You might have a few drinks to make the world nicer."

Shinobu had no answer for her. She might be a drunkard, but . . . wasn't she trying to be a good mother to Quin? He was still dizzy, so he obediently began to sip at the revolting tea.

There was a brisk knock on the front door. Fiona composed herself and walked out of the back room to answer it. Moments later, Shinobu heard official-sounding voices requesting access to the house. They were looking for a few young men who had been involved in a disturbance on the lower levels of the Bridge earlier in the week.

He could hear Fiona, in a calm and reasonable voice, her words hardly slurred at all, asking why they had chosen her house. Shinobu didn't wait to hear the response. The idea that he might be arrested by the Bridge authorities sent him into a panic. Bridge officials were very strict, and though they couldn't put him in jail, they could easily cut off his access to drugs—perhaps permanently.

He launched himself to his feet and went quietly up the stairs and out the balcony door. He never heard what was said next, because by the time he saw Fiona again, he was up in the rafters above her house, looking down at the Bridge thoroughfare from a dark perch inaccessible to anyone but a sewer rat like himself. His heart continued to beat frantically for a while. Being banned from the Bridge would make life quite unpleasant.

It was from this vantage point in the rafters that he watched Fiona leaving her house, still walking a bit unsteadily. She was surrounded by several men, two of whom had their arms linked with hers, almost like they were forcing Fiona to walk away with them. As he crouched in his hiding place and observed them moving out of sight, a small thought tickled at the back of his mind: *That's odd*.

It was not until his opium fuzziness disappeared, hours later, that he realized several things. First, the men who had taken Fiona were not officials from the Bridge at all—they'd had no uniforms. Second, one of the men walking with Fiona had been John. Third, Shinobu had been staying at Fiona's house with the idea of protecting her (though he hadn't wanted to admit it), but he had soaked himself in drugs and had run away at the slightest hint of danger—not even danger to himself but to his ready supply of intoxicating substances.

These three things made something else quite clear: he, Shinobu MacBain, former Seeker, current Scottish-Japanese salvage diver and opium addict, might tell himself he was still a good person, but he was, in fact, a completely worthless human being. He made the wrong choices when it mattered most, and others were left to pay: victims dead on his assignments with Briac, Akio nearly killed, his father ravaged by those dancing sparks, and now Fiona captured, right under his nose.

CHAPTER 49

MAUD

The sun was setting. Pain bloomed in the Young Dread's cheek as the Middle struck her across the face. She fell to her knees by the fire they had built near the ruins of the castle. She had chosen not to block the blow.

"Why did you help the girl?" the Middle asked. Before she could get up, he pushed her with his foot, sending her back to the ground. He was examining her as though she were a rat he was planning to slice apart very slowly.

"There is no need for anger," her master said.

Her master was on the other side of the fire, tending to Briac Kincaid. Since coming fully awake, Briac had been in agony. The Old Dread had dug the bullets from Briac's wounds, a procedure accompanied by great amounts of screaming. The Old was now packing the wounds with herbs they had gathered, and was binding them tightly with strips of cloth, while Briac continued to moan and thrash about.

She and the Middle had climbed down the steep path that led from the barn at the top of the cliff to the riverbank below. There, she had swum across to the far shore, where the athame had landed in thick silt, unharmed. Now they were by the ruined castle, where she had trained a hundred times over many hundreds of years, as the castle slowly fell to pieces and was swallowed by grass and soil.

The Middle Dread controlled his voice and asked again, "Why did you help the girl?"

She pulled herself up into a sitting position and wiped the blood from the corner of her mouth.

"She is not a *girl*," the Young Dread told the Middle. "She is a sworn Seeker, the last possessor of her family's athame, and she was in danger. Why would I not help her?"

Gently her master said, "Briac Kincaid is the oldest of their house. He considers he has a claim on the dagger."

"We believe the athame ends up with whom it belongs, do we not?" she retorted.

With great effort, Briac pulled himself to a sitting position and looked at her across the fire. She saw only hatred in his hard eyes.

"No," he said. "You interfered and gave her the lightning rod. You allowed her to leave with something that was mine." He was fighting to control his voice through the pain. "The Dreads must retrieve it for me."

"Do you understand?" the Middle asked her. "You have made an error. Because of that error, we must now recover Briac Kincaid's athame and set things right."

Again, the Middle Dread was coming to the aid of Briac Kincaid, bending the rules to suit him. The Young Dread wondered anew what secrets Briac was keeping for the Middle, what power Briac held over him. She herself knew of many unjust acts by the Middle, but Briac must know of more. She would wager that quite a few of those acts had been done by both together.

"Set things right?" the Young Dread scoffed. "Master, what is this word he uses?"

The Old Dread regarded her across the firelight, but said nothing.

"Are you a Dread?" the Middle asked. "Feared by Seekers for your justice? You have made an error and must correct it."

"And you?" she asked. "Will you see to justice?"

He struck out at her with his heavy hand, but this time the Young did not wish to be hit. She moved aside, twisting sinuously away from him. Without conscious thought, her knife was in her hand, like magic. Her arm flashed out at the Middle. It clashed with his own knife, which had appeared in his hand. Both blades glowed orange in the firelight.

"Enough," the Old Dread said.

The Young and the Middle froze, holding their blades still, but they did not put them away.

"Am I a person, Master?" she asked.

"A needless question, child," he answered.

"Am I a person, or a possession?" she demanded. "Do I have a will?"

"You have a will," her master said.

"You gave me into the care of the Middle and told me to obey him."

"Is that what I said, child?" The Old Dread's words were soft.

Her knife struck out. The Middle met it with his own. Then his left hand stabbed forward, another knife suddenly appearing there.

The Middle had properly bandaged the wound across his chest, but he was still injured, and the Young hoped this would give her an advantage. She thrust her body to the side and slipped away, pulling a second knife from a sheath at her waist.

"The oath of the Dreads: to uphold the three laws and to stand apart from humanity, so our heads are clear to judge," she said. "Master, do you know what happened to the Young Dread before me?"

The Middle slashed out at her with both hands. She blocked his weapons.

The Old Dread did not respond.

"Do you know what happened to the Young Dread before me?" she asked again. "And to John's mother? Has the Middle told you that? It is always *my* oath of which he speaks. What about his own?"

The Middle made no reply. The Young Dread's master, sitting on the other side of the fire, was equally silent. The Old Dread was regarding her quietly, and the Young Dread realized her master knew, or at least suspected, the things the Middle Dread had done in his absence. How could he not? He read the Young's mind as easily as he breathed. He must see inside the Middle's mind as well.

She had been overjoyed to find her master on the estate, sure that he would finally make things right with the Middle. But he knew what the Middle was, it seemed, and did nothing to stop him. In a flash of understanding, she realized the Old, her good master, was tied to the Middle somehow.

But she was not.

"Let me kill him!" she said.

There was no response from her master. And at this moment, his silence in itself meant something. If the Old Dread did not order them to stop, there was nothing to prevent her. She could remove the Middle from her life. She could repay him for so many injustices . . .

Her body moved into full battle speed. Her knives streaked through the air, orange arcs in the firelight. The Middle responded too slowly. He was not fully back to himself after his long stay *There*. She thrust forward. Then she saw her mistake.

He had maneuvered her onto uneven ground. She was losing her balance. In one swift motion, he yanked the knife from her hand and hit her ear with its pommel, sending her sprawling to the dirt.

Before she could recover, he stepped on her left wrist, pinning that hand and its knife to the ground. Then he leaned down and ripped the front of her shirt, tearing it carefully from her neck to her stomach and throwing the cloth aside. Her small breasts were exposed. She reached with her right arm to cover herself, but he stepped on that wrist as well. He was standing over her, staring down at her nakedness with a look of disgust. He bent over so his face was near hers and pinched one of her breasts hard. He smiled when an expression of pain moved across her face.

"Not a woman yet," he said evenly. "You are a little girl. A Dread only because we lack someone better, because your master knows that you are not worth the time to kill."

He stared down at her for several seconds, letting her know that she was at his mercy. Then he stepped away.

The Young Dread pulled her cloak around her, but she did not move from the cold earth. Anger and humiliation held her motionless for a long while.

Much later, the Young Dread still sat where the Middle had knocked her down, her cloak tight about her, covering the tatters of her clothing. She was rocking back and forth, but when she became aware of her motion, she stopped. She would control her hatred. She would be perfectly still.

Briac had fallen into a troubled sleep, his moans dying out, to be replaced with mumbled words in his dreams. The Middle Dread had wrapped himself in his cloak and lay near the fire, his eyes closed.

The Young's eyes were transfixed by the Middle now, watching his chest rise and fall. His heart was somewhere inside that chest, beating away, keeping him alive. *Until it stops beating,* she thought.

And yet, her master had done nothing to help her kill the Middle Dread. Perhaps he had allowed her to fight him only to teach her a lesson—a lesson that the Middle would always beat her and that she should obey.

Gentle hands were probing the side of her head, touching the ear the Middle had damaged with the knife hilt. The skin was split, that much she could feel.

"This is not bad," the Old Dread said as he examined the wound in the firelight. A moment later, she felt cool relief as he rubbed a poultice of herbs into the injury.

"Let me see the other," he told her. "The wound he pretends he did not give you."

The Young unwound her cloak and allowed him to examine the scar along the side of her abdomen, where the Middle had stabbed her. The tissue was thick and ropy under her skin, but the lines of the wound were fading. The medicine of this time had done strange things to her flesh, allowing it to heal almost perfectly. The Old Dread's fingers traced the thin scar.

"He is cruel," he said at last.

"He is cruel. And you have left me in his charge."

"He is mine," her master told her. "I have created him as he is. He fights well, for poor reasons. He kills unnecessarily and often. And he makes mistakes—such as traveling *There* with an injury serious enough to divert his attention. He might have been lost *between* forever."

The Young kept her face neutral as she considered this possibility.

Her master continued, "But there are things I have promised—" He stopped. "I am sorry you must live in his presence."

Let me kill him, then! she wanted to scream. Out loud, she whispered, "What happened to our noble purpose, Master?" It was the question Quin had asked, but it had been the Young Dread's own question for hundreds of years.

The Old did not answer immediately. His thoughts seemed to fold in upon themselves.

"The athame was meant to allow a great mind, a skillful mind, to move beyond the boundaries of human life," he said eventually, in a low and solemn voice. "Why should such a mind be bound to one location? If he could move freely, act freely, imagine what he could accomplish. A Seeker, using an athame, could appear anywhere— inside a guarded fortress, in the private chambers of a king, in a great university on the other side of the world. And so he could . . . help fate. He could seek the best way for mankind, could he not? It was my belief that great minds with the proper tools could change history." His eyes turned to her. There was almost a pleading in them. "We saw some of those changes ourselves. Seekers have determined the course of great battles, toppled tyrants . . ."

"But that is not all they have done, Master."

His eyes took in the campsite and the remains of the fire. "No," he agreed. "Some have used the athame for greed and spite and revenge."

"More than some."

"We have laws." They were words of protest, but his voice sounded hollow, as though it had been drained of life.

"You speak . . . as though we began with you," she said. "As though the athame came from you. Is it so?"

The Young turned her head slightly to watch one side of the Old Dread's mouth pull into a half smile.

"The athame . . . It's origin is a tale for a future time, child. If I am the first, I am also the last. But which side of our history is the beginning? Which is the end? Between now and the end—or the beginning," he went on, "I must spend much of my time asleep, stretched out, trying to remain alive in order to set things right. Our bodies are not intended for the things we Dreads make them do. There are seasons to our lives. When we defy them, we are not well. I have been woken too early again. It is always too early. I fear I would need a thousand years of sleep to catch up. But I do not have so long. We will set things right here, and I will stretch myself out again."

Silence fell between them, until the Young Dread finally dared ask, "Were you a great mind, Master?"

A real smile crossed his face. "You don't ask if I *am* a great mind, child? Because I speak gibberish now? Let me tell you—I once thought I was a great mind."

"And now?"

"Now it does not matter. Great minds are not what's wanted. Only good hearts. Good hearts choose wisely."

"How does one find a good heart?"

"It is luck, child. Always luck. With you, I have been very lucky."

CHAPTER 50

SHINOBU

"What makes you think I would give you such a thing?" Master Tan asked Shinobu. He was standing at a table in his office, grinding up a bright green plant with a mortar and pestle, his hands moving with the sure motions of an expert, his eyes free to study his shamefaced visitor.

"Our lives are a choice," Shinobu said. "I heard you say that to Quin."

"When did I say that?" With two fingers he tested the consistency of the plant, then continued to work it with the pestle.

"You know."

"Ah," Master Tan said, remembering. "Perhaps I did say it then. It was an eventful evening. Of course, she chose life."

The man was ancient, with gnarled hands that were both strong and soft, yet his face was almost unlined. He was staring at Shinobu with interest, as he might have studied a new herb for sale in the Kowloon market.

"You would have let her die if she wanted. You gave her the choice," Shinobu insisted stubbornly. "I heard you."

"Is that what you think? I am always letting people die?" the old man asked, as though fascinated with the idea. "Is that why so many come to see me in my shop? Because I am such an easy path to the undertaker?"

"You like to help people, old man," Shinobu responded, his voice low and sullen. "You should help me and give me what I'm asking for. I have . . ." He was going to say, *I have let good people down when it counted, and furthermore, I'm a killer.* But he couldn't make those particular words come out. They died somewhere in his throat before they were anywhere near the surface—just as his admission about Alistair in the disruptor field had died in his throat before he could tell his mother.

He had no wish to argue with the man. He had already decided what he needed to do, and he was experiencing a sense of peace at the dark inevitability of what was to come. *I should have done this a year ago,* he thought.

He stared at his feet, tried another tack. "I will not be missed, Master Tan, except by the owners of the drug bars—and they won't miss me much. They ask me to bathe, and I almost never do."

"What sorts of drugs, typically?" Master Tan asked with interest. "The ones you like to take—what sorts? Opium? Ivan3? Which drug bars will miss you the most?"

"What does it matter?" These questions were disturbing his even temper. He didn't want to talk anymore.

"I don't do this sort of thing every day. I have to have a reason to help you. Please explain how bad you've been. Which sorts of drugs?"

With a sigh, Shinobu came up with a long list. Master Tan patiently wrote everything down, all the while shaking his head and mumbling comments like "Terrible, terrible. Cigarettes as well? My, my. Vodka? Really, young man . . ."

Eventually, Shinobu felt they were getting off track. His hands shoved deep in his pockets, he said, "Look, I . . . My father . . ." He stopped, tried again: "My mother and brother and Fiona. I . . . want to protect them. This will protect them. Can you help me do one thing without failing?"

"Tell me. This one thing—killing yourself—it will fix the other things?"

Shinobu shrugged. "I can't fix those things. They're done. But I can stop everyone from relying on me. I can keep myself from wrecking things again. Because I *will* wreck them. Can you understand?"

Master Tan continued to study him in silence for some moments, as though weighing his decision.

"I'm afraid you do make a good argument," he said at last. "I won't try to stop you."

Shinobu, who had been looking at his shoes, was a little disappointed by the sudden agreement. But it was, after all, what he had hoped for.

The old man set down the mixture he'd been working on and moved to the enormous cabinet that stretched all the way to the room's vaulted ceiling. This cabinet was full of tiny drawers, more than a thousand of them, each labeled with Chinese characters. Master Tan accessed the drawers with a rolling ladder, which he pushed back and forth as he moved up and down, filling a large plastic bag. Every time Shinobu thought he was finished, Master Tan remembered something else and went back up. After nearly half an hour, the bag was almost overflowing. The healer was humming under his breath as he added the last ingredient and stepped off the ladder.

"I could have died of boredom faster," Shinobu muttered. He was grateful for Master Tan's help, but the man's cheerfulness was really getting on his nerves. Was it too much to ask for the healer to be a bit upset about the situation?

Still humming faintly, Master Tan walked past Shinobu and began to brew a tea with the heap of herbs.

"It is my wish that you *not* kill yourself," he told Shinobu, as though discussing the weather. "Actually, it doesn't matter much to me. But the medical authorities of the Transit Bridge require me to say that I would prefer you *didn't* kill yourself. It looks bad if healers are openly helping people commit suicide. I'm sure you can understand."

Shinobu nodded.

Soon the tea was ready and Master Tan was pouring it into a large thermos.

"You must drink this all at once," he said, "leaving no evidence for someone to find. I suggest you go somewhere quiet and safe, but near city waste disposal facilities. Perhaps a dumpster? Then your corpse will be easy to handle. And do it soon—the tea will not stay potent for long."

Shinobu snatched the thermos from Master Tan, and a very short while later he had it clutched to his chest as he worked his way outward along the Bridge's steel girders. He was near the Kowloon side and from his current position could see the lights of the city glowing through a deep fog off to his right. As he walked along a narrow beam, traveling away from the heart of the Bridge toward the edges of its structure, he began to see the water far below. It was inky dark tonight beneath the fog.

"'It is my wish that you *not* kill yourself,' he says as he scoops out the poisonous herbs," Shinobu said to himself. "He couldn't wait to get rid of me. You've sunk as low as you can go when a *healer* wants you gone."

The harbor was not as deep here as it was in the center of the Bridge. Shallower water would be better, he thought. They would find his body quickly, and his mother would not be left wondering what had happened to him. True, a dumpster would allow Mariko to be notified sooner, but jumping was insurance—two simultaneous methods of death were better than one. And he preferred not to die in a dumpster, no matter how charming Master Tan seemed to find the idea.

When Shinobu reached the end of the girder, he took a seat and let his feet dangle over the edge. Carefully unscrewing the top of the thermos, he sniffed the tea and gagged. It gave off an awful aroma and was nearly as thick as molasses. It was too bad this would be the last thing he ever tasted. He should have bought an ice cream cone to eat after drinking it. *I'll have to plan better the next time I kill myself,* he thought. *Ha ha.*

He looked down below his feet to ensure he had a clear path to the water—he didn't fancy bouncing off steel beams on his way down. The girder upon which he sat stuck out farther than its neighbors; below him were a hundred and fifty feet of empty air. Perfect.

There was no point in delaying. If he hesitated, he would change his mind, and he would end up betraying someone else—probably Quin this time. He refused to do that. *Now that I've found you, Quin, I can't trust myself to stay away.*

Shinobu plugged his nose and gulped down the contents of the thermos without stopping for a breath.

The effects were immediate. His stomach cramped so suddenly and so intensely, he doubled over and had to grab for the edge of the beam to avoid pitching off.

When the first round of cramps eased up, he crawled to his feet. He was beginning to shake. Violently. Another fit of cramping hit him, and it was all he could do to stay upright.

Propping himself up against another girder, he stripped down to his underwear. Then he threw away the empty thermos and his clothes, and several moments later heard a splash distantly below him.

His body was shaking and cramping so fiercely by now that he was forced to move his feet just an inch at a time, worried that he would lose his balance before he was ready. Finally he reached the farthest point of the beam and his toes were hanging off the edge. He took a deep breath, ready for the end.

And he jumped.

His stomach leapt up into his throat; adrenaline rushed into his veins. He was falling! He was going to die!

It was a long way down. Long enough for him to watch the steel skeleton of the Bridge flying by. Long enough to watch the dark water racing up to meet him through the fog. He had intended to hit the harbor in a flat belly flop, which would have killed him instantly. Instead, as he plummeted to the water, instinct took over. He had, in fact, jumped off bridges before—for fun. Unintentionally, he hit the water in a perfectly vertical stance, feetfirst, and he sliced down through the surface like a cliff jumper showing off for tourists.

His backup plan was to hit bottom so violently that he was killed by the second impact. Unfortunately, he was mistaken about the water under this portion of the Bridge. It might have been shallower here than it was at the center, but by the time he stopped plunging through its depths, he still hadn't reached the bottom. A few moments after jumping, Shinobu found himself alive, deep beneath the surface, with all limbs intact. The cold was a shock, but it was also making his stomach feel better.

His diving experience told him his body would soon force him to inhale, but right now, because he'd taken a breath before impact, he had half a minute of air left in his lungs, maybe more. So instead of surfacing, he dove deeper, swimming blindly down.

Stroke after powerful stroke, Shinobu pulled himself forward, and something strange was happening, something more than the terror and adrenaline of the jump. His stomach was twisting itself into knots and his muscles were shivering, but a more powerful sensation than either of these was taking over. His body was *humming*.

That was an odd word, yet it seemed to fit. He kept swimming toward the bottom, and as he did, it felt as though every cell were vibrating of its own accord, and in doing so they were shaking loose all sorts of things, some physical, some not.

First, the drug haze that had lain upon him for the last year and a half was rattled out of his head. As his arms pulled him through the dark water, he experienced a mental sharpness he hadn't felt in ages. Next his heart was shaken into furious motion, and it began to pump blood wildly, like a guerrilla warrior firing a machine gun on New Year's Eve. Shinobu's lungs began to complain, but he was still moving deeper.

Finally, memories started to shake loose:

He was on the estate, by the barn above the cliff. He had looked everywhere for Quin, had finally realized she must be here. They had done their first assignment as Seekers the night before. His new brand, the athame burned into his wrist, was throbbing beneath its bandage. He'd been sick to his stomach for nearly twenty-four hours.

He was going to find Quin and take her away with him. He would convince her to leave the estate today, with nothing but the clothes they were wearing. They could cross the river at the base of the cliff, and make their way down the opposite shore to the nearest village.

Quin probably still loved John, but Shinobu would make her see. John was leaving. Briac was getting rid of him. She and Shinobu were the two who should be together. They could put last night behind them, put the estate behind them, go somewhere where they would never look at their parents again. And one day, when they were safely away and alone together, she would turn to him and see him differently. And he would kiss her . . .

Reaching the barn doorway, he was startled to hear voices inside. He stopped at the threshold, listening. Quin was there and John was with her. John had gotten there first.

Moving silently, Shinobu stepped into the shadows of the barn. The two of them were up in the sleeping loft. They were speaking softly, but it sounded like they might be arguing. Shinobu thought they might be breaking up. He moved along the wall, and after a few moments, he could see John, standing by the round window up on that high platform.

He would wait in the shadows. She would send John out, and when he left, Shinobu would climb the ladder and convince her. Even if he were still just her cousin, that would be all right. The two of them could make a new life.

But John did not leave. As Shinobu watched, Quin stood up and moved over to him. In a moment, John's lips were on hers and their arms were around each other.

Shinobu was in the manor house, on their first assignment. He saw Quin moving down the grand staircase, the two children from the nursery following close behind her. He knew immediately what she intended. He and Quin had already been forced to participate in killing the parents, but Quin was refusing to do more. She was taking the children away, she was helping them escape. She was defying Briac. The idea gave him strength.

Shinobu turned to look for his father. He could steal Alistair's athame and lightning rod and join Quin. With those, they could save the children and then go anywhere.

But when he looked, his father was nowhere to be found. And when he returned to the staircase, Quin was sitting with her head in her hands, and the children were gone.

Shinobu was in the commons, practicing with John. They were using ancient metal swords, and the clang of the blades echoed off the trees. Shinobu was twelve years old, and John thirteen.

Shinobu was a better fighter than John, but not by much—John had learned to fight even before coming to the estate.

John made a good parry, then struck out nicely at Shinobu. He blocked the blow, but its force was enough to drive him back a step.

"You're learning," Shinobu told him, a bit arrogantly.

"I'm stronger than you," John replied.

"But I'm faster."

He slapped John's leg with the flat of his sword, causing him to jump backward.

"You grew up here," John said. "Of course you're faster."

"My father says the estate is the best place for a Seeker to grow up. There's something in the air, in the water, in the rocks."

"Could be," John said, "but my home's safer." At that age, John was always looking for ways to appear stronger, better, or more important—anything to make up for the fact that he'd come to his training four years late.

Shinobu neatly disarmed him and sent John's sword flying into the grass. Then he let his own sword fall to his side.

"Why is your home safer?" he asked, curious now. "How could anything be safer than the estate?"

John got a look in his eyes like he'd made a mistake and wasn't supposed to be talking about this, but the temptation to brag was overwhelming.

"*Traveler* was made for me," he said, searching through the grass to retrieve his sword. "A Seeker can't get onto it. So I'll always be safe from Seekers. Anyone could come onto your estate."

"But they'd have to fight my father if they did," Shinobu said, putting a hand to his chest. "And me."

Then John found his sword and they were fighting again.

Shinobu was younger, in the commons again, sitting hidden at the edge of the meadow in grass that was nearly four feet tall. Bees were moving from flower to flower among the tall stalks, and there was a smell of honeysuckle in the air. Summer was beginning and the day was warm. Quin sat next to him cross-legged, her dark hair tied with a ribbon. They were nine years old.

Without warning, Shinobu leaned forward and kissed her on the cheek.

"Are you allowed to kiss me?" she asked, giggling.

"Why not?" he said. "Our parents are related, so we are too, and I always kiss my family. And we've started our training now, so we're practically grown up."

Quin thought about this, then leaned over and kissed him back.

"Och," he said. "That's disgusting."

"Is not."

"Aye, it is."

He kissed her again. The two of them were eating bread and honey they had snuck from Fiona's kitchen, so the kiss was a bit sticky.

Shinobu lay back, looking up at a sky framed by the tall grass. "My da says as long as there are two of you together, things are all right. My ma is dead, but there are still two of us, Father and me.

And we're two," he said, taking her hand. "You and I make two, so that's all right."

With that, Quin kissed him one more time, and this time her lips brushed against his own.

"You got my lips!" he exclaimed.

They broke apart, and each began spitting furiously on the ground.

"Why do grown-ups like it?" she asked.

"They're strange."

"Will we be strange when we grow up, do you think?"

"Definitely," he said, and he kissed her again.

Shinobu's arm struck something as he swam. He felt mud and silt squeezing through his fingers. He had reached the ocean floor. He'd arrived at the bottom of the harbor and at the beginning of his feelings for Quin.

His lungs were burning. In a few moments, his body would force him to gulp in seawater and he would drown. Yet his body had stopped shaking and his head was clear.

You bastard, he thought, *that wasn't poison at all!*

At nine years old, lying in the commons with Quin, things had been good. Perfect, really. Between then and now, there had been a long list of very bad mistakes.

If I die now, he thought, *they will always be mistakes.*

If he took in a lungful of water, he would freeze the past just as it was. But if he lived . . .

Shinobu brought his feet down against the harbor floor and pushed upward with as much force as his muscles would give. He struck up through the water, his arms pulling him, his legs kicking. His lungs were at the end of their tolerance. He would have to take a breath, even if it killed him. His body would inhale whatever was available—seawater, silt, small fish, old diapers, anything. He must breathe, he must breathe.

And then he did. He drew in a great gulp and found that his face had broken the surface and he was sucking in the foggy night air of Hong Kong.

CHAPTER 51

MAUD

They left Briac Kincaid tied and blindfolded in what had once been the castle's courtyard. The Young Dread's master had packed Briac's wounds with herbs again and given him valerian root to chew, which eased the pain a bit. He now lay half conscious beneath an overhanging bit of castle wall, moaning to himself in the morning light.

The Young Dread thought of Briac much as she thought of the Middle, and had difficulty feeling sorry for him. Even so, she was relieved when they passed down into the remains of the castle crypt, well below ground, and his cries were cut off from hearing by the earth above her.

The crypt, which still held the stone coffins of the ancient Scottish lords who had been her relatives, was half in ruins. Much of the castle floor above had crumbled, burying large portions of the space from sight. Their path, however, had been kept clear through the centuries, and this had been done by the Dreads. The Young herself had moved rocks aside a dozen times, yet she had never gone deeper than the crypt. Today she would.

The floor of the burial chamber slanted downward until it ended in what appeared to be a solid wall of rock. They followed this wall all the way to the right, and there the Middle Dread's fingers felt along one of the natural folding seams in the uneven wall. After a moment, his hand slipped into a concealed channel—a handhold disguised within the pattern of the rock. The Old helped the Young place her own hands in the correct positions, and together the three Dreads, using all of their considerable strength, rotated a large slab of rock up and away from the wall.

Behind the slab were carved steps leading down into the earth. By the light of a burning torch, they descended far beneath the crypt, with the walls of rock pressing closer the deeper they went.

At last the steps opened on a larger space and the stairway ended. They passed through a long tunnel, its ceiling an arch of rough stones just above their heads. At the far end was another wall. Camouflaged between the stacked stones of the side wall and the smooth stone of the end wall was a jagged opening just large enough for a man to squeeze through.

Following her companions, the Young Dread slipped through the tiny gap to more stairs beyond. The walls of rock and soil were closer here, so close the men ahead of her were required to walk sideways. They continued down, soil brushing against their skin. The air was ancient and close, and their torch was filling it with smoke. But it was still possible to breathe.

At last, the stairs curved around in nearly a full circle. When the steps ended, the Dreads were let out into a space so large, it could only be called a cavern. It had the appearance of a natural formation, with a ceiling of rock hanging ten yards above their heads, its surface slick and wet in the firelight. Webs of tunnels branched off from the central chamber, but the torch showed only hints of how deep and far they might go.

As the Dreads moved into the cave and the Young's eyes took in the enormous space for the first time, she became aware of a stretch of rock that had clearly been carved by human hands. There, the cavern's natural uneven surface had been worked into a smooth wall. The other Dreads were heading toward it, and as they approached, the torchlight flickered over its even stone, revealing carvings along the surface. A group of images was chiseled so deeply into the rock that they would be visible for thousands of years. Perhaps they had been there for a thousand years already.

This place must belong to the Dreads, the Young thought. She wondered how much of the Dread knowledge was still hidden from her, and then, suddenly, she thought, *How long has my master lived? He speaks of ancient things as if they were yesterday.* Was this cave his doing?

She counted ten carvings upon the wall, most depicting an animal. They were arranged in a circle, the topmost figure above her head, and the bottommost near her feet. Beneath each was a rectangular hole where a large piece of stone had been removed. Under each hole, chiseled painstakingly into the wall, was a diamond-shaped slot.

The wall threw off unexpected sparks of light when illuminated by the torch. This was not dull stone she was examining but something more precious. The torch cast an orange light, but the wall, she realized, was probably a grayish white, and luminous, like . . .

Like an athame.

The carvings began to make sense. A horse, a fox, a ram, a boar, a stag, an eagle, a bear, and two creatures more fanciful: a dragon, and a wildcat with fangs. The final carving, the one at the very top of the circle, was not an animal but three ovals, interlocking. Like a flower perhaps, but more evenly shaped.

The Young Dread knew that symbol. It was carved on the pommel of the athame of the Dreads, which at this moment was safely tucked into a pocket of her master's cloak.

"The symbol?" her master asked.

They had been silent for so long, his voice came as a shock to her. It echoed off the distant ends of the cavern.

"A fox," she replied.

"You are certain?" This from the Middle.

"I am certain. The other, the one with the eagle, was broken during the attack. I had many chances to study it." *After you abandoned me to die on the estate,* she thought but did not add aloud.

Her master drew out the athame of the Dreads and slid it into the diamond-shaped slot beneath the carved image of a fox. The athame fit precisely into the hole, gliding in smoothly up to its hilt.

The other athames she had seen were all larger than her master's, and so would not fit into the slots beneath the figures. These ten slots, then, must have been made only for this particular athame, the athame of the Dreads.

The Old and the Middle began to chant. As they did, her master drew a small metal rod from one of his many pockets. It was an object the Young had never seen before. Not for the first time, she wondered what treasures she would find if she were to empty out all the hidden contents of her master's cloak.

The Old Dread tapped the metal rod rhythmically against the stone wall, next to the protruding hilt of his athame. As the metal hit the stone, the wall itself began to vibrate.

This went on for several minutes, the Old Dread tapping the wall in time to their chant. Soon the whole cave shook, as though the earth itself had taken up the tremor. When the vibration had become unbearable, and the Young was sure that rocks were about to start falling, the chant ended. The cavern steadied and the hum of the wall gradually died out.

When will he teach me all of this? the Young Dread asked herself. *I must know these things if I am to survive, if I am to be a true Dread.*

Her master replaced the metal rod into a pocket, then drew the athame out of the stone.

"Now, child," he told her, "we wait."

CHAPTER 52

QUIN

Quin emerged into the parkland behind Victoria Peak in Hong Kong sometime in the night. She had memorized those coordinates long ago, when her father had first taught her about the athame. The Peak was, her father had explained, like a freeway for Seekers—it had easy coordinates and it was sparsely populated around the athame's entrance point, but it was close to crowds of humanity in which to quickly lose oneself and hide.

She walked her way down from the Peak, along steep and winding streets, then through tall apartment buildings and office towers and eventually down to the waterfront. From there, she walked west along the shore toward the Hong Kong Island end of the Transit Bridge. On the way, she passed a sign blinking the date and time and discovered that it was Thursday, and nearly midnight. She had lost two days again.

Entering the Bridge, its canopy of sails rising above her in the night air, she presented her hands and face to be scanned, was confirmed as a resident, then walked into the gloom, joining the foot traffic.

She found the Transit Bridge less familiar, now that her memories were back. It no longer felt as much like a home, nor quite so safe as before. There were lights on within her house, though, warmly inviting her inside. She discovered she was eager to see her mother, more eager than she had been all year. Quin was seeing things clearly now. Fiona was a casualty of Briac Kincaid, as she herself was, and Quin wanted to make up for the coldness she'd shown her mother lately. She opened the door.

"Mother? Are you here?" She heard someone in the examination room as she headed up the stairs, and she called over her shoulder, "Did Shinobu tell you I was all right? Come upstairs with me!"

She didn't wait for Fiona's response. She was chasing an image in her mind and was scared she would lose hold of it—the image of three ovals.

When she reached her bedroom, she ransacked her closet, throwing aside folded blankets and smocks from the floor. But what she was looking for wasn't there.

"Ma?" she called. "I need your help!"

She paused for a moment, reaching her mind into the strange months when she'd been new to the Bridge and this house, when she'd been recovering from the near-fatal injury in her chest. Where had she put it?

She went to her mother's bedroom and opened the wooden trunk at the foot of the bed. It was full of silk dresses, hair clips, ornate slippers—items to make Fiona a beautiful companion for the men who came to visit her on the Bridge. There were also, she was sorry to see, at least a dozen half-empty liquor bottles.

And at the very bottom was a small metal box.

"There you are," she whispered.

For a year and a half, she'd tried very hard to forget about this box and its contents. Her hands were shaking as she removed it from the trunk and set it on the floor.

When she lifted off the top and examined the items inside, she was struck by a wave of dizziness. These were things she'd been carrying in her cloak on the day she arrived at the Transit Bridge. They were objects she'd never wanted to see again and yet couldn't bring herself to discard. In their early days on the Bridge, she'd given them to Fiona to keep, and had pushed them from her mind.

There was an old knife, very sharp and well balanced for throwing. At the sight of it, she recalled a man falling from a horse as he clutched at his throat. There was a lock of horsehair from Yellen's mane. The hair had been knotted around her fingers when Shinobu carried her from *There* into Hong Kong. There was a silk handkerchief with dried blood along the edge. It had been a gift from John, who'd brought it back with him after one of his yearly trips home to London. He'd given it to her beneath a tree in the woods, and then she'd kissed him . . . The blood along the edge was also hers, from the gunshot wound he'd given her on the night of the attack.

She forgot her purpose for a few moments, feeling light-headed. When the sensation eventually passed, she found what she was looking for. Beneath the other items was a thick book, bound in leather.

The cover had been worn smooth by the touch of many people over the years, but the dark smudges of dried blood along one edge looked more recent. Quin wondered if the blood was hers or if it belonged to someone else who'd had the book before her.

The volume opened supplely to her touch. Inside were pages and pages of diary entries, some in a modern feminine hand, others in the cramped and spidery scripts of former times. Entries had been pasted into the book, and there were loose sheets as well, some of paper, some of older and softer materials, parchment and vellum, folded and tucked neatly between pages. And there were dozens of drawings.

She flipped past simple illustrations of animals and rough ink landscapes. Then, in the upper corner of one page, she located the diagram she remembered: three interlocking ovals. This symbol had something to do with the origin of Seekers, of that she was sure. The script beneath the symbol was not in modern English but an older language.

Briac had always been silent about their history. Even the Dreads had been explained only briefly, as judges who would oversee the taking of their oaths. If Briac had been silent, it meant there were things he didn't wish her to know. This symbol must be one of them. How much more was there for her to learn? She felt as though she'd been shown only the tops of the tallest trees, and there was an entire forest waiting to be explored.

After looking at the diagram of the ovals for a while and tracing its lines with a finger, she forced herself to close the book. The leather volume deserved long and detailed examination, but first she wanted to see her mother, to tell her everything that had taken place in the last few days. Quin brought her mind back to Hong Kong and the room around her.

"Mother! Fiona!" she called.

Clutching the book, she stood and turned to leave the room, and nearly walked into the two figures standing in the doorway.

Startled, she took a step back. Neither person was her mother. One was Master Tan, small and tidy in his healer's smock. The other was a big Asian teenager covered in yellowing bruises. The excitement of finding the book evaporated. From the looks on both faces, she guessed at once what had happened.

"My mother—is she gone?"

Master Tan nodded solemnly. "Yes, last night."

"Was it John?" she asked.

Neither of them seemed to have any idea who John was, but Quin was already nodding to herself. Of course it was John. He wasn't going to give up until the athame was his. Fiona was a way to get it.

"Shinobu is very sorry about what happened," the large boy told her. "I know he regrets how stupid he was to run away. He realizes that even an idiot or a small child would have checked first to see who was at the door. Shinobu isn't a small child, but it's possible he's an idiot. I'm Brian, by the way. He and I were staying here."

"Shinobu was here? Staying with Fiona?" After the fight on the Bridge, he'd agreed to tell Fiona that Quin was all right. But she hadn't asked him for more than that. He'd seemed eager to get her out of his life.

"Yes. He saw your mother taken," the boy explained. "He was supposed to be guarding her."

"He was?"

Brian shrugged. "He thought it was a good idea. And it would have been—except for him running away."

"He has gone to kill himself to make amends," Master Tan added gravely.

"Kill himself?"

Quin looked from one to the other of them, hoping for a better explanation, or at least more urgency. When they both stayed silent, she said, "I never asked him— Is he— I mean . . . are you telling me he's *dead*?"

"Oh, I think not," Master Tan replied, shaking his head. "I would be very surprised."

"Unlikely," agreed Brian.

"Actually," Master Tan continued calmly, pulling out an ancient pocket watch and glancing at it, "unless he has done something very unexpected—"

There was a loud bang and a wild chiming of bells as the front door was thrown open. Quin pushed past both of them and ran down the stairs, the two men following close behind her. For a fleeting moment, she imagined it might be her mother returning. But it was not Fiona.

Framed in the doorway was the very tall and very wet figure of Shinobu, who was completely naked except for a pair of underwear decorated with comic book characters. Shinobu himself looked very like a comic book character. With his lean muscles outlined by the streetlamps behind him as he dripped onto the floor, he might have been a demigod cast to Earth by an angry parent. His short hair was plastered to his head, and he was shivering rather violently.

"You're still wearing my jeans," Shinobu said as Quin stopped near the bottom of the stairs.

For some reason, this made her blush deeply.

Aside from the lack of clothing, something about Shinobu was very different from the last time she'd seen him. He was not looking to the side, or away from her, he was not looking at her from beneath the hood of his leather jacket or while studying his worn-out shoes. He was looking directly at her, with an intensity in his dark eyes that she remembered. It was the look he used to wear when they were fighting together, a look that warned you how strong he was, how loyal, how deadly.

If he'd worn that look a few days ago, she would have recognized him immediately. It made her want to walk over and touch him, as if this moment were their true reunion.

"I promise you we'll get Fiona back. I have a plan. You won't like it. Maybe you will. No, you definitely won't. Quite, quite sure you won't. No way." The words were coming out of him in quick, erratic bursts. "But it'll do in a pinch, which is what we're in, since we don't know what John's planning. At least, I don't. And you probably don't either."

"You're talking strangely," Quin said carefully. She was embarrassed by a sudden urge to put her arms around Shinobu. She took a step toward him but restrained herself from getting any closer.

"He gave me something," Shinobu responded, pointing an accusing finger at Master Tan.

Quin turned to Master Tan.

"Completely natural, I assure you," Master Tan told her. "But effective. I told you to go somewhere safe, Shinobu. Did you *jump off the Bridge*?"

"I was trying to kill myself, remember? And as soon as I got back to the surface, all the thinking I hadn't done for the last year and a half was happening all at once." He looked at the three of them, who were still watching him warily. "Can I have a towel? It's not like they let me through the gate like this. I climbed back up. I'm freezing."

Master Tan went to fetch one, calling back over his shoulder, "It would have worked just as well in a dumpster."

Shinobu rolled his eyes. "The man and his dumpsters . . ." Then he turned to Quin and Brian. "My plan—"

"You'll be leaving me out of this plan, won't you, Barracuda?" Brian asked. "I still have a few ribs left that aren't broken."

"No, no, Sea Bass. You have the best part."

The basement space was narrow and long. It was filled with ornate cabinets and trunks stacked neatly along both walls, with a small aisle between them. There was a strong sense of Asia down here. Quin had grown up with Shinobu in Scotland, had seen the Scottish side of him for most of his life, but here, beneath his mother's house, she saw the Japanese half. There were no fewer than ten katanas, samurai swords, mounted in a shiny wooden rack above a black enamel wardrobe carved and inlaid with patterns of eagles—the symbol of Shinobu's family. The wooden trunks stacked around the room looked ancient, all of them decorated with scenes from samurai life and everywhere were cabinets with traditional Japanese designs of dragons and monks.

Shinobu had settled down a little but was still moving at double the ordinary human speed. This meant he was keeping himself occupied and didn't notice Quin's discomfort. He'd thrown on some old clothes, but her mind kept returning to how he had looked outside her door, and to that expression that had said he would do *anything* required to help her . . .

He was at the far end of the basement, prying open a large metal box. When he got the top off, the sides fell away, revealing a jumble of straps, clips, and metal tubing. His hands moved quickly through the mess, sorting and assembling simultaneously. In a few minutes, it had begun to take shape.

"What is that?" Quin asked. It looked a bit like a skydiving harness with rockets strapped to it, which, in point of fact, it was.

"I jumped off buildings for a while when I first got here. Very, very fun. Scared the daylights out of my mother, went to jail a bunch of times. That wasn't so fun, but I met loads of interesting people—jail's like that." The words were tumbling out, but he paused, noticing the way she was looking at the harness. "It's perfectly safe," he told her. Then he added, "No. Actually, it's not safe at all. I'm not sure why I said that. But I didn't die. Obviously. I'm right here!"

"How tall were these buildings?"

"Tall."

"As tall as—" She broke off. The athame was still concealed in the sheath running down her left leg, and now it was tickling her. She grabbed it through her jeans and found that the stone was vibrating, very slightly. As she touched it, the vibration steadily increased, sending a tremor through her bones, all the way up to her teeth.

"What?" he asked her.

"The athame's shaking."

He reached over and slid his hand up along her leg, trying to feel it. Quin found herself taking a step back, surprised by his sudden closeness.

"It—it stopped," she said. "That was strange. Something set it off."

"There's a subway line nearby," Shinobu suggested as he went back to fiddling with the skydiving rig. "Maybe it's picking up the vibration? I sometimes feel the subway in my feet when I'm down here. Except, when I've done Shiva sticks, it feels like everything is shaking, so it's kind of hard to tell. But you haven't done Shiva, so maybe that's it."

He was now pulling old rocket cartridges off the harness and setting them aside. When he was finished, he carried the rig to the front end of the basement and placed it by the door.

"Now clothes," he told her. "Luckily, my mother already did that planning for us, ages ago."

He threw open the wardrobe next to Quin, revealing an extensive assortment of body armor, some of it ancient and fit for a samurai, and some of it completely modern.

"My great-great-great—I forget how many greats—grandfather's," he said, nodding to the samurai armor. It had intricate pieces of lacquered wood held together with fine braids of silk.

"It's beautiful."

"It still works—against swords and things like that."

"And the other stuff—why?" She was looking at several sets of high-tech body armor.

"When my mother first came here, she thought Alistair might be following soon, and maybe Briac would be coming after him. She thought there might be, you know, a huge battle. She shopped accordingly. She thinks ahead like that. And she's the sort who buys three when one will do, probably because she has piles of money."

He flipped through the items and quickly pulled out several that looked to be Quin's size.

"This is sort of like chain mail," he explained, studying a full suit of something thin and shiny as he held it against her body. He pushed it into her hands. "And maybe these?" he asked, handing over a matching set of gloves. Then he retrieved a bulletproof vest, which he tossed to her.

"Go ahead," he told Quin as he began to assemble a similar pile for himself. "Put them on."

She hesitated. The space between the walls was small. Quin couldn't bring herself to take her clothes off in front of him, especially after she'd just seen how impressive his own body was.

"I just . . . I guess I'm shy," she said awkwardly.

"Sorry. Wasn't thinking. Of course I'd love to see you naked. I've been dreaming about what you look like since we were thirteen. Maybe earlier. Whenever I started being interested in naked girls. Maybe twelve. I got to undress a couple of girls down in the village, but you—" He broke off suddenly, blushing to the tips of his ears. He stared at her a moment in shock. Then he pushed the door of the wardrobe out, creating a kind of screen around her and hiding himself from view. There was a long silence. At last, from the other side of the door, he said, "I'm sorry. It's the tea." And then more quietly, she heard him mutter, "Unbelievable."

Quin smiled. She couldn't shake from her mind the image of him, unclothed and at her door. The idea that he'd thought about her filled her stomach with butterflies.

She began to undress, and she could hear Shinobu on the other side of the door, doing the same. She managed to get the shiny suit up over her legs and to her waist, but the upper half of the garment separated into several pieces that were supposed to attach to each other in ways that weren't immediately obvious.

"Quin? Are you all right?" he asked after a while.

"I'm trying to figure this thing out," she said, attempting, for the third time, to fasten the strips of the top together.

"Here, I can help."

He put his hand on the edge of the door, preparing to move it aside, and Quin scrambled to cover herself. When he came out from behind the door, he was wearing the same thin armor, which, like Quin's, wasn't completely attached and so left half of his chest bare. Obviously still embarrassed, Shinobu kept his eyes away from her face as he studied her suit critically.

"Uh, that part comes up and attaches to the front," he said, gesturing to one of the flaps hanging to her side. "Can you reach—"

She tried and nearly dropped the piece over her chest.

"Not quite," she said, attempting to look unembarrassed as she struggled to stay covered. "It slips—"

"Here—" He slid his hands around her back, and she felt him connecting two segments of her garment. Then he eased the suit up her back. It slipped once, and his chest accidentally brushed against hers as he grabbed for it.

"Sorry," he murmured.

"It's okay."

She found herself staring firmly at the floor as he smoothed the back piece up over her shoulders to attach it to the front. It was hard not to notice the warmth of his hands. And he was strong, she thought, strong enough to lift her if he wanted to, into his arms . . .

She stopped that thought. She kept her eyes turned away from him as she slipped her arms into the hanging sleeves, which he velcroed together into a snug fit. The suit was like thin, close-fitting long underwear with a metallic sheen.

"These connections give you a full range of motion in your arms, even if it's tight," he told her as she stepped back to put some space between them. "I've tried it out a couple of times when I've had to, you know, fight someone."

Quin made a couple of practice swings of her arms and found that the armor was surprisingly flexible.

"Will you help with mine?" he asked, still keeping his eyes away from her.

She figured out how to attach the front and neck of his shirt properly. Then she velcroed the bottom of the shirt to his waistband. This required putting her arms around him for a few moments, and her heart ignored her orders and began to beat faster.

"It's good for deflecting things like knives," he was explaining. "If someone stabs at you full force, though, it won't hold up. A straight hit will pierce it. But it'll keep you from getting burned. Unless it's really, *really* hot."

She nodded. It was difficult to concentrate on what he was saying. She hadn't really *seen* Shinobu, not since they were children. She'd been distracted by John. But she could see him now.

She made her hands drop to her sides. She had to stop this line of thought. He was probably right about the herbs making him say what he'd said. And anyway, they were cousins—of some sort. Was it third cousins? How related were third cousins? And hadn't one of their distant great-grandparents remarried? She remembered learning that, which meant they really shared only half the expected amount of common blood, didn't it? Their connection suddenly seemed distant—but Shinobu had always called her "cousin."

"Now we cover it," he said, turning around to face her.

They helped each other into ordinary shirts over the armor, still avoiding each other's eyes. Quin imagined reversing all of this—

taking off the shirts, taking off the armor, taking off the years that she had spent with John. Shinobu could carry her upstairs . . .

She turned away so he couldn't see her face, and pulled on a pair of trousers. Shinobu slipped woolen long underwear over his thin layer of armor. And all of it, she assumed, would go under some more elaborate outer armor in a moment.

Now he was pulling the bulletproof vest around her and cinching it tight.

"How does that feel?" he asked.

"It's good."

His face was inches in front of hers as he adjusted her vest. She could see the roots of his hair, which were growing out in that deep red she remembered. He had removed the piercings from his face, leaving his clean, perfect features unblemished. Without asking for permission, her hands moved to his chest and stayed there, feeling his heartbeat.

"You're warm," she whispered.

He looked down at her, his dark eyes close to hers. His hands were at her waist. Was she imagining it, or were they pulling her gently toward him?

Quin could not stop herself. She leaned forward, and her lips brushed his—

An unbelievably loud clanging sound erupted a few yards away, beyond the basement door, and they sprang apart.

The door was thrown open to reveal Brian Kwon, standing at the bottom of the stone steps leading up to the yard outside. One of Brian's hands clutched the handle of a large rolling pallet, which teetered at the top of the steps. This pallet was piled with several dozen metal canisters, many bundles of objects that looked suspiciously like fireworks, and a quantity of welding equipment that appeared to have spent a long time underwater. The noise had been caused by a very large and heavy canister rolling off the pallet, bouncing down the steps, and colliding with the metal basement door.

"Raided the salvage yard, Barracuda," he said, groaning as he lifted the canister back into place. "I hope you're not planning to ask for your job back. Also made a few other stops."

Shinobu smiled and clapped Brian on the shoulders as he moved past him, up the stairs, and began inspecting the items. Quin followed, feeling herself flush as Brian looked at her quizzically.

When Shinobu was satisfied with Brian's haul, the three of them packed all of the gear carefully into backpacks. Then they finished dressing, with Quin putting on Shinobu's old cloak so she could conceal the athame and lightning rod in its pockets.

When they were ready, she and Brian stood outside as Shinobu disappeared into the house. Quin's thoughts returned to the leather book she'd dug out of the trunk in her mother's bedroom.

"Brian, do you have a phone?" she asked.

Sometime later, Shinobu appeared through a nearby window. He stood in the hallway of his mother's home, his ancestor's samurai armor over his bulletproof vest and motorcycle boots. As she watched, his mother and little brother, Akio, bowed deeply and formally to him, and Shinobu bowed back.

CHAPTER 53

JOHN

"How is he?" John asked, looking at the image of his grandfather on the security monitor. Gavin was in bed, doubled over with a coughing fit, the burns on his chest and arm still bandaged.

"Better than yesterday, not as well as he will be tomorrow," Maggie answered.

Maggie, somewhere near ninety years old now, with long gray hair and a posture that was still upright, held Gavin's life in her hands. John had brought her back to *Traveler* the day he'd left for the estate. She had immediately begun administering Gavin's antidote at the highest possible doses, but it was taking a long time for Gavin's body to respond. He was old, and skipping the antidote for weeks had brought him close to death.

With his grandfather confined to his bedroom, John now had control of *Traveler*. It was true that Gavin's relatives were fighting in court for authority over the family's holdings, but Gavin had exaggerated the immediate danger they posed. The poison had made him see enemies at every turn. *As if we don't have enough real adversaries,* John thought.

"May I get you something to drink, Mrs. Kincaid?" Maggie asked.

Fiona was seated at a table in the corner, her hand cuffed to a chain, the other end of which was attached to the wall. It left her plenty of room to move about, but there was no question that she was a captive on the ship.

"No, thank you," Fiona said without turning her head from the window, through which she was watching London pass by.

The sight of the shackle around her wrist made John incredibly sad. *Somehow I have to make this happen without hurting her or Quin again.* The same words had gone through his mind a hundred times in the last two days, but he worried about his ability to keep Quin and Fiona safe when neither of them would do anything to help him.

He flipped through security channels on the monitor, catching short glimpses through *Traveler*'s exterior cameras, then watching images from the streets of London below. He had men prowling through the city, following *Traveler*'s path, waiting for Quin to arrive. She would come for her mother, of course she would.

"Can I make you comfortable in some other way?" he asked Fiona when Maggie had left the room.

"You could remove the handcuff and release me," Fiona suggested. "That would make me much more comfortable."

"That's the one thing I can't do just yet," John told her gently. He turned the monitor off and took a seat near her. "We're just waiting now. I don't want you to be frightened or ill at ease. Are you hungry?"

"For a kidnapper, you're terribly polite."

"I'm trying to remember my manners," he said, hoping she would smile, but she didn't.

"Unlike that evening on the estate?" she asked him, her voice cold.

"Yes, unlike that," he responded quietly, feeling a flash of the dread that always appeared when he thought about that night.

"I'm not hungry, thank you, John."

In spite of what she said, there was a kind of hunger around Fiona's eyes. John recognized it from his time as an apprentice. She'd been a wonderful teacher, in charge of languages and math, but by late afternoon, her mind had always been fuzzy.

From a cabinet at one side of the room, he pulled out a crystal decanter and poured a generous helping of brandy into one of his grandfather's heavy glasses. Without a word, he sat again and slid the glass across the table. Fiona lifted the glass and took a long sip, her eyes not meeting his.

"Even when I was twelve, I felt sorry for you, Fiona—with Briac as a husband," he told her, hoping she understood that he was sincere. He remembered her very clearly from his early days as an apprentice, her beautiful face and dead eyes. The way she had held herself back whenever Briac was nearby, the softness of her voice that hinted at tears. Quin and Shinobu had always seemed oblivious, but John had understood. He knew what it was to live under a cloud, to have someone near you who cared nothing about your own survival and wished you ill. "Briac treated you like he treated me—we are more alike than you might think."

"We're not at all alike, John," Fiona whispered.

"Don't say that. I only need a little help. I still believe Quin will understand and help me."

"Why would she? She's in no state to help anyone."

"She's come back to herself, Fiona. I've seen her. Can't you help me convince her?"

"Do you think kidnapping me was the best way to win us over?" she asked, her voice mocking him.

"I had to take you here so she'll bring me what's mine and teach me to use it. She loves you. She'll bring it to get you back. And then you'll be free to go."

"You think the athame is yours," Fiona said thoughtfully. She drank again from her glass, the cuff and chain weighing heavily on her wrist as she did so. "You're not the first person to claim that."

"Don't talk like Briac, please. You know the athame is mine."

"That depends how far back you're willing to look."

"That athame has belonged to my house for hundreds of years, probably more. You must know that, Fiona."

"A family becomes a large and twisted tree over hundreds of years, John. Some of its branches reach so far it's difficult to recognize them. How can you be sure you should have it?" She set the glass down. It was empty.

For some reason, the word "twisted" made him think of his mother, bleeding on the floor of her apartment, her limbs arranged awkwardly around her body. Suddenly he was losing control of his emotions. "Can't there be a moment when simple justice comes into it?" he asked her, hating the sound of despair in his voice. "When something is done because it's *right*?" He stopped himself. There was no point in moaning about justice to the woman who had been married to Briac Kincaid. She, like John, already knew that life was not fair—you had to *make* it fair.

He needed a moment to compose himself, so he crossed the room and poured her another helping of brandy. Then he changed the subject. "Why did you choose Hong Kong?"

He handed Fiona the refilled glass, and once more she brought it to her lips.

"We were there while Quin was healing. From the bullet wound. Perhaps you remember that wound?" Her eyes met his for a moment. One of her hands was at her throat, where the faintest traces of a scar were visible. *It was necessary,* he reminded himself about the wound on her neck. *But I went too far that night. Am I going too far now? Is it true what Quin said—am I becoming like Briac?*

"I thought we were only passing through Hong Kong," Fiona continued, "but Quin was very weak for a long time, and when she was better, she wanted to stay."

John let his eyes drift away from her.

"I imagine you were happy to be away from Briac, no matter where you were—no matter what you found yourself doing." It had been one consolation to him after that terrible night on the estate—that Fiona had gotten away from Briac. But the informer who'd helped him find Quin on the Bridge had spotted her mother with the yellow scarf of an escort around her neck. That had struck him as a particularly cruel fate.

Fiona's gaze went back to the window. The Thames was visible now, red and gold in a stray bit of sunlight breaking through clouds toward the horizon.

"I understand why you hated him, John," she said. "I often hated him as well. He took what we learned as apprentices and twisted it badly. But he was my husband. I tried to be loyal."

"Why do you use the past tense?" he asked, anger flaring up again at thoughts of Briac. "I still hate him, even more than I used to, if that's possible. The things he made Quin do . . ." Then he realized: the last time Fiona had seen her husband was that night on the estate, when Briac was lying wounded in the commons. "You think he's dead," he breathed. "You think I killed him."

Fiona turned sharply toward him, and the look on her face told him he was right. "I didn't know for sure, but I thought perhaps . . ."

"I'm sorry, Fiona." There were no words he could choose to soften the message. "Briac—he isn't dead. I saw him a few days ago on the estate."

Fiona set her glass on the table, nearly spilling it as she did. She studied him, the lines of her face growing ugly with a subtle but deep fear.

"Are you— Do you mean to . . ."

"Am I giving you to him? Is that what you're wondering? In exchange for the athame?"

Very solemnly, Fiona nodded.

"No. I tried that once, remember? Briac wouldn't accept anything in trade for the athame, even his beautiful wife." He said this as gently as he could. "But Briac doesn't have it. Quin does."

"He wouldn't want me now anyway," she murmured, not hearing anything else he'd said. "I know he wouldn't."

John understood then. Fiona was an intelligent and beautiful woman. After leaving the estate, she could have become many things, yet she had chosen to become an escort. She'd chosen a profession that would make her, in Briac's eyes, untouchable. She had believed he might be dead, yet she'd felt it necessary to protect herself even from the idea of him. By degrading herself, she'd hoped to escape his power, as they all had.

"No," John agreed, "you are free of him."

CHAPTER 54

MAUD

The Young Dread could not take her eyes off her master's face. He had shaved his beard and cut his hair, and the change was almost unfathomable. Somehow her master, who had, she suspected, been born so long ago that he'd seen the Romans in Britain, now looked like he belonged in this uncomfortable and crowded modern age in which they found themselves.

True, he had put on different clothes. Instead of his monk's robe, he wore trousers and a sweater, with modern shoes that looked to her quite painful. She herself had been given shoes and also a dress to wear. The shoes were intensely uncomfortable, and the dress hung about her slender frame awkwardly, giving her the appearance of a panther forced into a costume.

But it was more than the shaved face or clothing that made her master different. Something about the way he moved had changed as well. Even his voice was altered. He was speaking to the nurse, and his words nearly matched hers. He was even using the strange medical terms the Young Dread had heard so often when she lay in a hospital room like this one, recovering from the Middle's knife. He had been stretched out for hundreds of years and had woken only a few days ago, when Quin had pulled him from *There* and into the estate. Where had her master learned to speak this way?

The Old Dread and the nurse were discussing Briac Kincaid, who lay in the hospital bed, his leg and shoulder stitched and bandaged. The Young followed enough of the conversation to understand that Briac would mend perfectly well, given time. The doctors had even put something into his wounds that would heal them quickly from the inside. This did not please her. His moaning and thrashing had given her hope that the wounds would be fatal.

The Middle was standing in the far corner of the room, his arms folded, his cloak hanging from his shoulders. He'd allowed the cut across his chest to be stitched up, but he had changed nothing about his appearance. He looked rough and wild in the ordered surroundings of the hospital.

Eventually the nurse was done speaking to the Old Dread, and with a few final words to Briac himself, and a nervous glance at the Middle, she left the room.

"You will remain here," the Old Dread told Briac, his mannerisms transforming him, as he spoke now, back into the master she had always known. Somehow he could switch seamlessly between the ancient and the modern, like an actor pulling on different masks. "We will return for you when it is done. And then you shall have—"

The Old cut himself off. His hand went to the inner pocket of his overcoat, where the athame was hidden.

After a moment, the Young could feel the vibration as well. It was growing stronger. Somewhere in the world, Quin Kincaid was using her athame. The Old Dread's athame, after the ritual in the cavern, would now shake in unison whenever Quin's dagger was struck.

The Middle, who'd been as still as a piece of furniture all this time, slid into motion, crossing the room and pushing the door shut.

The Old drew the athame from his coat and held it lightly in his hands. The vibration intensified, until it had filled the room and the door began to shudder. Through the window panels into the hall, which themselves were vibrating, the Young saw medical personnel putting hands to their ears as the tremor reached them.

The Old was holding the stone dagger in front of his body, balanced on his palms. After a minute, the vibration began to fade.

"She has gone *There,*" the Young Dread's master said.

It was the next vibration, the second one, for which they must wait. That second shaking, as Quin struck her athame and stepped from *There* back into the world, would tell them where on Earth she had emerged.

The Young Dread knew it might be some time before Quin reentered the world. Getting lost *There* was one of the chief hazards of using an athame. Even veteran Seekers could find their minds wandering, then floating, then frozen into absolute stillness if they didn't carefully maintain their mental focus. Seekers used a time chant to achieve this focus, but even with such aids, athame was a perilous method of travel. Quin was still a novice, and the risk of losing herself as she stepped *between*—for a short while or a long while—was quite real.

It was two hours before the athame came to life again, a duration the Young Dread found impressively brief for a Seeker so inexperienced—Quin's mental control must be very good.

The Dreads had remained in the hospital room all the while. By then, night was falling. Nurses had come and gone, noticeably frightened by the Middle's stare. The three Dreads stood with their backs to the door, holding the athame between them as it began to vibrate a second time. The Young, the Old, and the Middle positioned their fingers around the dials.

The second tremor was much, much stronger than the first. It engulfed the room immediately, and a moment later panicked voices could be heard in the corridor outside. The shuddering of walls was disrupting medical equipment in neighboring rooms. Down the hall, a pane of glass broke.

Within the greater shaking, there were small, intense echoes through the athame's dials. The Old called out the name of two symbols, indicating that he had felt those vibrate more strongly than the others. The Young called out another two, and the Middle a third set.

The tremor ended, resonating in their ears for a moment longer, then disappearing completely. The Old replaced the athame into the pocket of his overcoat, then picked up a pen and paper from the side table near Briac's bed. To the Young Dread, he appeared to become a modern man again as he put the pen to the paper and quickly wrote out the six symbols they had spoken aloud.

Her master studied the paper, then held it up for the others to see. Together, the symbols were a set of coordinates—the location into which Quin and her athame had just emerged.

"London," he said.

"She's going to John," Briac responded from the bed. His words were drowsy, but he was pulling himself up to a sitting position.

There was a look in his eyes, a brightness there, that the Young Dread didn't like. Briac did not simply want his athame back—he was eager for revenge.

Briac turned to the Old Dread and asked, "Do you know about John's home?"

CHAPTER 55

SHINOBU

"It's windier than I'd like," Shinobu told her. "But once we get a little lower, we should be protected from the gusts."

It was nighttime and they were perched atop a 110-story building in London. Wind gusted about them, causing the building to drift gently this way and that, like the deck of a ship. And wind was not their only worry—judging by the clouds in the distance, there would be rain soon.

They stood near the parapet that encircled the roof. At their backs, rising steeply, was the decorative pyramid that formed the cap to the towering building beneath them. There was only a small border of walking space between the pyramid and the parapet, and on this narrow path they had arranged all of their gear.

Quin's athame had brought them to London, and then, through trial and error with all six dials, they had managed to carve an anomaly through to the inside of the building beneath them. From there, with their welding equipment and brute force, they had made their way up onto the roof.

Traveler's route through London was well known, and a quick search online had given them a map. From where they stood on this roof, Shinobu could see the massive airship turning at the bottom of its figure eight, preparing to make its way back toward them.

The breeze was whipping Quin's hair around her face in a way that Shinobu found distracting. He was tightening her harness—tricky work—as she tried to keep the strands out of his way.

"Are you going to fiddle with your hair, or are you going to pay attention?" he asked, pausing to adjust the chin strap on his ancestor's samurai helmet, which sat tightly on his head. All of the armor was tight, in fact. He was wearing it out of family pride and the secret hope that it might restore his own honor, but his great-great-great-grandfather must have been the runt of the family. "Or are you leaving the entire plan up to me?"

"This is not a plan!" she said, raising her voice over the wind. She dug in her trouser pocket and came up with a band to tie up her hair. "This is us throwing ourselves off a building!"

"We can still prepare. Stop playing with your hair!"

"You're doing it again!" she told him. She looked over to Brian, who was arranging their gear beneath the parapet.

"What—trying to keep us from being killed?"

"Yelling."

"It's noisy up here!"

Without comment, Brian handed a plastic bottle full of brownish-black liquid to Quin. She popped off the top and thrust it at Shinobu.

"Drink!" she ordered. "And not just a few sips this time. I want half of that gone before you say anything else."

"You want me to vomit all over you in a few minutes, then? I don't think that's going to make our landing any easier."

But he took the bottle and began to drink. He was, he knew, going through opium withdrawal, Shiva withdrawal, and probably a number of other withdrawals as well. Master Tan had brewed an enormous batch of a new and even more dreadful tea to help him overcome the absence of drugs, and Brian had bottles of the stuff stored all around their packs. The taste did not improve with continued drinking, but without it, Shinobu guessed he'd be curled in a ball somewhere, moaning and writhing. Which might, he thought, be better than what they were about to do.

Quin waited patiently as he gulped down half the bottle, then experienced a few minutes of cramping and shaking before his head began to clear.

"Sorry," he muttered.

The view of London at night was beautiful from where they stood, but he noticed Quin keeping her eyes on things closer at hand. Brian remained hunkered beneath the parapet, avoiding the view entirely. Out of loyalty to their Seeker training, Quin and Shinobu had agreed not to explain to Brian how they were getting to London, and he seemed willing to go along with this arrangement. But since they had blindfolded him and dragged him through the anomaly from Hong Kong, the big Asian had stayed rather quiet. He was now cutting the rocket fuses to size and arranging them carefully by the launching mechanism, muttering to himself. Most of his words were taken away by the wind, but every now and then Shinobu heard words like, "witchcraft" and "insanity."

"Does he actually know anything about rockets?" Quin asked, nodding in Brian's direction.

"He knows enough. We used explosives a lot for the big salvage dives."

"And fireworks?" she asked skeptically.

"They're similar."

"You do realize we're not underwater?"

"We're not? So we won't be able to use the inflatable life raft I brought?"

She smiled at that, and he was happy he was no longer snapping at her.

"I'm nervous," she admitted.

"How about some tea?" He offered her his bottle.

She smiled again. "No, thank you."

"Try to put your mind on something else as long as you can."

Quin's eyes lit up with a sudden thought. "What happened to my horse?"

"Your horse?"

"Yellen. When we . . . came through to Hong Kong."

Shinobu shook his head, remembering, as though from a dream, the tangle of arms and legs and saddle and reins they had been when they'd escaped to *There* after the attack.

"I honestly don't know," he told her. "I was worried you were about to die—which you did, by the way. I don't think Yellen came through with us. But if he did, maybe he's someone's backyard pet now. You know what those estates are like along Victoria Peak."

A thoughtful look came over Quin's face. Then Brian began tossing them canisters. These they hooked to every spare inch of their harness straps. On Shinobu's body, extra space was hard to find. He was already carrying rappelling rope and a plasma torch, with its huge fuel canister.

Once they'd managed to get everything attached, Shinobu moved experimentally, discovering that the gear bounced around like mad. It felt as though he were moving about with carpenter's hammers hanging all over his body. No matter how perfectly they jumped, the landing was going to be painful.

"Need my guidance system, Sea Bass!" Shinobu called.

Brian tossed him a cylinder that looked very similar to the array of fireworks he was preparing. This got attached at Shinobu's left hip. Then he and Quin pulled on their gloves.

Shinobu lifted himself, with all his heavy gear, up onto the edge of the parapet, where he took a seat, his legs hanging inward toward the roof. Quin followed, keeping her eyes up. The wind was stronger on top of the parapet, but the gusts were coming less frequently now.

Traveler was half a mile away, approaching from the south, its exterior reflecting the lights of the city. They put on their goggles.

When Shinobu had jumped off the Bridge in Hong Kong, he'd remembered what John once said about *Traveler* being "safe from Seekers." He'd realized then that the airship must have been designed so an athame couldn't get you on board. The coordinates they could reach with Quin's athame were all stationary locations. The dagger could not bring them to a moving point like *Traveler*, whose coordinates were changing all the time. So he'd formed a plan to arrive by a different route.

"Are you ready?" he asked her.

"You weren't lying to me, were you," she asked, "when you said you've done this before?"

That was a matter of opinion. Shinobu had jumped off high buildings in Hong Kong many times, but never with so much gear, in such bad weather, or with the intention of hitting a moving target. At this moment, however, he didn't want to split hairs.

"Of course I've done this before. Lots of times."

Very, very cautiously he stood up sideways on the parapet, facing along its length. The ledge was two feet wide, but Shinobu himself, with everything he was wearing, was wider than that. He found his balance. Then he pulled Quin up, so she was standing in front of him, her back toward him, as she also faced along the length of the parapet. Brian steadied their legs from below.

Shinobu watched her glance down. The building dropped off in a sheer face, plummeting a hundred and ten stories to the ground. Quin chose her footing carefully, edging backward until she was only a few inches away from him. Hooking the rear of her harness to the front of his own with carabiners, he drew her flush up against him.

"Oh, God," Quin breathed. She had turned her head toward the view, and he watched her eyes sweep the distance from where they stood to the approaching shape of *Traveler*. The ship was a quarter of a mile away and much, much closer to the ground.

"It's all right," he whispered into her ear.

Brian was standing at the parapet by their feet, also watching the ship approach. He hauled the launcher up onto his shoulder and slid the first rocket inside.

"Ready when you are, Barracuda," he said.

"I don't think I can do this!" Quin whispered. She reached back and grabbed Shinobu's hand. He squeezed it tightly in his own. He could feel her shaking beneath all her gear. What they were doing was, he had to admit, completely terrifying. There wasn't much he could say to change that.

"Quin?" he asked her.

"Yes."

"Were you trying to kiss me in the basement?"

Her head was turned from him so he could see only part of her cheek and her left ear, but when both blushed deep pink, he knew he'd successfully distracted her for a moment.

Without giving her warning or any more time to worry, Shinobu leapt off the building, pulling her with him.

And in one awful, gut-dropping moment, they were falling, plummeting at a speed that felt far too fast and completely out of control. Quin screamed. Shinobu's stomach clenched, and his insides tried to climb up his throat as his body told him that they were going to die for sure.

But he had jumped off buildings before. He assumed his free fall position, his body pulling hers into the correct stance beneath his own. *Traveler* was ahead of them. He could see it clearly. He angled toward it. Wind whipped at their faces, with gusts buffeting them.

"Pull the chute!" Quin yelled.

"Not yet!" he yelled back.

Thousands of windows streaked by in Shinobu's peripheral vision, skyscrapers blurring past as the huge shape of *Traveler* heaved closer.

"Pull the chute!" she screamed.

A streak of black tore by on their left, heading straight for *Traveler*. A moment later, a burst of pink filled their field of view and a boom echoed past them. The first firework had exploded in front of *Traveler*'s nose.

"Pull the chute!"

"I know what I'm doing!" Shinobu yelled, marveling at his ability to sound so confident when his words were only vaguely true.

The ground was racing up to meet them. They were almost on top of the ship, the pink flashes of the firework and acrid smoke all around them.

"Shinobu!" she screamed.

He pulled the chute.

CHAPTER 56

MAUD

Atop a smaller building, the three Dreads stood watching *Traveler*'s progress above the busy London streets. Briac Kincaid was with them. He'd insisted it was his right, as the owner of the athame, to accompany them on their quest to get it back. Apparently, Briac did not trust any of the Dreads to fulfill their promise.

He was walking, thanks to whatever the doctors had put into his wound and thanks also to a large quantity of white capsules he had swallowed just before making the jump to London. Privately the Young Dread was glad he'd come. Though Briac's leg was working better by the hour, he was still severely injured. In this condition, there was every likelihood that he would be killed.

The Young stood by the Old, peering out from beneath her leather helmet at the floating ship in the distance. She wondered what sort of machine could fly like that. Her master had told her, hundreds of years ago, that the world would be different each time she woke up, and yet the transformation she had seen in her last few wakings made all other changes look trivial.

The Dreads spent much of their time on the estate, or following new Seekers on their first assignments, so in her long life, she'd rarely been in a city. She had thought London was big the last time she'd visited, four hundred years ago. Now it must be ten times its former size, a giant forest of metal and glass stretching as far as she could see.

The Old Dread wore his monk's robe again, but his face still looked strange, bare of its beard. His eyes were following the ship closely, as his fingers made adjustments to the dials on his stone dagger. They had followed Quin's athame to London, and though she had moved from her entrance point, her ultimate destination was obvious.

From the Dreads' current location atop a building, they must first go to *that place,* of course, and from there her master must accurately determine the coordinates of the moving ship. No other athame could bring a Seeker to a moving point, and no man but her master could find his way into something traveling as swiftly as that vessel. The ship had been created, the Young Dread understood, to prevent attacks by Seekers with ordinary athames. Yet whoever had designed the ship hadn't understood that it could not keep away the Dreads, not when they had her master's particular athame and his skill in using it.

"I will not kill her, Master," she told him quietly.

She had moved close to him, while the other two were some distance away.

"I do not think you will kill her," he agreed.

"It would be unjust," she whispered.

"As you say."

"Will we truly give the athame to Briac Kincaid?"

He did not answer immediately, his eyes on the ship in the distance. *Traveler* was closer, gliding toward them between tall buildings.

"Our promise is to set things to rights," he told her, after some time had passed. "If that means putting the athame into the proper hand, should we not do that?"

"Who chooses the proper hand?" she asked quietly.

He did not answer her directly, but after a pause he said, "We three Dreads were not meant to be awake all at once. To decide what is just, one at a time should be sufficient—when all have been trained. An athame is a small thing. To give it to someone requires only one hand. Whose hand would that be?"

As *Traveler* moved closer, the Young waited silently for the Old to answer his own question. Instead he said, "Now is the time. Are you prepared?"

"I am."

With that, he called Briac and the Middle Dread closer, made a final adjustment to the dials, and struck the athame against its slender lightning rod. As the vibration engulfed them, the Young Dread's eyes caught movement far above, near a building so high that it was difficult to see the peak from where she stood. Throwing her sight, she focused on two shapes hurtling through the sky toward the floating ship. These shapes were people, a tangle of weapons and limbs.

Then explosions of color filled the night air, pulling her eyes away from the falling figures. Pink bloomed around *Traveler*'s nose, followed a moment later by blue, then green. Deep, rumbling booms rolled over them. Quin, it seemed, was arriving on the ship with tremendous fanfare.

The Old Dread carved a portal. The Young turned her eyes from the flashes filling the sky and stepped through the humming doorway after him. The Middle came next and then Briac, who pulled his bad leg behind him as he crossed the surging threshold between here and *There*.

Before the doorway had closed, her master's fingers flew over the dials of his athame. Then he struck the lightning rod again. With the first anomaly still hovering behind them, he carved a new doorway, which opened onto a hallway and a cross section of flooring. They were looking at the interior of *Traveler* through a hole that had been cut between floors, without enough room for them to safely enter.

Without hesitation, the Old Dread's fingers flew over the dials again, making a subtle adjustment. He struck athame and rod together a third time, turned slightly, and carved another portal. This one opened up into the same hallway, which was now directly in front of them. The Young experienced a moment of dizziness as she stared though both anomalies, each showing a slightly different angle of the same space.

Within both was chaos. The interior lights of *Traveler* were flashing, men were shouting, and bursts of colored light were coming in from overhead.

Drawing their weapons, the three Dreads and Briac Kincaid stepped through the doorway and onto the ship.

CHAPTER 57

QUIN

Shinobu pulled the rip cord, and the parachute yanked itself out of its casing, unfurled above them, and jerked them upward, abruptly slowing their fall. As soon as the chute was open, a gust of wind blew them higher and yanked them violently to the side.

They were going to die. Quin was fairly certain they were going to die. All around them, fireworks were exploding, sending burning embers everywhere. Her trousers were on fire. She tried to hit her legs together to crush out the flames, but a smolder of green firework fuel was eating through the fabric.

Traveler was just below them. Though it had seemed silent from far away, the enormous suspension engines made a thundering roar up close. Shinobu was cursing and yanking on their parachute's control lines, but the wind was still gusting, so it was almost impossible to steer.

Another firework went off, sending blinding golden squiggles across the known universe. The noise was deafening. Shinobu began cursing more loudly. Quin craned her neck back and saw that a burning stream of golden ash had set fire to the lace braids of his samurai armor. It was also eating a hole through their parachute. They'd been blown far behind *Traveler* now, and Shinobu was obviously losing control.

"Hold on!" he yelled. "Turn away!"

Quin's ears filled with the sound of igniting rocket fuel as they were sent into an accelerating spin. He had set off the thruster strapped to his left hip, and it was propelling them crazily toward the floating ship.

She was wrenched almost upside down, and then Shinobu had the thruster in his gloved hand, and he was aiming it behind them. They righted themselves, and suddenly they were above *Traveler* once more, its huge bulk hovering just below them.

"Hold on!" he yelled again as another firework went off.

Quin saw him throw the thruster away. Then he ripped their parachute loose, and they were both free-falling, no backup chute, no hope of recovering if they missed.

For two terrifying seconds, her insides turned to jelly. Then she and Shinobu hit the ship hard and began to roll. What had looked almost flat from above turned out to be a sloping surface. Quin's hands and feet scrambled for purchase, and the canisters attached to her harness bounced around her body like small anvils. She and Shinobu slid for yards, Quin thinking at any moment they would be at the edge, then falling over. Instead they came to a stop against the fins of the rear suspension engines.

Shinobu was on his knees immediately, pulling Quin up beside him and unhooking the carabiners that connected them.

"Are you all right?" he asked her, looking shell-shocked. It was still windy, and he was almost yelling.

She moved her limbs experimentally, noticing that her landing slide had conveniently put out the fire on her clothing, though much of her trousers had been burned away, revealing the shiny armor beneath. It had kept her skin from being scorched.

"Nothing's broken," she said, amazed that she still possessed the power of speech. "You?"

"I might have wet myself. Not sure."

They both laughed for a moment at the fact that they were alive and intact. Then Shinobu got to work. He located a burrowing piton in one of his pockets and slammed it into the hull. Its sharp metal point pierced *Traveler*'s skin, then automatically twisted deeper, giving them a solid handhold. They anchored themselves to this with the rappelling ropes and carabiners, as Shinobu had instructed when they were packing their gear back in Hong Kong.

Quin noticed his samurai armor was still smoldering, the embers flaring in the wind. As he adjusted the ropes, she pounded the armor with her fist until the fire died out.

"Thanks," he said.

From this position, they looked out across most of *Traveler*'s sloping roof toward the bow. Behind them were the four rear engines, and beyond the engines, the upper hull fell away steeply, then ended altogether.

Another firework burst near the ship's nose. They ducked, covering their heads with their arms as large clumps of blue sparks fell down around them like hail. Quin was momentarily blinded, and hoped the flash was blinding to *Traveler*'s security cameras as well.

"Get the torch!" Shinobu yelled against the wind, beating the burning sparks off them.

She unclipped the bulky plasma torch apparatus from his lower back, then handed it to him. Shinobu crawled forward, dragging it behind him.

When he'd gone ten yards, he called to her, "I found a hatch!"

Quin crawled toward him as he sparked the torch's blue flame to life, leaned over the hull, and began to cut.

Large raindrops were now splattering onto the ship, pelting her face and sizzling into steam as they came in contact with the flame. When she reached Shinobu, he was halfway done cutting a thick channel around the hatch.

He'd placed another piton, and still on her knees, Quin grabbed hold of it to steady herself, unbuckled her harness, and dropped it to the hull. She fastened her whipsword properly at her side, then located the knives she'd hidden around her body.

She unfurled Shinobu's cloak, which had been rolled and tucked at her back, pulled it about herself, and checked its pockets. After drawing the athame and lightning rod out, she fixed them on her waistband, then made sure her other items were securely hidden inside the cloak. The athame could not get her to a moving target such as this ship, but it would work perfectly well to get them off it—if only she could keep it in her possession.

She took one long strap off the harness, looped it around her shoulder, made it tight, and then clipped several metal canisters to it.

"Done!" Shinobu announced.

He had torched a path all the way around the hatch. It was raining harder now, which meant that the fireworks—while still blinding— were having a more difficult time lighting the two of them on fire. The rain was also quickly cooling the glowing cut made by the torch. In a few moments the metal had gotten cold enough for them to stick their gloved fingers down into the groove. The door was heavy and did not give easily, but with many curses from Shinobu and a great deal of effort from both of them, they managed to pry it upward and push it aside.

Beneath was a ladder down into the ship. Emergency lights were flashing, and Quin could hear panicked voices within.

Her heart began to race anew, with a mixture of fear and excitement. *I can do this. I can do this.* She fit her gas mask over her face.

"I'm ready!" she said.

Shinobu took hold of her shoulders, made her look at him. "Are you sure?" he asked.

"Yes!" Adrenaline was coursing into her bloodstream.

Shinobu nodded, and Quin lay down along the hull, pulling herself toward the opening. Shinobu grabbed hold of the strap around her torso and lowered her, headfirst, through the ragged hole.

She found herself looking down a wide corridor. There were men at the far end, running back and forth between two control rooms as the fireworks continued to go off around the ship.

Still hanging upside down, she unclipped one of the canisters from the strap around her shoulder. After twisting its release handle, she tossed it down the hallway toward the control room. The canister spun through the air, then bounced along the floor toward the bow of the ship, clouds of gas spiraling out of it as it went.

CHAPTER 58

JOHN

The corridors were filling with gas—thick, smoky curls of it drifting through the air. Holding his breath, John left the clean, sealed atmosphere of the upper control room and moved quickly down a gas-filled hallway, pushing his way past several men who were coughing and falling to their knees. He couldn't stop to help them now, or he too would be overcome.

He was trying to stay calm, keep his heart rate down, so he could make it to the end of the long upper corridor without taking a breath. He had to run the last twenty yards, his chest burning, but he reached his apartment, pushed inside, and quickly shut the door behind him.

Breathing deeply of the fresher air within, he began opening cupboards until he located the apartment's emergency kit. He emptied it onto the floor, dug through the supplies, and pulled on his gas mask. Then he retrieved the disruptor from his safe and secured its straps around his body.

As he headed back toward the door, he passed a mirror and he paused. His reflection was frightening—the mask blurred his features, and the disruptor looked like a medieval torture device strapped across his chest.

It should be frightening. Its purpose is to instill fear, he reminded himself. *I have her mother. I have the disruptor. No matter what she's planning, I can scare her into listening, convince her. She won't be hurt.*

When he'd taken Fiona, he'd expected Quin to arrive in London to try to negotiate with him for her release. Since her athame couldn't get her on board *Traveler,* he'd felt confident that he and his men would see her coming a long way off—this was the advantage of living on the airship. But clearly he'd been wrong. Half of his men were down on the streets of London, looking for Quin. But she had something else in mind.

Through one of his apartment windows, he watched fireworks burst against the ship's starboard side. Every few seconds the explosions of light outside overloaded all of their exterior cameras. He felt a moment of doubt and wondered: *Is it only Quin who's coming?* What if the Dreads were also after him? They had meddled with his family before, but now he had nothing of theirs—no athame, no book, and he was not even a Seeker. No, he had planned to lure Quin to London, and here she was, coming to get her mother.

He checked the seal on his gas mask and walked back out into the corridor. *Traveler* was descending further into chaos. Men were passed out now, sprawled across walkways. He knelt by two of them and felt for their pulses. Their heartbeats were strong—the gas was effective but not poisonous.

She's not a killer, he thought. *And neither am I. Together we would make good choices. We would spare the people who should be spared.*

He came to a group of three men who were still conscious, crawling toward a stairwell in search of fresh air.

"There are masks on the second floor, end of the corridor," he told them, helping them up. "Go. Find weapons—but don't shoot unless you hear me order it!"

The men staggered off down the stairs.

John slid his hand down the side of the disruptor, bringing it to life. Its unsettling electric whine cut through the noise around him, helping him concentrate. He was carrying a sort of fireworks of his own now. If he could terrify her into listening, he could put an end to this madness without a fight.

CHAPTER 59

SHINOBU

Shinobu clung to the aft end of the ship, his tether holding him in place as the wind and rain tried to pry him loose. His job was to throw *Traveler* into darkness, then join Quin inside.

He had torched his way through the outer layer of one of the ship's engines. Just below *Traveler*'s exterior skin was a tangle of valves and wires and tubes feeding into the engine itself and snaking off toward the body of the ship. The one thing he'd forgotten was a flashlight, and it was difficult to see into the well around the engine—except for the moments right after a firework went off, when it was so bright, he became half blind.

Online he'd found suggested electrical schematics for the famous airship *Traveler,* but he now realized, when confronted with the actual ship, that those drawings were completely worthless. He would have to rely on his own knowledge of wiring, which was based almost entirely on cutting up old machinery while underwater.

Squinting, he found a network of electrical wires and traced these until he located a bundle as thick as a man's arm. He reached in with the plasma torch and delicately sliced through the lot of them.

Except there was nothing delicate about the torch. It wasn't just the wires he'd severed. He'd cut through everything underneath them as well—nearly a foot of cables, valves, and other mechanical items that looked fairly important.

Immediately the engine beneath him began to make a stuttering sound, and through the windows off to his left, he saw the lights go off inside the ship. Then the entire vessel lurched, and an alarm began to sound, so loud he could hear it quite clearly out in the wind and the rain.

He waited, clicking the torch off as he checked his weapons in preparation for entering the ship. But the alarm died out a short while later, the lights came back on, and he felt the ship's engines right themselves. There were undoubtedly backup systems, and back-ups for the backup systems.

He looked around for other items to cut.

CHAPTER 60

MAUD

The Young Dread needed to breathe, of course. Yet she could go a long time without breathing when it was necessary. She and the others made their way through the smoky hallways of the great air-ship, following the noise of people not yet unconscious from the gas. The Young, like the other Dreads, had thrown her mind into her lungs and heart, and she was forcing her body to keep moving, her blood to keep circulating, without any further oxygen intake from her lungs.

She could not do this forever, but ten minutes was possible. She had held her breath that long once, underwater, with the Middle Dread holding her down.

Without warning, the ship lurched to the left, throwing them off balance, and all of the lights went out. A high wail began, so loud she wondered if her ears would survive it. They continued walking, disregarding the noise.

A moment later, the ship steadied, and different lights came on. These were dimmer, leaving the corridors in partial shadow. The wailing stopped.

Briac Kincaid was not keeping up. He'd held his breath as long as possible and now was gasping air through his cloak, which was wrapped tightly around his face. This did not completely filter out the gas. Coughing, he fell to his knees next to the Young Dread, then pitched forward onto the floor.

The Old Dread stared silently at the Young as if to say, *Briac has collapsed. What would you like to do about that?*

Before she could form an answer, the Middle ran up the corridor ahead of them. He returned moments later with a clear mask, which he must have taken off another man's head. After slipping this over Briac's face, the Middle pulled him to his feet, and Briac gulped in clean air. Eventually his coughing died out and they continued to walk.

Those two keep each other's secrets, she thought, yet again, as she pressed forward. *And they keep each other alive.* She knew what she would confront in her future, but had put off facing it. When her master went back *There,* to stretch himself out again for hundreds of years, she would be left alone with the Middle and with Briac. She'd now attacked the Middle openly and expressed her desire to kill him. There was no reason to suppose either he or Briac would allow her to live.

CHAPTER 61

SHINOBU

Shinobu had made several more incisions to *Traveler*'s wiring, which the ship had absorbed without complaint. He had expected to be inside helping Quin already, and he was now cutting more aggressively as he searched for the electrical lines that would shut off the internal power while still leaving the vessel aloft.

A thick twist of insulated electrical cables ran around the engine casing. He'd been avoiding it for fear of damaging the engine, but now, tilting the torch nozzle sideways to minimize its impact, he aimed it at the cables.

"Please don't hurt the engine, please don't hurt the engine . . ." he said aloud, the wind carrying away his words.

The torch made a long, deep gash, easily severing the electrical lines and instantly breaching the engine. For one moment he glimpsed the blue flame of the torch sinking deeply into the ship's whirling propulsion apparatus; then furnace-like air was gushing out around him, creating clouds of boiling steam in the rain.

"Dammit!" Shinobu yelled, ducking sideways to avoid the scorching blast. His goggles saved his eyes, but he could feel fiery streaks of pain across his cheeks where the steam had burned him.

The engine was making an awful noise, and now the ship bucked violently and Shinobu was thrown free of his tiny perch. He fell, then was yanked to a stop, dangling from his rope and piton as the immense bulk of *Traveler* appeared to tilt toward him. His vision was suddenly filled with the streets of London moving dizzyingly far below.

New pain shot up his leg, and he realized the torch nozzle was bouncing around by his ankle, burning through his samurai leggings, through his clothing, through the layer of armored heat-resistant underclothes, and right through his skin. He screamed and kicked at the nozzle, then tried to grab it, but he and the torch were swinging wildly through the air.

The ship caught itself, the other engines screaming as they worked to keep it stable. He kicked frantically at the flaming torch again and again, and finally it went out.

He hung at the end of his rope for a moment in relief, then scrambled to get hold of the ship. His ancestor's armor, though half burned from the fireworks earlier, was still so tight that he couldn't extend his arms fully. He dug his fingers into the charred sections of silk braiding, ripped the armor off, and tossed it toward the streets below, mentally apologizing to his mother.

Grabbing desperately for handholds, he managed to pull himself back up onto the hull. But before the relief of being on firm footing could sink in, another engine blew out with a deafening boom, and the ship swung nose-first toward the ground.

Shinobu was thrown up over the aft engines and found himself flying above the upper hull of the ship, far past the original hatch he had cut through, in the direction of its nose. His rope caught him, violently, and he slammed into the glass covering the bow. A moment later, the engines fired and arrested the ship's fall, as he struggled to fill his lungs with air after the impact.

His face was pressed up against the glass when he started to breathe again. It was dark inside, but something was moving. Rainbow-colored sparks were dancing around in the darkness. Suddenly the sparks were directly in front of him, whirling along the other side of the glass, inches from his face. Someone inside was firing a disruptor. And very likely, it was being fired at Quin.

The glass was slick from the rain, and Shinobu's feet skated around as he maneuvered the plasma torch in front of him. His ankle and cheeks were burning, his ribs were aching, but he hardly noticed these things as he sparked the nozzle back to life.

CHAPTER 62

QUIN

The corridor was smoky and dark from her own gas canisters as Quin made her way toward the enormous room up ahead. Her mask had also fogged on the inside, further obscuring her vision. Through her feet she felt erratic vibrations from the engines, and a deafening alarm was going off all around her.

Ahead of her, on the right-hand wall, loomed a large open doorway from the corridor into the great room. She could see figures inside that huge space, four of them beneath the glass canopy at the bow. There were two guards in gas masks, and near them was a figure slumped in a chair. Quin caught a glimpse of red hair—Fiona. Her mother was only yards away.

John was there as well, also in a mask and with a disruptor strapped to his chest, which gave him the look of something out of a nightmare. Would he really use a disruptor on her or her mother? Quin thought of that night on the estate, and a spasm of fear shot through her. *Yes, he might,* she thought. *He is desperate.*

No one in the great room had yet seen Quin, who stood outside in the corridor, her back pressed against the wall. She glanced down the hallway behind her. Where was Shinobu? What was happening to the engines?

The alarm stopped, but the vibration coming through the floor was now more jarring. Then a deep, unsettling tremor shook the entire vessel, and suddenly *Traveler* fell aft.

Quin was thrown to the floor as the lights went out again. For a moment, the ship teetered back into a level position, then was rocked by an explosion from one of the engines. *Traveler* began to dive, its nose tilting toward the London streets below.

She was sent rolling down the corridor, past the open doorway to the great room. She caught a glimpse of falling chairs, books, tables, all sliding toward the bow of the ship, with the four human figures flailing among them. A flash of light, then a swarm of multicolored sparks twisted through the air. John's disruptor had gone off.

Quin grabbed the edge of the doorway, heaving her body up the tilting hall, and crawled into the great room. With relief, she saw the disruptor sparks gyrating and dispersing along the glass canopy above—if the sparks were loose on the ceiling, no one had been hit. Not yet.

There was another roar from the engines as the ship caught itself, arresting the downward dive into a slow drift.

A figure was struggling up the slanted floor. Quin saw the red hair again. It was her mother, conscious, though she was without a gas mask and was coughing violently. Quin slid toward her as Fiona crept to the wall, arms and legs shaking, and hit her fist against something. There was a hum all around the room as vents opened up. Cold, wet air streamed in, quickly dispersing the gas.

Quin took a last deep breath of filtered air, then pulled off her foggy mask to see into the darker, lower corner of the room. John and his two men were tangled among the piles of furniture against the bow wall, but they were digging themselves free. The dancing light of the disruptor sparks was still moving on the glass ceiling. Except these sparks were all one color—in fact, they were the color of Shinobu's plasma torch.

Fiona was still on her hands and knees, breathing in the fresh air now. Quin was breathing it too. She grabbed hold of her mother, and together they slipped through an avalanche of books and crawled toward the door.

Halfway there, she looked up to see their path blocked by four figures—the Dreads and her father. They stood firmly on the tilted floor, taking deep, long breaths. Then all four pairs of eyes went to the athame and lightning rod at Quin's waist.

She pulled her mother in the other direction, toward the far doors, but one of John's men already stood there, blocking that route.

John himself had worked free of the piled objects and was climbing up the floor toward her, his hands busy searching for the disruptor controls on his chest. She knew she must act now, before he fired that weapon.

"John!" Quin called.

She pulled the athame and lightning rod from her waist and sent them spinning down the floor toward him.

The Middle Dread and the Young Dread turned immediately, following the path of the stone dagger. Shots rang out then, thunderous, the bullets caroming off the walls behind her. John's men were shooting at the Dreads.

To Quin's surprise, Briac didn't follow the athame. Instead he began walking toward Quin. He was injured, in a leg and a shoulder, but his whipsword was in his hand, and he looked ready to die as long as he could punish her. He slashed out with his sword, and Quin ducked.

"You have shown yourself worthless, girl," he said to her, his voice both soft and deadly, like the oily substance of a whipsword. "Why did your drunken mother provide me with a girl? You've weighed me down with your lack of skill. Your faithlessness."

Quin cracked her whipsword out and blocked his next blow, but she found herself hesitating. Years of training had taught her to follow Briac without question. Instead of stepping forward and striking him, she took a step back, into her mother.

Briac became aware of Fiona then, and like a spotlight, his anger tilted and focused upon her.

"You, Wife! Cowering as usual. All your training, and you were too cowardly to take the oath. Scared of what you saw in my mind? Frightened of a bit of blood and screaming. I should have rid myself of you both!"

Quin saw her mother staring at Briac with wide eyes, unable to move, an expression that said, *Don't hurt me. Please don't hurt me.*

And that was enough.

The look her mother wore—Quin had seen it countless times as a girl, and she'd tried to ignore it, had hoped she was mistaken. But hadn't she always known, somewhere in her heart, that there was no mercy or love behind Briac's eyes? Hadn't she sensed that if she crossed him, there would be no forgiveness? Even if she hadn't been as submissive as her mother, hadn't she also thought, *I'll believe in you, Briac, I'll do what you say, if only you won't hurt me.*

"Stand aside, Quin!" he ordered, gesturing her away so he could strike at Fiona. Even now he assumed she would obey him without question.

Quin stared at her father, with his sword raised, his face, his whole being, full of malice. And the spell was broken.

"Go ahead," she yelled at him. "Try to kill us!"

And with that she struck at him hard, her motions quick, fierce, and without warning. Briac caught her blow with his whipsword but stumbled back a pace, looking shocked that she would attack. She stepped forward, swinging at him again.

This time, Briac didn't hesitate. He slashed out to block her, then struck again. But Quin raised her sword viciously, throwing off his blade.

"You tried to kill me on the estate," he said, his voice acid, his whipsword hitting at her again, hard.

She caught the blow on her own blade, one of her hands at the hilt, one at the tip, the force of his strike bending the middle of her whipsword until it almost touched her nose.

"What kind of a daughter kills her father?" he asked, his sword pressing harder against hers, his face close. "What kind of monster did I raise?"

Hatred welled up in Quin like a tidal wave. Looking into his dark eyes—so like hers on the surface, and yet entirely different underneath—she wondered, *How could I ever have followed you?*

"You're the monster," she said. "And I'm through with you."

She twisted her shoulders and thrust her hands forward, her whole body behind the sudden motion. Briac's sword slipped to the side, and then he fell, off balance, sprawling onto the floor.

His head hit the ground hard enough to stun him, but still he was coming after her. Quin lifted her whipsword high, ready to strike down and split her father's head in two.

Before she had the chance, Briac disappeared in a blur of limbs as something large and flailing dropped through the air directly onto him. Someone was on top of him, punching him again and again, in a fury equal to Quin's own. Briac was twisting his body and cursing beneath the rain of blows, clawing at the floor to get away.

Then the punches stopped abruptly, and Briac crawled off, scrambling out of Quin's reach as quickly as he could.

His attacker rolled over, clutching a bleeding gash in his side.

It was Shinobu. He'd fallen through the ceiling. He looked up at Quin, his eyes full of pain but also triumphant.

"I really hate him!" he whispered to her.

CHAPTER 63

MAUD

Along the slanted floor, the Middle Dread and the Young Dread approached John and his two men. She could see the athame and lightning rod several yards behind John. The stone objects had come to rest against an upturned desk.

John's men were firing guns. The range was close, and the Dreads should have been easy targets for the bullets. Yet the Young and the Middle had slowed their sense of time to that point she often felt in battle, when a heartbeat took a minute, and a breath an hour. She saw the bullets as they left the barrels of the guns, and her body was no longer in their path by the time they reached her. They themselves would appear as blurs of motion to the others in the room.

The Middle cracked out his whipsword and stabbed forward at the first of the men. The Young's sword was already out, preparing to engage with the second man. She swiveled to the side as a bullet tore by her head, then she raised her sword. This would not take long.

Before she struck the man, she spared a glance at her master, who was standing behind them, keeping himself apart from this fight. As the Young met the Old Dread's eyes, her mind shifted even higher.

Images poured through her. He had trained her for years, been a father to her, taught her about the hum of the universe. The athame was to move a great mind beyond the bounds, but there were no great minds, only good hearts. Was she a possession? It takes only one hand to place an athame. Only one mind to decide. Where was the justice of the Dreads?

She saw it then. Her master could not rid himself of the Middle Dread. The reason was a mystery, but the fact remained: her master was tied to the Middle. He had been looking, for a thousand years perhaps, for a Young Dread who would do what was right.

Without another moment of hesitation, she turned her sword away from John's man and thrust it straight through the Middle Dread's back, as she had imagined doing so many times. As he lifted his own sword to deliver a death blow to John, she neatly pierced his heart.

The Middle reeled backward, her sword all the way through him, and the Young Dread caught him as he fell. John was staring at her, eyes wide, shock and gratitude chasing each other across his face.

Her master was by her side now. He leaned his head close to her ear.

"That was right," he whispered.

CHAPTER 64

JOHN

John was seeing the moment of his own death. The Dreads had boarded *Traveler* with Quin, and though they didn't seem to be helping her, their presence had destroyed any hope of avoiding a fight.

The athame and lightning rod were on the floor some yards behind John, and the Dreads were out for blood to retrieve them. In a cloud of motion, the Middle Dread was raising his sword to kill John.

Then something long and thin sprouted from the man's chest, covered in red. As John watched, it snaked its way back into the Middle's torso and disappeared. Then the man fell backward into the arms of the Young Dread.

For the briefest moment, John's eyes and the Young Dread's eyes were locked upon each other. She had saved him, she had helped him. Then the Young was gone, dragging the Middle away.

John turned toward the athame and found Briac Kincaid heading right for him. Briac was limping, and his face was bloody, but this didn't seem to be slowing him down. The bright light of revenge was burning in his eyes.

A gun went off, and John's shoulder jerked back. He could see the gun clutched in Briac's left hand. The man was going to kill him. Except that John had something worse than death in his own hands. Ever since that day, so long ago, when he'd glimpsed the flash of rainbow-colored light from his hiding place beneath the floor, he had been waiting for this. Ever since that day in the old barn, when Briac had stood before the withered figure in the hospital bed, lecturing the apprentices about the dangers of disruptors, he had been waiting for this.

John's remaining guard lunged forward to stop Briac, just as John's own hand slid down the edge of the disruptor. There was a high, piercing whine as the disruptor launched a thousand sparks.

The room was filled with multicolored light again, and the hiss and snap of electricity. The web of sparks collided with both of the men, John's guard and Briac, who were now locked in a fight.

His own man jumped backward, beating at his head, which was swimming with electrical flashes. Briac fell to the ground, falling out of the cloud of sparks as he did. But he was not completely free of them. A small handful—maybe three or four—were still dancing around Briac's head. The disruptor field had split between the two of them, something John had not known was possible. Briac rolled along the floor, swatting the flashing lights like they were flies.

John turned away, searching frantically for the athame and lightning rod.

Quin threw me the athame! he thought, filled with a relief so profound and a happiness so intense that they were almost overwhelming. *She chose to give it to me!*

His hands closed around both stone objects. But they were wrong. They didn't feel as they should. Instead of cool stone, his skin felt something softer, warmer. He hit the athame against an overturned table, and it crumbled to pieces in his hands.

It was a trick. She hadn't thrown him the real dagger. She hadn't chosen to help him. He stood quite still for a moment, despair flooding in. And then came anger.

He could see Quin and Fiona farther up the steep floor, kneeling by another figure. As he approached, he recognized this figure: Shinobu MacBain. Quin's rescue on the Bridge suddenly became clear. Shinobu had been there. He had been helping her. Perhaps, in Hong Kong, Shinobu had taken John's place. Perhaps he and Quin had been together for the last year and a half. He could imagine her touching him, kissing him, helping him, as she had refused to do for John. The idea made him furious.

"Can you move?" he heard Quin ask him.

Shinobu was clutching his side, and one of his legs was bent in the wrong direction.

"Sure," he whispered. "I can move."

"We're going to pull you," she said. "Hold my arms."

Before Shinobu could grab on to her, John grasped his whipsword with both hands and drove the butt of it into the side of Quin's head as hard as he could.

She dropped to the floor, stunned.

Then there was a tremendous groan from the back of the ship, followed by the sound of a great amount of metal tearing away from itself.

Traveler began to plummet.

CHAPTER 65

QUIN

The room was swinging madly. Something had hit Quin, hit her head so hard she couldn't see properly. Her vision was spinning, but she was fairly certain the room was spinning as well. There were sky-scrapers outside, whirling across the huge glass canopy like the lights of a carnival ride.

She and Fiona and Shinobu were sliding across the floor together, and someone else was there. She could feel him breathing near her face. He was clutching her as they slid, keeping her with him. And his arms were searching inside her cloak.

"No," she breathed.

"Why wouldn't you choose me?" he whispered. "Just once?"

She had to stop him from searching her pockets. Her head was throbbing and her arms weren't working properly, but she struck out. He pushed her arm away like it was a stalk of wheat.

"There," she heard him say. "There it is."

It was John, and he sounded *happy.* She could see him now. He was holding the athame and lightning rod, the real ones that she had concealed.

"No, John . . ."

He continued to search inside her cloak. She tried to push him away, but there was no strength in her arms.

He was taking something else from her pocket. She heard him draw a breath in surprise.

With great effort, her head pounding, Quin turned toward him and made her eyes focus. John was staring at a thick book with a leather cover and a leather tie holding it shut. She grabbed for it and was confused to see her hand move in the wrong direction.

"You don't want that," she whispered. But the words seemed wrong: of course John would want it. She watched as he flipped through the pages, a look of joy crossing his face. She made another grab for the book, but her arms came nowhere close.

It's all right, she told herself. Even in her dazed state, Quin remembered that John taking the book was not a catastrophe. She'd brought it as a potential bargaining chip, hadn't she? There was a reason she could let it go. Somehow she'd taken steps . . .

"How do you have this?" he asked her. He sounded like a child on Christmas.

"Briac . . ."

They were sliding again. John leaned over her so she could see his face clearly.

"You *have* helped me," he whispered, his words kind, grateful. "Thank you, Quin. Thank you."

His lips were on her cheek, warm and soft. And then John was gone, sliding across the floor and away from her.

The ship was screaming. *Traveler* began to rock back and forth. There were hands on her arm. Someone was pulling her. She turned. Shinobu was there, trying to bring her closer. Her mother was lying flat on the floor, tying a thick wad of cloth against the deep cut in Shinobu's side.

When Shinobu had fallen through the ceiling, Briac's whip-sword had caught him in the center of his chest. The thin layer of armor under his burned clothing had deflected the tip, which had slid across his torso, then finally pierced the armor at his side. There was warm wetness along Quin's leg. Shinobu had been saved from instant death, but he was still bleeding all over the floor.

The ship was lurching upward now, like a wounded animal trying to pull itself back to its feet. The engines were roaring in different keys. Shinobu was grabbing Quin's shirt.

"We're crashing," he whispered.

"Hold on to me," she told him. Her head was pounding, but she was no longer dizzy, and her arms were starting to work again. "I'll pull you out of here."

"I crashed the ship," he said. "I think I'm bleeding . . ."

"It's okay. Hold on to me."

The ship was tilting more severely, as some engines cut out completely and those remaining tried to lift the vessel back into the air. Shinobu and Quin slid sideways until they hit the wall. Gravity pressed her tightly against him.

"Keep talking to me," she whispered as his eyes started to droop.

"Did he take the athame?"

"He did. It doesn't matter . . ."

"Am I dying?"

"You're not dying."

"Quin . . ."

"It's just a little blood, I promise. Hold on." She grabbed him more tightly, as if her own arms could protect him from the falling ship. His cheek was pressed against hers.

"Quin, we're only third cousins, you know."

"*Half* third cousins," she whispered, her lips close to his ear. "Hardly related at all."

"Did you want to kiss me . . . in the basement?"

"Yes," she breathed, "so much."

The buildings outside were lurching around the glass canopy drunkenly. The ship was bucking and falling at the same time.

Shinobu pulled her so their faces were level. Then he kissed her lips, very slowly and tenderly, as if they were not lying in a spinning, crashing ship, as if they had all the time in the world.

"I love you," she whispered.

"I love you," he whispered back.

Then Shinobu threw himself over her. With one final scream, the ship's engines pulled the nose up, and *Traveler* crash-landed in Hyde Park.

The glass canopy shattered into a thousand spiderwebs, and the large sheets began to fall. Shinobu was pinning her down, protecting her. She saw her mother in the corner a few yards away, hunched in a sheltered space where two walls met. Quin tried to roll out from under Shinobu, to push him closer to that corner and to safety. There was a thud as a sheet of glass landed on top of them, crushing him into her. Quin felt the breath knocked out of her lungs.

There was stillness then. But not quiet. The ship was settling beneath them, and there were sirens everywhere. Every ambulance, firefighter, and policeman for twenty miles was converging on their crash site.

"Come," a voice said as Quin struggled to breathe.

The Young Dread was lifting the glass sheet up. Quin didn't pause to wonder how so small a girl could lift so heavy an object. As quickly as she could, her breath returning, she wriggled out from beneath Shinobu. The Young Dread was holding up an athame. A deep tremor flooded over Quin as she and Fiona and the Young Dread dragged Shinobu's limp form through a dark circle in the dark room, the energy of its edges surging inward toward complete blackness. A moment later they were not in the ship at all; they were *There*.

CHAPTER 66

QUIN

They emerged back into the world a quarter of a mile away. No one paid them the slightest attention. Every human for miles was looking at the crashed bulk of *Traveler,* framed by the greenery of Hyde Park.

Fiona teetered unsteadily on her feet, then fell into a sitting position. Quin and the Young Dread knelt by Shinobu, who lay unconscious on the sidewalk. Quin tied up his wound with a strip of wool from her cloak. He had blistering burns across both cheeks, his leg was broken and also badly burned, and she was certain he had other broken bones as well. But he was breathing and his heartbeat was strong.

She looked up, at the chaos of emergency vehicles near the crash site. Grabbing her mother by the shoulders, she pulled her closer to Shinobu.

"Stay with him," she ordered. "Don't let him move."

It took her mother a moment to understand, but at last she nodded.

"I'll be right back!"

Quin had a splitting headache, but she found she was able to jog.

She started off toward the mess in the distance, searching for the closest ambulance. Halfway there, she noticed the Young Dread running along with her. When they came to the edge of the crowd, they both stopped, hunting for someone who could help.

"Look," the Young Dread said quietly, pointing through the mass of people.

In the distance, near the ship, a man was being loaded into an ambulance. Tall, strong, and wild-looking, he was thrashing around furiously as the medical personnel pushed him into the vehicle. It was Briac. Her father had survived.

The Young Dread put a hand on Quin's arm and pointed in another direction. Quin followed the girl's gaze to an alley off to their left, below the park. As they watched, the figure of John Hart, just recognizable at this distance, slipped into the darkness between buildings and disappeared.

"Here we part ways," the Young Dread said softly.

Quin nodded.

The girl withdrew from her cloak the athame of the Dreads and held it loosely in her hands.

"Where is your master?" Quin asked.

"Sleeping," the girl said. "It is past time."

There was something different about the Young Dread's cloak. It seemed too large for her and also more threadbare than the last time Quin had seen it. Its interior pockets appeared to be crammed full of hidden items whose bulk she had not noticed before.

Before Quin could wonder about this change, there were sirens behind them, and she turned to find several emergency vehicles heading their way. She waved her arms.

"My master says I am Young, Middle, and Old now," the Young Dread told her, her eyes downcast, looking at the athame in her hand. "Or perhaps I am none of those. We shall see."

An ambulance pulled to a stop by Quin, drawn by the sight of Shinobu's blood, which covered half her body. She moved toward the vehicle, but the Young Dread caught her arm.

"You will have this," the Young told her.

Quin watched as the girl placed the athame into her hands. She looked down at the stone dagger's slender shape, saw the symbols lined up along its dials. Her thumb went to the back of the blade, where the thin lightning rod was fitted neatly into place. This athame was far more delicate and somehow, she sensed, more powerful than her own.

She noticed the design carved into the pommel. It was not an animal. It was three interlocking ovals. It was a carving of an atom. Quin's heart began to beat more quickly.

"Why?" she asked.

"It is my choice," the Young Dread said. "The gift is not permanent. But this athame's power does not solely belong to me. You will take it for a while. I have a debt to pay, and business with the other athame."

"John has it."

"Yes. John has it," the girl agreed. Then she put out a hand, as a modern person would upon being introduced. "You are Quin," she said. "I am Maud."

"Maud," Quin repeated, shaking the girl's hand. The name fit. "I'm pleased to meet you, and sorry to say goodbye."

"Not goodbye," Maud replied. "We will meet again. Soon. Be sure of it."

Something about the way the girl said this was not entirely pleasant, as though the next time they met, they might or might not be on the same side. Then Maud, the Young Dread, the fifteen-year-old girl who was nothing like a fifteen-year-old girl, was gone, weaving through the crowd in the direction John Hart had been running.

Quin returned with the ambulance, and the medics swarmed over Shinobu. When they'd loaded him into the vehicle, she took a seat beside him, with Fiona next to her. She gripped Shinobu's hand tightly. He was unconscious, but she could feel his warmth and the steady beat of his heart.

It had taken her too long to realize that he was half of her, as she was of him. It had been that way since they were nine years old. She would not be whole until he was out of danger.

As they pulled away from the chaos, Quin could feel her own future lining up clearly in front of her. At one side of her waist was the athame, at the other her whipsword. On her left wrist was the brand that marked her.

Without turning away from Shinobu, she spoke.

"What am I, Mother?"

The answer was obvious, but still, Fiona took a moment to respond, as though made uneasy by the words she would say.

"You are what you were always meant to be," she said carefully. "You are a Seeker."

"Yes," Quin agreed.

John had taken the leather journal. But Quin had studied it again as they'd prepared to come to London, and she knew some of what it held. There were ten images drawn in sequence, and among these had been a fox and an eagle. The fox was John's athame, the eagle Shinobu's—the one that had been destroyed. And there was a diagram of three interlocking ovals—that was the athame hanging at Quin's side. That left seven other symbols. If each one represented another athame, and each athame belonged to a separate family . . .

Catherine, and many others, had been gathering knowledge for a long time, and the book was a trail a Seeker could follow . . . But to where?

Quin looked out the back window of the ambulance. The streets were getting quieter the farther they traveled from the crash site. London was growing dark around them.

"I am a Seeker, as we were in the beginning," she said. "What do I seek? The truth. The beginning and the end. Our knowledge began somewhere, sometime. And one day it will end."

Before they'd left Hong Kong, Quin had taken pictures of every page of the leather journal and each folded piece of vellum tucked within it. The pictures were safe, a complete copy, waiting for her. And now she had an athame as well, one that no one would be trying to steal, at least for a while.

"Seekers have lived long before you, and they'll continue to live long after you die," Fiona murmured. "We don't have a choice in that, Quin."

It was like a chant, the way her mother said it, or like a prayer she'd been taught as a girl. Quin imagined generations of Seekers all saying the same thing, all assuring their children and their children's children that they could survive anything, that their power over life and death would last until the end of time. That killing whomever they chose to kill was within their rights.

"No," Quin said, lacing her fingers through Shinobu's. "We have a choice. I'm going to put an end to it. Starting with John."

Is it the end or simply the beginning?
Find out in

TRAVELLER

Spring 2016

ACKNOWLEDGMENTS

My first instinct is to take all the credit for this book. Is that done?

I feel sure that you, the reader, don't need to know about the desk-pounding, karate-chopping conversation in which my agent, Jodi Reamer, lectured me with great passion about how *my own character* would or would not behave in a certain situation. I wanted to say, "Jodi, I don't want to tell you how to do your job—scratch that, I totally want to tell you how to do your job. I created these characters. I'm like a god in this universe. A god!" Actually, it wasn't so much that I "wanted to say" that, but that I really did say that, or some slightly less brave version of that.

Unfortunately, you begin to realize that you may be the creator in the universe of your book, but you're not the only one who lives there. And an agent who is willing to take up residence in your world so thoroughly that she gets *ferociously angry* with you when something doesn't seem right is absolutely priceless. An agent like that is like the best friend you've known since grade school, who stops you from taking drugs or sits you down to have a serious discussion about your unfortunate choices in hairstyles. She makes the world of your book better, and she makes you a better creator in that world. So, um, you know, (cough), thanks and all that, Jodi. I did pay for dinner once, so we're probably square.

Krista Marino, if you're reading this (that's a joke—as my editor, I know you *have* to read this), you are an entirely different sort of creature. I'm pretty sure you fight on the side of good, but you're so very quietly devious. Devious! You pretended to let me talk you out of several notes, but somehow *I ended up doing all of them anyway.* How did that happen? Voodoo? Hypnotism? Or was it that you gave me the space to realize that your note-giving ability is a subtle superpower? Sure, it's not all flashy and in-your-face like flying or telekinesis, but it's equally potent.

You secretly moved into the universe of my book and furnished a house there for yourself before I'd even signed with Random House. I showed up in the world of *Seeker* to do a new draft and you were already standing there, glancing at your watch and tapping your foot like, "Where have you been? I've been waiting for ages."

So, you know . . . thanks and everything.

This is getting a little easier.

Thank you, Barbara Marcus. You left me such a nice message back when this all began. Please don't tell anyone, but I kept that message on my phone and I listened to it from time to time when the book was giving me trouble.

Thank you, Beverly Horowitz, for teaching me about the publishing business. I love your simple explanation that "Everything about a book is the result of a decision." And in that vein, I want to thank those very talented decision makers on the Random House team who gave shape and life to this book:

Thanks to Alison Impey for giving *Seeker* its marvelous cover, which seems to glow with an inner life of its own. Thanks so much to John Adamo, Kim Lauber, Stephanie O'Cain, and Dominique Cimina for figuring out how to get *Seeker* into the wide world. And thanks to Judith Haut for all your support and enthusiasm.

Thank you to my children, to whom I have already dedicated this book, and who therefore don't really need to be mentioned a second time, especially since they are constantly distracting me from writing.

But they keep me on my toes and fill my life with love and adventure, and those are very important when working through complicated and sometimes violent plots.

Thank you, Sky Dayton. I may be naming you last, but I want to give you the most profound thanks. It would really be far too personal to name all the ways in which you make my life better. Luckily, you already know.

ABOUT THE AUTHOR

Arwen Elys Dayton spends months doing research for her stories. Her explorations have taken her around the world to places like the Great Pyramid at Giza, Hong Kong and its many islands, and lots of ruined castles in Scotland.

Arwen lives with her husband and their three children on the West Coast of the United States. You can visit her at arwendayton.com and follow @arwenelysdayton on Twitter and Instagram.